Minahi ON, June 2021

Dear Deborah,
I hope you enjoy Moral Hazards!
Thanks for choosing it and I really
look forward to our discussion.
With best wishes,
Tim

MORAL

A Political Thriller by

TIM MARTIN

HAZARDS

◆ FriesenPress

Suite 300 - 990 Fort St
Victoria, BC, V8V 3K2
Canada

www.friesenpress.com

Copyright © 2020 by Tim Martin
First Edition — 2020

ISBN
978-1-5255-6277-8 (Hardcover)
978-1-5255-6278-5 (Paperback)
978-1-5255-6279-2 (eBook)

1. FICTION, WAR & MILITARY
2. FICTION, THRILLERS

Distributed to the trade by The Ingram Book Company

Dedicated to Fatima for her constant love,
sacrifices, and support in navigating
our beautiful and turbulent life.

HELL IS OTHER PEOPLE.

—Jean-Paul Sartre
No Exit

1

Mogadishu, Somalia,
JANUARY 1991

FINANCE MINISTER OMAR KHALIL'S driver followed the armed escort through the war-blasted streets of the capital to the beleaguered presidential compound. He was going to a meeting about how President Barre would survive the death of his state. Therefore, it was about money—or more precisely, how much money was left and who would get it.

As an elite technocrat, Omar always wore a blue suit. His sense of self did not permit him to see the president in anything else, even though the pants were threadbare at the knees and seat, the suit made the crushing heat worse, and white crescents of salt showed under his arms.

He had been unable to sleep the previous night. In fact, he couldn't remember when he last slept. His pulse beat a rhythm of dull pain in his temples. He was thirsty.

Omar struggled to control his nerves as the steel gate swung open. His official vehicle entered the compound and pulled up to the entrance with the other ministerial vehicles. Stooped with worry, he got out and went inside, heading toward the cabinet room.

The ministers took their usual seats around the massive, ornate cabinet table. They didn't trust each other, and they didn't talk to each other as they waited for President Barre. Barre always made others wait.

At last the leather-upholstered door to his office opened smartly, and the president strode to his place at the head of the table. He held Omar in his gaze for an excruciating minute before he spoke.

"What is the current cash position of our government? In liquid assets, that is." The president's baritone voice was flat. His words had bureaucratic precision but no human connection to the ugly catastrophe surrounding them.

Omar had agonized about this encounter for an interminable week. Barre radiated a palpable dominance that Omar tried to resist, but it was impossible. The others would take his shaky voice as a sign of weakness.

"Your Excellency, I've reviewed the status of your gold reserves. There are two hundred ingots of four hundred troy ounces each. The current value is twenty-eight million—US dollars, that is."

Omar searched for a reaction in President Barre's perfectly oval face. Like his voice, his features were closed, composed, and impassive. He had the complexion of a corpse.

Omar's palms were slimy. His large frame folded in on itself. His head ached with remorse for the steps he had taken along the path that made him the minister of finance on his country's deathwatch.

"Because of the informal and clandestine methods that will be required to liquidate our national holdings in gold, I estimate a 25 percent discount will be necessary. Unless your friend, President Moi, gives us a preferential rate," Omar added.

Barre looked from Omar to the minister of defence. Omar turned away from the table to gaze out the dusty windows. The sun appeared over the presidential compound's concrete perimeter. The new cement blocks were topped with coils of concertina wire. Its razors flashed in the sun's glare. He turned back to Barre. The president's photosensitive glasses darkened, obscuring his thoughts.

"General, can we take more than this cargo?" the president asked. "I'm thinking of dollars and other valuables. We must safeguard as much of the Somali people's financial patrimony as possible."

Even though the question was directed to the head of the remaining rump of the army, it was the central bank president who answered. "Your Excellency, there is nothing else. The dollars were exhausted for arms purchases. Our national currency lost its convertibility. No one outside Somalia will take our shilling."

The ministers were startled by the throaty grunt of assault rifle fire outside. Then there was a deep thump and a mild shockwave from the explosion of a rocket-propelled grenade on a nearby building. The minister of defence turned to the president with a submissive and apologetic expression. "These are small-scale probing maneuvers by the enemy. We still have some time, but we cannot delay your evacuation plan, Excellency."

"I approve the plan you submitted for the transport of my first wife, Mama Khadija, my daughters by her, and myself," President Barre said slowly and deliberately. "There is one change. The only advisor I require is the minister of finance. Please issue the necessary orders. You are all dismissed—except for the minister of finance. Omar, come with me."

The other ministers sat in a stunned silence at their abrupt abandonment as Omar and Barre left the room.

President Barre had an enormous office. The aide-de-camp closed the heavy wooden door behind them. Like the door, the walls were upholstered with overstuffed green leather to prevent eavesdropping. The metallic chill and noisy buzz suggested the air conditioners were on maximum.

After crossing ten metres of carpet, Barre motioned Omar to sit across the antique mahogany desk from him. Behind the desk was a life-sized official portrait of the president flanked by two Somali flags of bright sky blue with a single white star in their centre.

Barre looked at his picture with Secretary of State Jim Baker. "We can't expect any more help from the Americans, not since the collapse of the Soviets. Well, it was a useful rivalry in its time. Now they're obsessed with getting Saddam out of Kuwait, and we're on our own. So, Omar, how will this be done?"

Omar's throat constricted, and he feared he could not speak. His eyes could not meet the president's iron gaze. Cramps knifed his gut; it was his body's reaction to betrayal utterly beyond forgiveness.

"May I have a glass of water, Excellency?" His words came out in a whisper.

"No. Time is of the essence; you can have a drink after our meeting."

Omar gathered his dwindling willpower and composed himself. "Mr. President, I suggest we deliver the gold to the government of Kenya. This will increase their reserves, against which they will make deposits in a set of international banks. We can instruct them to transfer funds anywhere in the world for the purposes of your government in exile. Moreover, we can withdraw cash to be remitted through trusted friends in the hawala[1] system. Our friends can move cash to our officials and fighters in the homeland. Hawala has served us well for hundreds of years and continues to transfer money up and down the coast, from Zanzibar to Bombay." Omar took a few deep breaths before he

[1] Hawala is an honour-based money transfer system dating from the Middle Ages that connects Asia, the Middle East, and Africa.

continued. "Legal banks—especially international banks—might freeze any assets under your control."

Barre took off his glasses. His eyes were tired. His face went from tense to flaccid. The presidential smile was one of cynical amusement. Omar had never seen Barre remove his mask of command before. He had failed to understand that the hypocrisy was total.

"I'm glad it's you coming with me. I groomed you, and I selected you. You always knew that, didn't you? I needed someone smart to run the money, but I needed a Marehan clansman like you even more. We can't trust anybody outside our clan. You are like my kin. Everything you have, you have because of me. I don't worry about your loyalty. I can't say the same for your colleagues."

Barre got up, moved around his office, and selected the photos of him with world leaders he would take as souvenirs.

Omar cursed the fate that had anointed him for leadership from the beginning. First the Soviets taught him engineering and sociology. Then the Americans gave him a Fulbright scholarship for a PhD in economics. His jobs with the UN and the World Bank seduced him with an illusion of virtue. He was happy to be called to serve in the highest positions of his government and had a policy prescription for everything. For a long time he deluded himself that his position and power were earned, even deserved. When did he realize that corruption and cynicism were not temporary flaws subject to technical correction? Why hadn't he found an exit before he was irretrievably lost in this labyrinth of moral hazards?

"You worry too much," the president said. "I'm looking forward to our journey tomorrow. For now, you're dismissed."

2

IBRAHIM HUSSEIN CLIMBED THE stairs to the second floor of the family villa in Mogadishu. He always bathed as soon as he returned home from work. The water supply had been cut off for months, so the servant left a bucket of tepid water in the shower with a small cup next to a plastic stool.

Black exhaust rising from the generators at the presidential compound across the street gave him the depressing knowledge that other government leaders were comfortable.

He carefully folded his uniform as he undressed. He looked at himself in the mirror, displeased with the languid droop of his eyes, long lashes, and full lips. Then he sat on the stool, lathered his head, and delicately pulled the razor across his scalp. His father had bird-of-prey eyes and was treated with the respect due an apex predator. So, like his father, he shaved his head to eliminate frivolity from his features. He wanted to look older than his twenty-five years. His authority must be absolute at all times. He wasn't sure if it was. Ibrahim had adopted this severe look when his father made him an officer in the military intelligence service.

Ibrahim loved his father. As a toddler, he cried when his father went to work. It took him a long time to understand that the man returned every evening. Later, little Ibrahim begged his uniformed father to take him to work, tugging on his olive-green pant leg as the tall general climbed into his military sedan. A desperate need for paternal approval spurred ambition and excellence in his schoolwork. On Ibrahim's fifteenth birthday, his father said to him, "Come with me, and I'll show you what I do."

He had quietly followed his father into the official vehicle, and off they drove.

"Son, our president has selected a few men of wisdom and courage to discover our enemies and their conspiracies before they harm loyal citizens. Before they disrupt our social tranquility and the nation's path to development. This is my work. You'll see it today." That was the end of conversation in the car.

They drove a long way to a scruffy, poor neighbourhood on the edge of the city. The unmarked compound was large. It had no street number and had a vaguely commercial appearance on the outside. *Perhaps it's a kind of warehouse or storage building*, Ibrahim thought as they drove through the grey entrance gate.

His father was the only one in uniform, but the busy men inside stood to attention and saluted with rigorous discipline as soon as Ibrahim's father got out of the car.

"Stay by my side, and say nothing," his father said. "Lieutenant, take me to enemy thirty-eight H." Ibrahim admired his father's imperative language and took pleasure in the soldier's unquestioning obedience.

They walked past a well-tended flower garden and big house to a plain cement-block building, two stories high. It looked like a small school, but the windows were tiny, about the size of a brick. A dented metal door with a peephole swung open from the inside.

As he crossed the threshold, Ibrahim was puzzled by the darkly intimate odour of human feces and the acrid ammonia scent of urine. It was at odds with the tidy order of the rest of the compound.

The hallway was lined with doors. One staircase led to the second floor and one to the basement. He followed his father down. At the bottom of the stairs was another hallway of doors, though underground and dark.

They approached a metal door with "38H" stencilled on it in black paint. The lieutenant unbolted the door, swung it open, and switched on a bare light bulb hanging from a wire. A chubby middle-aged man squinted up from the floor at them. With a squirm of discomfort, Ibrahim saw he was naked. He had the expression of a supplicant. He knelt like a beggar on a damp, filthy piece of foam rubber.

"*Salaam walekum,*[2] dear General. I'm so happy to see you." The man smiled hopefully. "But I still do not know why I'm here."

"I've come to tell you the reason you're here in my house. They tell me you received bribes from merchants seeking to rob the republic of its legitimate customs duties. This is why you're here. Who are these merchants?" His father spoke calmly and with precision. His tone was not unfriendly.

The man licked his lips. He looked warmly at Ibrahim, as if they might be good friends. "How could that be?" He chuckled nervously. "I know nothing of this matter."

Ibrahim's father stepped forward. He reached down and gently took the prisoner's right hand in his left. With an expert motion, he grasped the man's little finger in his right fist and broke it with a sharp snap. The man looked like a fat fish ripped from the sea. The whites of his unblinking eyes shone incandescently. His mouth gasped in a slow rhythm.

Ibrahim's father took his time, observing 38H with care. "It begins with a finger. It can end right now if you tell me. I'll continue until you give me the names of these men. We both know how this goes. Everyone does."

2   Peace be with you.

The man struggled to control his panic. "General, it's true." Names tumbled from his lips. He had lied and deserved his punishment. His father's wisdom gave Ibrahim a warm satisfaction. He was happily secure in his father's confident control of the situation. Just like this, when his father beat Ibrahim, it had two benefits: it corrected his behaviour and hastened his understanding of his father's power.

They returned to the general's office. Ibrahim was made to sit in front of his father's desk.

"My son, when fear is great, the application of a small measure of pain, like I demonstrated just now, will obtain positive results. But fear needs belief. This man is lucky. I'll return him to his home and government position. He will tell others, and they will share his fear. Sometimes more is needed. Sometimes our enemies may not return to their homes.

"With women, a different approach is required." His father smiled knowingly at Ibrahim, as if he was old enough for grown-up secrets now. "We remove their honour." Ibrahim's cheeks warmed at his father's mention of sex. Could it be in Ibrahim's power to make this happen? "This serves as a lifetime punishment to them and to their family. Done properly, it's an encouraging incentive for our men."

"How does this happen? Do they agree?"

Amused, his father chuckled. "They do not agree. They have no choice in the matter. The important thing is to direct your men. Do you wish to learn more?"

The question made Ibrahim happy and eager to please. He looked at the flag behind his father and the picture of President Barre. He wanted these things and the success they signified. He wanted the comfort and gratification of his father's approval. "Yes, Abba. I'll learn it well. You'll be proud of me."

When Ibrahim nicked himself behind the ear with the razor, the sting of soap jolted him back to the present. He lathered his body and rinsed himself with the little cup. Cleansed and renewed, he wrapped his *kikoi*[3] around his waist, stepped into his leather sandals, buttoned his white shirt, and climbed the stairs to see his father on the rooftop.

Sitting cushions had been placed there in the hope that some slight air movement could relieve the crushing heat. There was no air conditioning inside the sprawling family villa because there was no fuel for their generator. The powerful family had never suffered a shortage of any kind before.

"I've just returned from work, Abba. How are you this evening?"

"I'm concerned about your safety and future, my son. You are a talented intelligence officer and have brought honour to our family and to me. But we are entering a time of great peril."

Ibrahim knew the enemy's movements and conspiracies. His captives told him everything. The news was bad. He concealed his panic by projecting authority downward and obedience upward. He kept walking his tightrope of command. To waver was to fall into a bottomless pit. "You can count on me. The enemies won't win. I won't let you or the president down." What alternative was there?

Ibrahim watched his father light a cigarette and reach for his grapefruit juice. It disturbed him to see frustration and anxiety come over the old man's face.

"Don't be an idiot. This government is a hollow shell balanced on a matchstick. Any fool can tell that it will not survive longer than a matter of days." He gathered himself and lowered his voice. "Listen to me, son. I've learned of a great humiliation about to disgrace us."

Ibrahim's eyes widened. "And the president, surely he will protect us?"

His father shook his head slowly. "The president has betrayed us. He is preparing to abandon the country. He is leaving

3   In Somalia, men wear a cotton kilt called a *kikoi*, which is much cooler than trousers.

everything behind, except for what money he can steal and take with him."

They both looked up as the crescent moon began a timid appearance on the eastern horizon. "We will be face-to-face with those who know who we are and what we have done to them," his father continued. "Many people will have bitter memories of their time with us. We will be exposed to them. And alone."

In the milky air of dusk, colours faded to charcoal and ash. The bellow of high-powered diesel engines intruded on their conversation. Father and son could make out the convoy of two armoured personnel carriers. They were escorted by two pickups stuffed with soldiers. The vehicles bumped over a road that was more pothole than asphalt.

"The president is leaving us earlier than I thought," Ibrahim's father said. "He needs only two things now, money and protection. He thinks he can hang on to those despite his treason. The money will be handled by that ridiculous Omar. He is basically a white man, a calculating coward like the rest of them. He could not last one minute without the president's protection. Remember what Omar did to you?"

Ibrahim immediately recalled Omar's humiliating joke about "military intelligence" made at his and his father's expense in front of foreign dignitaries. He would never forget Omar's smug face.

"And I can just see him maneuvering his soft ass next to the money to escort it out of the country and into Swiss bank accounts," his father continued. "I would give everything to have him in my prison."

He had never displayed such angry cynicism before. If President Barre were gone, what would happen to the chain of command? Where would the orders come from? Who would obey Ibrahim now? The tightrope had snapped. His eyes stung. Some tears broke out of the secret prison where he locked up his feelings.

"Abba, what will we do?"

"There are two things you must do. Go to the compound, and kill each prisoner. If they get out, they will give dangerous information to our enemies. Then take as many weapons, vehicles, and men who will follow you to our hometown. If you get there soon, you will be the power amid the chaos."

The family's hometown, Merka, was on the coast, about one hundred kilometres distant. Only three hours' drive, Ibrahim figured.

"You and I have been utterly humiliated," his father said. "Our honour could not have been more deeply wounded if the president and Omar had fucked your mother and sisters on state television. Remember this always—unavenged shame stinks of weakness. The only asset you have left is fear—the fear you inspire because of what you have done, because of what you're capable of doing, and because you're my son.

"Go now. It's better to do these things at night."

3

OMAR SAT ON THE edge of his bed and threaded a new set of
laces through the four eyelets of his old Bata desert boots. He
wore khaki trousers and a thick cotton, long-sleeve shirt. It would
be better to travel without ID.

The houseboy came in with Omar's day bag and opened it for
him to inspect. His pants and shirts were carefully pressed, as
were his underwear and socks. The houseboy had been with the
family for most of his seventy or so years. No one knew his birth-
date. "Be careful when I'm away," Omar said. "Here is an advance."
He handed the houseboy an envelope with enough money to see
him through several months. A tear from the old man fell on the
proffered envelope. "I'll be back soon," Omar lied. He tried to
deceive himself that it was a small mercy not to burden this vulnerable and solitary man with the knowledge that he could never
return. But really, his conscience was just too drained for another
regret. The houseboy must have known this was the end.

He had paid off the driver and sent him away a week earlier.
The driver was family—a cousin from the desert who wanted to
stop driving camels and start driving a car. Omar told himself that

his cousin's loyalty was absolute—at least it always had been; he could only hope that he could trust him for one last task.

"Take your wages for the next year," Omar had said. "I have one request. Tell your brother to wait for me at this location. I'll be there soon." Omar had handed the driver an envelope with the money, a map, and instructions for when they met. "Keep the Land Cruiser, and save yourself."

Now a detachment of presidential guards waited right outside his door to take him to the convoy. Mogadishu's wrecked streets murmured cruel threats in the evening shadows as they travelled to the presidential palace.

At the compound two squat Russian armoured personnel carriers (APCs) crouched to receive their passengers. The rear opened like a giant steel maw. Grey exhaust puffed lazily from the idling brutes. They had eight big fat tires. Clumsy yellow-and-brown camouflage was a flimsy impersonation of the African desert. The drivers peered through slits of heavy bulletproof glass. Jerry cans of diesel fuel and drinking water were slung on the sides.

Standing next to the APC, Omar felt alone, small, and weak. A young major approached. "I'll take your bag, sir. President Barre is coming."

One Toyota Hilux pickup was at the front and another at the rear of the four-vehicle convoy. Heavy machine guns were bolted to the beds. Gunners checked their large-calibre ammunition feeds over and over.

"This is the order of march," the major said. "My truck will lead. The presidential APC will be second in line. Next is the APC with the president's wife and daughters. My deputy's truck will be in the rear position."

Evidently, the calculation was that any threat would come from the rear, when the president's flight became known. The women behind would act as a buffer.

Omar craved a human connection before his confinement in the APC's belly. "What is your name?" Omar asked the major.

"Moussa."

"And your first name?"

"Major. Please get in the presidential vehicle. His excellency will be here soon."

Omar entered. He heard a hydraulic whine, and then the rear gate thumped shut. High-powered air conditioning was on maximum for the cold-blooded president. In the darkness, Omar strapped himself into the nylon webbing seat, shivered, and tried to summon the presence of mind he would need for the journey. Finally, the rear gate fell open, and Omar squinted into the setting sun to see the approach of Barre's silhouette, accompanied by Major Moussa.

Barre entered and looked at the vehicle's occupants: Omar, the driver, the gunner in his turret, and two other soldiers. The president frowned. "I need to be able to speak to the minister in confidence."

"We always have a crew of a driver, a gunner, and at least two men in case of trouble," the major said.

Barre scowled. "They can do more good outside. Put them in the truck. I only need the driver and the gunner." The commander ordered the other two soldiers to climb into the crowded lead pickup.

Barre opened the built-in refrigerator, installed where ammunition used to be kept. The president nodded with satisfaction when he saw his favourites: Coca-Cola, cashews, and Cadbury's chocolate. He took his seat—the leather one with the single star on the back—strapped himself in, donned his headset, and ordered the convoy to proceed. The 260-horsepower turbo diesel growled, and fifteen tons of steel loaded with two tons of gold rolled south. Omar looked straight ahead, avoiding eye contact with Barre. It was good that the president despised small talk.

They drove through the night. At every turn in the road, Barre requested an update. Over and over the driver reported, "All clear."

At around midnight, Omar sensed the president relax. He took a long pull on his Coke and gazed at Omar in the faint blue interior light. "It's working out nicely when one considers the alternatives. What would you say, Omar?"

Omar struggled to mask his heaving disgust. "What do you mean, Excellency?"

The president reached down and tapped one of the olive-drab ammunition cases under his seat. He pulled his lips into a grin, and his eyebrows rose above his glasses. "I mean we will be all right, you and me. We will be just fine. I can have a fresh start, and so can you. I'll never have to worry about another war with those infidel Ethiopians. Tiresome famines can be somebody else's problem for a change. And those political midgets who conspired to take my power . . ." he caressed the ammunition box affectionately, "Aideed and Ali Mahdi, let them have it. They can receive the visits from self-righteous ambassadors whimpering about so-called human rights. They can have the World Bank hypocrites telling them all the things they can't do because of all the money they don't have. You know that game pretty well, eh, Omar? Don't forget. Money is the best weapon of all."

"Yes, sir." Omar wanted to say, "Shut up."

"And the hours we work barely leave us the time and energy to service our wives. There are beautiful women in Nairobi and not expensive. You see, I've decided to get out of politics. This is why we can speak like this, like two friends. I want to go into business. And I want to play the role of elder statesman. That can be useful in Africa. Maybe a UN contract here and there, or speaking engagements. It's important to maintain just enough profile. The way things are going, there will be more room for smart businesspeople in the arms trade. With no police or army, everyone will need guns. You'll help me. I want you to think about the opportunities when there is no government. Please prepare a memo to me on that as a priority."

He continued, practically talking to himself. "No matter what, we have enough to live like presidents for the rest of our lives." Barre finished his drink, closed his eyes, and started to snore. Omar hugged himself against the cold and quivered through the night.

At dawn the convoy stopped for a break. Omar walked into the bush to relieve himself after the long night's journey.

"Stop! Come back!" He froze in his tracks. Did they think he was trying to escape?

"I just need to piss."

"You are in a minefield. We planted them here to punish an enemy village. It's on the way to their water. Retrace your steps exactly," the soldier said.

The scrubby ground radiated deadly menace. He tiptoed back to the side of the road, and then dashed to the far side of the convoy, out of sight of the women as they chattered and performed their ablutions behind a sheet they took turns holding.

He needed to take himself out of this moment and recompose his thoughts to make the urine pass.

When he was seventeen, the old women in his family had agreed which cousin he should marry, but he never cooperated in closing the deal. He wanted to go far, and the marriage would hold him back. Omar had grumbled, sidestepped, and ultimately evaded that commitment by studying overseas.

As he urinated, he thought back to his life as a graduate student in California. He had basked in the fascination of Stanford University women who told him his poise and good manners were sexy. Finding partners had been easy and unencumbered by long-term expectations. He sighed as he zipped his fly. Then he stooped and tightened a double knot on both shoes.

Barre had used the presidential chamber pot in his vehicle and was talking with Major Moussa while he ate his breakfast. It was something about coordination with the Kenyan troops who would meet them at the border to take them to Nairobi. Omar sat on a campstool by the fire and thanked the corporal, who handed him tea and a piece of bread. What would be the fate of this young man? The soldier followed orders and maintained his military routine as if this mission was just like any other. Surely his commander had told him there was no return. Maybe Barre thought he could keep them as his personal bodyguards.

Major Moussa finished his consultation with the president and then turned to address the group. "Load up! We move in ten minutes." The turbo diesels thundered to life, and soon they were rolling toward the border again.

"Soon we will be in radio contact with the Kenyan military," Barre said. "President Moi has pledged full cooperation. You were right about that 25-percent discount. He requested a personal gift of five million."

"It was to be expected, Excellency. We will make the arrangements when we are settled in Nairobi," Omar said.

"He will put us up in the government guest house for VIPs as a gesture of brotherly friendship," Barre replied.

More likely to keep us under surveillance, Omar thought.

An explosion shook the APC, and it stopped dead.

"What happened?" Barre screamed. "Don't stop! Keep going!"

An ear-splitting *boom, boom, boom* came from the turret gun above them. Assault rifle fire chattered outside, then smacked into the gunner atop the turret. He slumped from his perch and slid to the floor.

"We're under attack!" Omar heard the driver say through his earphones. "The lead vehicle was hit and disabled. The driver is wounded. They need our help . . . and they're blocking our way forward. What are your orders, sir?"

Omar knelt by the gunner. Bullets had ripped a hole in his abdomen. "Stuff it with something!" the driver yelled. "Stuff the hole!" Omar grabbed a shirt from his bag and stuffed it in the wound. The soldier was paralyzed with shock.

"Get us out of here!" Barre howled through the pandemonium. "Full speed! Don't stop for anything!"

The APC roared back to life, leapt forward, lurched to the left, and then the passengers felt the nose fall off the road and dive into a ditch. The gunner was thrown forward. The engine spun past its red line and shrieked in mechanical agony. Eight frantic wheels found no purchase. Then, like a fighting bull just before the coup de grace, it idled in defeat, motionless. They were stuck.

The driver shouted what he was seeing through his slit of bulletproof glass. "Ten fighters with RPG launchers and assault rifles are approaching. They have separated into two groups. One in front of us. He's motioning us to get out. I lost sight of the other. They're pouring fuel over us. They want us to come out." He bent over his fallen comrade. "Dead."

"Shoot them! Shoot them!" Barre was furious. "Call for help. Call for reinforcements!"

"We will suffocate if they ignite us. And burn alive. I've seen it before. I won't die that way," the driver said. He flipped a switch, and the back of the vehicle opened. Piercing white light blinded Omar momentarily. Then he saw Major Moussa on the ground looking up with an incredulous stare.

The man's lower body was smashed from the waist down. His pelvis and legs were tread marks of green fabric, bloody mud, flesh, and splintered bone. His lips stretched tight across his gleaming white teeth. His agony was silent. They had run him over.

Ragged fighters with machine guns and RPGs yelled at them. Omar could summon nothing to say to Major Moussa. He turned toward his captors.

Guttural voices yelled at them. "Get out! Move to the side of the road! Barre! Down! Lie with your face down and your hands at the back of your head where we can see them. You move, we kill you!"

Barre lay on the ground, his face turned toward the vehicle. He had lost his glasses, and his feeble eyes shifted from side to side in confused rage. He would soon realize that he had been made a fool by Omar's deceit. Omar could never be safe again anywhere.

Fighters lashed the ammunition boxes to six camels, several boxes on each side. Barre shot Omar the murderous glare of a thief who has been double-crossed. Then he closed his eyes to await his fate.

Omar turned to sit next to Major Moussa and held his hand. The man died quietly. Perhaps his comrades would bury him. Probably they would run scared and leave him for the birds and hyenas. The assailants were unconcerned. It was a relief to Omar that they ignored the fluttering women hovering outside the second APC.

A boy led Omar's camel to him. It knelt, and he mounted.

4

....
Ottawa

THE DEFENDANT'S WATERY OLD man eyes made Anik Belanger mad. The spittle scum at the corner of his cracked lips also irritated the elegant young prosecutor. His dumpy daughter shot her a malignant glare. Anik averted her eyes to the white acoustic tiles of the courtroom ceiling and composed herself for the jury's decision. Anik hated losing.

The case was political dynamite. The Jewish community demanded action on Nazis like Otto Schuman who had hidden their past to sneak into Canada. Schuman's small town didn't think that way though. He was a jovial neighbour, churchgoer, and loving grandfather. Had he run a brothel of sex slaves in a Nazi concentration camp? No way.

Anik had been living and breathing Schuman's rotten past for a full year. It started when her childhood friend, Sophie, rushed into their weekly coffee date clutching her briefcase to her chest.

"What's wrong?" Anik asked.

Sophie's mascara ran with tears. She sat down without taking off her winter coat, opened her briefcase, and pulled three old notebooks from a manila envelope. "You need to help me. I can't read it. You need to read it for me."

"Take off your coat, catch your breath, and I'll get the coffee. Then tell me about it."

Anik returned shortly with the hot coffee, and her friend took a few careful sips. Sophie was still staggered by the sadness of losing her mother to cancer a couple of months earlier.

"In her last days, Mom just wanted to make sure everything was in order before she died. After she was buried, I needed to take a break from it all."

"You were such a wonderful daughter. You were holding her hand at the end. Edith didn't die lonely or alone. It was hard on you too."

"Mom wrote a letter to me. I didn't read it until today. Emotional procrastination, I know." Sophie's nose began running, and she rustled around in her handbag for a tissue. Anik took one from her purse and gave it to her. Then she reached out and held her hand. The two young women were quiet for a minute.

"She always worried something horrible would appear out of nowhere and hurt me. I thought it was just, you know, a personality problem." Sophie started sobbing. "I wish we didn't fight so much."

"What was it? What did you find?" Anik asked.

"A whore." Sophie looked down at the table. "She didn't want me to think she was a whore, but she needed me to know what had happened. After she was dead." Sophie looked straight into Anik's eyes. "You need to read her journals for me. Then you can tell me what to do."

"It's okay. It's okay." Anik put the notebooks back, pulled the thick envelope across the table, and slipped it into her briefcase. "I'll read it tonight, after work. I'll call you first thing in the morning. Let's not talk about it here, like this."

Sophie sniffed and then nodded. "Thanks for the coffee. Sorry. I really don't have anybody else I can talk to about this."

"Just take your time."

They sat in silence for a couple more minutes. Sophie's sadness was a lead weight in Anik's heart. She gently held her friend's hand and willed comfort with her touch. Sophie slowly raised her eyes and returned a small smile. Anik silently pledged to do something for her friend, without the least idea of what was in the journals. Then Sophie had to go back to her job at the bank and Anik to her job at the Department of Justice.

At that point she had been in the department a year, stuck at her desk working on a boring inter-provincial transportation law. She was sure this was not the right project for her and was looking for a way out. Anik craved something with action and profile. She was distracted by Sophie's envelope and unable to concentrate on the management of highway maintenance. After work, Anik rushed home to her downtown apartment. It was in a new building with hardwood floors and white walls. Besides Italian leather furniture, chrome track lighting, and IKEA dishes, there wasn't much else yet. When she had time she would think about getting some oriental carpets and modern art reproductions.

She poured a big glass of sauvignon blanc, put some rye crackers and cheese on a dish for dinner, threw on old jeans and a Rolling Stones T-shirt, lounged sideways on the sofa, and pulled out the contents of the envelope. It contained a letter and three dated notebooks. The notebooks were undamaged except for the grey of age, unlined paper bound between black cardboard.

The letter was dated November 11, 1991, just before Sophie had taken her mother, Edith, to the hospice for palliative care. Death came soon after.

Anik remembered Edith as delicate, thin, and often ill but always possessed of a silent dignity. She must have been beautiful as a young woman. Whenever Anik played at Sophie's house, which was next door, lunch was strangely proper with formal settings and always three courses. Edith was the first person Anik had met with a manicure. Her clothes were fashionable yet mournful. Anik's best friend, Sophie was a pretty blonde, perfectly groomed, and her clothes were always new, sunny, and bright. Anik was a tomboy, and her mom sent her out to play in cutoffs and a T-shirt.

The letter from Edith was short, and the writing was shaky.

> To my darling daughter,
>
> I could not tell you this while I was alive. I was afraid you would judge me harshly, as others did. I couldn't face you thinking I was a whore, and I did not want my ugly pain to hurt our little family.
>
> Perhaps you will have children, and they will need to know what I hid from you. In these journals I've written what happened to me in Ravensbruck camp.

The idea that Edith could have been called a whore was unfathomable to Anik.

> I survived, and I'm joyful because you came into my life. You were a strong girl, and you will be a strong woman, ready to read this. I wrote down everything I could remember as soon as I was free. Maybe you will want to talk to others. If God is willing, you will find a husband and have children. They should know what I learned. It's possible to find love and consolation after great hardship.
>
> I love you so much. I wish I could have brought happiness into our home. I hope this will explain why I was not a better mother.
>
> With my dearest hopes for your bright future,

Your loving mother,

Edith

Could these notebooks explain the mysterious sadness of Sophie's mother?

She looked down at the first one. The label's adhesive gave up and slipped off when she passed her fingers over the faded cover. Old paper dust clung to her fingertips. She worried that bending the pages would break them.

November 3, 1942

> The Germans took me out of France and put me in the Ravensbruck camp for women. They gave me striped prison clothes with a red triangle. Inside the triangle was P for political. I was in the Association of Communist Students in university, and we helped the resistance. They gave other colours and letters to Jews, Russians, and Gypsies.

> They took twelve of us to the men's camp at the quarry. I was confined in a little room by myself. The guards put men in a line outside my room. I was a sex slave for the best workers in the labour camps. It was a reward for them.

Anik's heart stung with guilt for having been uninterested and dismissive of Edith. This testimony required attentive reading. She sat up straight. Anik looked for Edith's presence in the words on the page. The letters leaned forward with formal precision. Old-fashioned loops adorned the beginnings of capital letters. Royal-blue ink lent an elegance of expression to an unspeakable experience. This was the handwriting of someone for whom penmanship was a sign of character and respect for the reader.

At law school, Anik had taken graduate seminar courses in war crimes. She researched the brutal atrocities of the Nazis for a paper on the Nuremberg trials. What she was reading now about systematic sexual assault at the Ravensbruck concentration camp for women was new information to her.

Edith listed the events that happened to her with remarkable recall. When other women spat on her and called her a whore, she had a date, names of the offenders, and if it was morning, afternoon, or night. When it came to the German guards who woke them up in the middle of the night to assault them, she put the names and the ranks, which she must have been able to tell from their uniforms. Sometimes she even included the names of their units and their command relationships up to the camp commandants, Max Koegel and Fritz Suhren. Anik recognized those two names. After they were captured, Koegel killed himself, and Suhren was executed.

Now the ghosts that had haunted Sophie's home were made visible. Anik had an idea of how she could help Sophie, and how this could help her. She took the journal to her desk and started putting every name she encountered into her IBM PC with a backup to a brand-new floppy disk.

At 3:00 a.m. Anik made herself a strong coffee and turned to the third journal. It began in the winter of 1944. Edith said she got less food as spring approached.

> I was beginning to starve. Sergeant Schuman said I was useless for my work, and a replacement prostitute required my bed. He sent me back to Ravensbruck, to die I supposed.
>
> April 23, 1945
>
> The guard told me to get up, go outside and get in line. I moved slowly. I thought it was the end. When I was outside, it was bright and hard for me to see at first. There were other women in striped prison uniforms. At the end of the line was a white bus. On its side was the yellow-and-blue flag of Sweden. When we reached the bus, a

soldier in a Swedish uniform asked for my name. He wrote it down and said I should take the triangle off. I pulled it off, threw it in the dirt, and got on the bus. They took me to Malmo, and then I went to Canada.

That was the last entry.

Ravensbruck wasn't covered by the Nuremberg trials. Maybe one of the Allied forces that occupied defeated Germany dealt with it. Probably Britain. Then it hit her. There could have been no justice for what happened to Edith because it was not a crime in the law of war. This could be big. It was an opportunity to create an international precedent about sexual assault and crimes against humanity.

Anik put the journals back in the envelope. Then she took a long shower and let the hot water flow over her tense shoulders and down her back. She towelled off, put on her flannel pajamas, and slipped under the duvet. She slept fitfully for a couple of hours until the radio alarm clock woke her up with Bryan Adams singing "Everything I Do, I Do It for You."

Anik called Sophie before she went to work.

"Did you read it? What did it say?" Sophie's voice was hoarse. Anik needed to handle this properly. She needed to get something from Sophie, and it would not be easy.

"Terrible things happened to your mother in Ravensbruck."

"Like what?"

"I'm coming to see you. Let's meet at the coffee shop at ten thirty."

"Why can't you tell me over the phone?"

"I want to be with you when I tell you. It wouldn't be right for you to be alone."

Sophie was silent for a moment. "Okay. Bye."

Anik skipped her makeup, pulled on her suit dress, threw her high heels in her briefcase, put on her Nikes, and hurried to her office. She needed to photocopy some forms for Sophie to sign.

Anik filled out as much of the information about Edith and Sophie as she could, put the papers in a folder, and then grabbed a cab to the coffee shop. She dreaded the idea of describing what was in the journals and rehearsed in her mind what she should say.

Sophie was already there with two lattes when Anik arrived. She looked puzzled and worried.

Edith must have known that hurt would be inevitable. Anik decided that softening the reality would not be right for either of them. "You should read it too. She wanted you to know what they did. She was forced to be a sex slave in a Nazi camp. She had no choice."

Sophie covered her face with her hands. After a long moment of silence, Anik continued. "But she was strong. She decided to survive and make a new life. We should be inspired by her courage."

Sophie removed her hands from her face. "She never told me about that." Sophie sounded angry and confused. "She must have been ashamed."

"But it's amazing your mother made this journal. She did it for a reason. What we do with it can give meaning to her suffering."

Sophie nodded. "She wanted to explain it to me. She always said the war years were difficult. I guess that's why she was always so sad and why her marriage couldn't last. I'll read it, and then I'll know. I don't think anyone else needs to know. I'll take those journals back. Maybe I should burn them, and this sad story can stop right here—before it goes any further than our conversation." Sophie looked into her coffee cup and took a long sip.

"No, you can't burn them," Anik almost shouted. "I need them—I mean, we need them. They're evidence."

Sophie looked at her in surprise. "This is a family thing, and I'm the only family. I don't know what you mean." Anik felt Sophie's eyes searching her face for a clue about what was happening. Anik pushed as much kindness and concern into her expression as she could muster.

"Listen to me, Sophie. There's something we can do. There's something we have to do." Anik was talking too fast and needed to regain her breath and her composure. "Your mother named the war criminals responsible, including their rank and role. If we can find any of these men in Canada, we can take them to court. We can charge them as if what they did to her happened in Canada."

Sophie shook her head. "But it didn't happen in Canada. It happened a lifetime ago. It's humiliating It's . . . over."

"I think we can do it. They changed the laws to include war criminals. Let me try to make the case for her. Criminal Code 273, sexual assault—aggravated sexual assault—and probably conspiracy too. I want to run the names from your mother's journal against our database. Don't you think that's what she would have wanted? What about all the other women? This would be for them too."

"I think she wanted just me to know this. I don't want to have kids, so nobody else needs to know." A dark mass of sadness pushed words away. Finally, Sophie spoke again. "You knew her. She was a private person."

"This would honour her memory and her strength. Trust me. I'll be careful."

"Are you sure about this?"

A little too quickly, Anik reached into her briefcase and pulled out a file with the permission forms. "Just sign where I put the sticky notes. That's all you need to do. I'll take it from there."

Sophie's concerns and reluctance gave up in the face of Anik's confident insistence. "I'm trusting you to do the right thing. You're my best friend." She pulled out a ballpoint pen and signed in a flustered rush. Looking emotionally disoriented and unsure if this was a wise thing, she stood up. "Goodbye," she said, and then she left.

Back in her office, Sophie's signed permission form in hand, Anik's ambition was fired up. She booted up her PC, turned on the monitor, and logged into the Department of Justice war crimes database of postwar German immigrants to Canada. It was a secret list for investigating war crimes allegations. One by one she input the names that Edith had written in her journals. At the forty-sixth entry, Anik stared at the screen until her eyes stung. There was a hit: Otto Schuman.

Anik hated Schuman with satisfying righteousness. Edith wrote that he was present at all her forced couplings. When pregnancies inevitably occurred, Schuman escorted Edith and the other women at gunpoint to the clinic and oversaw the abortions. She imagined him as a stupid brute. He must be the kind of man who, secure in his obedience to superiors, indulged cruel appetites on those below with greedy abandon. She made a vow to the illuminated green letters on the screen that he would pay.

Anik felt a thrill of adrenalin. This case could make her reputation.

5

THE DEPARTMENT OF JUSTICE needed a war crime. Anik
hoped her superiors would think this was a good one, maybe even
one for the legal history books. Schuman hadn't even changed
his name—just his background story. She had checked out his
immigration records and worked up a memo for departmental
approval to arrest and prosecute Schuman on the basis of the
journals as evidence. Today was the day to find out whether her
case was going forward.

Anik got up from her workstation and walked down the hall
to see Don Burroughs. He was the team leader for war crimes. It
would be his call. She would only get one shot at this. If there was
a stumbling block, Sophie might change her mind.

Anik stopped by the washroom to check her appearance. She
put on mauve lipstick and some subtle eyeliner. She straightened
her long black ponytail. There were dark circles under her dark
brown eyes. That was okay. Everyone in this office was supposed
to be over-worked. She got a nice warm feeling and imagined
telling her family about an early promotion.

"He's in. Just knock on the door," the secretary said.

"What is it?" Don asked.

Anik stepped in, and Don looked up from a disordered desk covered in files and several dirty coffee cups. "I have got a good case for us." She held out the memo she had prepared for him.

"What?" Don said with disinterest. Anik assumed he would be at this same desk, in this same role, for the next eight years or so until he retired. This job was beyond his abilities and his imagination. She could do it better than him. She would do it with passion and creativity. His hair needed a trim and his suit a dry clean.

"I found new evidence about Ravensbruck and a Canadian citizen. We have the power to apply the Canadian Criminal Code for acts committed outside of Canada when it comes to war crimes. That's what I'm proposing."

"Aren't you supposed to be doing a copyedit of the transportation regulations?"

She ignored his comment. "This is the match I found. Sergeant Otto Schuman. Listen to this." Anik opened the journal to one of several places where she had placed bookmarks and read. "November 24, 1941. It was cold and snowing. After the midnight bell, Sergeant Otto Schuman came into my room. He woke me by placing his knife at my throat. 'If you make a noise, I'll cut your throat. One less communist. It will be no loss. It will be good,' he said to me. Then he forced himself on me. He pulled my head up by my hair and said, 'Not a single word, or you will go with the others to the gas chambers.'"

Anik looked up. "Schuman is here in Canada. He came in 1948. A contact of mine in Citizenship and Immigration pulled his file, and it checked out. Their fax is attached to the memo. He lied about his Nazi military background—said he was a civilian mechanic. Now he's retired in Southern Ontario."

Don spread his arms over his messy desk. "Do I look like a guy who needs more work?"

"I know how busy you are," Anik said, "so I'll take this on. I know the issues. The transport regs can wait. If the department doesn't get some good war crimes cases, it will be embarrassing for the government. Remember, our new minister said he wanted to be aggressive on finding the war criminals who snuck into Canada."

She handed him the memo, and he motioned her to take a seat in the chair across the desk from him.

"You got the Immigration Department to pull the file without asking me? I don't like that kind of surprise." He scanned the memo with a frown. "What about the daughter?"

"We have her permission, in writing. A copy of that is attached too. Edith has no other survivors."

He shifted a file and grabbed the copy of the Fourth Geneva Convention he always kept on his desk, reading from it in a pedantic voice. "Willful killing, torture, or inhuman treatment, including . . . willfully causing great suffering or serious injury to body or health, unlawful deportation or transfer or unlawful confinement of a protected person, compelling a protected person to serve in the forces of a hostile power, or willfully depriving a protected person of the rights of fair and regular trial . . . taking of hostages and extensive destruction and appropriation of property, not justified by military necessity and carried out unlawfully and wantonly."

Don looked up with a skeptical squint. "Fourth Geneva—ratified after this shit, but it's the gold standard by which to judge a war crime. Doesn't sound like what your little Sergeant Schuman got up to. Maybe we could work with unlawful confinement, but it would be a stretch. Edith is dead. There's no such thing as genocide against communists. We need to concentrate our limited resources on cases we can win. This is a borderline case at best. And this guy was a small fish." At least Don was talking to her like it was her business. He didn't totally dismiss her. That was a good sign.

"Rank doesn't excuse anything," she said. "He'll give us leads about the chain of command—including where they are now.

Anyway, we don't have any other cases for investigation and prosecution right now."

Don looked her straight in the eye and chuckled. "You think
this will make you a fucking hero, right?" He was right—and
probably jealous too. It would make her a hero. Her case would
redefine sexual violence as a war crime. That's what the legal
history books would remember.

"It's not about me," Anik said. "It's about Edith and the other
women like her."

Don initialled his approval on the memo. "We can send it
upstairs, I guess. You found it, so you can lead it. I'll send it to
the deputy. We do need at least one case." The deputy was the top
bureaucrat in the department and the gatekeeper to the minister.
Anything with political implications went through the deputy.
Anik didn't know him, and he didn't know her.

Don looked down at the papers on his desk. "Win or lose, this
will define your career. Be careful what you wish for."

A year later in the courtroom, Anik remembered his warning.
And what was the balance on the scale? She had started this
case buoyant with righteous virtue. It hit the press as soon as
Schuman was arrested and charges laid. Then invitations to
better and better dinner parties from more and more senior
lawyers and mandarins kept on coming. The Israeli ambassador
even hosted her as a guest of honour at a diplomatic dinner. Her
ego swelled accordingly.

Then things changed. Her forward-leaning confidence turned
into apprehensive uncertainty, and the invitations stopped. The
business community in Schuman's town created a legal defence
fund for him. Top-line Toronto lawyers took on his case for its
notoriety and played it for maximum media profile. The burden
of Nazi war crimes didn't belong on the shoulders of a poor
conscripted soldier, they said. Schuman had no choice but to
obey orders.

His cute grandchildren took the stand and told the jury every-body loved Schuman.

"He never killed anybody. He wouldn't hurt a fly."

"Wouldn't you need to kill at least one person to be a war criminal?"

The defence cast doubt on the journals as valid evidence. The journals were not sworn testimony, unlike the gushing of Schuman's grandchildren.

It was time for Anik to sum up the case for the prosecution. She had done the best she could with the evidence she had. What happened to Edith was an irrefutable historical reality. She brought an East German historian to corroborate the consistency of journals with the admittedly scant facts about Ravensbruck.

Anik knew there were two weak links in her strategy. First, there was no witness (besides Schuman) to what happened to Edith, no witness of Schuman's crime. Second, if the crime was systemic, why hang it on Schuman? She decided to compensate for evidentiary weakness with moral force.

Anik stood before the jury and tried to present the stance and expression of a lawyer with far more experience than her few years. It felt like standing on thin ice. *Fake it till you make it,* she said silently to herself.

"The court has seen what happened at Ravensbruck to thou-sands of women. We have before us the case of one of these victims. Out of thousands of women and incalculable suffering, one criminal case makes it across the world, across half a century, and sets this crime in front of me and in front of you, the jurors. We wish we could do more for the women who have suffered and died without a shred of justice. In anonymity. Without retribution for the horror of sexual violence to which they were subjected as an instrument of war."

The twelve jurors all gave Anik their full attention but in dif-ferent ways. A chubby middle-aged man looked defensive and skeptical. That was bad. A young woman radiated righteous indignation. That was good. Anik would turn up the temperature.

"Fate has put but one opportunity for justice before us. Here in Canada, in this court, on this day in 1991. Yes, you must decide based on the evidence, but you must also express the moral horror and repugnance with which we view the violation of Edith's body and spirit by Otto Schuman. Attainable justice is limited to the crime of one man against one woman. A guilty verdict may seem small compared to the enormous scale of the horror. But consider this. What if Edith was your daughter? Your decision will be a historic moral landmark in condemning sexual violence as an egregious violation of the law of war and a crime against humanity."

She tried to read the faces of the jury members. The skeptical man was listening carefully now. Maybe he was moving to her way of thinking. A wave of sadness passed across the face of a short, stocky man with the rough hands and sunburn of a blue-collar worker.

Anik looked in the eyes of the elderly woman with blue hair who was forewoman of the jury. "What if Edith was you?" she said in closing.

The jury forewoman reacted badly to being cast in the role of a victim. She must have thought this could never happen to her. She rolled her eyes in disgust. Anik had overshot the mark, and her heart sank.

Then came the defence lawyer's statement. He looked like he could have been the husband or pastor of the jury forewoman. Although he was a publicity-seeking member of the moneyed elite, often appearing in tuxedos at high-powered events, he was wearing an everyman's rumpled brown suit.

"Otto Schuman is the kind of guy we want as a neighbour," he said in a relaxed conversational tone. "Upstanding, responsible, and hard working. A wonderful father and grandfather. We heard that firsthand, not from some old journals."

He received some knowing smiles in the jury.

"We don't really know much about the accuser. She's not here. She never complained in person. We don't know if Edith received special benefits for sleeping with the enemy. We don't know if the sex was non-consensual."

Anik stood up. "Objection! This is total speculation—completely unfounded. I request that it be struck from the evidence." The judge sustained her objection, but the seeds of doubt were scattered all around now.

"My learned colleague said you had a moral choice to make. Of all the dubious, unsubstantiated, and immature ideas she has introduced, this one is the most cockeyed of all."

There were a few laughs from the jury. Anik was losing them.

"Here in Canada, do we need to worry about our moral fitness? I'm pretty sure we fought and died on the side of the righteous, our brave fathers giving up their lives in the fight for freedom against the Nazis. I'm pretty sure we are the ones who have taken in and sheltered Edith plus millions of others in our beautiful country. We still do that—look at all the Africans and Asians coming here every day to benefit from our generosity."

The all-white jury nodded knowingly.

"And even if we did accept these journals—unsigned, I might add—as evidence, does the moral weight of the Nazis' crimes really rest on the shoulders of this one upstanding senior citizen? Of course not. No crime has even been proven.

"You might even think that—if there was a little non-consensual sex fifty years ago—this case kind of cheapens the idea of crimes against humanity. Your duty is to find Mr. Schuman innocent.

"Thank you for your attention, and thank you for your service," he concluded and then moved back to his seat beside Schuman and his daughter.

The judge dismissed the jury to deliberate. Anik was paralyzed by an overpowering anxiety that she had never felt before.

After about an hour, the jury filed back into the courtroom. She scanned their faces, looking for indicators of what she would know in a matter of seconds. It felt like an infinity of time as the judge read from a card in front of her. "The defendant has been charged with sexual assault, conspiracy for sexual assault, kidnapping, and conspiracy for kidnapping. These charges have been laid by the federal government under the 1987 amendments of the Criminal Code that permit the federal government to prosecute Criminal Code violations committed outside the borders of Canada. What is the decision of the jury?"

The jury forewoman stared at the small piece of paper in her hand. "Ma'am, Madame Justice, not guilty."

Schuman's daughter stretched her arms to the ceiling and looked at her father with ecstasy. "Thank God! Praise the Lord! Daddy, we can take you home now!" Tears seeped from his cloudy eyes.

"Order. Order!" the judge demanded.

"Yes, ma'am. My father would never do such things, you know."

"Mr. Schuman, you're free to go, now."

Anik turned to see Sophie walking out the door. *I've betrayed Edith and Sophie*, she thought, floundering in a mire of guilt and shame. Anik's head fell into her hands.

Don, who had been sitting along the back wall with the few official observers permitted by the judge, approached her. "No comments. Just come with me. The minister needs to know about this before he sees it on the news tonight."

Don hailed a cab and opened the door for her. She scooted across the back seat. This could not be over—not like this. Giving bad news to the minister and losing Sophie's friendship filled her gut with an acid compound of anguish and frustration. "We need to appeal. He's guilty, and there's more to this case," Anik said in desperation.

"Doesn't matter," Don said. "I know it. You know it. The judge knows it. Your case just wasn't good enough. The victim is dead and can't testify. This is over."

"Let's try—or at least keep working the case. Please support me on this. And we should broaden it. We could find the general who planned and approved the sex crimes and God knows what else. That's who needs to pay. We have leads we can take back to Germany."

"What part of 'no' don't you understand? This is done. Nobody in Europe wants to pick old scabs like this. Just forget it. You get the cab. I'm short of cash today."

Her disordered frustrations heated into anger. The taxi arrived at the Department of Justice, and she handed the driver ten dollars without waiting for change and shoved the door open.

"Watch out!" the taxi driver screamed. Wheels screeched, and a horn blared. A teenager at the wheel of a fluorescent muscle car howled "You fuckin' idiot!" She pasted herself against the taxi as the car barely avoided smashing into the taxi door and her.

"Sorry. I'm sorry," she muttered to no one in particular, then stepped behind the cab and onto the sidewalk. Road salt from the dirty cab smeared her black suit dress. Anik was dizzy with disorientation. She couldn't trust her instincts anymore.

"Pull yourself together, Anik," Don said. "It won't be an easy meeting."

Anik wanted him to tell her not to worry. She wanted him to tell her that it would be okay.

"How do you think we should handle it?" she asked.

"You'll see the deputy minister first. He'll decide how you should handle it. He'll be pissed."

"You'll be with me, right?" Anik asked as they stepped into the elevator. Don pushed the buttons for floors four and nine.

"I don't need to be there." He stepped off at the fourth floor, and Anik rode up to the ninth floor by herself. The top floor housed the minister, his political staff, the deputy minister, his support team, and the government's chief counsel. A hush of stress was in the air.

A sign hanging from the ceiling in front of a suite of offices said, "Deputy Minister." She walked in, and the secretary told her to sit on a bench outside the door. Anik looked at the numbered doors up and down the hallway. They were labelled with acronyms with which she was not familiar. The faceless maze of the place felt strange and unforgiving.

She looked at her watch and saw that she had been waiting for twenty-five long minutes. Finally, the deputy stepped out with a broad smile over his bright red bowtie. His wavy grey hair was carefully coiffed. She stood up and smiled back with relief. Anik had expected him to be angry, but he didn't look that way.

"You must be Anik. It's on the news already. The minister is waiting for us. The media is quite sympathetic to the defendant. What happened?"

"The defence manipulated the jury into sympathy for Schuman. The judge shouldn't have permitted it. It was inappropriate and unfortunate." She had rehearsed this line over and over in her mind.

His smile turned grim, and Anik had a feeling she was alone in unfriendly territory. "Unfortunate indeed—terrible, in fact. Embarrassing, you might say. We're not supposed to lose. When the government loses against a senior citizen, everyone thinks we're mean and incompetent. It looks like a persecution instead of a prosecution."

Suddenly Anik was scared that she had landed on the wrong side of the powerful forces at the summit of government. Her breath shortened. "Schuman got off, but this case . . . a victim came to Canada and became a citizen," she said in an uncertain voice. "I believe we need to pursue this as a matter of policy."

"Believe what you want, but you don't set policy, and don't you dare say that to the minister. Deciding what to do next is far above your pay grade. This minister is new. He doesn't understand the department or his role yet. Just give him the facts of the judgement. He'll get used to hearing bad news before long. Let's go."

They got up, and the deputy recovered his cold smile. "You know, I was surprised you wanted that job in the first place. Most yuppies want corporate, taxation, or constitutional law—something that's a path to partnership in one of the big Toronto firms. But not you, I guess."

They stepped across the hall into the ministerial offices. "Good morning, Deputy," the secretary said. "The minister is waiting for you. Go on in."

An enormous plate-glass window offered a vista of the snowy Gatineau Hills across the icy Ottawa River. The sun's glare was painful. Opposite the window, flanked by Canadian flags, the minister was hunched over a stack of documents to sign as his political advisor quietly muttered pros and cons to him. They both looked up at her.

Minister Sandy MacDowell was a tall, slim man with a shock of wiry red hair shot through with grey. He looked older than his pictures in the news. His formerly athletic frame was stooped now. Anik didn't know what to expect. She desperately wanted his kind smile to be authentic.

Standing as if at attention, the deputy spoke. "Minister, I have some bad news. Schuman was found not guilty."

"Just as well," the political advisor said. "Hauling an old cripple off to jail is not exactly on party message."

The minister furrowed his brow and looked at his political advisor. "I disagree. It was an important case to prosecute. It was a matter of political principle. We haven't met, but you must be Anik Belanger, the prosecutor."

"Yes, I am." The minister stood up and extended his hand. Anik stepped forward and shook hands with him. She felt a physical lightness of relief at the minister's reaction.

"I used to work in your area but at the UN," he said. "We lectured countries on human rights but never got so far as prosecutions. I plan to change that as minister. It's the right thing to do.

But it won't be politically easy." He looked intently at her. "What happened, Anik? What next?"

She had the minister's full attention for a critical instant. There may never be another opportunity like this. The words came spilling out of her mouth. "This is a small setback in a bigger picture. It goes far beyond Schuman. We have leads about the intellectual authors. We can find the generals who issued the orders. I recommend we make a statement regretting the judgement and calling for an international inquiry. There is no time limitation for prosecution of crimes against humanity. It would be a political precedent and show your government's leadership on human rights. It would be a first. We would make sexual violence in war a crime against humanity," Anik said.

The minister looked thoughtful. She could tell he liked the idea. Maybe the year of emotional drain and late nights was leading somewhere after all. Somewhere better. She had a faint hope that a successful appeal could restore her friendship with Sophie.

"I read about what's happening now in Sudan, El Salvador, and Bosnia," the minister said. "How are our peacekeepers handling this stuff on the ground? I have no idea. You're right. My political intuition tells me this issue is not going away."

This was exactly the conclusion that she needed him to reach. Warmed by relief, she started formulating the announcement of a new initiative she would develop. As she was about to open her mouth to speak, the minister turned away from her.

"Deputy, what do you think?"

The deputy's moist complexion flushed red with alarm, even as his smile stayed calm and even. She had probably made an enemy of him, but what difference did it make if the minister was on board and could see the big picture?

"Minister, we all want the same thing as Anik," the deputy said in a soothing, cultured voice. "At the same time, this doesn't make strategic sense. Before proceeding, you would need to consult with your colleague, the minister of external affairs. As you know, all eyes are on the fall of the Berlin Wall and German reunification right now. The prime minister is on his way to Bonn, and Nazi war crimes are not in his talking points. Trade and security are on the leaders' agenda. The issue is not ripe for moving forward at this time. Don't forget we have to worry about Canada splitting up if the Québec separatists have their way. It's not the moment for our department to create a distraction from government priorities."

The minister sat back and thought about it. "Hmm . . . Good points. Okay. Maybe we can come back to this once the dust has settled."

The minister's secretary walked in. "Prime minister's office on the line. They want to talk about the legal strategy for the North American Free Trade Agreement. They say it's urgent."

"They always say it's urgent. Anik, I want to continue this conversation with you. Come back in a couple of months, and give me your ideas. Thanks everybody." The minister's phone rang, and he picked it up before she could reply. The minister's secretary hurried Anik and the others out of the office

"Anik, I need to talk to you. Privately," the deputy said. Anik's nerves were rattled, and she wanted to be alone, some place where she could let down her guard. The cool composure into which she had forced her face trembled from the anxiety and anger coursing through her emotions. Her entire professional future was in play.

She followed the deputy into his office. He slammed the door. The man was rigid with tension and raised a hand as if to strike her. "Never do that to me again," he hissed. "Never surprise me in front of the minister. You know why you got that case, don't you? You're junior. It was a dog. But we needed to do something, and I couldn't expose my top talent to that kind of risk." He turned his back and moved to his desk. "It was a learning opportunity for you, but you didn't learn anything."

Anik felt unbalanced, as if she were swaying on the edge of a precipice.

"The minister doesn't understand what the hell you're talking about!" the deputy continued. "I have to protect him from your silly adventurism. You lost. You need a break. Take a year off. Take a leave of absence. Go."

She sat there, stunned. Could he really do that? Couldn't she complain or appeal?

"You're dismissed. I'll have your leave processed by the end of the day. I'm busy, just go."

In a state of confusion, Anik got up. Her legs shook with frustrated anger as she stepped out of the office and walked down the hall. She looked at the closed door to the minister's office. A chapter of her life was over. It had ended in a failure that cost her reputation and her best friend. Government—*it's all about dominance and submission*, she reflected bitterly.

She walked to the elevator and went down to her spartan workstation on the fourth floor. It looked small and pathetic compared to the deputy and the minister's offices. She would feel her anger in its fullness when she was at home, by herself.

When she recovered her ability to think clearly, Anik made a promise to herself. This would be a tactical defeat only. She would find a way to redeem herself.

She sat down at her desk and flipped through her Rolodex. Amnesty International, London Office. Human Rights Watch, New York. United Nations Human Rights Commission, Geneva. Justice Before Peace, New York. She had really hit it off with Ruth, the executive director. They were cutting edge on sexual violence. They were working on the war crimes of today, not fifty years ago. She would go to the field, where the action was. She would return to the minister with fresh ideas from the battlegrounds of today's war crimes. That's how she could make her mark. She would call Ruth tomorrow.

Anik put on her Nikes and walked home with her personal possessions in a single filing box.

6

....

The Somali Desert

WHEN THEY WERE WELL away from the defeated convoy, Omar dismounted and stumbled on trembling legs. With deep relief and respect, he embraced the man leading the caravan.

"*Salaam walekum*, Bilal," Omar said. The man was about forty, like Omar, but the lines of his burnt leathery face told a long story of life under the desert sun. He wore a red-checked *kikoi* skirt, a faded khaki shirt, and a white skullcap. "Thank you, my dear cousin. You got my message, and you came. Was no one injured?"

"*Salaam*, Omar. The message found us, and we came," Bilal replied with distance and slow caution. "Yes, these are our winter grazing grounds. We were not far away. No, no one on our side was hurt. The boxes of ammunition are heavy, but the camels are strong. It was difficult. You asked much of us. Maybe too much," he added in a whisper that was almost inaudible to Omar. "What is in these boxes? Bullets are not so heavy as this."

"Gold," Omar said. If Bilal had a reaction to this news, he kept it hidden.

"You ride behind me," Bilal instructed. "We will join the old slave route east. Few use it these days. Let's go." The long line of animals strode off. "It's your own camel that you ride, Omar. He's old, and he's bad tempered, but he knows this route." His animal was ugly for a camel. He had scars from fighting with others— perhaps also from beatings. Its hide was mousey grey, and its old teeth were orange.

"He does look familiar," Omar said. "It's been so long I forgot his name."

"Saeed," Bilal said. That was it. His name meant "Happy." "You misjudged his character when he was a calf," Bilal reminded him.

Omar accepted Bilal's offer of a muslin cloth. He wrapped it around his head. Then Omar pulled a pair of Ray-Bans out of his shirt pocket.

Happy kept his place as second in line. Omar tried to lose himself in the timeless rhythm of the caravan. He had imagined this moment as one of personal liberation. He tried to push out the oppressive guilt of betrayal with the astringent scent of the thorn scrub. He meditated on the subtle sandy undulation of the landscape. It didn't work. The terror and desolation of Major Moussa's face smoldered in his head.

Omar's hands were sticky with the gunner's dried blood. Razors of guilt shredded his self-worth. He tried to rationalize honour into his actions, but it was all in vain. Instead, he turned his mind to the simpler matter of why he was riding with Bilal.

When he was six, his father decided that every year for a month, Omar would be a desert nomad, like his forbearers. The first time, he was petrified to leave the soft, fat, closed world of his privileged family home in Mogadishu. His father took him to the edge of the city. They walked up to a line of camels, laden with trading goods. A young boy approached Omar and took his hand. "They told me to be your friend," the boy said. "Come, we're ready to go." This was Omar's first introduction to Bilal, son of one of his father's cousins.

Six-year-old Omar felt the judgmental gaze of his clansmen sizing him up. He feared they assumed he was delicate and cowardly. He barely held back his tears when his father gave him a stiff, formal farewell. Omar carried no baggage, no water, and no prior knowledge of this alien and frightening way of life.

In time, as his father intended, he came to understand the ancient bonds of mutual obligation that held families and sub-clans together. The limits of his physical and psychological endurance stretched. He stuck close to Bilal, who openly shared everything he knew with Omar. Bilal also made sure he was fed and clothed.

They slept side by side in Bilal's family tent. Until Omar learned to control thirst, Bilal gave him more than his fair share from the leather water bag. It tasted of old camel skin and dirt. With each year's journey, Omar absorbed more and more of the cruel beauty of their austere life, absolute Islamic faith, and implacable sense of justice in a zero-sum world. He felt sure that this was the way the first prophet, Abraham, had lived. Then and now the nomadic life was a source of virtue and merit.

The caravan and the gold slowly wove through the wicked thorn wasteland. Before long they joined an ancient trail to the abandoned Arab slave ports on the Indian Ocean.

At nightfall they stopped at a clearing spotted with the remains of previous campfires. The women assembled five round tents made of branches and skins, one for each family. Omar was given a small amount of water to cleanse his bloody hands. After a meal of flatbread and dried meat, Omar sat beside Bilal to join him in a glass of cardamom-spiced tea. They looked into the expiring embers of the cooking fire.

"I did what you asked," Bilal said. "I couldn't refuse you. Nor could you refuse me. I never asked you for anything despite your wealth and prestige of position. I'm responsible for my family and for the animals. Tell me, what will be the consequences for me and those I protect? What comes next? I'm uneasy."

Hyenas grunted and laughed in the distance. "I understand your worry," Omar replied. "The capital is in chaos. Our country has fallen off the end of the world. Our president abandoned what he had already destroyed and stole the little that remained. Foolishly, I thought things would be otherwise. But when I learned of his treasonous plans, this was the only remedy I could think of. Bilal, terrible times are upon us. I pray to God I've acted correctly. Our trouble will become worse and will endure. But you must know that you have acted honourably, that Barre has no power to reach you. He does not know my family was involved. This is a safe secret, and your people must keep it that way."

Bilal chewed thoughtfully on a twig. "I made a mistake. If I had known this was about gold, I would have killed Barre. We should have killed them all. The survivors must have reached the Kenyan border post by now. Barre will think about finding you through your family first. I would. Any of us would. Who else knows?"

This was an uncomfortable question. "Many people know Barre took the gold. Only you and I know who has it now." He looked at his hands. There had not been enough water to clean all the blood off them. Moussa's blood was still under his nails. "We hope. We hope our secret stays hidden until we are safe in our graves. It's a curse." He spat in the dust.

"Bad times are not new. My brothers and cousins have suffered the sacrifice and danger of service in the army," Bilal said. "And yet our men came back with weapons and the knowledge to use them. You saw their work this morning. I keep my faith in Allah and the truth of his messenger, Muhammad, peace be upon him. I trust that our old ways and ancient paths will continue to provide pasture, and a good camel will always fetch a good price. This is my plan. What is yours?"

Omar had a sketch of a plan in his mind, and it involved a long journey to a remote island off the coast of Kenya. He was unsure how his cousin would react, so he spoke carefully. "I believe that Lamu is a safe place, and I ask that we continue there. This is where I'll hide the gold in safekeeping. I owe you an enormous debt and will provide a gift to you every year as my thanks."

Bilal drew circles in the sand with his fingers as he pondered Omar's plan. He nodded. "It should be a small gift. It's bad to look rich. Goodnight."

Pasture was decent, and the animals stayed healthy. They did not encounter other caravans on the route to the coast.

After a week of travel, the desert gave way to sporadic fields. Kenyan trucks shattered the desert calm with the bray of unmuffled exhausts and the howl of air brakes. Omar felt the nervous tension of the nomad approaching a settled world where he had no place. In this borderland between a state that had failed and one that muddled along, they passed small ghettos of Somali refugees huddled around makeshift tents covered in flimsy blue plastic tarps.

Earlier in the day, at a village on the trail, Omar had bought three young goats, a bag of rice, and a four-litre can of cooking oil. His purpose was a big festive meal to thank the five families who had risked their lives as a matter of automatic obligation to him. Three roasted goats should be enough, and the rice would fill stoic bellies accustomed to meagre rations of dried camel meat, tea, and flatbread cooked over an open fire. Looking at the USAID insignia on the rice and oil in the shop, he wondered how many other Stanford graduates had bought and tasted food aid.

He found a telephone in the village and told his friend he was coming to Lamu.

In the hours of meal preparation, children watched in suspense and fascination as the men killed, skinned, and butchered the kids. Their dying eyes, spilled entrails, and blood seeping into the sand reminded Omar of Major Moussa, and his stomach turned. Women roasted the meat slowly over a carefully tended fire and simmered oily rice. Kidneys, liver, heart, and testicles were grilled separately as special treats.

The meal was eaten quickly and with great relish. Omar was heartened to see Bilal and his family satisfied, relaxed, and drowsy.

He stood up to address the group. "My brothers and sisters and sons and daughters, I'm leaving you now. I owe you a debt, and I want you to know that Bilal and I have agreed on a fitting repayment. May God keep you and your animals safe and healthy in your travels."

Bilal nodded as uncertain eyes looked to him to confirm the truth of Omar's words.

Ten of the strongest camels had been loaded with the heavy ammunition boxes. They covered the metal boxes with straw mats. Eight young men shouldered their weapons and walked silently into the dark with Omar and Bilal.

7

THEIR LOADS HAD BEEN heavy, the journey was long, and they drove the camels hard through the night on the last leg. Urgency is contrary to a camel's nature, and they bleated their reproach. Happy moaned disagreeably at Omar, who felt some sympathy for once. When they reached the shore, the camels sank to their knees.

Bilal and Omar looked out to sea. An ugly stench of the previous day's catch wafted from the scruffy fishing boats that bobbed on the water. "What a disgusting way to live. These people are stuck in the same spot. Surrounded by their own filth." Bilal viewed the world through the proud chauvinism of his ancestors. "I'll never know how fisher-folk preserve any self-respect." Omar was wound tight and envied his cousin's ability to relax at any time and in any circumstances. "Don't worry," Bilal said. "The police know better than to disturb a group of armed Somalis. We will be left to our business."

Omar checked his watch. It was just past five in the morning. He breathed a sigh of relief when he spotted a small dot on the horizon. It grew into a large fiberglass boat with an outboard motor as turquoise dawn peeked above the black ocean.

The boat sped quietly to the shore. The driver raised the motor, and two muscular men jumped off the launch to pull it onto the beach.

"Omar, where are you?" asked a well-dressed Swahili[4] man. He was seated in the front of the boat, peering at the opaque profiles on shore. His well-laundered white skullcap shone in the moonlight. Omar realized his own sun-darkened face, tattered clothes, and a week's worth of trail dirt made him indistinguishable from his skinny black companions.

"It's me, Mohammed. Tell your men to help my clansmen load these boxes as quickly as possible."

"It looks heavy. How much does your baggage weigh?" Mohammed asked.

"Two thousand kilos. Maybe a little more," Omar replied.

Mohammed placed his hands on the top of his head and slowly pulled them across the gloomy expression of his face. "Allah protects the righteous."

Omar turned to Bilal. "This is Mohammed Dinar. He lives on Lamu. In Stone Town. Every year, the week before Eid al-Adha, you must go to him. He will have your gift."

"*Salaam, salaam walekum*, Bilal," Mohammed said and then turned to Omar. "I have what you asked. Five thousand dollars." Mohammed handed a fat envelope to Omar, who handed it to Bilal.

"I'll come back at the time you say. May Allah go with you," Bilal said.

4   Swahili people inhabit the East African coast of the Indian Ocean and share a distinct language and culture. They are proud descendants of an ancient Islamic trading culture connected to Arabia and the Indian subcontinent.

They hastily embraced. The loaded boat was ominously low in the water. Mohammed rapidly fingered his prayer beads. Omar climbed in gingerly.

They could not speak above the rumble of the outboard motor. Light chop slopped over the gunnels and puddled over their feet. One of the men bailed, and Omar worried why it was taking so long. After an agonizing hour, the hull crunched against gravel on an isolated beach.

Omar was alarmed. "Why is there an ambulance here?"

"You told me you had heavy luggage. We need to take it to my house. Did you think we could just pull up to the main dock with a fugitive finance minister?" Mohammed asked. "Anyway, this is the only vehicle on our little island. I give money to our clinic, and they let me use it when I need it. Get in." He turned and barked at the stevedores to unload faster.

The ambulance groaned under the weight of the cargo as it crept toward the edge of Stone Town. It could not fit through the narrow lanes, and the workers rushed in the early morning to stow the cargo out of sight. Hunched over, two to a box, they jogged down a narrow alley to the back of the house, past a beaten iron door, under an arched medieval passage, and down roughhewn coral stone steps into a corner of the damp, fungal cellar. When Mohammed was satisfied with the arrangement of the boxes, he led Omar around to the ornate front door. A servant opened it as soon as they stepped on the threshold.

In the ample front hall, Mohammed paused to address Omar. "I've become fat. A man of business should be fat. You look hungry for a minister of finance. Follow the houseboy. He will help you wash off the honourable but unappetizing smell of camel. He will find some respectable clothes, and then we will have breakfast, and you will explain those heavy ammunition boxes."

"Thank you, Mohammed. I'll do exactly that," Omar said. "By the way, I'm hungry." He managed a smile.

After he showered and dressed, Omar looked in the mirror. Hi eyes were bloodshot with fatigue, but the rest of him looked refreshed. A hand-woven cotton *kikoi* wrapped around his hips and a white cotton collarless button shirt made him indistinguishable from the other townsmen. Mohammed's sandals were too small for Omar, so the houseboy loaned him a pair of flip-flops. He sat across from his friend on the carpet facing a large embossed bronze tray brimming with food.

"Sit down. I'll pour you a nice milky tea. Help yourself to *mandazi*[5] and pigeon peas. Cook is bringing an omelet," Mohammed said.

Omar took the warm fried dough, tore it open, and scooped up the soft savoury beans cooked in rich coconut cream. He closed his eyes, comforted by the food and a sense of safety that he had not enjoyed for a long time.

"The weight of those boxes makes me think of gold, but it would be too much gold for one person," Mohammed said. He sipped his tea and waited for Omar to speak. It was time for Omar to share the story with his friend—and then one more person would know the secret upon which his life depended.

Omar ate another bite, and then took a deep breath. "Our families have known each other for generations. We performed Haj together as young men. This is why I'm here. There was no one else I could trust. You have two hundred ingots of gold in your cellar. It belonged to Somalia. I stole it." Mohammed's eyes went round and wide. The rest of his face was immobile. Omar explained to him the events of the last few days as Mohammed sipped his tea and listened. "I . . . I understand what I did," Omar concluded, "but I prefer not to think that I'm a thief. I prefer to think that I'm custodian and have kept the gold safe from evil purposes."

Mohammed chewed his omelet thoughtfully. "Well . . . because you rescued what remains of your nation's wealth from a cruel hypocrite—your president, that is—your action is moral up to

5   A form of fried bread that originated on the Swahili coast.

now. It's good the gold is in my house. However, the manner in which you employ this money is equally important."

"I don't have the faintest idea of what to do next," Omar admitted. His shoulders drooped forward, and he plunged his face in his hands. He was a homeless fugitive, complicit in a criminal government that had brought disaster on his nation. His emotions escaped control with a salty sting to the eyes. Stones of guilt weighed heavily in his gut. Sobbing, he pushed his food aside.

A moment later, he felt his friend's gentle hand on his shoulder. "You're exhausted. You must rest. This is your home, and I'm honoured to provide you with protection and hospitality. For now, you're like my little brother." Mohammed called the houseboy, who led Omar upstairs to a bedroom.

8

UNTOLD HOURS LATER, OMAR surfaced from the black nirvana of slumber. It took him a moment to orient himself. Coral walls aged by the passage of centuries said he was in Stone Town. Fading light sifting through an ornate wooden lattice confirmed that he was safe in the house of his friend, Mohammed Dinar. The call of the muezzin[6] meant Mohammed would be in the prayer room.

Omar quietly descended the stairs and stood at the doorway. It was furnished with fine Persian carpets brought by wealthy fore-fathers as one of two acceptable luxuries. Their worn blue-and-red patterns were diagonal to the walls, oriented toward Mecca. The other acceptable luxury was fine food. Mohammed knelt on the carpet and spread his knees to make space for his ample belly and broad rear end.

Omar rinsed his hands, face, and feet in the basin outside the entrance to the prayer room. Then he entered and performed his prayers next to his friend. When they were finished, they sat beside each other in silence.

6   The crier who, five times daily, makes the call summoning Muslims
     to prayer.

"This is the second time you have given me hospitality and shelter when I needed it," Omar said. "Thank you."

"God is great. We were boys then. Now, like then, you were uninvited." He chuckled. "You stowed away with your goats."

"You made good money selling our goats to those rich Arabs for the feast of Eid al-Adha, and I wanted to see Aden." Omar had snuck onto the boat while his family haggled over the goats. The Dinars discovered him after it was too late to return. Mohammed's family took him in until they could arrange passage for him back to his own family. In the meantime, the two boys became like brothers, and Mohammed sealed the relationship by giving Omar his most precious possession: a Yemeni knife with a rhinoceros-horn hilt.

"Allah is the mysterious engineer of our destiny, and here you are again." Mohammed's gaze sharpened as he looked Omar up and down. "How do you feel?"

"I feel clean on the outside, but filthy on the inside. And I feel grateful for your help and hospitality." He sounded unsure, and he felt uncertain of Mohammed's intentions.

Mohammed nodded at his friend's feet. "Those flip-flops will not do. My boy will take you to the sandal maker for footwear that befits you and your wealth." Mohammed's eyes narrowed to a calculating squint. "And what do you plan to do with this orphan treasure, my friend?"

"I don't know. I prevented Barre from taking it. It's only now as you ask me that I see I need a better answer." Mohammed ran a hawala network up and down the coast, into Dubai, and across to India and Pakistan. "What do you, as a financial expert, advise?"

"It would not be the will of God for wealth to sit idle when it could be used for the virtues of industry or charity." His eyes lit up. "I work with gold merchants and goldsmiths from Massawa to Zanzibar. Probably about two million dollars' worth could go to them and earn some 12 percent profit. I could bring a sample to my cousin the goldsmith and ask his counsel. A gold brick is four hundred troy ounces. Gold is trading at three hundred and fifty-three dollars an ounce."

Mohammed fell silent as he did the math in his head. "There are twenty-eight million dollars in my basement." Joy and anxiety flickered across his face, until anxiety prevailed. "Secrecy is paramount. You must let no one know," he whispered.

"As your Wall Street friends in America must have told you, diversify. For a start, we should invest it safely but productively. This will take time. We don't want to raise eyebrows by placing too much too soon. It's safe here for the time being. We will move gradually. I know some gold merchants. We can sell some to them to generate cash.

"You are obligated to perform virtuous acts. A tenth, a zakat, would be appropriate. This is my initial thinking, but twenty-eight million is a great deal, and these ideas are not enough."

"I'll do whatever you advise," Omar said. "And I must go to the mosque today."

"By all means. Put your spiritual health first. But you cannot go to mosque as the minister of finance of Somalia. You must be a simple traveller or refugee like so many of your sad countrymen." His frank smile eased Omar's mind. "But you're a refugee with millions of dollars."

The neighbourhood mosque was a small stone box. The irregular concrete dome shone with a new coat of green paint. The muezzin's call to evening prayer came with a splatter of static from a loudspeaker wired precariously to a rusty steel pole. A simple waterspout served for ablutions. Omar pumped the handle for a family who was also going to pray.

The man for whom he was pumping water was accompanied by his wife and son. The little boy wore an old T-shirt that did not reach below his genitals. The man's clothes were tattered and his face haggard. The woman was in a faded polyester dress that she must have bought from a peddler of discarded clothes and looked pained by her immodesty. The crunchy, urgent sounds of the Somali language told Omar that they were compatriots.

"Thank you for helping us with the water. You are also Somali? What clan and from where?"

Omar thought quickly. "Marehan. I've been many years in the Gulf, where I was born to my Somali parents. I'm just coming back now. And you?"

"We are Marehan too! I was a teacher. We left, and I don't have to tell you why. Sometimes the people who attend this mosque give us food. I'm looking for work. We were in Dadaab camp." He fell silent. His wife stared at the ground.

Omar knew the man was referring to the UN camp for Somali refugees. "Why did you leave? Is it not the place for refuge and aid?"

"Dadaab is terrible and dangerous. We could not stay. Now we are looking for a school for our son. Without an education he is without a future. I've heard that there are religious schools that take poor boys for free. Do you know of any? I come from an educated family. He can read."

"I've just arrived, and I do not. Excuse me, I'm going to pray now."

"You must be rich, coming from the land of oil and money." The man's eyes were bright. He struggled to layer an expression of friendly persuasion over naked imprecation. "It's indeed auspicious that we should meet at the entrance of a holy place. Surely it's so you can help my son."

"Unfortunately, I'm travelling and need to shepherd my savings. I'm sure you will find others. I have no money on me at this time," Omar lied, his feelings of shame and guilt mounting. "I'm a refugee like you."

"He's a good boy, a good boy, and smart too. In the camp there is nothing but disease, ignorance, and humiliation. We are like the cattle of a poor farmer who feeds them just enough to keep his herd alive. They become skinny and sick, and no one wants them." He gripped his son by the shoulders and twisted the boy to face Omar. The boy was baffled and confused. "You must keep my boy from this fate. I have an idea—you can have him!" The boy tried to get away and turned toward his mother, but she pushed him toward Omar.

"He will do anything you tell him. You can afford to feed and educate him better than us. Do you have a wife? A son? Start now, and take him!"

"I'll pray for you and your family," Omar said in a quavering voice.

The man's face went blank, and he shuffled into the mosque, as did Omar. The boy was about seven, so he sat with his mother in the women's section.

Omar evaded the man's eyes and tried to lose himself in the sounds and rhythms of prayer. After prayers had finished he still lingered on the carpet in order to avoid another conversation with the refugee family. The words "without an education he is without a future" repeated in his mind. The bloody image of Captain Moussa reappeared. How could Omar ever atone for his sins?

All the faithful had left except for Omar and the imam.[7]

"My dear brother, I must close, and you must go," the imam said.

"I can't go yet. I need an answer. I think it will come to me here," Omar replied.

"You are troubled. My counsel is that prayer and good works bring spiritual harmony. You cannot stay here. Go now."

With nothing to say in response, Omar left.

7   The prayer leader of a mosque.

9

....

Washington, DC

ITALIAN DEFENSE ATTACHÉ BRIGADIER General Giancarlo Cristiani had just returned from high-level military consultations at the Pentagon. They had talked about getting Saddam Hussein out of Kuwait, the disintegration of Yugoslavia, what to do about the former Soviet Union's nuclear arsenal, and various other global threats. The chief of Italy's armed forces led the delegation of senior officers from the army, navy, air force, and intelligence. When it was over, the American chief of defence staff took his Italian counterpart aside for a tête-à-tête about Somalia. Cristiani ached to know what had been said, and if the chiefs had talked about him.

In his spacious embassy office, Cristiani selected a Dunhill cigarette out of the silver box on his antique mahogany desk and lit it with a silver Dunhill lighter. Being defence attaché in Washington gave him privilege, prestige, and proximity to those who would decide his next promotion. It also freed him from the frustrations of command in an egalitarian social democracy. Soldiers these days lacked the obedience a commander required. He took a long, soothing drag and admired the bust of Julius Agricola on his desk. That was the Roman general he sought to emulate: the one who conquered Britain. He shared a certain resemblance to the illustrious hero with a small overbite, prominent lower lip, and sloped forehead.

He was scanning the *Washington Post* and diplomatic cables when his aide-de-camp asked permission to enter. The young man gave a crisp salute.

"Brigadier General Cristiani, the chief of staff requests your presence in the ambassador's office. The debriefing is about to begin."

Cristiani took two more quick puffs, and then rose from his leather armchair. Erect with purpose, he crossed the rich oriental carpet to the door. He did not dismiss the captain, who would stay at attention until Cristiani was out of sight. This was his way of training junior officers in the primacy and mystique of rank. The even rhythm of his hard leather soles on the corridor parquet transmitted a sense of gravitas and confidence proper to his level.

The heavy oak door was open, and he entered the gentle illumination of the ambassadorial office. They had started without him. The chief leaned back on an ornate sofa and rubbed his eyes. He was tall and overweight. Too much wine at lunch inflamed his nose and jowls. His pomade had lost control of his grey curls in the humid Washington summer.

The ambassador leaned forward from the edge of an antique Chippendale chair, caught deep in thought. An acid cloud of tension floated between them.

Cristiani sat on the leather sofa with his chief.

"It's an internal and intractable conflict," the ambassador said. "The American military is arrogant. Admit it. They think they always win. They don't. Italy has never done this type of operation before. There is no military solution to Somalia. This is something new . . . and ugly."

There was an uncomfortable pause, and then the ambassador continued. "I have to tell the prime minister what I think. Even though it's awkward. You and I agree about our role in Iraq and Yugoslavia. We have no argument there. But I counsel against joining the Americans in Somalia. Yes, the situation pulls on our heartstrings, but it will end in tragedy or farce for Rome. General Cristiani, you told me you had doubts about this mission too."

Cristiani needed a maneuver to elude the line of fire. Intellectually, he agreed with the ambassador. The old man had a perspective shaped by decades of experience, and Cristiani respected that. At the same time, a combat command position was a necessary condition for his next promotion. To side with the ambassador against his chief could be fatal to his career. Geopolitical crises carried military opportunity. This mess in the Horn of Africa might be a good one.

"I agree, it's a risky mission, as you say, Ambassador. Political and military risks in a place where our direct national interests are, well, not obvious," Cristiani said. "What's the best way for us to help the Americans, Chief?"

"Somalia is on CNN all the time. Thousands of people are dying every day. Politicians can't just stand there and do nothing. The Americans said it's a political imperative. Bandits are harassing the aid workers, and we need to stop that." The chief dabbed his sweaty face with a handkerchief. "We won't face anybody who can fight back. Militarily, it's simple. The political risk is if we do nothing. And just because we got our balls cut off in Ethiopia a hundred years ago doesn't mean we're still eunuchs. One look at a modern NATO soldier, and these so-called warlords will roll right over. I don't see any risks."

The ambassador winced at this humiliating reference to the disgraceful end of Italy's nineteenth-century colonial adventure in Africa. He stood up and began to pace. "General, people will stop at nothing to resist foreign invaders. We were defeated in Ethiopia because we went to war in a place we didn't understand.

The Somalis haven't attacked us or our allies. We don't need to do this. There is no strategic objective. Sending in troops to deliver humanitarian aid? That's not what soldiers are for. Our soldiers are for defending our country. They will die for that."

"The Americans are going into Somalia, and they want some of their friends there too," the chief shot back. Cristiani was disconcerted by his vehemence. "Eagleburger, the deputy Secretary of State—"

"I'm well aware of who he is," the ambassador said.

"Anyway, Eagleburger just told UN Secretary General Boutros Boutros Ghali that with the right Security Council resolution, the US will take the lead. The Americans want to bring along a few friends, like us. The Americans will do the heavy lifting. It's not about the hungry Africans and their failed country; it's about Rome and Washington."

The chief loosened his tie and the top button of his shirt. *He's putting on more weight*, Cristiani thought. *He needs a bigger uniform. He'll retire soon, and opportunities will blossom.*

"It's simple geopolitics. There's fucking chaos across the Adriatic from us," the chief said. "Our national interest is to have Americans in the Balkans. You don't give, you don't get." Cristiani observed how the chief deployed aggressive eye contact and casual vulgarity to dominate a conversation. Cristiani stroked his finely trimmed eyebrows. The ambassador was overdue for a haircut.

"Look at it from a diplomatic point of view," the ambassador said. "In Somalia there's no government. Nobody to talk to. We know nothing about why they're always fighting. Who are our Somali allies? You know the old saying, 'Choose bad companions, and you're bad too.'"

"Julius, I already told the Americans that we don't know the terrain or the people there," the chief said. "They told me that Somalis eat spaghetti, not hotdogs. That was the end of the conversation." The chief was like a ton of concrete in the room.

The ambassador shook his head gravely. "Go back and tell the Americans they're asking us for something we can't give. Tell them to retract their request."

Cristiani was horrified. It transgressed military honour. He had to speak out. "We can't do that. When others say yes and we say no, there will be a national price to pay. We can't let our American friends down. It will be embarrassing if the Italian armed forces are on the sidelines. We need the right military posture for this crisis."

"That's an excellent point, Giancarlo," the chief said. "And the Pentagon knows exactly what we can and can't give. They even told me what battalion they want—and they're right. It's not busy right now. A few casualties would not be such a bad thing for our country. Fallen heroes remind us that bravery and the military go hand in hand." He switched to English. "Soldiers die for their country . . . and diplomats lie for their country."

Cristiani felt a twinge of regret for the dignity of the ambassador, who was being outmaneuvered by the chief.

"Tomorrow Bush is calling the prime minister about this," the chief said. "I told the Americans we can do it, and we will do it."

"The president is calling him tomorrow?" the ambassador exclaimed. "I must inform the prime minister immediately and prepare him. He needs balanced diplomatic advice. He needs to see the pros and cons. He needs options."

"Julius, this can work for both of us." The chief's eyes brightened as he spoke. "It will be good for you if the PM says yes. The Americans will say you can deliver when it counts. If he says no, your channel to the White House closes right down."

It would be suicide for the ambassador to land on the wrong side of this, Cristiani thought. He felt a thrill at being in the centre of geopolitical decision-making.

"When the CIA intercepts the message you send the PM, and they see you're undercutting them, they won't sit on their hands," the chief said. "There'll be a leak, and you'll be finished in this town. I can just see the headline, 'Top Italian Diplomat Says No to Starving Babies.'"

The ambassador closed his eyes. "I see your point."

"Well, I think you'd better report your diplomatic advice to the PM right now," the chief said. "Cristiani, there's something I need to talk to you about—let's go to your office. Goodbye, and good luck, Julius."

"Goodbye, General. You'll need luck too. More than me."

In his office a few minutes later, the chief addressed Cristiani. "I know you, and I trust you. I told the Americans I'm giving you command of our troops in Somalia."

Cristiani's heart climbed into his throat. The rocket of his ambition was passing through the turbulence of performance anxiety. He needed this to get promoted, and he needed it before he was too old. However, nobody had trained for this kind of war or operating theatre. He wasn't ready.

"General, we don't even know if the prime minister will send us in."

"I told the Americans that we can do it, and we will do it as long as Bush makes the call to PM Amato. The rest is just bullshit. I need the best piece of that shitty country we can get. I won't be screwed by the Americans because they want to be nice to the French, the Germans, or the Canadians. You can't let that happen, Giancarlo. I'm putting you in charge of that right now. Get the real estate with the best PR for the least amount of grief."

"Yes, sir." It was an involuntary military reflex and came out of his mouth even before he knew what he was getting into.

"And I want a direct line to the CIA. We need to know what they know. That's an order. That's what you're here for," the chief said.

"Yes, sir."

"The Americans asked if you had ever commanded men in combat. I said you could. How hard can it be to discipline these ridiculous Africans anyway? And you need this, so I can give you your promotion to major general," the chief said. "I know I can count on you to be a good soldier, like the Romans you admire so much. You do this right, and you get whatever job you want." Cristiani nodded silently as the chief continued. "Two things. One, keep the Americans happy—I don't want their chief calling me with complaints about you. Two, don't send our boys back in body bags. Any casualties, and the politicians will stick their noses in our business. Any questions?"

"No, chief. No questions. You can count on me."

"Good. Make me proud. Ciao."

Still a little tipsy from lunch, the chief struggled to get to his feet. Cristiani moved to the door, opened it, and saluted the old man. Now he needed to be alone, so he could absorb this new development. He looked down and saw his hands trembling slightly. Cristiani wasn't as young as he used to be.

His aide-de-camp nervously cleared his throat at the threshold.

"Captain, you have an uncanny knack for showing up when you're least wanted," Cristiani snapped. "I'm tempted to include reference to this doleful habit in your evaluation. What do you want?"

"Sir, you have a call from the CIA. Mr. Randy Samson is on hold."

10

CRISTIANI NEEDED TO GET the best piece of real estate from Samson. Making the appropriate impression was of capital importance. He had studied how American presidents dressed for leisure activities. He carefully selected a white button-down shirt. The stiff, crisp cotton felt right. He left the top button unfastened. His aide-de-camp had pressed his khaki chinos impeccably and shined his Sperry topsiders to a deep gloss.

The backyard barbecue is confusing terrain, Cristiani grumbled to himself. *It's the worst place to begin this strategic relationship with the CIA.* Italian family dining al fresco was infinitely superior. Everyone wore nice clothes and knew their place. The optimal sequence of dishes from antipasto through primero, secondi, dolce, coffee, and grappa had been established long ago. Children knew to keep quiet. Any attempt at improvement could only have the opposite effect.

Thinking about his family made him gloomy. He had just received a letter from his financially incompetent brother asking for money to keep the ancestral estate running—a lot of money.

The big problem was the hat. His Tyrolean roots came with an Aryan complexion, and his bald spot needed protection from Washington's molten summer sun. A baseball cap was inappropriate for his rank. He put on his jaunty alpine homburg with the feather.

Cristiani told his driver to arrive exactly at the appointed time of 17:00. Why did Americans have dinner at teatime?

The house presented itself to the street with a dumb, blank face of double garage doors and a number. A girl of about twelve years old opened the door for him. "Hello, General, won't you please come in?" She looked at his homburg, clapped her hand over her mouth, and ran up the carpeted stairs.

The interior looked more prosperous than he expected for an American civil servant. It had hardwood floors, European leather furniture, and African art displayed in the manner of a discerning collector. Samson jogged up to greet him. When they shook hands, Samson applied pressure that hurt across the metacarpus.

"Giancarlo, come on outside, and let's have a beer."

They walked through the kitchen and out the back door to a deck overlooking an extensive and carefully landscaped backyard with a sizable swimming pool.

Samson wore knee-length shorts, an oversized T-shirt, and a baseball hat. What was that artificial grey substance his sandals were made from? Cristiani had a theory that infantile vulgarity was taking over American men. They wore pants that shortened the appearance of their legs, untucked shirts that elongated their torso, and hats that exaggerated their head size. *He looks like a big three-year-old*, Cristiani thought, *except for the mirrored aviator sunglasses.*

Samson put an arm around him and drew his face too close. Cristiani did not recoil from this excessive male intimacy because he sensed Samson was about to confide something to him. A cold wet aluminum can of beer was thrust into his hand.

"We think it's good for you guys to be on the team, but the operation is higher stakes than you think." Cristiani saw his face reflected in Samson's sunglasses and tried to look like a major general as Samson continued. "This Somalia thing is not about the Somalis. It's about America and our ability to prevail wherever and whenever and forever. It's dress rehearsal for a bigger drama." Samson released him and took a long pull of beer. Cristiani wished he could read the expression behind the sunglasses.

"The Cold War had a huge fringe benefit: adult supervision for all these places that don't deserve to be countries," Samson said. "And now look what's happening. Things fall apart and land in our lap."

Cristiani liked the way the discussion was moving to an intellectual plane, where he felt more comfortable.

"Just so, Randy, very much so. Global stability requires an imperial centre of gravity. Rome fulfilled this historical mission first, and Britain took a turn. Today it's the burden of Washington along with its NATO friends, such as us," Cristiani said.

Samson nodded. "That's going back a ways, but . . . yeah . . . I guess so. If we fail, think about what it means for our Western Christian civilization, Giancarlo. Especially if we lose to illiterate black Muslims. Bad people will get the wrong idea. They'll sense weakness and exploit our fears. That's not the world I want for my little girl."

"Randy, we understand each other completely," Cristiani said in a careful, even, and deliberate voice. "It will be a pleasure working with you."

"That's good, because I'm going to be responsible for your turf. Intelligence-wise, that is."

Cristiani was elated that he had built a close working relationship so rapidly with Samson. His uncertainties were giving way to images of a wildly successful operation and his future promotion.

"What's your background, Randy?" Cristiani asked. "Where have you worked?"

"Oh, I've been around the block, and I like to be where we can, you know, make a difference. I've done a couple of missions in Afghanistan, helping the patriots there against the Ruskies. Lots of work in Honduras and Nicaragua containing the evil empire. And I like Africa, especially our friends in South Africa. We can count on them to keep the commies on their back foot. Don't get me wrong; I love my job here at Langley. But I'm really much happier in the field without all the bureaucratic bullshit. It's good to be in the kind of place where anything can happen. That's where opportunity comes knocking. Why don't you tell me a little bit about yourself—how come you speak with that English accent?"

It was good that Samson recognized his social rank.

"I come from an old family with a military tradition. The roots of our family tree go back to the Romans."

Randy turned to him. In the space between the visor of his hat and his sunglasses Cristiani saw his eyebrows rise. He took it as a sign of admiration. "We come from the north, near Austria," he continued. "Men in our family prefer the German military tradition, but events made that unworkable for me. So, I attended a boarding school in England from age twelve. In England they know one's class by the quality of one's accent. Then I went on to the Modena Military Academy and the Turin Military Institute. You know them?"

"Rich?" Samson asked.

"Excuse me?"

"Is your family rich? Do you have a castle or something? Don't you have to be rich to go to a fancy English private school?" Samson stabbed the meat sizzling on the grill with a long fork.

"My family is old money, and yes, there is a small castle." Cristiani felt wistful. "It is, in fact, beautiful." Then he caught himself. Americans were egalitarians. His superior social rank might be a barrier for Samson. Maybe revealing a personal challenge would help Samson confide in him. The sun was lower in the sky, and he removed his hat to emphasize his sincerity.

"Not so rich now. My brother has spent down our inheritance instead of building it up. I worry about the future of our estate. It's expensive to keep up, but this is a matter of honour, and there will be a way. I am, of course, committed to the army and to Italy. This does not lead to great fortunes."

Samson flipped a burger. "I'm not so sure about that. You never know when opportunity can come knocking. Tough luck with your brother. What about Africa—ever work there before?"

"My specialty is peacekeeping operations. Cyprus, Sinai, Jerusalem, Golan Heights, and Western Morocco," Cristiani said.

Samson nodded. "Nice. No combat, right? You want cheese on your burger?"

"No, I prefer it on the side, with the third course," Cristiani said.

Samson coughed.

It was true. Cristiani had not operated where shots were fired in anger. His hands began to flutter, and he clasped them behind his back. It would be damaging if the American sensed this slight weakness in his confidence to lead.

"Subtlety and savoir faire are called for in these peace operations. The cultural and political dimensions are the centres of gravity in multilateral settings. This will be a contribution I can make to you, Randy. You Americans, of course, don't wear blue helmets."

"No. No, we don't really feel comfortable unless American soldiers have American commanders. Maybe it's one of those political and cultural dimensions you were talking about," Samson said. "Giancarlo, you're going to find that working with these cats in Somalia is way different from those UN gigs you were on. Is that a chicken feather in your hat?"

"No. Pheasant. You have been there?" Cristiani asked.

"Yeah. A bunch of times. I've been all over the horn—you know, the Horn of Africa. Until I went to Somalia, I thought the Danakil were the worst. You hear of them?"

"Vaguely," Cristiana lied.

"They're neighbours with the Somalis. You gotta be tough and mean to live in that desert of theirs. They are too. They have funny, uhhh, customs. Anyway, I had my Danakil interpreter helping me check what was going on with the Cubans in Ethiopia, and one day he comes back from visiting his family as sad and blue as he could be. 'Why so glum?' I asked. He said he was going to get married. 'Why's that a problem?' He told me that you can't get married unless you take a guy's dick."

Cristiani was confused. He checked his fly. Samson snickered.

"Yeah. You need to impress dad-in-law first, and you do that by bringing him another guy's dick. Interesting kind of natural selection. Well, my guy was non-violent, so couldn't deliver, even though he liked the girl. Actually, the Danakil girls dig it too. They wear necklaces with little rows of silver dicks."

"What happened?" Cristiani asked.

"He made a mistake. He asked if he could have mine. I didn't feel we should go desert camping anymore, just the two of us. One day you think a guy's your friend, the next day he wants your dick. Half the time in these places, you really don't know what the fuck is going on. Anyhow, I fired him. Next interpreter—I made sure he was already married. Had a coupla wives, so I knew he could take care of himself. Trust is so important. Anyway, those hotdogs look just about ready now. What was it you were saying?"

Cristiani advanced to his objective. "Randy, I want to explain to you the kind of operations we prefer. My chief of staff instructed me to work with you on this. We want an area of operation that will be positive for Italy."

Samson shifted the spatula from his right to left hand. He took off his sunglasses, and his blue-grey eyes gripped Cristiani with steel intent. "You don't have to worry about that," he said, punctuating his message by tapping Cristiani in the sternum with his index finger. "We have a plan, and your guys are going to love it. It's a place on the beach and quiet. They call it Merka."

This wasn't good. Was Samson giving him orders? Was he being outmaneuvered by the spy? He was supposed to be the one with rank and initiative. Cristiani wanted to look down, but breaking eye contact would be like surrender.

"I think I should ask Rome."

"Don't. Just tell Rome this is the place. You do this for me, and it will be a cakewalk. You gotta know who's who in the zoo. If you don't, some joker is gonna walk away with your dick. Maybe mine too."

The poking . . . and now this talk about cakes and a zoo. Dicks again. "How could animals survive in a zoological garden?" Cristiani asked to regain his bearings. "If the people are starving, the animals must be the first to go."

Samson pulled back from the barbecue. "It's an expression. It means reliable knowledge about the people you're dealing with is fundamental. This is the hard part of our mission. It's difficult to understand the human and social terrain in Somalia, but it's absolutely vital. The good news is that I've established a good working relationship with the leader of Merka. We can make it a win-win situation for us and him. His name is Ibrahim."

Cristiani felt humiliated by the way Samson dominated him. He took a drink of his beer. It was sour and viscous on his tongue. Then he saw a warm smile come over Samson's face.

"Giancarlo, maybe I came on a little too strong there. I didn't mean to make you uncomfortable. I guess it's just because I care too fucking much. I mean you and me—we're in this together. We really need each other. I just know Merka is the best place for you and your men."

"It would be much better for me if it was our decision," Cristiani said.

"I can see why you would feel that way. I can see why you would say that. I really can." Samson turned off the gas on the barbecue. "Let me help you. I can make sure you have the support of the locals. You know what will be positive for the people of

Italy? You on TV with skinny little African girls and boys. They're gonna be smiling, 'cause you'll be giving them food. Finally, somebody is on their side, and it's you. You'll be a star. I have an idea. Make Merka your recommendation. You tell Rome the CIA gave you a personal briefing on the options, and this is the best one. Tell them we haven't briefed the other countries yet. You got to choose first."

Cristiani thought for a moment and then nodded. "I'm glad you can see the issue from our perspective. I appreciate that very much." This would be something the chief would like, everything he asked for. He was feeling better now. The food smelled good, and he began to salivate.

"It really is a beautiful part of the world, even if the situation is a piece of shit," Samson said. "There's a fringe benefit too. A place you should go for a break now and again. It's a little island where movie stars and hippies go called Lamu. Good place to get laid once in a while. You gotta live a little. Okay, let's eat."

11

....

Merka, Somalia

CRISTIANI'S CHOPPER CROSSED THE bright blue Indian Ocean and flew over wide golden beaches into the dusty sky over Merka. The city was a labyrinth of medieval lanes winding between low stone dwellings. The structures had merged into one another over centuries. It looked like a strange geological extrusion.

Strategic communications in Rome agreed that Cristiani's first photo op would be critical to setting the tone for the mission. The arrival should be by helicopter. An Italian MV Agusta helicopter should come from an Italian ship because the message was about Italian national pride, sovereign choice, and military capability. At all costs, any images of dependence on the Americans were to be avoided. Cristiani was told his speech should be about humanitarian aid, period.

The location of the military base was suggested by the UN. It was a long-abandoned villa surrounded by crumbling stone walls next to the sea. They flew over the site. Rows and rows of dark-green tents for enlisted men were set on the sand by the beach.

Dozens of trucks and armoured personnel carriers were parked just outside the wall. Next to them were hundreds of barrels of fuel. Men worked to install coils of razor wire and chain-link fencing around the perimeter. Larger tents were placed at the front of the compound for headquarters functions. Two enormous diesel gensets belched grey smoke.

A simple plywood structure housed Cristiani's command office and quarters. Next to it was a circle of stones painted white for the helicopter landing pad. A huge shiny white bladder to the side of the compound stored the battle group's water supply. It all looked quite satisfactory. Exactly according to the site plan he approved. It was rewarding to see that his military engineers had followed his detailed orders to the centimetre. Maybe this wouldn't be hard after all.

Cristiani patted his pocket where his speech was. There would be no questions allowed. They had told the journalists he had to get right to work.

"Pilot—do you read, over?"

"Yes, General. I hear you loud and clear, over."

"Good. Remember, you must land with my door to the cameras. Please confirm, over."

"Yes, General. That is in our flight plan, over."

The helicopter began a rapid descent and sped to their destination over the rooftops of Merka. Chickens and drying clothes went flying, and people took cover. The chopper lifted its nose to brake and settled onto the landing pad in a cloud of brown dust.

Cristiani unsnapped his helmet so he could doff it on camera with extra flare. The pilot gave him a thumbs-up. Cristiani opened the door and stepped into his new domain.

The high-decibel whine of the turbines wound down and came to a stop as he reached the prepositioned lectern and microphone. His command team was lined up in a row behind him. To present a humanitarian image, they did not carry sidearms. No weapons were in sight. A battery of cameras and microphones from Italian and international media pointed right at him.

"Today I take supreme command of the Italian forces in Somalia. This is a multilateral humanitarian mission in which I have a special leadership role, as does our country. It's a mission about humanitarian concern for our Somali brothers and sisters, with whom Italy has a strong historical tie.

"My message to our Somali friends is that we come here to help. That is our only motive. We will give you the food you need. Together we will rebuild your country, your economy, and your future."

He paused and then continued. "Most importantly, troops will work with Italian and international NGOs to help them deliver humanitarian assistance. We will work with UN agencies and, of course, the International Committee of the Red Cross."

Journalists' hands went up, and they shouted questions at him. "Will there be casualties?"

"What about the warlords who are stealing the aid?"

"Can your men shoot to kill?"

"Will you protect civilians?"

"Will you take prisoners?"

"My press officer will answer your technical questions," he replied. "Now I must go to work. Goodbye." He walked toward his operations centre with a decisive stride. His officers stepped in line behind him.

His operations centre was a dark-green tent. It was designed for a conventional war against the Warsaw Pact in northern Europe and was unbearably hot on the African coast. The officers assumed their places on each side of the long table, and he took the head. Sweat streamed down their faces, and dark patches spread on their chests and under their arms. Banks of communications equipment on one wall crackled with static and chatter from two patrols out on reconnaissance. On the other wall, operational maps sheathed in plastic were covered with notes about patrol routes and village locations.

Cristiani addressed the commanders upon whom he would depend for the mission's success. "You are my council of war. We will share a chapter in our nation's profession of arms unique to our generation. We will make our nation proud, and we will prevail. I want to begin my command by giving you my five objectives for this mission."

Five was a good number. It allowed one to count in a way that resulted in an open palm. It was not too much to remember or communicate down to the lower ranks.

"Number one, Somalis respect force. As of today, we are the strongest clan in town. Number two, establish relations with the strong ones, and make them fear you. Number three, casualties are politically unacceptable. If we lose the battle for public opinion at home, we have lost the campaign. Number four, strategic-level decisions are made in Rome and Washington. Everything we do and say as commanders must be in line with that. Number five, money is a weapon system, and it's often the least expensive one." He wanted to come across as clear, confident, and commanding, and he did.

"Give me a briefing on the status of our operations, starting with the chief of intelligence and concluding with the doctor on the health of our men."

Cristiani liked the look of his intelligence officer. Colonel Mariotti was athletic and serious. He was a long-distance runner with a doctorate in political science. His file said he loved his work and believed that knowledge and objective analysis were indispensable to a military organization. However, Cristiani also heard that Mariotti was a man who said what he thought, even if it was inconvenient.

"General, as you know, Operation Restore Hope was mandated because warlords diverted and extorted food and medicine,"

Mariotti said. "Heavy fighting in Mogadishu made it impossible for aid workers to get food to the population.

"Here in Merka, information is still sketchy. The humanitarian situation is bad. UN reports say food stocks are exhausted. Medical facilities have completely collapsed, except for one Red Cross clinic. As a military operation, we keep our distance from that clinic because of the principle of humanitarian neutrality. The delegate said he would brief us when the emergency calms down.

"There are approximately twenty-five thousand displaced people concentrated in three clusters in the vicinity of the town. We estimate this represents 10 percent of the city's population. Reports indicate that they are completely destitute." Mariotti pointed out the displaced centres on a detailed aerial photograph.

"Communication with locals is a big problem. We brought two translators from Italy, but we need many more. Patrols are out trying to learn the city. They report skepticism and hostility about us. We have identified the primary humanitarian organizations in the region and are assembling the relevant dossiers on their leadership structures."

Was that all? Cristiani needed more and better information—a lot more.

"I want the people in Merka to feel safe now because we're here," he said. "Increase the pace of patrols. I want everyone to feel our presence, to know we're here. Make the patrols regular and predictable, so they're not a surprise to anyone, and they'll get used to us as soon as possible." Cristiani started to get impatient. Would he have to think of everything? "Well, who's the local leader in charge here, Mariotti? Surely we know that!"

"There is no governmental authority here. Local fighters control the dock, and logistics was able to negotiate access for our supplies. The price was high, but we were in a hurry. Local fighters are also located at key intersections. We have not established communications with them yet and don't know their command structure.

"Our analysis of aerial photography shows a large compound on the west side of town with thirteen technicals.[8] It's six kilometres distant from our base. Ten are Toyota Hilux pickup trucks with heavy machine guns mounted to the rear bed. Three are Land Rover Defenders with the top chopped off. One of these has what looks like a salvaged anti-aircraft cannon on the back.

"There are multiple structures and a large amount of activity in the compound. I assess that this is the location of the dominant militia here. We don't have any information yet on their commander. There are no reports of recent clashes. We can't tell if their intent is hostile or friendly or what their outside alliances are. They have not approached us.

"General, we do not have capabilities for offensive operations. If their intent is hostile, they will be a formidable enemy. Especially here on their home turf," Mariotti concluded.

It was a credible threat, and Cristiani wished he had more armoured capability than the twelve APCs in his battle group. Planning the logistics and taking care of his move back from Washington had not left time to get to know much about the place. He had expected his men to take care of the local element while he kept his focus on the big picture.

"This situation is unacceptable, Mariotti! This is not enough! I want to get to know this militia boss as a top priority. You know my intent! You all heard me state my intent to the press. My goal is to help the people. We come here as friends. Obviously, there is a local leadership, and I want to recruit them to our mission immediately. That's an order. Understood?"

"General, in my opinion, the people should see us as impartial. Also, we need to know more about the leadership structure before we engage. Give me some time to collect intelligence and provide you with an analysis. The operating environment is still permissive for us. A mistake at this stage could have repercussions for

8   A technical is a pickup truck with a tripod-mounted large-calibre machine gun bolted to the bed.

the entire mission. There may be other leaders and notables who can help us. The traditional elders have great influence in this culture. So do religious leaders."

"You are trying my patience, Mariotti. Did I not give an order?"

"Yes, sir," Mariotti said.

"Next—operations. Tell me what the men are seeing out there. What is our perimeter security plan? This is a starving city, and I want to make it utterly clear that we are not a target for theft and pilfering. We cannot show any vulnerability."

"Sir. There's something else," Mariotti said. "The CIA has requested a meeting with you tomorrow. I can take it for you, if you wish."

Cristiani hadn't seen Samson since they closed the deal on Merka for the Italian mission in his backyard. This was good. "No. I'll see him," he said.

12

CRISTIANI HAD A LARGE, complicated diagram of the clans and sub-clans of Somalia on the wall that Mariotti had prepared for him. It reminded him of the bloody family rivalries of Renaissance Florence. Cristiani was pleased with the office that his engineers had prepared. It was an insulated plywood structure with high-power air conditioners. He had a modern executive desk and a swivel office chair. Cristiani had his personal oriental carpets arranged on the floor, and there was a meeting table with room for eight. His plywood walls were covered with multicoloured maps showing details of humanitarian and military operations.

He heard Samson's Black Hawk helicopter arriving early. Shortly after, the CIA agent walked in with his flak jacket in one hand and a helmet in the other. He looked different. He was in jeans and a polo shirt. He had beige desert combat boots and a holstered Glock sidearm.

"Hey, Giancarlo. Here we are!" Samson dropped his gear by the door, slapped him on the shoulder, and gave him that painful handshake. "Nice office. Looks like your base is all buttoned up.

Good fence, razor wire. Tidy helicopter pad. Ready to get down to work?"

Cristiani nodded. "Everything is going according to plan. I arrived yesterday, and we are completing our setup."

There was a knock on the door. Cristiani nodded. "You may enter." Mariotti and the lawyer saluted smartly and then hurried in.

"Hi, Mariotti, I know you. Who's this other guy, Giancarlo?" Samson pointed to the lawyer.

"Captain Batista is my legal advisor. I thought it would be prudent to have legal advice to underpin my command decisions at this juncture."

"Not really. Why don't we just keep this between the three of us? This is need-to-know only. Batista doesn't need to know. Nice to meetcha, Batista. Have a great day. Goodbye."

With the puzzled look of a dog that had just been punished for an unknown reason, Captain Batista looked at Cristiani. Perhaps Samson was right—this conversation should be on a need-to-know basis only.

"You are dismissed, Captain. It's good to see you again, Randy," Cristiani lied. Now that he was getting settled in his base, he was not so sure he wanted Samson looking over his shoulder.

"I want to talk to you about KLE—Key Leader Engagement, Giancarlo. And I wanted to have this meeting right away to tell you how we're gonna to play this. Hey, can I get a coffee or a Coke or something?"

Colonel Mariotti got up to fetch a coffee and left the two men alone. Samson spoke quickly before he returned. "Our guy here is Ibrahim Hussein. He's been on our payroll for about a year now. He's not cheap. So, we have an investment in his success as the number one—and I repeat—number one key leader in your area of operation. He speaks English, which is a big plus. He calls the shots here, and we don't want any confusion about who's in charge. He's young and has great potential. He's with the big clan in Merka, and family means a lot to these cats."

Why hadn't Cristiani been told this critical information before? What else did Samson know that had been kept from him?

"How did you select this man? What is his background?" Cristiani asked.

"He's kinda coy about what exactly he was doing before this mess broke out, and we haven't quite figured it out yet. Something with the government, I guess, but that's ancient history now. Most importantly, he has a pretty decent bunch of gunfighters working with him—about a hundred of these guys with serviceable weapons that they know how to use and more than a dozen vehicles. That makes him the mayor, the sheriff, and the judge around here. I think he has a bright future."

Colonel Mariotti returned with the coffee.

"Well, that's interesting," Cristiani said, "but why do I need this Ibrahim Hussein? My battalion is over six hundred men. I have modern weapons and tactics. My men have everything they need to get food aid to the people here. That's the job we came here to do."

Samson shook his head and frowned. "It doesn't work that way. You can't just parachute in here and expect everyone to fall in line just like that. You need to start with some allies. Some friends, like Ibrahim."

Cristiani didn't like the idea that his photo opportunities giving food to children might include some unsavoury local. They wouldn't understand it back in Rome.

"Why do I need this . . . local . . . person involved with me?" he asked. "There are no indications of active fighting in Merka. The conflict has burned itself out here—that is my conclusion."

Mariotti looked nervous. "Mr. Samson, we don't know much yet, but . . . I've seen some references to this Ibrahim Hussein. I've received mixed reports about him, some rather disturbing. I advised General Cristiani we should be impartial in the eyes of the people. It could be risky to get too close to people we don't know too soon."

"This is good coffee. Maybe I should come here for breakfast next time, Giancarlo. They even told me you serve wine with dinner." Samson savoured another sip of espresso. "Mariotti, you seem to be easily troubled for a person in your occupation. But like I told your boss, we have an investment in this man and his organization."

"With all due respect, Mr. Samson," Mariotti said, "I prefer to do our own intelligence assessment, at our own pace."

Samson turned directly to Cristiani. "I did not come to debate this," he said, his voice rising. "I want you to work with him. If you help him, he'll help you. We need local leaders to step up and take responsibility. By the way, the fact Ibrahim hasn't gotten himself killed yet means a hell of a lot. In my books, survival is a pretty fucking big qualification. Don't you agree, Giancarlo?"

Before Cristiani could reply, Mariotti jumped in. "General Cristiani, I propose that we go through our procedure of preparing a profile on this individual and his background for your situational awareness. Then I can interview him personally and make a recommendation based on the best available intelligence on whether you should have high-level exposure to this man. There are many war criminals out there."

This was becoming uncomfortable. Cristiani's instructions were to get along with the Americans. He didn't want any friction reported back to his superiors.

"Look, Mariotti, bureaucracy never won a war," Samson said. "But it's a good idea for you to meet him, Giancarlo. I see him all the time. I'm bringing him to see you tomorrow, and I'm handing over my relationship to you. I think you have a lot to offer each other. Mariotti, I need a private word here with the general. Excuse us."

Cristiani felt he had no alternative but to agree. Radiating tension, Mariotti left the room.

"Ibrahim is rough around the edges; I admit it," Samson said with soothing tone. "But he has a lot to offer. He's high value. We had some arrangements with him. Financial arrangements. He provides services to the community, like the port and the airstrip, and we pay him. He earned it, and he's a good troubleshooter when shit happens. There's something else you should keep under your hat. We didn't think he really needed all that money. So, we had him chip into our pot too. In my experience, it comes in awful handy to have some cash off the books—for all kinds of things. Anyway, think about it. You might want to continue that arrangement. Ibrahim might too."

88

13

THE ITALIAN GENERAL SHOULD have come to Ibrahim. That would have been good manners. This was Ibrahim's town. He kept it under control. It would be dangerous if people thought Ibrahim shared his power with others—or worse, if they began to feel safe.

When his driver slowed at the gate, Ibrahim told him not to stop. "I want to see how they react."

With slow-burning humiliation, he remembered the day the president abandoned him and his father like old whores. "The only asset you have is fear," his father had said. Ibrahim had learned to be a wise steward of fear. He started with small local terrors. He secured land through intimidation, extortion, and assault. Well-targeted rapes provided sex and entertainment for his young fighters. It had a multiplier effect on fear and created useful community divisions between violators and victims. At first he was careful not to provoke dangerous opponents prematurely. He took them on later when they could be extorted, co-opted, or killed, safely.

Merka was his town. The Americans knew that. But these new people, these Italians, they needed to learn. He had prepared a lesson for them.

He had told Samson he expected to be treated properly if the newcomers wanted cooperation. If they did not want to lose men. He had told Samson his red lines. "They cannot search me. They cannot touch me."

All the same, Ibrahim was relieved to see that the peacekeepers were prepared for his arrival. The tire-shredding dragon's teeth[9] were smartly pulled out of the way, and he rolled into the Italian compound. His three accompanying technicals stayed outside the gate. Ibrahim wore a light khaki jacket with the four gold stripes of a full colonel hand-sewn to the sleeves and epaulets; it looked cheap and rough against the peacekeepers' tidy new fatigues.

Ibrahim's bodyguard hopped out to open the door. Ibrahim stepped out, determined to project pride and confidence. Samson was at the building entrance, just like he said he would be.

A peacekeeper stepped forward to greet him. "Colonel Ibrahim, welcome to the Italian base. Brigadier General Giancarlo Cristiani is waiting for you in his headquarters." Ibrahim heard disdain in the tone with which the peacekeeper pronounced Ibrahim's rank. *Never mind superficial things*, he told himself.

"Please hold your arms out from your side. I'll give you a quick pat down. We do not allow weapons or listening devices for visitors. This is the security procedure."

Ibrahim was incensed. Thank Allah his men did not understand English. Otherwise he would have to violently reject this insult in order to recover his honour.

"Mr. Samson. What this is? Fix it!"

Samson came running. "For fuck's sake! Hold on there, soldier! This guy is here for the general. Don't do that." Samson put his

9   A row of sharp steel blades positioned at entry gates to shred and deflate the tires of intruders upon entry.

arm around Ibrahim's shoulders and led him away from the puzzled lieutenant.

"Hey, Ibrahim. Thanks for coming. Don't worry about that. Forget about it. They're new here. I'll get it sorted out. Let's go meet my friend, Giancarlo." They walked together into the general's spacious office.

Ibrahim noticed that the military maps were covered with Italian tourism posters. They did not trust him about operational security matters. Ibrahim squinted at a beach picture of women in bikinis. "Your women wear little. Exposed." He smiled. "General, I'm Colonel Ibrahim."

"*Salaam walekum.* I'm happy to be here in your beautiful country."

It wasn't beautiful, and Cristiani didn't look so happy. Maybe he thought Ibrahim would be flattered. Ibrahim tried to take the measure of this man. Was he hypocritical or stupid? Looking at the orderly layout of the base and the unimaginable resources behind this deployment, he felt small. Ibrahim had to wrest his survival and his position with nothing but wit, terror, and pain. Did they think that was simple? Did they realize the sacrifices he had made and the risks he had taken? Did they know he had been through hell? These peacekeepers had it too easy.

"I've prepared tea; won't you have some?" Cristiani said.

"I like coffee." Ibrahim took the biggest chair in the room and sat down.

Cristiani barked an instruction to his aide-de-camp. "Coffee will be here soon. Colonel, do you have a military background?"

"Merka is my city. Nothing escape me," Ibrahim said.

Cristiani leaned forward, as if to explain something to a dim child. "Mr. Samson mentioned your name to me. I would like to help you learn about peace and security. I'll be your mentor. I'm sure you will benefit from my experience." Cristiani's mouth bent into a curt smile. "Now that I'm here, we should make our decisions together. Keep me informed of what you're doing, and I can advise you about the right way to do things, the modern way. You see, I've commanded peace operations in many countries."

"I told UN no foreign army needed in Merka," Ibrahim said. "In other Somali places, maybe yes. Not here. My men and me do the job better. Much cheaper. I sure they tell you this before you come. So, why you here?" Ibrahim asked with a forced smile.

"Colonel, with all due respect, this goes far beyond me. It's even beyond my country." The Italian spoke slowly. "We are here under the authorization of Security Council resolution number seven nine four. It's a resolution to protect humanitarian assistance to the Somali people. Your people. It gives us the power to use all necessary means. All necessary means gives me the power to use force. This is why I'm here with my battle group."

Cristiani arrogantly looked at Ibrahim's face for signs of comprehension. Of course Ibrahim knew about the UN mission. He had heard the unwelcome news long ago on the BBC. It was unbearably patronizing. He kept his steady gaze fixed on Cristiani's eyes. "That council is in New York, I think. Yes?"

Cristiani nodded.

"They forget something."

"I'm sure you're wrong. This mission has the backing of the international community. It has been carefully planned. What could they have possibly forgotten?" Cristiani asked.

"They forget to ask me. You ask people before you come in their house. Me, I protect the people in Merka. This my house. Not your house." Ibrahim stopped smiling. He took a sip of coffee and looked at the carpets. With envy, he admitted to himself they were a nice touch. So different from his ragtag street fighters and rough, dirty compound. He took a mental note to make some improvements at his place.

Ibrahim turned to Samson. "We really like Americans. They help us with money and new trucks. Some guns too. We tell them what is going on and who doing what. Thank you, Mr. Samson."

"You are welcome, Ibrahim. I want you to work with the general now," Samson said. "The general will be a good friend to you. He will be your best friend now. You should work closely with him." Samson turned to Cristiani. "Real close."

"Everybody ask me now—Is Italy poor like us? Why don't they give us dollars? If they don't wanna help us, why they here?"

The door swung open, and a soldier whispered in Cristiani's ear.

"Gentlemen, please excuse me. I must step outside for a moment. There is a problem."

Ibrahim looked for and saw a flash of distress on Cristiani's face.

After Cristiani went out the door, Samson turned to Ibrahim. "Look, Ibrahim, don't give Cristiani a hard time. We should all be on the same team."

"I give my opinion. Mr. Samson, you know us. We push a little. We always push a little. Is our way. Maybe too much for him."

"That's right, Ibrahim. You're coming on too strong."

"How strong they are? How many men the general have?" Ibrahim inquired.

"This is a combat-ready infantry battalion. It's well equipped. They have twelve armoured vehicles with heavy machine guns. Offshore they have a supply ship with a helicopter. Cristiani has a big footprint."

This was extremely valuable information to Ibrahim. "The Italian battalion," he rhymed. They both chuckled. "So, maybe six hundred men?"

"That's right. It doesn't feel that way because they're just getting started. They only have a few recce patrols out there getting to know their way around. But don't fuck with them, understand?"

"Six hundred. Most of them for support—logistics, I think. Then they need to sleep. They need to eat. Fix trucks. Cook food. The general need people get coffee for guests. Some soldiers watch the fence and the gate. People gonna see their nice things and wanna take them. Maybe one hundred for fighting. Same like me."

"Yeah, but that won't be necessary. Like you said, Merka is under control."

"They know to fight?" Ibrahim asked. "The general, he know how to fight? Where he fight before?"

"You know as well as I do that they're trained to fight the Russians. That's why they're cooking in camo meant for the fucking Black Forest." Samson shot a hard look at Ibrahim. "Who would they have to fight anyway? You?"

Ibrahim laughed. "No, no, no. Don't worry about me."

Cristiani came back and remained standing. He was agitated. "Excuse me," he said, his voice wavering. "I'm afraid I must postpone this meeting. Perhaps tomorrow we can resume. Randy, would you stay, please?"

"What happened, Giancarlo? Trouble?" Samson asked.

"One of my patrols had an accident in the market." Cristiani said.

"Your guys okay?"

Cristiani looked down. "Yes. Somewhat shaken, but no injuries. My men responded to a threat and opened fire. A child was hit."

"Who attacked them? Was it a formed unit?" Samson asked. "Ibrahim, is there somebody on your turf we don't know about?"

"Somebody always making trouble. That's why the people need me and my men," Ibrahim said.

"The threat came from the child," Cristiani said. "The child was hostile. My men opened fire in self-defence."

Alarmed, Samson stood up. "You better contain this right away. You're the new guy in town. When a stranger hurts one of their kids, they flip out. They get pissed off, and they need to get even. Is the kid okay? Is the kid here with the doctor?"

"The situation became hostile. My men acted in self-defence, and they were ordered back to base. The child may have been fatally injured. I'll send a report to Rome for instructions. We did not expect civilian casualties. I need legal advice."

"Keep your shit together, for fuck's sake!" Samson said. "Don't be so quick to call Mom. There has to be a better fix. A local fix. And whatever you do, don't get lawyers involved."

Samson turned to Ibrahim. "Can you help us with this? We can count on you to keep a lid on things. Outsiders don't have to know about it. What do you need from us?"

"This bad. We love our children. They gonna wonder why you come, why you shoot children."

"It's just one little kid. They die all the time," Samson said. "Let's keep it in perspective. What the fuck do you need to fix this?"

"Money. When you kill somebody child, then you pay them. Money solve many problems," Ibrahim replied.

"We have money. How much do you need?" Cristiani asked.

"I gonna find out. It depend. I go now. I send you back my deputy Abdi Rahman, with a message how much." Ibrahim's calm helped the other two men settle down. "Nobody outside gonna know. You guest in my house. I take care about it for you."

Cristiani nodded. "I agree—nobody needs to know about this. Please come back any time, Colonel. You and your men are welcome here. Now I must go." Cristiani hurried out of the room. Samson jogged after him, cursing under his breath.

Ibrahim's bodyguard was standing at attention to open the vehicle door for him. The back seat on the right-hand side was where he preferred to ride—like a VIP. They rolled out of the gate, and the technicals fell into formation: one in lead to cover the road ahead, and two behind for both flanks as they raced back to his compound.

Abdi Rahman was waiting in the room he used for meetings. Ibrahim looked at the small body, torn and bloody, on a tarp in the corner. "Give me your report," Ibrahim ordered. He was relieved to be speaking Somali again. Speaking English made him feel slow and dim. It also gave him a splitting headache.

His deputy stood up. "It went well, Colonel Ibrahim. We found a little girl on her own and gave her a toy gun and some food. We played with her for about half an hour. She became happy when she saw us all fall down and then get up laughing. She was tall for a seven year old, which was good."

"What clan?" Ibrahim asked.

"She came from some far place. She is not our clan. She looked Bantu." He sneered. "Maybe Mushunguli."[10] Abdi Rahman gestured toward the corner of the room. "They have a *tukul*[11] on the edge of town with the other beggars."

"Continue," Ibrahim commanded.

"It was just as you ordered, Colonel. We told her she was good at this game. She should play it with the peacekeepers. We went to the market at the time of their patrol. It's like a clock. Yesterday and the day before, same patrol, same time, same place." This was an important tactical detail for Ibrahim.

"We told her after she plays with them we will give her and her family a nice big lunch. She ran up to the soldiers with the plastic gun shouting like we showed her."

"How did they react?" Ibrahim asked.

"The soldiers opened fire immediately. She was hit by many rounds. Of course, the people in the market were enraged. They stoned the armoured vehicles. Then the soldiers closed their hatches and retreated back to the base."

"They shot immediately?" That was good news. It meant they were afraid.

"You give the girl's family this $100 bill with the body. Tell them it's my gift to them because their daughter is a holy martyr. Tell them I said it's God's will that she should reveal the evil intentions of the infidel invaders. There will be a small burial. Your men are to keep the street calm."

"Yes, Colonel." Abdi rose to leave, but Ibrahim motioned for him to stop.

10   A minority group in Somalia that some sources say descended from fugitive slaves.

11   A round, thatched hut.

"I'm not finished. Then go to the Italians. Tell them I've paid from my pocket twenty thousand dollars in blood money for the girl. Say it's a large amount because the family is powerful. I want only ten thousand back. The rest is a welcome gift. It's my gesture of hospitality to General Cristiani."

14

·······························

Dadaab Refugee Camp

ANIK HAD BEEN IN Dadaab for one week. Earlier in the day, she had explored the vast camp again, searching for just the right place to start interviewing women. Roasted brown dust hung in the stifling heat. Particles of animal and human dung joined the sand and soil in her nostrils, throat, and lungs. As far as the eye could see were random clusters of little round huts. The *tukuls* were separated by winding paths of dust—not a tree, hill, or land-mark of any kind in sight. Dadaab was the largest refugee camp in the world. With hundreds of thousands of people, it was bigger than most cities in Kenya. Was it located in this ugly wasteland so nobody would want to stay?

Here her work was needed. Not like back in Canada. All the same, she was dying to wash the dust out of her hair and the sweat off her hot skin. Her combined office and bedroom was right next to the UN compound, and they let her use their toilet and shower facilities.

At six the sun completed its torment for the day. In letters to friends, Anik said the sunset at Dadaab refugee camp looked like a drop of blood in a café au lait.

The long, cool shower refreshed her and marked the end of her workday. She carefully put on a clean bra and underwear. She would spend her year of forced leave in Dadaab. Roll-on antiperspirant was easier to stock up on than aerosol. Chanel No. 5 was not necessary or helpful for this work. She was fascinated though by the practice of Somali women to perfume themselves by standing in their long dresses over burning incense, so the smoke scented them from the inside out. She wondered how the smoke felt on their skin.

Her nails were growing faster. She folded her towel and placed it on the wooden bench between her toiletry bag and neatly arranged clothes. She carefully clipped her fingernails and toenails, then placed the clippings in the garbage and picked up her clothes from the bench. Back in Canada, it mattered for ambitious Québécoise lawyers to look sharp, and Anik had enjoyed the frequent occasions when she was the best-looking one in the room. She had considered carefully how to relocate her modern fashion sense to a refugee camp next to a war zone.

The loose white cotton blouse with long sleeves was set off by her olive skin and natural tan. New blue jeans would not look right, so she pulled on pre-washed straight-leg Levis, form-fitting on her long athletic legs. Not too provocative for the Islamic culture of Somali refugees, she hoped. The sticks, broken glass, and shit mixed up in the dusty paths made ankle boots more practical than sandals. Since she would work with traditional Muslims, she covered her long glossy black hair. It was hard to find a good-looking hat, so she chose a silk scarf with a paisley pattern that contained the same deep blue as her eyes. She liked the way it all came together.

After Anik got kicked out of her job, the first place she called was the small human rights NGO, Justice Before Peace. The head of it, Ruth Freeman, was a contact from human rights conferences. At first Anik couldn't believe her luck that Ruth had this job to research human rights with Somali refugees ready to go and was looking for a bright young lawyer. Anik said she was particularly interested in the problem of rape as a weapon of war. Ruth was delighted with the idea and told her she was free to be creative in her approach—just send in a CV for the files. Sometimes Anik wondered if she should have waited and checked out other job possibilities, asked more questions, or negotiated a better salary. But the timing for the Dadaab project was perfect, and she was frantic to get a new start after her humiliation at the Department of Justice.

Justice Before Peace gave her a couple of vests with its initials and logo on the back. The letters "Jb4P" and the scales of justice were overlaid on the dove of peace. Ruth said Anik needed to wear it at all times so that she would be visibly protected by humanitarian principles. Anik thought it made her look like a socialist fly fisherman on a tight budget, so she didn't use it. She didn't see why she might need protection anyway. She was there to help people, not fight.

The flush of a toilet told her that she was not alone in the women's bathroom. She had finished her shower a while back, so this individual had been there for some time.

A thin voice came from the cubicle. "They talked about you again today." Sandra, the English UNICEF worker, had that gastro thing again.

Anik would never initiate a conversation from inside a toilet cubicle—and probably not in a bathroom, either. She liked Sandra, but Sandra's naive faith in the goodness of people bugged her. As a lawyer, and after Schuman, Anik's expectations about human nature had slipped down too many notches.

"And another thing—there's a Somali bloke I want you to meet," Sandra said.

"Oh, *bonjour*, Sandra. That might be nice. Who is he? Are you feeling better, I hope?"

Sandra gave a small belch, followed by a sniff. "I think the worst is over—there can't be much left in there. I'm going to pop a few more Imodium just to be safe."

She came out of the stall adjusting the elastic waistband on her pants. "He calls himself Haji Omar. Sounds funny to me, so I call him Joe. Nice sort of chap. Been here about a year. Speaks English almost as well as a Brit. He has a sweet little religious school project. I like him because he uses our primary school curriculum for refugees. After all those consultants took years and a million dollars to put it together, I'm bloody glad someone uses it."

Sandra peered up at Anik with a knowing look. "Plus, he doesn't undress me with his eyes. It gives me the heebie-jeebies when they do that. Can I use your towel?"

Sandra rolled up the sleeves of her khaki safari suit and gave her pudgy hands a perfunctory rinse. "It's the first time I've seen one of these people trying to do something for themselves instead of waiting for us to help them." Sandra sneezed into the towel, and then wiped her runny nose with the back of a moist hand. "Maybe he could help you."

Anik was mildly interested but didn't feel like changing her plans for something tangential to her mission. She was fastidious and a little unhappy about Sandra's use of her towel. She did all her laundry by hand in a bucket in her room, and towels took a long time to dry. "That sounds like a good partner for you, Sandra. But my translator comes tomorrow, and I need to start interviewing victims right away. My boss in New York is waiting for my first report. Can I get a rain check?"

"*Pas de* problem," Sandra said, a little crestfallen. "I just thought . . . you don't know anybody here, do you? Isn't it all a little bit . . . iffy? You drop in here like some kind of skydiver and . . . this work you do. You don't speak the language; you haven't been here before. Should you do it all by yourself? What if something happens?"

This challenge to her competence stung, especially after the bitter failure from which she was trying to escape. Anik bristled. "I don't understand—what do you mean, a bit iffy?"

"Our chief of mission, Dr. Miroslav, talked about you at our security meeting today. He worried that . . . he said if people saw you in our compound, they would be confused. They would think we're taking sides. He said your work might involve you in the conflict. Then they might think we support what you do. We wouldn't be impartial humanitarians anymore. He sent a memo to New York for instructions. He said you're interesting and appealing though." Sandra gave a hopeful smile. "Some of us like you, Anik. That might be a point in your favour."

Anik forced a smile, gingerly recovered her towel, and walked out the door.

15

THE NEXT MORNING, ANIK went to meet her interpreter. The camp entry checkpoint was a jagged steel tube controlled by an old yellow rope in the hands of a young policeman. Well-worn paths skirted both sides of the checkpoint. A handful of other police officers sat in front of a rusty corrugated tin shack. The Kenyan constable with the rope in his hand leered at her through bloodshot eyes. She guessed he was drunk.

Soon a lime-green *matatu*[12] pulled up to the gate, blaring heavy reggae music. A tall young woman in a traditional Somali wrap with alert eyes and a suitcase gracefully stepped down. She was the only passenger to get off at Dadaab. The woman scanned the checkpoint, saw Anik, and smiled.

"Dr. Anik? I'm Ubah, your interpreter."

She extended a sleek brown hand graced with delicate henna patterns. Subtle decorative scars framed calm almond eyes that looked out from under the turquoise chiffon covering her hair. She looked past Anik to survey the camp. Anik was encouraged

12   A privately owned minibus that provides public transportation.

by the young woman's poise. There was a quiet intelligence in her serene face.

"Every year it's bigger," Ubah said, "and more shameful."

"I didn't know you had been here," Anik replied.

"Yes. I know this place. We all know this place. We hate it."

"Let's drop off your suitcase." Anik pointed to low concrete buildings painted blue and surrounded by a chain-link fence topped with barbed wire. A bright blue UN flag flew in front of the main entrance. "This is the UN compound. We stay outside of it, but close."

Anik's quarters were on the other side of the fence. Next to that were more modest, unpainted concrete buildings with rooms, a kitchen, and an eating hall for the UN interpreters and guards. Shabby doors and windows looked directly onto a dirt road through the camp. Across the road, the camp extended into the far distance.

"I've arranged a room for you with the other interpreters."

"Thank you for this work. You are brave to do it. Why do we stay outside the fence?" Ubah asked with a puzzled look.

"They told me only official United Nations staff with blue passports are allowed to live inside the compound security fence. I don't think it really matters though. Nobody would want to hurt us."

When they turned to walk into Dadaab, the young policeman shouted to them to stop, and then called them over. He demanded Anik's ID, even though Ubah was the one entering. He took it to the two older police officers, and they lingered over her passport photo, laughing in a language Anik did not recognize. They looked her up and down.

"You with UN?" the young policeman asked. "This not UN papers."

Anik figured a friendly look would get the quickest results. She flashed a smile at the man but did not get a reaction. "No, no, I'm with another organization." Anik said.

"Why no visa?"

"Canadians don't need a visa. It's just a small tourist visit," she lied.

He did not look satisfied and watched her face with calculating curiosity for a long minute, and then returned her passport.

After putting Ubah's luggage in her small room in the building for local staff, they went to Anik's place for tea.

"I saw on your application that you want to be a lawyer," Anik said.

"That is my hope. I'll save the money you give me for the University of Nairobi law school."

"What kind of law do you want to practice?"

"Human rights. Like you do. I hope. I'll learn so much from you." Ubah's admiration inflated Anik's pride and determination to succeed.

"Well, let's get started," Anik said. "I've been exploring the camp to find the best place to begin our work. There's a water pipe where the women gather. It's not far."

Ubah nodded. "No man would ever carry water. It's better if there are no men where we work."

"Are you ready for our interviews? Do you have any questions for me?" Anik asked.

Ubah assured Anik that she had read all the project information she had received. "I know the talking points and the interview plan. I'll follow the instructions you sent to me. But I do have one question."

"What is it?"

"They don't know us. Maybe they want to keep secret what happened to them."

"We will protect the information. We'll explain that I'm a lawyer specializing in war crimes. I won't share what they tell me without their permission. We'll say that too. They have not had this kind of project before. I think it will be good news for

them. I'm bound by my professional ethics to keep information confidential."

"I understand," Ubah said. "I'm ready to get started as soon as
you wish. Thank you for the nice tea." Ubah spoke in a dignified
contralto. Her smooth face carried a courteous smile, and her
confident bearing reassured Anik that she could be trusted.

Ubah looked straight ahead as they walked along the paths that
meandered between the *tukuls*. They passed children, women,
and men sitting outside their dwellings. No one made eye contact
with them. There were no greetings, no social interaction.

"They are too ashamed," Ubah said. "That is why they don't
look at us."

The water pipe was on a slab of wet cement in an open space.
The refugee women stood erect on cracked, leathery feet and
wore wild patterns of bright colours. They patiently waited their
turn at the pump and then worked the long lever to draw water.
Old, empty oilcans served as vessels. Anik scratched at a sand flea
that found its way up her jeans and then slapped at a fly tangled in
the fine hair at the nape of her neck.

Small children hung onto their mothers. Many women had
babies slung on their back with a cloth. Despite the heavy drudg-
ery of lugging water back to their *tukuls*, the women appeared to
enjoy each other's company.

"They need to talk as much as they need water, Dr. Anik. Here
they can find out who is sick, who died, and who was born. People
are always coming to Dadaab with news from home. Sometimes
they send Dadaab news back. This is a good place for us to work."

The women stopped talking, and the water stopped flowing as
Anik and Ubah approached. Suspicious eyes looked at Anik.

"*Salaam walekum*," Anik said. The women looked wary. They
did not respond. She turned to Ubah. "Could you explain our
project, please?"

Ubah respectfully greeted them and then spoke with increasing animation to break through the impassive and impatient looks coming from the dozens of women at the water pipe.

This language erupted from the back of the throat. Anik watched Ubah's hands gesturing with more urgency. Then the women started shouting questions and comments. They were agitated. Words were thrown like stones, blunt and direct. Were these people as angry as their language sounded? Ubah's voice went up a register, and she matched the vehemence of the shouting women in her answers. Everyone spoke at the same time. Anik worried that the critical first encounter had spun out of control. At last, the cadence of speech slowed. The volume fell, and there was a pause. All the women looked at Anik.

"I told them our greeting, Salaam walekum, and that we have a new program," Ubah explained. "But then they asked me how much their benefit will be. Will there be food or money or medicine for their children? They were unhappy that we had nothing for them. They told me they liked the kind of program that gives goats and chickens to the women. This is what they want you to give them." Ubah looked down. "They don't want to talk to you if you don't give them something."

"Tell them our project is so there will be justice, one day," Anik said.

Ubah's translation set off another round of shouting. Ubah nodded, as if she expected the answer she was receiving.

"They want to know if there will be punishment. For them, justice must have punishment."

There was a tense silence. The gaze of the women chilled Anik. She was terrified of failure, as if she was taking a final examination in a subject she had never studied. If she failed again, she would be shamed and adrift.

She tried to guess a good answer, and words tumbled out. "I hope there will be punishment one day. For punishment, you need to tell me your stories. The truth must be known for punishment to be justified."

Ubah translated this to the women.

"*Haa,*" they said, which meant, "Yes."

The women conversed among themselves. Then one called out a question.

"They want to know if you will protect their stories," Ubah said.

"Tell them yes, we will protect them carefully and keep everything secret until we give reports to proper authorities. The authorities will also protect the stories. You'll be safe."

Ubah explained this, and one woman stepped out of the crowd. Her hard face framed a trembling mouth. Her eyes were moist and sad.

A cement bench was next to the pump. Ubah motioned the woman to sit down. She carefully set her water can beside her on the bench. It said, "Castrol Motor Oil" on the side. Ubah motioned for Anik to sit with them too. Women and children stood around them, listening.

Ubah asked the woman questions in a soft tone. Sometimes she reached out and touched the woman. She took her time, carefully writing notes as the woman watched her. Sometimes the woman traced her finger along what Ubah had written and suggested corrections. Anik figured the woman wanted to make sure it was exact. Ubah asked follow-up questions to confirm the information. This went on for an hour or more.

The other women listened intently and nodded from time to time. Some of them gave words of encouragement. When the woman concluded, Ubah gave her a respectful hug. The woman silently lifted her water can to her head. She said something to Ubah and then disappeared down a dusty track.

"She said thank you," Ubah said.

The sun was getting hot. A number of women approached Ubah and spoke with her briefly. Then they hefted their water cans to their heads, chose their paths home, and melted away into the destitute labyrinth.

A wave of relief hit Anik. She had not failed after all. "It sounds like we're off to a good start. Let's go back to my place, and you can explain what we learned."

Ubah nodded. "It was good, Dr. Anik. Tomorrow there will be more. I think many more. They say the same happened to them."

Back at her room, next to her bed, Anik had a plastic table with two chairs. She offered a chair to Ubah and a bottle of water. Ubah took a long drink and then read from her notes.

"Dr. Anik, this woman had terrible trouble. This is why she wants to participate in our 'punishment for rapers' program. That is what she called it." Anik gave a start at the name given to their work but decided not to interrupt. "She said she has nothing to lose. She lost everything already."

Ubah looked at Anik, sighed, and then continued. "On December 3 at 10:30 a.m., this woman, Jameelah, was making tea and listening to the radio. Everyone listened to the BBC station, she said, because it was the only station that did not lie all the time. She had the volume on low because there was no electricity. She lost her job at the hospital laboratory, and there was no money, so she wanted the batteries to last. I wrote down her full name, date, and place of birth, plus she remembered her national identification number."

Ubah concentrated on her notebook. "This is exactly what she said to me. It's like her statement. A man in a uniform came to the house. He had other men in uniform behind him. Jameelah knew him; he was her neighbour, Abdi Rahman. Her husband used to be a government worker. He was an honest one. His job was to register land and give permits to buildings. He was the top man in the Merka land registry department. But then, when the government had no money, people stopped going to work. So, he took the papers to his house, and people came to him and asked him to put their land in his books—you know, if their father had died and they inherited it, or if they sold it.

"But this young man . . . Abdi Rahman . . . " Ubah squinted at her writing ". . . said he wanted to take her husband to see his boss, Colonel Ibrahim."

Anik was following closely. "Where is this place, her town? Is it far?"

Ubah thought for a while. "Merka? Once my uncle went there. It's quite far—hundreds of kilometres—but not as far as Mogadishu. It's on the sea, and old.

"It was bad and clever what Abdi Rahman did. He called Jameelah into the street, so everybody could hear and watch. He said he would take her husband to Colonel Ibrahim Hussein to settle arguments about land titles. He told Jameelah that her husband must do this. If her husband did not do it, Abdi would come back with his men and rape her in front of the neighbours, so the family was shamed forever. So she would lose her husband and her home. Her husband got his books and went with them. He couldn't even say goodbye to his children. But they really wanted to steal the land and the houses.

"The next day they came back. Abdi Rahman called her into the street, in front of the neighbours. He said her husband didn't do what they told him. He said that now she was a widow. He told her to take off her clothes, or they would kill her children. What could she do? He pushed her on the ground, and they raped her. Nobody could help her. She understood that. It was too much disgrace for her husband's family. Nobody wanted to take a chance that Abdi and his men would return.

"So, what could she do? She left with her two small children, and they walked west. They met others who heard about Dadaab and told her to go there. Sometimes she travelled on a truck, sometimes walking. Now she is as we saw her. With nothing."

Ubah took a drink of water. She was not looking at her notes anymore. Anik asked Ubah where Abdi Rahman was.

"Jameelah does not know. He might be still in Merka. But maybe he's here in Dadaab camp. His people, sometimes they visit here. They watch what happens here."

Later that night, Anik and Ubah carefully prepared their first case file with all the details and fastened the papers in a manila folder. The label read:

Jameelah Ishaak—Victim of Sexual Assault.

Assailant—Abdi Rahman

Accomplice—Colonel Ibrahim Hussein

Crime—Aggravated Sexual Assault: Canadian Criminal Code Provision 273—Maximum sentence 10 years imprisonment. Canadian Criminal Code Provision 271 (1) (a).

"This is little," Ubah said. "Ten years is not enough. He took her life. He must pay more. He should pay with his life."

"This happened three months ago. It must be different now," Anik said. "Now that the peacekeepers are there, maybe there's something we can do."

Ubah nodded. "Maybe. We hope."

"What are the names of the children?" Anik asked. "We should have that in the file."

Ubah touched her eye, where a tear was forming. "I asked her that. Jameelah said it did not matter because they are not here. It's a difficult journey, too difficult for children, and they could not make it all the way to Dadaab. What time do we start tomorrow?"

16

ANIK'S BOSS, RUTH FREEMAN, pulled strings in New York and got herself a UN car and driver for her trip to Dadaab. The white-and-blue 4x4 pulled into the camp, and Ruth stepped out wearing a Jb4P baseball hat with a long peak and a matching khaki photographer's vest covered in pockets. Her sunglasses covered the top of her face. Her upturned nose protruded over her thin-lipped frown and sharp chin. Anik hoped one of the many pockets on her vest had sunscreen. From the blotchy red on her nose and distressed pink of her cheeks, it looked like Ruth's Manhattan skin burned quickly and badly. Anik was glad for the Algonquin genes that gave her a deep bronze tan.

"Anik! It's wonderful to see you. How are you doing?" She embraced Anik and gave her a kiss on each cheek. "This is so fucking hot. Unbelievable!" Ruth turned from one side to another, taking it in. "What a wasteland! Let's get going. I can smell my own BO. I need a shower. Is there air conditioning in my room? I have a lot to talk to you about. Tell the driver to put my bags in the room. Do these guys speak English? How much do we tip here? Can you take care of that for me? Do they have Diet Coke?"

"Ruth, welcome to Dadaab. It's great to see you," Anik said.

Ruth's urgency flustered her. It clashed with the leaden patience of the refugees. Anik shook herself into the moment. "This way to your guest room. I hope you like it. The conditions are . . . let's call them austere compared to what you're used to. The UN was nice to provide this for you. There is an air conditioner." She wanted Ruth to be comfortable, but she didn't like the way these arrangements made her feel inferior to her boss.

"Good. It's our taxes that pay for this stuff."

They stepped into a nice cool room inside the compound reserved for infrequent high-level visitors. It had its own bathroom with a toilet and shower. "It's two o'clock now," Ruth said. "Let me relax for a couple of hours. Maybe it won't be the seventh circle of hell by then. Come back at four. We'll go over your work."

Anik joined Ruth a few hours later and brought a box of ten case files to review with her. They sat on the porch outside Ruth's room. A dusk wind came up, and the heat began a small retreat.

"The first file is the first woman we interviewed, Jameelah. She was brave to provide details on her sexual assault in front of the other women. She inspired others to come forward. We couldn't have done this without her. I owe her a lot."

Ruth took off her hat and glasses. She had brought a bottle of gin in her luggage and was sipping a couple of ounces from a plastic cup. "Want a drink?"

Anik tried valiantly to sip the hard liquor without coughing and sat in expectant silence while Ruth flipped through the material. Anik had skipped lunch, and the alcohol wormed around in her head, dulling her attention.

"Your work is better than I expected. As a fellow lawyer, I would say this is professional." The recognition gratified Anik.

"I'm a good leader because I don't pussyfoot around," Ruth said. "I'm going to tell it like it is. Come on! What the fuck were you thinking? Okay, it's true. This is serious information. You have the names of the victims, their birthdays, where they were born, and their clan and sub-clan—I guess that's like an address in its own way. It's cute you added references to the Canadian Criminal Code and the penalties a prosecutor should argue. You could use it in a court—if there was a court. It's clever—but it's not smart." Ruth rolled her faded brown eyes up to look at Anik over the frames of her glasses.

"Anik, there is no court for these poor victims, like what's-her-name—Jameelah. This is too much. If we were going to court, it would be good. But look where we are." She waved her arms at the endless expanse of refugee huts. "Frankly, it makes me kind of nervous. I mean, what's your exit strategy?" Ruth got up. "I'm going to pee, then we can talk."

Anik kept her outer cool as the words stung and confused her. Ruth had said she would have free rein with this work, and now she felt exposed and alone.

Anik thought back to when she had accepted a professional lifeline from Ruth the day after the deputy minister forced her to take a leave of absence. She had assumed it would take time to get through to the president of Jb4P, but she was put directly through to Ruth on her first call.

"Hello, Ruth. Do you remember me? Anik Belanger? We met at the contemporary war crimes conference. When you came up to Ottawa last year."

"Why yes, yes I do. That was a great visit, and I remember we had a great conversation. You were interested in our work. How are things going? Sorry about the Schuman verdict. Would have been nice to see that bastard behind bars. What are you doing these days? Will you be in New York any time soon?"

"Thank you so much for those kind words." Anik always said that when receiving a compliment. But this time Anik was thirsty for reassurance. "I really enjoyed meeting you too. Actually, I'm looking for a change in direction, and you were the first person I thought to call."

"Your timing is impeccable!" Ruth said. "Have you ever been to Africa? We happen to be opening a new project, and you would be perfect. It's about refugee women and what happens to them. And it's about the biggest crisis in the world today. You know, the Somalia humanitarian catastrophe. It's on the news all the time. You'll probably get on CNN if you take this job. When can you start?"

Ruth's enthusiasm energized Anik and gave her a feeling of hope and self-worth that she sorely needed at that point of her life. She yearned to make a difference. It was also time for her to get some distance from Ottawa and government work. A new start at the epicenter of a human rights catastrophe would remove the dreaded problem of explaining that she was on forced leave. It would also divert attention from the Schuman humiliation. And this wasn't about senile Nazis; this was about the fulcrum of world events. That was where she wanted to be and be seen as an activist—a humanitarian activist. When she needed it most, a spark of self-righteousness radiated warm comfort against the chill of her failure.

That warm satisfaction didn't last. She had had to do everything herself. The salary was poor, and she had to use her own money for travel expenses. Now she didn't feel the support from Ruth that she deserved. Had she been naive? It was discouraging that her work disappointed Ruth's expectations. Worst of all, were these women she interviewed just plain out of luck and on their own? Her mouth and eyebrows wouldn't obey her decision to stay cool. Stones of doubt scraped across Anik's mind.

"Don't feel bad," Ruth said. "There's some material we can use here. The human dimension of our work is what connects with our funders."

"I appreciate the constructive criticism," Anik lied. "I'm so glad you're here, so I can get closer to your vision. What are you thinking about the justice part in our name Justice Before Peace?

When people ask you about justice, what do you say? What does it mean to you?"

"Good question." Ruth smiled as if Anik were a good pupil. "Money. It boils down to money. When you do something wrong, you have to pay, and you pay with money. I want to take this to the next level. Victims should get something for restitution."

The sun skulked over the horizon. In the dark distance, a man started chanting at the top of his voice.

"I don't like that. Sounds threatening. Should we leave?" Ruth asked. "What's going on?"

"It's the call to prayer. The muezzin doesn't have a loudspeaker, so he yells."

"Do you know what he's saying? I think he's angry."

"He says the same thing every sunset. 'God is great. Allah is the only God. Come and pray.' You look around at this place, and you might think people would start to doubt God, but they don't."

"I would," Ruth said. "But getting back to my way of thinking, I believe in moral justice. I mean that I believe in social justice across borders." She opened a file. "There's a compelling human interest story here. Rich countries need to hear about Jameelah, how she lost her kids and has nothing now. That way we can get at the guilt of the international system.

"My message is—compensate suffering. If we play this right, we can get funding for projects for these women. Teach them to sew, buy pipes to bring water closer, even teach them to read. How great would that be?" Ruth smiled with satisfaction at Anik. "Let's not forget to get a photo of Jameelah and me before I leave."

"I thought justice was about putting criminals in jail. That's what the refugees think we're trying to do here," Anik said.

Ruth put her hand on her forehead and then poured a couple more fingers of gin. "Oh, come on. Don't raise expectations. When you do that, you take responsibility for what people do with those expectations." Ruth tapped Jameelah's file with her index finger. "I mean this perp—Abdi Rahman. He must be long gone. Out of the picture. It's chaos in Somalia. It's all over the TV news. So, let's do what we can now to help them rebuild their lives. Here in their new home of Dadaab."

"What happened to Jameelah—that brutality—it destroys a person's life," Anik countered. "Evidence has value. When it's documented in a legally valid way, it can last forever. It's worth something to Jameelah that what happened to her isn't just forgotten. If we do this right, women like her will get justice. One day."

Ruth set down her gin. "Look at it from my perspective. I've been fucking trying my best to get the message across in New York, but it's like banging my head against the proverbial brick wall. And if I don't get donations, this project is toast. We need stories from the field from people like you, but it has to be the right story—with a happy ending. There's no money for a wild goose chase to find Abdi and his henchmen."

Ruth downed the last of her gin before continuing. "Is everything ready for the dinner tonight? Are community representatives invited? I want a sense of Dadaab. I can get your reports any time. The value for me is getting to the grassroots. They say it's the largest refugee camp on the planet. I'm going to have another drink—how about you?"

"Yes, we have people from the UN, the police, and community representatives. No, no thank you about the drink. I better go now and make sure everything is ready. Sandra, the UNICEF representative, will come by and take you to the dinner. All these UN buildings look the same, and I wouldn't want you to get lost here." Anik excused herself and hurried through the dust to the building where dinner preparations were being made.

17

THE LOCAL POLICE CHIEF, John Kithunga, arrived first, along with two of his constables. He was wearing his dress uniform. A crust of sweaty dust circled his peaked cap. He asked for a warm Tusker beer and nursed it silently. He must have been looking forward to free drinks because he came fifteen minutes early.

Zanov Miroslav, the manager of the UN camp, came into the room right on time.

"Anik, good evening to you. But where is Madame Freeman? I normally delegate UN representation with NGOs to my deputy, but I feel this is different."

His meaty face was coarse, oily, and pale. He looked at his watch and then looked at Anik. Ruth was late, and her discourtesy bothered Anik. His tone softened. "My goodness, you look elegant this good evening, Anik."

She was wearing black ankle-length skinny jeans, a scoop-neck red leotard top, and a light cotton jacket with sandals. Her sleek black hair was pulled tight over her head in a high ponytail. Before she could formulate a response, she heard the barking laugh of her approaching boss.

The dinner was held in a cement-block UN meeting room. Three moulded plastic tables were placed end to end and surrounded by the white plastic chairs they had managed to scrape together. Bright flowered Chinese oilcloths had been newly purchased for the event, and artificial flowers in jam jars had been carefully placed in the middle of the tables.

Jameelah caught Anik's eye, brought her hand to her chest in greeting, and nodded with a grateful smile. She was with two other Somali women, and all were dressed in the full-length traditional dress of bold, brightly patterned fabrics. They stood beside the tidy row of plastic serving bowls full of the savoury food that they had prepared for the special event. Soft drinks, wine, and beer were also available. The meat cooked by the women in the open air over charcoal was separated into crunchy ribs, neck, legs, liver, and kidneys. Anik told the ladies they could keep the goat's head, testicles, lung, and trotters for themselves. A bunch of small bananas was placed next to a large bowl of spaghetti with oily tomato sauce. The dish of stewed okra looked slimy but smelled delicious. At the end of the line was freshly baked flatbread.

Sandra waddled into the room and eagerly guided Ruth straight to the top UN authority at Dadaab. "Dr. Zanov Miroslav, I would like to present Dr. Freeman, who is visiting us on an important mission in her capacity as executive director and chairperson of Justice Before Peace. She has so much to tell us; I'm sure it will be a wonderful evening."

"Call me Ruth, Zanov. My, what an enthusiastic officer you have here in Sandra."

Miroslav set his drooping shoulders back, hooked his thumbs in the belt of his beige safari suit, and licked his moist lips. "And we really enjoy your field person, Anik. I would love to know what she actually does wandering around in our camp." He chuckled. "As the ranking UN official, I officially welcome you to Dadaab. I'm with the refugee agency, but as the senior executive I lead and direct the entire team, including Sandra, who does the little children and lady projects. You might say I'm the mayor of the biggest refugee camp in the world. The big picture—security, political affairs, finances—is my job. Everyone reports to me. Anik, there's wine, yes? Sandra, please open some for us. I would happily—how do you say—closely coordinate with Anik too—but she is non-governmental and doesn't have to listen to me. I'll need to be highly convincing to make her do what I want!" He giggled.

"Ruth, what I really want to know is the gossip in New York. Do you know your American ambassador to the UN, Ambassador Pickering? Secretary Baker? General Powell? I'm sure a dignitary like you does. What are they saying about us out here in Africa? The humanitarian work we do is so important. We only get about fifty cents per refugee per day to run this place, so please help us increase our budget."

"Well as a matter of fact, I'm closer to the Democrats. I'll see what I can do. But it might not be a good time. You heard about that attack on the twin towers? Lucky for us they didn't bring it down with that truck bomb in the basement! Six dead and closed the place down for a week. Some crazy Islamic fundamentalist Egyptian sheik, they say. Who are those fundamentalist guys anyway, and why are they mad at us?" Ruth asked. "But more importantly—a glass of wine would be wonderful."

Two Somali men entered. They were the community representatives. Anik didn't know them. Their dress was identical, a traditional calf-length *kikoi* skirt, safari shirt, and white leather skullcap. They were talking, but their body language was stiff. The older one had eyes that were permanently bloodshot from a life lived in the sun. His black irises were indistinguishable from the pupil against his pink eyeballs. Accompanying his suspicious red eyes was a leery frown and a bright red beard. The skin behind the beard was also stained red. His teeth were tinted olive from chewing the green leaves of the qat[13] plant. They matched the colour of his dirty khaki shirt. Anik had heard qat was addictive and that qat hangovers spiked a propensity for violence. The other man had clear, lively amber eyes. His clothes were clean and pressed. He sported a neatly trimmed beard and had a demeanour of cheerful curiosity.

"The red beard guy is Uthman," Sandra whispered in Anik's ear. "They say true believers dye their beards with henna like the prophet did. Uthman knows everything that goes on. They say nothing can happen without his say-so. Dr. Miroslav considers him to be a leader of the refugee community. He sometimes helps by telling us who to give food to and who doesn't need it. I think of him as the godfather around here. Like in the mafia movie." Sandra gave a nervous chuckle. "The other fellow is Joe, the one with the little school I told you about. His real name is Haji Omar. I think you'll like him."

Anik found Uthman disturbing and repellent. She didn't want and didn't think she needed a relationship with him. She turned away from him and approached Omar. "We haven't met. My name is Anik Belanger."

Omar took Anik's hand in a friendly handshake. His hand was strong, his fingernails carefully clipped, and his skin felt clean and dry. His grip was soft and sensitive. It seemed out of time and place in a good way. She felt a strange frisson when they touched.

"Hi, Anik. It's nice to meet you." He touched his skullcap, looked around, and then released her hand. His tone shifted to distant and formal. "*Salaam walekum*, Miss Belanger." He pronounced her name perfectly. "I'm Haji Omar. I run the New Light Madrassa. Do you know of it?"

---

13 Qat is a shrub native to northeast Africa and the Arabian Peninsula. Chewing qat leaves produces a stimulant effect similar to amphetamines and is addictive.

"Yes, Sandra has said nice things about it, and I would love to visit." A question nagged at the back of Anik's mind: *Why would a cosmopolitan type like him be in a place like this?*

"Excellent! In the morning is best. The students are most active before it gets hot. And what brings you here from . . . Canada, I guess. Is your accent Canadian?"

"Well, I'm from Québec, actually. My job is field officer for Justice Before Peace. I'm interviewing women about the crimes they suffered. Sexual assault." Anik felt uncomfortable and unsure of how he would take any talk about sex. Would he be threatened, insulted, or maybe indifferent?

"What for?" he asked.

"That's what this dinner is about. Thank you for coming. My boss, Ruth Freeman will explain things. Let's get some food and sit down before it gets cold."

When they had all served themselves at the buffet and sat down, Ruth held forth.

"My name is Dr. Ruth Freeman, and I've come from New York, where I direct an important human rights organization serving the international community by giving voice to victims. Assault victims like Jameelah and her friend who prepared this colourful local food." Ruth pointed them out with a smile. They smiled back. "Our current campaign is about sexual assault and refugees, which is, as you know, a huge problem here in Dadaab. What happened to women here is a terrible stain on the international community."

Miroslav was looking nervous, the Kenyan police chief was indifferent, and Omar had a quizzical expression.

Anik tapped Ruth on the shoulder. "Slow down," she whispered. "We need to give Ubah a chance to translate." Ruth waited impatiently as Ubah translated into Somali with an even and deliberate cadence.

Upon hearing her name, Jameelah looked at Ubah with fearful disquiet. Anik had a shot of anxiety about the casual violation of her promise of confidentiality for the women.

"As I was saying, our purpose is to give voice to the victims, and Anik here has been doing a wonderful job. Thank you, ladies, for your collaboration and for sharing your stories. Even though it must be difficult to talk about all those horrible rapes, the important thing is that you have survived!" Ruth emptied and refilled her glass of wine and then continued. "I believe our work here will have a big impact on American opinion makers and donors. Ubah, translate that please."

Uthman spat on the floor, and then held Jameelah and her friend in a long, angry glare. Shamefaced, they stared down at their feet.

Oblivious to the storm clouds gathering around the table, Ruth said, "I came here to see the ground truth of our programs from people in the field. What are the opinions around the table? Let's start with you, chief."

The policeman looked up, startled and displeased to be interrupted from his eating and drinking. "Madame, it's nice to share this tasty food with you." He paused, and then his voice rose in volume and register. "You must understand that my country is paying a huge price for the hospitality we give our troublesome Somali neighbours. You rich countries need to help us more. Maybe you noticed my Kikuyu[14] complexion. I'm a black man, but I'm carrying the white man's burden of these refugee peoples."

The hostile and sarcastic tone was totally unexpected. Anik had thought the dinner and beer would be enough for a little gratitude. The policeman saw the discomfort of his table companions who spoke English. He changed tack.

"Your Excellency, Dr. Ruth, my government cannot change what those crazy people are doing on the other side of our border. We cannot do much about what happens inside this camp. We

14   Kikuyu is the largest ethnic group in Kenya.

need more help to manage this so-called humanitarian disaster. On behalf of the police, I formally request your financial support to improve the living conditions of my men here." Kithunga guzzled his beer and stared at Ruth. "By the way, it's better here than in the Kariobangi and Kibera slums we have around Nairobi. You should go and help there."

Ruth swayed in her seat a little. Anik remembered that she had started on the gin early. Ruth didn't eat anything. She just pushed the food around on her plate. Perhaps the African food alarmed her. Anik also knew that Ruth was not in the habit of justifying herself. Nor did she have anything to give the police.

"Well, you know, I do have contacts with groups that do human rights training. I'm sure your policemen could benefit from that." Police Chief Kithunga looked doubtful and returned his attention to his dinner.

Miroslav stepped into the breach. "Chief Kithunga, on behalf of the United Nations Organization and all of us international professionals in Dadaab camp, I want to thank you very much for the support and security you bring us. Rest assured that your contribution and that of your government are fully recognized and greatly appreciated. Would you like another beer?" Miroslav's oily diplomacy reduced the tension. The chief and his deputy both accepted another beer.

"Anik, why don't you give us a little presentation on what Jb4P is doing here in Dadaab, so everyone is in the picture," Ruth said.

Anik explained she had interviewed fifty-four victims in the previous month. She spoke slowly and clearly, pausing from time to time so Ubah could translate. "More women are coming forward now, so my translator, Ubah, and I are busy every day. I'm interviewing them and documenting the crimes that have been committed against them. It's pretty much always sexual assault." Some of the guests shifted in their seats and looked uncomfortable, but it was more important to lay the facts on the table.

"Sometimes it's a garden variety criminal rape where one or two men attack and have forced intercourse. Usually, there's something else—what I call rape as a weapon. The women tell me they are raped in order to intimidate a neighbourhood, to force women and families to flee, or to punish and humiliate if warlords don't get what they want. Every case breaks your heart and ruins lives.

"It's astonishing how many details the ladies remember. Times, places, and names. These interviews are generating solid evidence. I've created case files. When we analyze our case files, a pattern comes through. There is a concentration in one city much more than others. Sometimes it's the same rapists in multiple cases.

"I'm doing this work according to Canadian criminal law, because that is what I know best. Ruth will use these reports to raise awareness and money in New York."

"Yes, thank you, Anik. The purpose is to raise awareness, and I see the people around this table as strategic partners. Ubah, could you please ask our two Somali friends to share the view from the community? That will give Anik some time to eat!"

Ubah quietly translated Ruth's request for views to Uthman. He spat on the floor again and then scolded Ubah with angry comments.

Ubah's voice quavered, and after every phrase she needed to stop to catch her breath. "Mr. Uthman says he speaks for all the refugees. He said it was unwise and unwelcome for this shameful woman to spy on Somali families. If there is a problem, he will fix it in the traditional way. If you need to know something, ask him, and he will advise you. He said he will give you what you need. He wants you to stop talking to the women, Dr. Anik. He says that you must come see him. Everything should go through him."

Uthman noisily sucked the marrow from a goat femur and looked at Anik with a lewd squint. He wolfed down some more food, wiped his hands on the tablecloth, and then left.

After a weighty pause, Omar spoke up. "Welcome to Dadaab, Dr. Freeman, and thank you, Anik, for sharing your work with us. My name is Haji Omar. I run a school here for refugee girls and boys that is financed with gifts from wealthy Gulf Arabs. In my way of thinking, the only things that you cannot take from a person are education, knowledge, and faith. So, this is what I try to give. It's a religious school, yes. This is because some of my brothers and sisters believe religious training is the only thing more valuable than helping with family chores. Sandra provided us with special curricula, so we include modern teaching.

"About Uthman, he has a traditional outlook. You took him outside his comfort zone. Talk of sex in mixed company, especially rape, is taboo. It's not discussed openly here. I think our community needs to change its attitude about that, and I welcome your work. You should know that he is probably a better representative of community attitudes than me. Anyway, I spoke to Anik about a visit to my school. Why don't you come too, Ruth? Maybe we can do something together? I also have a question for you, Ruth. Is raising awareness all that can be done? That seems inadequate to me."

"Omar, I'm afraid I don't have time to see your school, although I'm sure it's wonderful," Ruth said. "Anik will go. Look, what we do is more than adequate. It's the international community that needs to wake up and do something. Don't you think so, Zanov? And what about those peacekeepers you have over there in Somalia?"

Miroslav looked like his mind was elsewhere. Sandra had told Anik that her boss had been angling for a posting back at headquarters in Geneva. He heard his name but had to ask Ruth to repeat the question before he replied.

"Well, the international community's first obligation is fully financing our UN budget, so we can—ha-ha—deliver groceries for the refugees. I don't have a mandate outside the camp, so these crimes you talk about are none of my business. Anyway, it's the Kenyan police who take care of that sort of thing when they happen here in the camp.

"The soldiers next door in Somalia are not policemen. International peace and security is their mandate. It wouldn't be appropriate for them to get involved in this kind of ummm . . ." He closed his eyes and concentrated, then opened them and smiled, obviously pleased at his formulation. ". . . family problems between men and women."

Anik contained her exasperation at Miroslav's prevaricating. She was thankful Jameelah did not understand English. She summoned all of her diplomatic reserve. "Really, I thought sexual assault would be exactly the kind of insecurity the peacekeepers would need to stop. They do call it a 'humanitarian mission.'"

Miroslav gave a smug smile. "It's a technical military matter. It depends on the rules of engagement. It's doubtful that countries that contribute troops would endanger their soldiers to protect individuals in the course of their conjugal disputes. Of course, the military side of things is the responsibility of peacekeeping operations in New York."

Miroslav opened his arms in an expansive gesture of generosity toward Ruth. "This is well outside my mandate, but I want to help you. I want to do a favour for you, Ruth, through my personal connections. I know the UN political officer in our office in Mogadishu. He's a friend, someone I served with in Geneva. I'm sure he would find your work most interesting. Bring your documentation to my office, and I'll gladly forward it."

"It's a deal!" Ruth said happily. "Anik, I want you to take your reports to Dr. Miroslav tomorrow, after I leave. I have a positive feeling about this. With the community support that we heard from Omar and high-level cooperation from the UN, we are breaking new ground."

Anik hesitated. She didn't trust Miroslav, and Ruth's offer had caught her off guard. Uthman's ominous comments seemed to be some kind of warning. Was she ready to share the women's sensitive information more widely? She felt the eyes of the table on her. She couldn't contradict and embarrass her boss in front of these people. That would probably be the end of everything she had been working to put together. Actually, Ruth had made the decision for her, she reasoned, and if she didn't take this opportunity, there may never be another chance to get her information into the hands of people who could really do something about it. Anik started to visualize the praise and profile she would achieve for shaping a peacekeeping operation with a women's rights mission. It would compensate for the humiliation of the Schuman case and be a big win for human rights and justice. She was kind of surprised to hear support coming from Miroslav. He was notorious for keeping precisely inside his bureaucratic mandate.

"That sounds great, Ruth. Dr. Miroslav, I'll put together a report for you tonight and bring it to your office tomorrow morning," Anik said.

The UN functionary grunted his assent. "Very well then. It's all settled. I'll see you tomorrow morning at ten o'clock sharp. I bid you all a good night." He pushed away from the table, and the other guests also rose to leave.

"Why don't you come for a morning tea?" Omar asked Anik on his way out. "Day after tomorrow? It's so nice to see the children coming to school. That's my favourite part of the day. Say seven o'clock?"

"That sounds wonderful, Omar. I'll do that," Anik said. She was intrigued to know more about him and what he was doing in Dadaab.

18

ANIK WORKED THROUGH THE night to prepare her report and arrived at 10:00 a.m. on the dot, right after seeing Ruth off from Dadaab. Sandra had told Anik that Miroslav Zanov was a "High and Mighty D1." That meant he was a first-level executive in the UN system. Anik introduced herself to his assistant, who told her Miroslav had not arrived yet. Thirty minutes later he walked past them without a greeting and entered his office. The secretary spoke into the intercom. "That NGO person Belanger is here to see you. She said you would be expecting her."

"Very well, please escort her in."

His office was large and panelled with cheap plywood. Zanov sat behind a wide desk in a high-back leather swivel chair facing the door. An old sofa was against the wall. The official portrait of UN Secretary General Boutros Boutros Ghali was installed behind him. He looked down at her through his thick spectacles as if lending awesome authority to whatever Zanov might say. Next to the portrait was Zanov's doctorate in sociology from the University of Belgrade. Zanov was eating a breakfast of sausages and boiled eggs. A cloth napkin covered his generous belly. A hangover gave his jowly face a bleary, grouchy expression.

Anik approached his desk. He did not invite her to take a seat. There was no chair. She saw a pile of statements from the Chemical Bank of New York. He quickly turned them over.

"Bonjour, Dr. Miroslav. Good morning." She put a cheerful tone in her voice but observed that he had been much friendlier the previous night. "I came to follow up on our discussion about my work and your UN contact in Mogadishu." Anik was both weary and elated. She had stayed up all night going over her notes to prepare this special report for the UN. "Ruth insisted that I come right away."

"Very well. Please remind me what you think we agreed upon."

"Yes, of course. We talked about a pattern of sexual violence that emerged from my interviews with women here in Dadaab. You and Ruth both thought the UN must have this information and act on it to stop these human rights violations. You said a friend of yours—a political officer—working in Mogadishu can give the report to the special representative of the UN in Somalia. I've prepared a full brief on what we are seeing, with the information on the witnesses and the testimonial evidence on the crimes we have collected. It must be treated with high confidentiality. I think you should also send it to the members of the Security Council, so they are aware of how grave the situation is."

Anik carefully placed the typewritten document on his desk. He read it as she stood there. She was proud of her work. It was an excellent report, with the rigour and disciplined analysis she learned in the Department of Justice. It was the kind of information and findings that would naturally trigger an investigation and prosecution in any serious jurisdiction. She expected him to be impressed and give her the respect she knew that her work deserved. She watched as he read.

Crimes of Sexual Violence as Reported by Refugee Women in Dadaab Refugee Camp: Observations and Recommendations for the United Nations

Introduction and Summary: The Dadaab field office of Justice Before Peace (Jb4P) conducted structured interviews with fifty-four (54) refugee women who were displaced as a result of strife in their native Somalia. Forty-nine of the interviewees have reported being victims of sexual violence. In many cases, these assaults appear to have been intended to force their displacement through intimidation or terror. There is a concentration of assaults reported in the area of the coastal port town of Merka.

The quality and the specificity of the evidence obtained are of a good standard. In most jurisdictions this evidence would be sufficient for prosecutorial actions. Unfortunately, in the case of Somalia, the absence of government authority is such that there will be no prosecutions. Somalia has no judicial branch or court infrastructure. The purpose of this report is to formally convey the information obtained by Jb4P to the competent UN authorities for investigation and human rights action.

Maintaining the confidentiality of this information is of utmost importance to protect the identity of the women involved. It's likely that most of the alleged assailants are at large and would view this information as a threat. A primary concern is preventing retribution against interviewees for sharing this information and naming names . . .

Miroslav scanned the discussion of the results, the patterns that suggested systematic use of sexual violence as a weapon, and the recommendation that the UN peacekeeping mission initiate a program of investigation and action against the criminals responsible. A tabular annex included the names, birthdates, and addresses of the victims, alleged perpetrators, the crimes committed, and the appropriate sentencing according to the Canadian Criminal Code. It was signed "Anik Belanger, Field Officer, Justice Before Peace, Dadaab Camp."

After he had scanned the document, Zanov carefully sliced a piece of sausage. His mouth opened as he chewed, looking at the plate in front of him. "This is unusual and surprising information. In these kinds of things, the technical approach is best. I would like to get this information into the hands of the people who can properly evaluate it. We don't need to involve the Security Council in New York."

He picked up a hard-boiled egg, sprinkled salt on it, and took a bite. He looked directly at Anik. "Did you know there are fifteen countries on the council? They never agree on anything. It will be too complicated. There will be delays." Zanov's lips gleamed with breakfast grease. He stretched them back in a smile. "Your document will be sent next door. Like you just said, I happen to be good friends with the political advisor to the special representative of the secretary general. I'll send it to him. He will do the right thing."

It wasn't everything that Anik had been hoping for. She really wanted to get it to the Security Council ambassadors in New York. That would come later, she supposed. This would be a good start anyway. "Dr. Miroslav, can you please assure me that this will be treated in confidence? The information is sensitive. If it fell into the wrong hands, somebody could get hurt. These women still feel vulnerable." She had promised them over and over that their information would be protected, and it would be devastating to her and her project if she lost that trust.

"My friend is a trustworthy person. He is junior to me and will follow my instructions. If you do not trust the UN, who can you trust?"

"Thank you, Dr. Miroslav, but I need to know exactly what you're going to do and what happens next."

With some impatience, he put down his knife and fork. "I'm going to send this through our special system. It's strictly confined to UN users. I'll send it directly by fax to the office of the special representative of the secretary general. That means it will be seen by my friend first. I'll recommend that he undertake a special review of this information, and, if you permit me, I'll add that the field office of Jb4P is disposed to collaborate fully with the United Nations. In my personal view, I believe this information is of capital importance to the peacekeeping operations in Somalia. Their mandate should include the prevention of sexual violence against women. I'll personally recommend this."

"Dr. Miroslav, this is my only copy. I wanted to get it to you right away. Could you return it to me when you're finished?"

"In due course." He dropped the report in his empty plastic inbox on the right side of his desk. "I'm afraid I must move on to other things. Have we finished here?" Zanov looked at her and raised his eyebrows to confirm she understood.

Anik nodded her assent. It was good news, she told herself. She was about to make a real difference. "Yes, thank you for helping me, Dr. Zanov. You'll tell me the outcome, won't you?"

"No doubt, no doubt. I'm sure you will be among the first to know the results of your initiative. Good day."

19

THE NEW LIGHT MADRASSA was about a kilometre from Anik's quarters, so she got up early. She chose an understated ivory-coloured scarf and a long skirt. She worried about making the right impression on Omar and the children at the school. She put on a little makeup. Ubah had obtained the directions and met her in the dusty dirt road outside her quarters at 6:30 a.m. to guide her and translate.

"He seems like a nice man. What do you think?" Anik said.

"Maybe. Something is strange. It takes a Somali about two minutes talking about clans, uncles, cousins, and great-grand-parents before we connect. Haji Omar doesn't do that. It's like he comes from nowhere. For me, it's difficult to trust someone like that."

They walked in silence. Anik didn't want to pursue that line of discussion. It was soiling the good opinion that she wanted to have of this man.

Around them the camp bustled with morning activities. Men and women squatted to relieve themselves behind make-shift dwellings. Girls stumbled along under vessels of water and bundles of sticks. Babies screamed. Flies buzzed, and an acrid haze of smoke from cooking fires stained the cool morning air.

Off the main road, they saw a large compound surrounded by a tidy chain-link fence and recently planted jacaranda saplings. The Somali flag flew on the pole in front. A couple of young girls holding hands and wearing backpacks skipped by. Anik smiled when she heard the happy sound of camp children laughing. Kids clamoured over the colourful slides, swings, and climbing frames in front of the long, narrow concrete school building. It was painted in the national colours: white and blue.

Anik and Ubah joined the stream of children pouring through the gate into the playground. The girls wore blue jumper dresses and white headscarves with brown canvas running shoes. The boys were in white T-shirts with blue trousers. A couple of boys were shooting baskets, and pairs of girls were absorbed in a complex clapping game. A number of kids accumulated outside the fence. They didn't have uniforms. With longing, they looked inside.

Beside the building, Anik and Ubah saw Omar beckoning them with a wave. He stood beside a table with three chairs and small glasses for tea.

"Let me guess—one sugar?"

Anik nodded. She was relaxed and refreshed to be in a place that was self-sufficient, thriving, and optimistic.

"This is fantastic, Omar. Tell me all about it." The man impressed her. He wore polished sandals, a tidy *kikoi*, and a clean white shirt. A gold pen peeked out of his shirt pocket.

"There is not so much to tell," he said with a gleam of pride in his eyes. "It began with a sad story. I met a man at mosque. He was a refugee, and he wanted to abandon his son to me, so I could give the boy an education. The father was educated, but he had lost everything. Can you imagine the desperation it takes to offer your son to a stranger?" Omar spoke with real feeling, and Anik sensed that this memory held special significance as a pivotal event in his life. "Then I said to myself, we must educate children, so they can start fresh after our generation sent everything to hell."

"What did you do before? Where do you find money?" Anik thought it was admirable but also strange that a sophisticated person like Omar would leave everything behind for a little school in Dadaab.

"I have money from doing business, and I have friends in the Arab Gulf who wanted to help. So, here I am," he said. It seemed pretty vague, but this was not the time to probe. "I'm sorry there's not enough room for everyone. We only take the ones with basic literacy and numeracy, and we are at capacity right now. That's why you see others outside the fence. They'll wander back to their *tukuls* after classes begin."

At the trill of a whistle, the children formed lines in front of their classrooms. Omar turned to Anik. "Excuse me, it's time for morning prayer."

Attentive eyes focused on Omar. Ubah translated his words to Anik as he spoke to the children.

"In the name of Allah, most beneficent and merciful, I welcome you to another day of school. Children, we are of the desert. We know that water is life, that it must be preserved, honoured, and shared among our people. Learning is like water. You must cherish it and never waste it. Like rain, learning contains the grace of Allah. Like love, it can be shared infinitely without diminishment. As I say to you every day, Allah has given us hands to create and senses to hear, see, and feel our world around us. Intelligence to discern the right path and a voice to share our knowledge and opinions. Today and every day I ask you to use Allah's gifts to their fullest in our little school. Have a happy day, my children!"

"Have a happy day, Haji Omar!" they replied in unison and then filed into their classrooms.

Anik wondered about this man. He spoke English with a natural and neutral accent. He appeared relaxed and comfortable with her. He had accomplished something remarkable with this fine school in the midst of misery and failure.

"You know, Anik, I'm so happy I could show you this," Omar said. "I'm so proud of our school. But I really wanted to talk about your work. How did you come to this insane place? Why here?"

"Like I told you last night, I'm Québécoise; that's where I'm from. But I was in Ottawa before coming here. I'm a criminal prosecutor. My last job was with the federal government. I investigated war criminals in order to bring them to trial under Canadian law." Anik decided not to mention that she lost her big case against Schuman. "It bothers me that in our day and age there is complete impunity for war criminals in Somalia and so many other conflict zones. So, I'm trying to investigate and build cases here. Maybe the work I'm doing in Dadaab on rape as a weapon of war can be a precedent for other places. You know, they talk about something like a war crimes court for Bosnia."

"I don't want to sound cynical, and I really do want to support your work with our women. They probably feel better when they have someone to talk to. Someone who listens to what happened. But I thought chasing war criminals was finished with Nuremberg, and, well, the Americans dealt with Japan too. Catching war criminals in this part of the world? Maybe in Europe they will do something. But in Africa? War crimes are normal here. They happen all the time." Omar poured more fragrant tea into their short glasses, then delicately added a leaf of mint.

Anik didn't expect him to dismiss her idea so casually, and it upset her more than it should have. "They are not normal!" she exclaimed. "We can't let them become normal. If there are no limits on war—well, you know what happens. Civilians are the victims. Especially women." She was getting hot in the morning sun.

"Sometimes people are caught in impossible situations despite their best intentions," Omar replied. "Sometimes it's a matter of survival. When everything collapses, and there are no rules, can you really hold people to account? How can you put the blame on individuals when entire countries fall apart, like ours did?" His brow furrowed, and his fists clenched. "Your problem is that you don't understand. You couldn't."

In the pained silence that separated them, Anik thought about Edith and the network of cruel complicity that violated her. Jameelah and the other women were just pawns in the greedy games of powerful men. It had to stop.

"After the Second World War, every single Nazi minister was tried for war crimes," she said. "Even the finance minister."

Omar winced and turned his face away for some reason Anik didn't understand. She paused until she had his attention again.

"You can always trace the people responsible. I'm pretty sure you and every other educated Somali know who the architects of this catastrophe are—the ministers and generals and politicians. Even that bastard President Barre couldn't stay in Kenya. He got expelled from Nairobi and is stuck as an exile in Nigeria. There's nowhere to hide. Those warlords who are taking advantage of this terrible situation with raping and looting will be held to account too. I have their names and have given the report to the UN. Yes, like in Nuremberg." Anik was vibrating with emotion.

Omar's face closed. "Uthman doesn't like what you're doing." Anik remembered Uthman as the hostile community leader who rejected her work. "You better be careful. I bet there are hundreds of your war criminals right here in this camp. Around here, you never know when you might be talking to one."

"That sounds a bit like a threat."

"It's a warning. I just want you to be careful." He sounded contrite and concerned, but his face was a mask, and Anik felt him pushing her away.

She regretted her tone and wanted to find common ground. "Maybe we're both looking for the same thing. You're making a difference in the future of these children."

He didn't respond for a while. "Go back to Canada," he said finally, his face grim. "This is neither the time nor the place for you. You shouldn't be here."

Anik caught sight of a skinny little girl swimming in a uniform that was far too big watching them from a distance. Why was she not in class? Omar called her over. The girl padded up silently, furtive and fearful, like an unwanted stray cat.

"*Salaam*, Kamiis," Omar said. The girl said nothing. Omar's face softened. Anik was grateful for the break in tension.

"She doesn't talk and can't participate in the classes. 'Kamiis' means Thursday. She came here on a Thursday, so I gave her that name. I tried to find out where she came from and what happened to her family, but she won't speak, at least not to me. We don't know her real name. She won't say it." Kamiiss's jet-black eyes were wide open. Her shaggy hair retained the bleached-out beige of near-death from starvation. It should have been glossy black like her eyes.

Ubah smiled at Kamiis and held out a hand. Tentatively, Kamiis touched the palm of Ubah's hand, and looked in her eyes. Then she withdrew her hand. Ubah asked her something.

"*Haa*," Kamiis replied. It sounded more like a breath than a word.

Anik thought the girl's bicep could fit in the circle made by her thumb and forefinger. "What did you say?" she asked Ubah.

"I asked her if she liked being here at the school. She does. Maybe she feels safe here with Haji Omar. But maybe she is too shy or too afraid of men to talk to him."

"She came to the school one morning," Omar said. "I saw her naked, alone, and scrounging for scraps of food in the school garbage. She came up to me and held out her hand. She was starving and would die if I didn't do something. I let her stay here in an extra room next to mine. I don't know if that was wise, but how could I push her away? She must have been separated from her family somehow. Nobody has come to claim her."

Ubah was surprised at the news. "Doesn't someone here know her?"

"I asked Uthman. He said no one should take her. He must have meant no one was willing to take her."

The girl's eyes stayed wide open, wary, and alert.

"She looks young, maybe four," Anik said.

"I think she's older than that," Omar said. "Malnutrition makes them look younger."

Ubah nodded. "I think she's more like seven."

"If I knew anything about her, maybe I could help her find some relatives," Omar said. "She's safe here, but she can't stay here forever." They sat in silence.

"Sometimes what they can't say, they can draw," Anik said. "Why don't we try it? Maybe you could give her something to make a picture with."

Omar went into a classroom and came out with a box of crayons and a piece of paper.

Kamiis sat down on the floor and gently took out the crayons, laid them beside each other in a row, and looked at the colours. *She has been to school before*, Anik thought.

Kamiis started to draw some people. There was a female in the centre. She wore a long red dress. She was horizontal and had a sad mouth. Perhaps she was lying down. To the right, three green people were facing the prone woman with smiles.

The tip of Kamiis's tongue slipped between her teeth in concentration. She bowed her head closer to the paper, completely absorbed in her picture. On the left side of the paper she drew a small female figure. It was facing away from the others.

She looked at her picture for a long minute. The picture was a message of some kind.

"Are you in this picture?" Ubah asked.

"*Haa.*" She pointed to the small figure facing away from the others.

"Is this something that happened?"

"Haa."

"Who is this?" Omar touched the prone figure in the picture.

Kamiis sniffed, and her nose began to run. Anik took a Kleenex from her pocket and gave it to Kamiis, who clutched it in her tiny fist. Her nose dripped onto her picture, and she delicately wiped it off with the tissue.

"Hooyo."

"Mother," Ubah whispered to Anik. The little girl picked up her picture and walked quietly away. They watched her go along the edge of the building. Sounds of teachers asking questions and children chirping answers came out the classroom windows. Kamiis sat on the ground in a shadow and gazed at her picture.

"I think she saw the death of her mother," Ubah said. "Then she left."

"This is the first clue I have about what happened to her," Omar said. "The kids don't talk about what happened to them. It would be better if they could."

"Maybe they can draw about it," Anik suggested. "Can we come back and talk to Kamiis again?" She dreaded rejection from Omar.

He nodded. "Please. Please come back."

In her relief Anik realized that she needed Omar as an ally, someone who might be able to understand her and what she was trying to do. In another way she didn't trust him, but she wasn't sure why.

20

AFTER THE SCHOOL VISIT, Anik and Ubah went back to the water pump and conducted a few more interviews.

Later, alone in her room at the end of a long day, Anik picked up a book that Sandra had recommended to her, *Birdsong* by Sebastian Faulks. It was about two lovers against a tragic backdrop of injury, war, and longing. She wondered what kind of love she would fall into after she finished her year in Dadaab.

A knock on the door startled her. At night the camp was dark and dead, and she kept her metal door locked and bolted.

"Who is it?" Anik asked.

"It's Ubah. Good evening, Dr. Anik."

Anik unlocked her door. Ubah looked like she was concerned about something. She stepped in, and Anik closed the door behind her.

"Dr. Anik, do you remember Jameelah? We interviewed her. She helped serve dinner to Dr. Freeman." The question worried Anik.

"Is she all right? What happened to her?" Anik felt a stab of fear that her interviews could cause harm, that the women could be subject to reprisal, especially after Uthman's ugly reaction.

Ubah looked down. "No, nothing happened to her. Please don't worry. She is outside, and she wants to see you. But you're an important person and a busy person with your project. She wanted me to ask you first. Ask if you would see her."

Anik opened the door right away. "Tell her to come in. Please tell her to come right in."

Ubah stepped out into the light that shone from above Anik's door and spoke. A ghostly form appeared and then materialized into a slight woman wrapped in faded fabric. Anik recognized Jameelah. She smiled and motioned her to come in. Jameelah sheepishly put a bare foot across the threshold. She carried a dirty plastic bag and said something softly to Ubah.

Ubah looked at Anik. "She is so sorry to disturb you."

"Tell her I'm happy to see her. Would she like to sit down? I'll make us tea."

At the translation of these words, Jameelah looked up with a faint smile and opened her bag. Inside was a small shiny tablemat woven from strands of plastic. It had an orange, yellow, and red flower pattern bordered with nylon lace and plastic beads.

"It's a gift for you, Dr. Anik. A gift from Jameelah to thank you for your project. She made it especially for you," Ubah said.

Anik gently took the mat and put it on her table. She had secured acceptance, and perhaps trust. She was suddenly elated. Anik faced away from the two Somali women and composed herself. She took her time to carefully spread the lace and place the beads perfectly.

"How beautiful. I needed to brighten up this room, and this mat is absolutely perfect. Tell Jameelah I love it! Have some tea. I'll get some biscuits to celebrate your visit."

Ubah translated for Jameelah, and both women relaxed visibly. They took a seat as Anik made tea and placed some gingersnaps on a plastic dish in the center of the mat. Jameelah held herself with dignity and removed her head covering: a sign that she was comfortable in Anik's room. A happy smile and alert expression showed she was excited about being with Anik and Ubah.

"Jameelah wants to help you. She says that some of the women were injured, and they suffer. But they are too ashamed to go to the clinic. She wants to work with you, so they can get help." Anik sipped her tea in silence, wondering if it would be wise to accept the help of an untrained person in this sensitive work.

Jameelah looked around Anik's room. She focused intently on Anik's little bookshelf, where she had a few of the books from Québec that she loved most. Then Jameelah looked Anik straight in the eyes. *"Est-ce que vous parlez français?"*[15]

Anik and Ubah were stunned. *"Oui! Bien sûr que je parle français!"*[16] Anik exclaimed.

"Do you remember I told you I worked in a hospital?" Jameelah said. "I was trained in Djibouti, in French." Then her face opened into a broad smile. "Thank God! We can speak!" Jameelah melted in a combination of tears and laughter.

Ubah became animated too. "The women really appreciate so much what you're doing. It makes them feel different now. It makes them feel better that they do not have to carry this heavy load alone. You are with us. You feel what we feel. You didn't have to come here, and you're not afraid. We think everyone in your country must be very good people."

Anik basked in the nourishing affirmation. Any doubts about working with Jameelah evaporated like spilled water on hot sand.

"The women have injuries but no one to advise them what to do," Jameelah said. She spoke a lovely formal French, only it started a little more from the back of the throat than the way people spoke in Paris. "They should go to the clinic. After these attacks there is shame. They will not go by themselves for the

15   Do you speak French?
16   Yes! Of course I speak French!

shame of it. Now we see how it has happened to so many of us. Antibiotics and minor surgery is all they need. I can support them. I want to do this."

It will be a wonderful help," said Anik. "But let's talk tomorrow. It's late."

They left happy, and Anik smiled as she listened to them chattering into the distance.

21

ON THEIR WAY TO the New Light Madrassa the next morning, Ubah and Anik talked about Kamiis.

"I think she wants us to know what happened to her. I felt she was holding something inside so tightly." Ubah stopped for a moment, searching for words. "Like she's afraid something will happen to her if she lets it out."

When they arrived school had already begun, and the children were in classrooms. A woman stood by the gate looking inside.

"I told Jameelah about Kamiis," Ubah said tentatively. "I told her we were coming today."

Jameelah turned to them, unsure. "*Est-ce que je peux aller avec vous?*"[17] The lost, searching look in her eyes told Anik this request came from a deep place.

"*Mais, oui. Biensûr. Viens,*"[18] Anik said with a warm, reassuring smile.

17 Can I come with you?

18 Yes, of course. Come.

Omar had arranged a room for them. "She is fearful," he said. "She is too scared to be in a classroom with the other students and the noise." A straw mat was on the floor. "Please have a seat. Kamiis always sits on the floor." He held her hand and spoke to her as she looked up at him. Her flip-flops were on the wrong feet.

As if they could read each other's minds, the three women sat down in unison with Kamiis.

Ubah leaned over toward Anik. "He said we are friends. That we want to draw more pictures. He said we want to be friends with Kamiis too."

Anik carefully laid out paper and five crayons on the floor—yellow, red, green, blue, and black. Kamiis looked at the crayons, moving her eyes from one to the next. She held Omar's hand in her right, and in her left she clutched a crumpled, dirty piece of paper.

"She hasn't let go of the picture she drew yesterday," Omar said. "Not for a minute. It got a little wet last night. She tried to keep looking at it while she drank a glass of water." Omar smiled at Kamiis.

The girl searched Jameelah's face and received a gentle smile. Anik had not seen that expression on Jameelah before. What kind of smile was it, anyway? It seemed to comfort Kamiis. She let go of Omar, walked slowly to Jameelah, and showed her the picture. The two of them gazed at the picture for a long time.

Kamiis touched her finger to the picture, on the horizontal woman. "*Hooyo*," she whispered. Her faint voice was more air than words. She turned to look at Jameelah and saw the smile. Then Kamiis leaned her head against Jameelah's breast.

Jameelah began to hum a melody as she stroked the girl's hair. She sang the words, and then Kamiis, almost involuntarily, joined in.

"It's one of our lullabies," Ubah explained. "We call this one, 'Oh Perfect Child.'"

Jameelah's face radiated the love of a mother, as if Kamiis was her own child. After a while, Jameelah reached down and fixed Kamiiss's flip-flops as she spoke to her.

"Jameelah asked her to draw a picture of where she comes from," Ubah whispered.

Kamiis handed the previous day's drawing to Jameelah and then drew a box in the upper-left side of the new piece of paper with a black crayon, followed by two rows of little black squares. She put the black crayon down and looked carefully at the other colours. She chose a blue one and drew a square on the other side of the page. On top she put a green semicircle. Then she used a blue crayon to scribble wavy lines across the bottom.

Jameelah's eyes widened in astonishment. "Is that your house?" The girl nodded. Jameelah pointed to the blue box. "Is that your mosque?" Kamiis nodded. "Is this the sea?" She pointed at the blue scribble. Kamiis nodded again.

Jameelah took some deep breaths. "I know this place. This is the blue mosque. She comes from a wealthy family with a big house, I think. This is my town, Merka." Jameelah spoke to Kamiis and then gave her a hug, as if she was proud of the girl. Kamiis smiled up at Jameelah.

"Ask her to draw a picture of her family," Anik said softly. "Maybe it will help us find them."

Following the request, Kamiis's smile turned into an expression of sadness and concentration. She drew stick figures. Some had triangles for bodies. They were probably female. She drew a big one and then some little ones. They were horizontal. Above them she drew some figures that looked male. They were larger and green. Some of them had blue heads. Last of all, there was a small female—facing away from it all. She touched the small stick figure and whispered, "Kamiis."

"What happened to your mother?" Jameelah asked. .

"Soldiers hurt her," Kamiis whispered in a broken voice, like a small bird fallen out of the nest. "She couldn't get up. I ran away."

Suddenly, she shuddered and gasped with sobs. Kamiis buried her head in Jameelah's chest and wrapped her arms around her. Jameelah looked stricken.

"This is the first time I've seen her cry," Omar said.

"It's what she was afraid to let out," Ubah said. "She couldn't show weakness if she was all by herself."

The wrenching sobs subsided into long keening. Jameelah rocked her in her arms.

"Omar, you said Kamiis stays in a little room here at the school," Anik said. "Could Jameelah stay there too? I think they need each other right now. For a few days, anyway."

He nodded. "That would be good. It would be so good for Kamiis to have someone take care of her."

Ubah explained to Jameelah, and a wave of relief crossed the woman's face. Anik's mind began to churn. What did the drawing mean? Was it connected to what the women were telling Anik?

"Ubah, will you please stay with Jameelah and Kamiis while I speak with Omar?" Anik asked.

They walked into the schoolyard.

"Poor Kamiis. She was trying to keep this horrible experience inside. Trying to hide it. I could tell something was . . . was killing her psychologically," Omar said. "I think she saw the rape of her mother and the death of her family—and then the ordeal of her journey here. It's starting to make sense to me now. Except for the men with blue heads."

"Maybe they're not heads. Could they be blue helmets?" Anik wondered aloud, appalled at the thought that peacekeepers could let something like that happen. She would go see Zanov the next day to confirm that her report had arrived and see what was being done.

"Will you come back tomorrow?" Omar asked. "You can keep working with Kamiis. I know some other children who need this. We have so much work to do together." Omar held out his hand to Anik. She took it and felt the possibility of a new friendship in his gentle grip.

22

IBRAHIM SAT ON ONE of the long garish cushions placed against the walls. There were no chairs or tables. Heavy curtains covered the freshly painted glossy pink concrete walls. For security reasons, there were no windows behind the curtains. His receiving room still fell short of the traditional look he wanted to project of himself as a natural leader at home in his culture. He was spending money. He had to.

He wished he could talk to his father. He wanted to explain how hard he had worked. How every step of the way he had followed his father's advice. The night the president deserted the country, he struggled and succeeded to fulfill his father's command.

When he arrived at the prison, his men's faces told him they might not be loyal. They might not follow his orders to process the prisoners. To start but not finish would be a disaster. He had to do it himself.

When he had organized executions before, it was orderly. It was done in the middle of the night. The condemned were gagged and silent. The hood over the enemy's head prevented eye contact. There was a physical distance between the firing squad and the men against the firing wall. By the time his men pulled the trigger, the condemned had ceased to be individuals. Nobody was watching.

That final night at the secret prison, there were forty-three prisoners. He had his soldiers open their cell doors one at a time. The first man sat motionless, blinded by the flashlight beam in his eyes. The mixture of confusion and hope on his face was indelible in Ibrahim's memory. He killed him with one pistol shot to the forehead. That was the face that haunted his dreams. When the other detainees heard the shot, they started screaming. They panicked and jumped around their cells, sliding in the foul slop. Some tried to crawl past him. He changed from his pistol to an assault rifle. The air was electric with high-decibel terror. It took forever to resolve into dead silence.

His men were in shock after the massacre. It was not a victory; it was an undignified retreat from discipline to nihilism. He was ashamed when he thought about it. His father was right though.

Ibrahim was the first to arrive in Merka with guns and ambition. He arrived at his uncle's villa with six pickup trucks and thirty desperate men. Then his uncle told him whose houses to take. Now he had over a hundred fighters and plenty of room.

Abdi Rahman entered the sitting room. Ibrahim had given him the rank of lieutenant colonel, second-in-command. Ibrahim did not take pleasure in cruelty, like Abdi. Abdi was utterly loyal. He was also feared, he gave good counsel, and he had an encyclopedic knowledge of the people and sub-clans of Merka. But he was flawed by an immature lack of self-restraint. Ibrahim also wished his deputy was less addicted to qat. He gestured for the jumpy young man to sit down beside him.

"Colonel Ibrahim, there are more waiting for you today. Every day more are coming." Ibrahim should have known people would come to him with their problems. They brought him disputes to settle. No one would dare challenge him, but everyone begged him for help.

"It's good that people come to you. This is what we want," Abdi said. "We need more money soon. Or we need to send them away."

Ibrahim stood up. "Let's walk, and we can discuss. We'll go out the back door."

His compound was a sprawling Arab villa. Decades of bad times had crushed its former grace. The yard was dusty and dry. The only remnant of the ornamental garden was a broken fountain fallen on its side. For the sake of security, he had blocked the elegant arched windows with cement blocks.

Ibrahim and Abdi exited from the back door because the front waiting room was full of supplicants. People asked him for money for medicine, to settle feuds, and to marry their daughters. The more his power grew, the more the people came to him for solutions. It was starting to get more expensive than he could afford.

His parade ground was the size of a basketball court. One of his men with formal military training was shouting at some boys in rags.

"Who are the new boys?" Ibrahim asked. "How old are they?"

"They are brothers from the country. Their village was taken by an enemy clan, and they were separated from their family. They came here three days ago begging for food and a place to stay. They will do anything and are strong enough to hold a gun. Twelve and fourteen." This was the ideal age: young enough not to question orders or motives, and old enough to handle an AK-47. Nobody was looking for them either. These boys needed to join the side of the predators before they became prey.

"On your belly!" Ibrahim shouted. "Crawl to the far wall! Faster! Get up! Run back! Food for the one who is first!"

They staggered on bloody bare feet though the dust and gravel of the parade ground. The boys would continue without complaint until they collapsed. Good.

"Keep going. Work them hard. Tell me if we should keep them," Ibrahim said loudly enough for the brothers to hear.

They walked through an opening in the compound wall into the neighbouring space. A house had been converted into barracks for the fighters. Those not out on patrol lounged on dirty mattresses they had dragged onto the veranda. They bickered with each other and were slow to stand at attention. Ibrahim nodded to his men, and they sat down.

"They need to chew to keep up morale. Why is the qat delivery late?" Ibrahim asked.

"This is bad news. Our qat flight from Kenya was held up. Maintenance problems. They said it will come, but later tonight," Abdi said.

Ibrahim ran his hand over his shaved head. "Take their guns away until it comes. Fights are going to break out, and I don't want things to get out of hand."

They walked past the sleeping quarters to Ibrahim's rudimentary prison and interrogation unit. He watched as his men pushed two babbling captives into the steel shipping container that served as a jail. Then they slammed and bolted the doors shut. Bullet holes provided the only ventilation. Beside it was an open shipping container with a table and a couple of chairs plus implements for interrogation. They were the same things a carpenter might use: hammers, chisels, pliers, and an electrical drill. There were also car batteries with cables connected to alligator clips.

"There should be ten in my jail," Ibrahim said. "Is that right?"

"It was hot yesterday, and two didn't make it. There are eight now, plus these two. They were trying to steal from the Italian base and were handed over to us."

"Why did the peacekeepers do that?" Ibrahim asked. "Is it the first time?"

"Yes, the first time," Abdi said. "They said they have no permission from Rome to keep prisoners. Their instructions are to hand over criminals to local authorities. That's us."

Ibrahim nodded. "Good."

On the other side of the compound was an open-air kitchen and dining area for the men. Generous servings were an important fringe benefit for the militia and a powerful incentive for the hungry street boys, who were an excellent source of recruits.

"Let's inspect the girls," Abdi said with a grin. Females were in another house in the neighbouring compound. The female presence was a unique perk for Ibrahim's fighters, especially the adolescents. Ibrahim and Abdi walked through the gate and saw the women sitting on the ground and leaning against the rough concrete wall of their quarters. Their heads were uncovered. Ibrahim rationalized that it was better to be a sex slave than starve.

"Abdi, come. Come inside, Abdi. Come chew with us. Come inside and lie down." A slender girl beckoned with serpentine gestures.

"I'll be back tonight, my sweet. Don't worry. Save yourself for me tonight!" Abdi called.

"Ignore her, and keep going," Ibrahim said. Abdi was oversexed. It annoyed Ibrahim.

When peacekeepers came around, Ibrahim explained that they were the sisters and cousins of his men and that it was his duty as leader to provide them with safety and shelter from the treacherous storm of the civil war. If visiting peacekeepers wanted a girlfriend for a quick half hour, that was different, and it could be arranged. Anyway, the girls had food and a place to sleep. They formed a kind of collective harem that serviced the men's need for sexual release, and they cleaned the place—except for the jail. Cleaning the jail was unnecessary.

He strolled over to the motor pool. His fifteen vehicles were lined up in an orderly way under the shade of corrugated iron roof sheets on wooden poles. His armoury was in a shed close to his office, guarded by two of his most trusted fighters. He kept an inventory and checked it personally and meticulously. It was mostly AK-47s and ammunition for them. He had a number of American M16s, which were prestigious but difficult to obtain.

When Ibrahim carried a gun, he chose an M16. He had also managed to steal three Italian Beretta AR70 assault rifles and was pleased to discover that they used the same standard NATO ammunition as the M16s. He also had five RPG launchers and ten RPGs. Ammunition for the anti-aircraft guns on his technical was scarce, and Ibrahim didn't have a resupply source. This bothered him because he could not sustain a serious fight for long. He had managed to obtain a stock of some twenty land mines from a group of ex-government soldiers who had joined his militia. Maybe they would come in handy one day.

Surveying his base, he had the happy thought that his father would be pleased with his accomplishments and proud of the way that Ibrahim had overcome adversity and adapted to new circumstances. He had secured a respectable position in this new kind of world without government. His father had said that fear was his greatest asset. True, but he needed money too.

Back at his quarters, Ibrahim issued orders to Abdi. "You'll go to the Italians and tell them they have some serious problems that we can help them with."

"What problems? They patrol where we advise them and avoid the places we say are too dangerous. They do not interfere with us. It's good."

Ibrahim looked at his second-in-command. Abdi's face was filling out. He had acquired a layer of baby fat. He was not hungry anymore. "The problems are coming," Ibrahim said. "The translators that they brought from Italy speak with the wrong accent, and people don't like it. We think they may be corrupt too. They need translators from Merka. I'll select them."

"How much do we charge for them?"

Ibrahim thought for a minute. This was an important business decision. "Not too much. The value is in the information they can give us. Next, tell them that we have intelligence about enemies of the UN operation who are organizing to attack and steal humanitarian assistance. We will tell them the UN must help us find these men. They should give me any information that they have. Very bad war criminals are at large, and it's the duty of the international community to punish them." He handed over a rough piece of blank newsprint with newspaper photos. He had drawn an organization chart of the failed government. At the top was pasted a picture of President Barre. Below him were his ministers and senior officials.

"This is my only copy, so tell them to make one hundred copies for me and one hundred copies for them. Post them around town. I want the original back."

Abdi studied the paper carefully. "Someone is missing."

"My father is a patriot," Ibrahim said. He had no basis to say his father was still alive, but he refused to concede his death without proof.

"Tell them also that the enemies of the UN are against the western Christian presence in Somalia. They have targeted the port, the airstrip, and the aid convoys. The situation is dangerous and could result in many peacekeeper casualties."

"And what is the solution to this problem?" Abdi asked.

"Contracts. It's simple. We'll protect these facilities in exchange for contracts. It won't be cheap because solving these problems is dangerous work. This way their men don't get hurt. We'll need vehicles too," Ibrahim added. "I don't think they'll give us weapons. The UN arms embargo is inconvenient. We need to buy those on the open market. I want to sign these contracts with the general soon. Let's say in one week's time. Say it's urgent. Our informers tell us that something will happen soon. It could be an incursion from the south. It's better if they think there's a threat. Also, ask them for the details of the aid convoy routes and timing. We can use land mines for that. You are dismissed. Go there now."

"Yes, Colonel." Abdi saluted with a grin.

Ibrahim rose and placed his notebook in his pocket and his gold Cross pen in his bright white finely pressed shirt. He adjusted his white leather skullcap and donned his jacket with the four stripes. *I should promote myself,* he thought.

23

CRISTIANI REVIEWED THE DAILY situation report before it was transmitted to Rome. Fuel supplies were satisfactory. Water was getting low and would have to be replenished from the supply ship. Two armoured personnel carriers were out of commission. Heat and dust had blown out the bearings. Five cases in sick bay: three malaria, one gastroenteritis, and one broken nose from a barracks brawl. Not too bad. One humanitarian convoy would be travelling through his area of operations that day. It was strange he hadn't issued orders for it to be escorted.

He called for his aide-de-camp and pointed out the troubling item in the report. "What is this? Why is the aid convoy going without our escort? What will people think we're here for anyway? I don't like it. Well?"

"Sir, the convoy was going to make deliveries in no-go areas for us. We had no intelligence and were unable to assess the threat level. Standing orders are to follow approved routes that have had a prior threat assessment and reconnaissance patrol. This was your order after the mishap with the little girl. The commanding officer of the APC fleet declined the request for escort. The NGOS went ahead anyway because they said the humanitarian situation was desperate, sir."

"I don't like it. I want to be informed of each request for escort from now on. In fact, I want to be informed of each shipment of aid that lands at the port. Understood?"

"Yes, sir. I'll convey your intent to the planning cell, and orders will be issued."

Cristiani nodded. "Good. Dismissed."

The following week he was going to Mogadishu headquarters to make a presentation on his operations in front of the top UN commander and his multinational peers. It was an important career opportunity, and he needed to work on his speech. The theme was building local leadership. He had come to think of this as "the Cristiani Doctrine." Military intervention was not about military occupation. It was about creating conditions conducive to exit and handover to local authorities. Nobody wanted to own the place.

His relationship with Ibrahim was coming along nicely. It was creative and mutually beneficial. Other commanders had adversarial relationships and no end of headaches with local leaders and elders.

He lit a cigarette and took a soothing drag. Two documents were on his desk. If he was going to work with Ibrahim, the accountants would want to see that his expenditures were supported by contracts. Paperwork was an eternal burden of command. The contract was short and open. It was a personal contract with Ibrahim for services to be mutually agreed. The lawyer, Batista, put in a clause protecting the Republic of Italy from any legal complaint that might arise from Ibrahim's actions. Another clause prevented Ibrahim from making any binding obligations on Italy. An English version was appended to the Italian original. Did Ibrahim have a last name?

The contracts were arranged for signature. Maybe Ibrahim could help with this issue of food delivery instead of those unreliable NGOs.

Mariotti burst in without knocking. He looked frantic.

"What happened, Mariotti?"

"General, you're needed immediately in the operations centre!" They both ran out of his office and into the dimness of the dark-green tent. The radio crackled. "What is your location?" the radio operator said. "Repeat, what is your location? Over." Cristiani's officers huddled around, listening.

The responding voice was high-pitched, speaking English with a strong Somali accent. "Helb! We neet helb! Lead truck hit mine. They tellin' us ged oud. When you be here? Ofer."

"Who is it? Are they threatening you? Over."

"Fife technical and twenny arm men. When you coming? What to do?"

"Message received. Stand by. Over," the radio operator said.

Mariotti pointed to a location on a large aerial photograph on the wall. "We haven't patrolled this area yet. We told them we were unable to escort. There are no international staff accompanying. Four trucks with food supplies headed west for a displaced persons camp in the interior. It's an aid convoy for a small British NGO. Only Somali drivers and local logistics staff. We could get a quick response team there in two hours. That won't be enough if they're hostile. It'll be dark by the time they arrive."

"Where you are? We need helb, helb! They are—" The voice was cut off by the sound of a gunshot.

"This is Merka Battalion, Merka Battalion Operation Restore Hope," the radio operator said. "Do you copy? Do you copy?"

The operations tent fell silent.

"Order the supply ship helicopter to make an aerial reconnaissance of the location," Cristiani said. "Do it now!"

He walked back to his office to wait for the report, but he knew what it would say. No trucks and no survivors. Thank God no international staff were on the convoy, or the press would be all over him.

24

THE ITALIAN GATEKEEPERS WERE prepared when Ibrahim rolled up for his 9:00 a.m. meeting with Cristiani. It was a new vehicle he had shipped in from Mombasa at great expense. The blue Land Cruiser gleamed in the bright morning sun. As they opened the gates and pulled the dragon teeth out of the way, he was pleased to see that the peacekeepers noticed his new uniform. Instead of the four stripes of a colonel on the cuffs and shoulders, he had the single gold star of a general.

The intelligence officer, Mariotti, received him. Ibrahim stepped out smartly with his notebook in hand and waited for a proper recognition of his new rank. It didn't come. He would have to prompt Mariotti.

"Good mornin', Colonel. You'll please see now I'm brigadier general. This is what Merka people want. They want me same level like General Cristiani. This time you did not know. Next time you salute me. When we go in, introduce me the right way." He spoke in a tone that was clear, firm, and serious. Ibrahim knew that Mariotti would not like this, and that Mariotti was suspicious of him. Never mind—the important relationship was with the other general in town, Cristiani.

"Very well," Mariotti said and then led him to Cristiani's office.

"General, the general is here to see you," Mariotti said with an insulting undertone of irony.

"So I see," Cristiani replied as if playing along. Ibrahim's promotion was not sufficient to dampen Cristiani's insufferable superiority. Still, Ibrahim was confident in his move. It would have been untenable to be seen as subordinate to the foreigners. Any sign of weakness or inferiority, and his authority might start to unravel. He had started to receive reports that troublemakers were grumbling and calling him cruel and greedy. If the peacekeepers looked more powerful than him, people might go to them with such complaints. A conflict between Ibrahim and Cristiani would put him in an impossible position. He didn't think he could win a firefight, and the Italians could call in American reinforcements if needed. He would lose everything. The situation was delicate.

Cristiani gestured to a seat at the meeting table, and the three sat down.

"So sorry you have problem with you food trucks," Ibrahim said with maximum sincerity. "I hear they got hit bad. My people tell me they lose trucks and food. Thanks be to Allah, your soldiers not hurt. Where they were? What happen?"

"I would imagine you know what happened," Mariotti said, his tone frosty. "The lead truck of an aid convoy struck a land mine. Four trucks with rice, oil, high-protein biscuits for children, rehydration salts, and medical supplies were attacked and hijacked. Our aerial reconnaissance after the event spotted several bodies on the ground. I assume the aid workers were executed."

Ibrahim shook his head to feign commiseration. "That a bad area. I wish they ask me. Or you ask me. But nobody did." He looked at Cristiani with a sympathetic smile. "I wanna help you be success. Be better than other countries here. The Belgians, Canadians, and even Americans have so much problems where they are." Ibrahim spoke with as much sincerity as he could muster. This was a time for persuasion and building relationships. "It's going good here in Merka, to now."

Ibrahim tore a sheet out of his notebook, on which a list of troublemakers and local ingrates was carefully written. "These the guys stole the food. I think they sell it to the militia in Kismayo. The food is not in Merka." He handed the list to Cristiani, who passed it to Mariotti. "What we need is get these guys. You should catch them and put them in your jail." It was an audacious move. Convincing Cristiani to be part of his cleanup of dissidents would be insurance against any locals looking to side with the peace-keepers against him.

Cristiani paused and thought deeply. "We should work together to stop these bandits. When we work together, I believe there is a great deal we can achieve." Once again, he failed to address Ibrahim by his rank.

"General Cristiani, we do not have a mandate to detain, judge, or sentence Somali individuals," Mariotti said. "We have no legal authority under the Security Council resolution. This is not possible. We have no jail."

"I can help," Ibrahim said. "Remember you had robbing problems on your base? You give us two prisoners."

"What happened to them?" Mariotti asked. His suspicion was annoying, and Ibrahim wished he would be quiet.

"They guilty, and they off the street. They won't bother you no more," Ibrahim said. "We need to do same thing again. We catch them together. I know where to find these robbers. Then we keep them at my place. People should see you catch the bad guys. They need see you keeping us safe. They need see that you don't just let these bandits humiliate us. My men will be with you, my transla-tors too. There will be no problem. Plus also, I can deliver the food. You see, these poor hungry people that need food are my people. Maybe I care about them more than you. We know who need what."

"I like this approach," Cristiani said. Ibrahim sensed that Cristiani saw some benefit for himself here. What could it be? In any case, it was time to lean forward and close the deal.

"You have the papers for sign?" Ibrahim said.

"What papers?" Mariotti asked. "We have no papers to sign." Ibrahim hid his exasperation as Cristiani opened a manila folder and removed two documents.

"Colonel, this is not a concern of the intelligence unit," Cristiani said. "It's a financial and administrative matter." He pushed one contract to Ibrahim, who flipped the pages until he reached the English section.

"Where it say how much?" Ibrahim asked.

"It doesn't have a limitation. We decide what you do and how much we pay. It's flexible."

This was confusing. Ibrahim had expected a menu of tasks with a generous payment for each one. His cash situation was worrisome, and he had hoped this contract could bring some quick relief, not ambiguity and delay. "What you want me do? Telling you what we know? Protecting food? It could be for running port or airstrip?"

"It could be for those things. Maybe we will have other ideas," Cristiani said.

"Why would we give you money for the port?" Mariotti asked. "You already charge a large fee on the few ships that dock. The same with the airstrip. Your men are already there taking landing fees."

"We keep it open and safe. I happy you see that." Ibrahim tried to think of a way out of this problem. "It would be better for the food to come in free. You pay us, and that way we don't take money from NGOs. Put some your soldiers with me. Is good the people see us together."

Cristiani nodded slowly. Ibrahim wanted to know what he was thinking. This all seemed too easy. "Yes, we can do that. I'll station

some men there, so people can see we are working together."
Cristiani said. "How much do you need?"

Ibrahim thought fast. He would simply arrange for his usual
port fees to be paid at his compound, out of sight from the peacekeepers. The contract would be extra income.

"You pay me fifty thousand dollars per month. I need this
much. And then I take no charge to boats, more business for
everyone, and I promise security. Same for airport. I proteck food
for free. Other things we think about and talk later."

"Agreed," Cristiani said surprisingly quickly. He signed both
copies and passed them across the table. Ibrahim took his Cross
pen out of his pocket to write his signature on the dotted line:
"Brigadier General Ibrahim Hussein." Cristiani suddenly looked
a little nervous.

"We have a good deal. Thank you," Ibrahim said.

25

THIS WASN'T ABOUT RANK; it was about real power. Cristiani was not happy about being summoned to the office of an inferior rank, but he didn't feel that he could fully exercise his authority when it came to Samson. He walked in and sat down on the chair across from the American's desk. Such a small, shabby office for a man with so much influence over Cristiani's circumstances and future. Samson pushed a document across the desk. They were both in a bad mood.

"Read this." He dropped a long fax on Cristiani's lap. "You have a problem that you need to fix. I'm getting a coffee while you read. Want one?"

"No, thank you." He couldn't stomach the brown dishwater Americans called coffee, and he wanted to keep working on his Cristiani Doctrine presentation for the commanders' conference. He had been fine-tuning his talking points about putting the doctrine into practice. The best example was the structured contractual relationship he had with Ibrahim. It showed that he was mentoring emerging leaders on good governance, transparency, and proper administration of taxpayer funds. Then Samson interrupted his plans with this urgent meeting. He hadn't even provided an agenda. Cristiani felt the humiliating needles of Samson's arrogant stare and struggled to concentrate on the report in front of him.

After reading and re-reading the disturbing report by somebody he had never heard of, he asked Samson for a cigarette. He had been in such a hurry he forgot his.

"Who is this Anik Belanger? What is Justice before Peace? Do you know this organization?"

"Buncha do-gooders. This fucking battlespace is infested with NGOs. Never heard of this one before. Must be a small outfit. I mean, I could find out if I wanted to. But that would mean sending the report around, getting a lot of other people sticking their noses into it. Some people might not be as understanding of your predicament as I am."

"But so many of these crimes happened in my area of operation—some of them even after I arrived. Do you think this report is credible? Was this going on when you were handling Ibrahim? Could it still be happening?"

"It's a convincing report," Samson said. "Names, dates, locations. No opinions, just the facts. This Anik Belanger knows her stuff. But she has no idea what she's getting into."

Samson was right. The report was good—and damning. There was no point trying to refute the information. Cristiani was disoriented, and then a sense of betrayal nibbled at his confidence. Surely Samson would help him deal with this. After all, he was the one who had started the relationship with Ibrahim.

"Oh, and by the way, that report came to me through the special rep of the secretary general and the US commanding general. I don't plan to get back to them about it. Maybe you'd like to discuss it with them, except that would be a terrible idea—for you."

Cristiani looked up. "How do you suggest we deal with this? This kind of . . . thing is outside our rules of engagement. I don't think we have a precedent for intervening in such situations. It's not really a military concern."

"No, I guess it's not a military concern, but it looks pretty fucking bad and would be an unwelcome surprise back home. This is not what your nation expects from their brave men in uniform."

Cristiani got a sinking feeling in the pit of his stomach and could think of nothing to say.

"Look, this sorta rough trade is how all of these cats operate," Samson said. "You should know that by now. I even recognize some of those names—especially that sleazebag, Abdi. Can't keep his dick in his *kikoi*." Samson pushed the report back across his desk to Cristiani with a hard, humourless expression. "You need to understand this clearly, General. He's your management challenge now. Personally, I have no fingerprints on this militia. Everything I did with Ibrahim's outfit is deniable. Don't tell me you let him get away with his ridiculous self-promotion to your rank. And hey, is it true you signed a contract with him? People are talking about that."

"Well, I thought that would be prudent administratively—you know, to have our arrangements in writing."

"Doesn't look so fucking prudent now. What are you going to do?"

Cristiani was dizzy with sudden vertigo. His non-conventional relationship with Ibrahim was thanks to Samson's introduction. Didn't Samson's involvement insure him against this kind of political risk? The connection with Sampson had trumped the advice of his lawyer and Mariotti's misgivings. Their advice had stopped after he told them not to be bureaucratic, unhelpful, and risk-averse. Now he felt abandoned and manipulated. It was so unfair.

"Let's be reasonable. This is your man, Randy. You paid him. You introduced him to me."

"Yes, indeed. I was trying to help you. When you took over your area of operation, I thought he could be useful to you. And

I guess he has been, judging by the way everyone says you're doing such a bang-up job without even firing a shot. But really, Giancarlo, the due diligence is incumbent on you as area commander. With jokers like Ibrahim, it's my policy to maintain plausible deniability. I'm gonna deny like a motherfucker if word about this hanky-panky gets around. Anyway, why do you keep depending on a juvenile delinquent like Ibrahim if you have an entire fucking army at your disposal?"

There was a hollow space where Cristiani's courage used to be. He had to urinate badly, and he didn't know what to say or do next.

"I guess that report wouldn't be too welcome in Rome," Samson said. "I can just imagine the headlines. 'Rape Epidemic under General's Nose.' Maybe even an official inquiry. Ouch." He grabbed the report and waved it in the air, then dropped it in Cristiani's lap. "Frankly, I don't think Ibrahim is your problem. It's that fucking bitch who wrote this shit. Anyway, you need to go talk to Ibrahim. He's resourceful. If he created the problem, maybe he can solve it."

Finally, some constructive advice. With a way forward, Cristiani felt better. "I see." He held up the report. "And this will go no further?"

"Nope. You have the only copy in this shithole of a country. I've forgotten about the entire thing already. Let's never talk about it again." Samson bared his teeth in a quick grin. Cristiani hurried to the bathroom, then returned to his base.

26

CRISTIANI TOOK A DEEP breath as he got out of the armoured personnel carrier. It was the first time he had called on Ibrahim. This was not a conversation he could have on his own base. His men conducted liaison visits to Ibrahim's compound on a regular basis, but he had hoped to postpone a personal visit indefinitely. It confused the proper order of things. The optics weren't good.

Cristiani walked past an honour guard that Ibrahim had assembled for the occasion. There were more fighters than he expected, about a hundred. Their blank faces radiated sweaty malevolence. They had uniforms of a sort, hand sewn in faded green polyester. They held their AK-47s with confident familiarity. Obviously, they knew how to use them. He couldn't tell if the safeties were engaged. Ten fighters shouldered RPG launchers. No ranks were indicated. Some had ropes instead of belts to hold up their pants. Like a herd of predatory cattle, they slowly chewed wads of qat in their cheeks. To the side, Ibrahim's fleet of technicals was lined up. Snaky yellow spray paint scribbled over a dirt-brown background mimicked military camouflage. Their heavy machine guns were aligned and pointed upwards. Cristiani counted fifteen. That was two more technicals than his intelligence unit had reported.

Ibrahim was giving him a show of military capability, and his firepower was considerable. Cristiani started making tactical calculations. If this were the enemy, how would he engage, given the forces at his disposal? Theoretically, a helicopter missile attack followed by an assault with his armoured vehicles could take most of this out. Eight were operational, of which three should be held back in reserve. But if some fighters escaped and started harassing actions, and if his armoured column got bogged down in the narrow streets, it would turn into a bloody quagmire. If the population turned hostile toward the peacekeepers, there was no path available for retreat. Besides, the Security Council resolution authorizing the mission did not permit offensive operations. He shook all options of confrontation out of his mind.

As he crossed the threshold of Ibrahim's villa, the warlord took his hand. "You are my special guest. We are brothers in arms. Come in. Come in."

They walked through an entryway crowded with lounging soldiers into a large receiving room.

The pink walls and heavy curtains were garish. He was disconcerted by the lack of chairs. Ibrahim sat on a cushion covered in loud velveteen fabric and patted the spot next to him. "Welcome to my house. Sit on my right side. The place of honour is for you." Ibrahim looked comfortable, alert, and focused. "Very nice you want to be just the two of us together. We get to know each other like friends. Take a grapefruit juice with me."

A fighter brought in two tall glasses. Cristiani worried that accepting hospitality would diminish his ability to deliver a difficult message, but he took the drink anyway. The sour tang of the cold pink fluid was bracing. He sat down and turned to his smiling host.

"Here we say what we want," Ibrahim continued. "Nobody listen. Nobody write it down. We just talk. How you want me help you? Now we have contract, we can do so many thing."

"Thank you." Cristiani took another sip, then realized there was no soft entry to what he needed to convey. "There's a problem. A report. It comes from Dadaab camp. It lists crimes against women from here. It mentions your deputy, Abdi Rahman, and it mentions you as an accomplice. This is embarrassing for me and could jeopardize the success of my mission here."

Ibrahim's confident smile crash-landed into a confused frown. "Crimes again women? Like what?"

Cristiani decided to be brutally clear. There was no room for miscommunication. "Rapes of women. By your men." Cristiani hoped Ibrahim would deny this information. He hoped there was a slight chance that it was all a horrible mistake.

Ibrahim's confusion gave way to anger. "What you mean? I doan think this your business, General. I doan think you should come into the house of your friend and say this. You need let us do things our way. Maybe you don't understand our customs. Fucking the women is crime to UN? Not here in Merka." The sparks of high-voltage rage in Ibrahim's obsidian eyes made Cristiani realize what the man was capable of. He sensed danger and averted his gaze.

"I don't want details. You do your business according to your rules and your . . . customs. I understand that. But I can't have your, shall we say, 'non-conventional methods' stain my mission and my reputation."

"I'm good for your mission, my friend. Don't forget that. But who made this report? They make more reports?"

"It's a woman who lives in Dadaab camp. Her name is Anik Belanger. I assume she is white. I also assume she will continue this intrusive behaviour."

"What she say?"

"She made a report to the UN about women who were raped and who did it. Most of the women came from here. You probably know many of those she accuses."

Ibrahim thought about this and seemed to settle down. "Hmm . . . I doan like it. She not helping you. So we stop her reports. I gonna get a message to my friends in Dadaab. An' I'm gonna send some of my guys to visit. Stop your worry, there woan be no more reports."

Cristiani nodded. "Yes, I want the reports to stop."

"You want this be part of contract?"

The man's gall was astounding. Then a new fear edged in. What would Ibrahim do to stop the reports? It was better not to ask. Like Samson, he would adopt a posture of plausible deniability.

"No, no. This does not belong in the contract."

"But I'll have expenses to fix your problem for you." A sharp tone entered Ibrahim's voice. "You have to pay me."

Cristiani knew he was on thin ice with little or no bargaining power. "We'll add something to the port payments to cover your expenses."

27

CRISTIANI ARRIVED BY HELICOPTER to the commanders' conference in Mogadishu. The country headquarters had the crude kind of name only Americans could conceive of using: MogBase. It was a plywood complex next to the airport with an auditorium set up for an audience of officers, UN officials, and civilian staff. Everything looked temporary and disposable.

Cristiani entered the room and located his seat. In the front row facing the plywood lectern was a line of chairs marked with national flags for the contingent commanders in alphabetical order, from Australia to Zimbabwe.

He nodded to his Indian and Kuwaiti neighbours and then pulled his speech out of his briefcase. His public affairs officer had been instructed to bring lots of extra copies to distribute. Those officers with area commands like him were all to present their achievements, challenges, and opportunities. Each contingent commander would give his report, and then the American general commanding the entire Restore Hope operation would sum things up and give his direction.

As Cristiani waited for his turn, his colleagues talked about their challenges.

"No locals are stepping up to show leadership."

"It's like catch-and-release fishing. When we catch bandits breaking our perimeter and stealing stuff, all we can do is let them go."

"We're sensing growing resentment to our presence. We need projects to buy hearts and minds, but these humanitarian agencies won't give us any aid to deliver. They won't get with the military program."

"Dysentery is at 10 percent, and we're worried about the psychological impact of that malaria medicine, Lariam, we use. Anybody else having this problem?"

Cristiani could not have asked for a better backdrop for his presentation. He took energetic and purposeful strides to the podium and placed his written remarks upon the lectern.

"Gentlemen, as the preceding comments so eloquently demonstrate, we face daunting challenges. That is because we are at the beginning of a new era, and we must adapt to a completely new operating environment. We need to face the fact that we are not well prepared in terms of strategy or tactics, much less doctrine for this new era."

He looked out into the audience. His move was bold, and he had their attention, as he had intended.

"Let's be realistic. You do not field the finest armies in the world to deliver groceries. Our armies are intended to prevail over our adversaries. And yet, we do not have an enemy to defeat. We do not want to occupy this territory. Our governments do not want responsibility for a long-term military government in Africa. Elections, my friends, are not around the corner." He was gratified by the laughter this raised among his colleagues.

"It's a principle of military planning to begin with the desired end state in mind. In my view, our exit strategy must be to hand responsibility over to the leaders who can, in turn, defend themselves and keep the peace. They will be harsh, but who would deny that this is a harsh place? Look around you. We are in the landscape of the Old Testament. It's unfair and unwise to impose our morals, values, and the delicate sensibilities of our civilian politicians in this part of the world."

He could see that the mission commander was intrigued. So was the secretary general's special representative. His battlefield colleagues were listening, their curiosity sparked by the novelty of what he was saying.

"In my battlespace, Merka, we have found a workable operational expression to this dilemma. The traditional government structure here is clan based. We must embrace the authentic leaders. They're still here. They did not leave, even though President Barre did. Through a deliberate and careful approach, my team identified Colonel Ibrahim Hussein." Ibrahim would never know of this slight against his new self-appointed rank. "He is a young but effective local leader. The fact that he has the benefit of some military training, discipline, and skill of command makes him an ideal local partner.

"Gentlemen, our work must go beyond stabilization. That's why I'm working to delegate some of our tasks. Routine patrols to accompany aid convoys are a good example. Who better than members of the community to provide protection? I also see a positive role for this nascent local security force in policing and maintenance of public order. With carefully targeted contracts and projects, we are injecting financial sustainability into the equation and moving away from what had been a criminal economy based on extortion and theft.

"We manage our coordination at the command level and one tier down. Operational planning and intelligence sharing are the key points of contact. The benefits have been extraordinary and have allowed us to swiftly target the troublemakers, who are the reason the Security Council sent us here in the first place.

"As we all know, we are working in a strategic political environment with a low tolerance for casualties. After all, we are not protecting our homelands. This approach has resulted in greater security with fewer casualties than we see in other areas of operation. In fact, we have had zero battlefield deaths and negligible civilian casualties."

His public affairs officer suggested that the last comment about casualties would rankle his colleagues, who had not been so fortunate. Cristiani overruled him because the entire point was to put the success of his mission on the official record and in his own words.

"Thank you. I'm happy to take your questions."

There were no questions. Admittedly, it was a lot to absorb for his colleagues, who were unaccustomed to innovation. He was hopeful that his orders to the public affairs officer to selectively send his presentation to some friendly journalists would raise his profile back in Rome. He returned to his seat. Feeling fortunate and superior, he listened to the next presenters continue with a litany of problems.

28

"I LOVE THIS WORK, and I feel this is where I belong." Anik liked writing letters on the blue airmail paper that folded into a tidy envelope. Just enough space for some news, but not so much that she had to go on and on. She imagined how happy her parents would be when they found the letter in the beat-up old mailbox nailed to the wooden post by the gravel road in the scruffy neighbourhood where she grew up.

Photographs of her family were arranged on her bedside table. She picked up her favourite picture and set it on her desk, looking fondly at her mama and papa as she composed her weekly letter to them. It was a picture of them on the dock, floating on a clear blue lake under a bright northern sky. They offered squinty grins to the camera. Anik was in a red racing swimsuit. She had just gotten out of the water, and her black hair glistened in the sun. She was taller than her parents, who were a little pudgy and did not photograph well in swimsuits. They always had fun when they were together at their uncle's lakeside chalet. It was the happiest piece of her life for as long for as she could remember.

The picture was taken the previous summer, when she had come up from Ottawa to be with them. It had been taken by her Uncle Benoit, a lawyer, who got her out of the little town where she was born and into a legal career. It was the weekend when she told her family she was moving to Africa.

Anik's mood shifted when she recalled the sting of their disapproval. Her parents couldn't understand why anyone would leave a good government career for a crazy job in a country they had never heard of. Were there no people closer to home she could help instead? For the first time in his life, Uncle Benoit said he was disappointed in her decision. She cried a little bit about that later when she was alone.

Anik craved for them to be proud of what she was doing. "I had a great day today," she wrote. "The women are comfortable with me now. They are happy to see Ubah and me when we arrive every morning."

She remembered what a sacrifice it was for her parents to support her through law school. Her mom served in a local restaurant, and her dad pumped gas. Every dollar they sent to her was hard-won, and Anik felt a heavy responsibility to show her parents that their sacrifice was justified. For her mother, seeing Anik receive a law degree and find government work with a pension was more than enough success. Anik wanted them to understand that for her it was different. Success was what a person accomplished. It wasn't just a job title. She struggled for the words to say this in a way that they would understand.

"Last month I told you that my report went to the UN. This will make women's lives here better and safer," she wrote, hoping they would be impressed. "I'm also helping a little girl who lost her family." Helping real people would have real meaning for her parents.

Suddenly, Anik was in a beautiful moment that she wanted to embrace forever. The kind of moment that is fleeting at best and goes extinct when the innocent loves of childhood stumble, fall, and fail in the march toward adulthood. In that moment, so far away from them, Anik felt whole and fulfilled in the knowledge that she could recover her parents' admiration.

There was a knock on the door. It was probably Ubah. She probably wanted to talk about what they could do with Jameelah the following morning. Anik wished Ubah would not take the risk of venturing out at night for things that could wait until morning.

Anik got up from her desk and stretched after sitting so long. She slid the bolt open and turned the doorknob.

As soon as the latch clicked, the door flew open. A man in a Chicago Bulls jersey pushed in and placed a huge hand over her mouth and nose. He was at least a head taller than her. She couldn't breathe and tried with all her strength to pull his hand off her face, but he was too strong. He was not angry. He took his time. Anik had never seen him before.

She was about to bite his hand, drive her thumb in his eye, and kick him in the balls when he removed his hand. But she gasped when an open-hand strike on the side of her head stunned her. The blow forced her canine tooth through her lip. She fell down, dazed and disoriented. He had to be a robber. Blood wept over her tongue.

Stay calm, don't panic, she thought. She looked up from the floor. "Take what you want."

Chicago Bulls looked down on her. "Your name is Anik Belanger?" He spoke with an American accent. She nodded. "Shut up or I'll kill you," he said. "Stay still." He had no weapon, and Anik assumed he would beat her to death if she disobeyed. Adrenalin flooded her galloping heart.

Three other men came in. She recognized one. It was the man with the red beard—the community leader, Uthman. He had an eager smile on his face.

"I need the other two women. Where are they?" Chicago Bulls said something in Somali to Uthman.

"Ubah *ijo* Jameelah," Uthman replied in a nasal whine.

"Leave them alone!" Anik yelled. Her desperate fear spiked when she realized they would rape or kill Ubah and Jameelah, and it would be her fault "Leave them alone. They didn't do anything!"

"Never mind, we'll find them. You first."

In Somali, Chicago Bulls called Abdi and instructed a young man dressed in a *kikoi* and khaki shirt. Abdi was overly excited. He made quick, unnecessary movements. His voice was loud, high, and angry. He held a dirty rag in his hand. The young man pulled Anik off the floor to a sitting position against the wall and gagged her tightly, her mouth forced into a pained grimace. The punch had lacerated her cheek against her teeth, and blood pooled in her mouth. She probed a loose tooth with her tongue.

Anik was in a state of heightened awareness. Everything was vivid despite the low light in her room. Time crept. She kept still and watched the men with intense concentration. Survival instinct reigned in the wild gallop of her heart.

Uthman opened her toiletry bag. He held up a tampon and asked a question. When he heard Chicago Bulls' answer, he snickered uncontrollably. The young man guffawed. Anik wondered why they were in no hurry.

Another man was guarding the door. He talked to some passersby. They didn't stop. His voice was calm and without emotion. Uthman opened her deodorant, smelled it, and put it in a bag he had brought. He collected her other things of possible value, then came over and took the Swatch from her wrist. He smelled like rancid sweat and cooking fire smoke. A dribble of green spittle ran down the side of his mouth. He was chewing a wad of qat.

Anik thought of the warnings she had read for travellers to Kenya. Robberies were often violent. *Stay still. Don't argue. Let them have what they want.* This was clear in her mind. *Please, please leave now.*

Chicago Bulls picked up a file from the table. He opened it and read it. Then he nodded and looked at Anik again. He flipped through the file and looked around the room. He went to the two cardboard boxes in which she had organized all her work. He opened the boxes and scanned the files, nodding the entire time. He picked one up and then turned to the young man and said something. Anik thought she heard "Jameelah?" and "*haa.*"

Chicago Bulls instructed the young man to pick up the boxes and carry them out the door. Then he took her computer. His blue flip-flops gently slapped his heels as he padded out the door with all that she had done there.

Chicago Bulls spoke to Uthman. The elder pointed at things in the room, speaking as if reciting a list. He pointed to the teakettle, the towels, and Anik's clothes.

The man at the door stepped away. Then Anik smelled kerosene. *This is what they came for*, she thought, *to destroy my files.* Wisps of smoke entering the room enraged her. She got up and reached to pull off her gag. Chicago Bulls slapped her across the head, and she fell to the floor, trembling and helpless.

"Get up," Chicago Bulls said. He pulled her to her feet and dragged her by the arm toward the door. She pulled back and tried to scream, but the gag was too tight, and she could not breathe through her mouth. Nasal grunts were all she could manage. They had the files they came for. What more did they want? She summoned her courage and told herself that she was strong, but her heart raced with unbridled terror. Her vision was blurred by the tears streaming from her eyes.

She yanked back with all her strength and pulled away, but the door was blocked. Anik retreated to a corner of the room. She recoiled from another blow to her head. Her ears rang, and her vision blurred.

Do what they say. No one will come. Her will to resist crushed, she went with Chicago Bulls and the three others into the night and down a path between the *tukuls*. Men and women watched her go by in silence, their faces pained. Did they know what would happen? Why didn't they try to help her?

The men eagerly asked questions of Chicago Bulls, who answered in a tone of authority. A thin blade of moon shone meagre light on the terrible crime about to occur.

She tried to call for her father and mother, but she was voiceless. The stones on the path cut her bare feet. Her wounded mouth felt like it was full of rusty nails.

The handle of the pump where she came every day looked like the grim reaper's scythe. This was where the women told their stories. It was obvious now why they brought her there. Anik's spirit plummeted with the knowledge of what would come. She decided to survive.

Chicago Bulls shoved her down on the concrete pad against the pump. He joked with Uthman and then instructed the two others. They grabbed her by the arms and held her down. Uthman roughly but cheerfully pulled off her jeans and then her underwear. Her skin was chilled by the dank cement. Anik closed her eyes tightly and felt rough, scratchy hands on her skin. Uthman's beard prickled her face. His fetid breath invaded her lungs.

And then excruciating pain. She clenched her teeth and fastened her eyes shut. She stiffened and then lay still, waiting for it to end. The others shouted encouragement to Uthman. After an interminable wait, she felt his spasm, and then it ended. He panted to catch his breath and then pushed himself off. She told herself that she had survived.

There was movement at her side. She felt the hands change on her arm. Anik opened her eyes. Abdi leapt on her in a frenzy. He pounded her remorselessly. The others laughed and shouted things she could not understand. Her lower body went numb. Things started to turn grey. She was thirsty. Cold.

She left her body. Looking down, she saw herself under the thrashing man. One of her eyes was open but unfocused and without expression. The other was swollen shut. A stream of blood was flowing from her nose. The gag across her mouth was pink with blood. Then everything went black.

29

OMAR'S ROOM WAS AT the back of the school. The floor, walls, and ceiling were concrete. It had one window and a metal door to the playground. He had a desk, a bookcase, a single bed with mosquito net, and a chest for his clothes and personal things. Everything was painted in a soothing ivory colour. In the evening he took a long solitary shower in the boys' washroom. Refugee parents valued the school, so security was not a problem.

Mohammed Dinar had just sent money from his gold for the school, and there was a gift of food. The fruit was mangos, pineapples, and bananas. Because Mohammed loved *mandazis* so much, he thought everyone else should too. He sent a dozen portions of the chewy fried dough along with a creamy dish of pigeon peas cooked in coconut milk. There was always a big frozen fish, but it had to be eaten the next day because the school lacked refrigeration. The deliveries fit into Omar's explanation that he financed the school through philanthropic contributions from wealthy Gulf Arabs.

These gifts found their way into lunch for the students and the meals that Jameelah made for Kamiis. Having Jameelah and

Kamiis next door provided an emotional fulfillment he had not known before. He had a new sense of strength and honour from helping and protecting them.

Sometimes he reserved a modest treat for himself. Mangos were his favourite. The one that night had a fine fragrance of roses. A piece of fruit now and then should not disturb his moral equilibrium. Omar lived in humble austerity and was building the future of 134 children.

With the silky sweetness of mango flesh on his tongue, Omar relished the satisfaction of turning over a new leaf inside and outside. Motivating teachers, giving the school direction, and watching it prosper were cleansing. He was helping the very people his government had betrayed. His alter ego, Omar the schoolmaster, was real now. Omar helped real children in the real world. The things he did now were good things. He would build another school soon.

Standing in his doorway, he looked up into the black equatorial night and remembered what the imam had told him on the day a despairing father tried to give his small boy to Omar. "Good works bring spiritual harmony." Omar convinced himself that his virtue was accumulating in line with divine truth. He had atoned. The good he did now cancelled out the evil from his past. Things probably would have been even worse for his country if he had not been minister of finance, if it had been someone with fewer scruples.

An emaciated crescent moon was too weak to challenge the brazen stars glaring down on Dadaab. He tried to fight back his memory of the punishments the refugees wanted to exact if they ever laid hands on President Barre or his ministers. He was unable, and his black dread of discovery descended on his spirit again.

Everyone knew what had happened in the government torture chambers, some firsthand. They knew Barre had fled the country and, like all presidents, would live to a ripe old age with complete impunity as a guest of the government of Nigeria. Omar and most of the other ministers were still fugitives.

Sometimes on Friday afternoons when the New Light Madrassa was closed, Omar went to the corrugated tin shack that served as a ramshackle camp mosque. Uthman held court, giving the men advice, direction, and instruction in the right way to think about things. There was full agreement that Barre and his ministers deserved the worst kind of death, but one that must be religiously correct. Tongues should be pulled out by the roots in retribution for lies and hypocrisy. Hands should be cut off for robbery. Eyes that had coveted the property and daughters of respectable families must be plucked out. And then stoning. With death by stoning the maximum number of refugees in Dadaab could join in the satisfaction of justice, in accordance with God's will. Uthman exhorted vigilance by all in case traitors were among them in Dadaab camp. If Omar was discovered, if someone recognized him, his hands would probably be cut off before his tongue.

He closed the door quietly but left the latch open in case Jameelah or Kamiis needed something. It was dark after he extinguished the kerosene lantern. He closed his eyes. Against his will, the despair of insomnia joined the flying stones of his imagination, just like the previous night and the one before. He whispered over and over, "Don't worry, nobody knows. Don't worry, nobody knows. Don't worry . . ."

There was sudden banging on the door. "Haji Omar! Haji Omar!" a boy shouted. Omar snapped alert and yanked on a white T-shirt. He opened the door to find Hamed, a student. "Come now! You have to come! There is a bad problem. Hurry!"

"What is it, Hamed? It's late, and you should be at home with your family. "

"My mother told me to get you. Everyone else is afraid to help. She said you wouldn't be afraid."

"Help who? What happened?" His thoughts darkened into worry.

"The white woman. The pretty tall one who talks to the ladies. I think she's dead. Come with me! Run!"

It was hard to follow the path in the dark. From some huts amber kerosene lantern light filtered through blue tarps and meagre thatch. Most people were asleep.

Omar was panting and sweating. The boy was fast, and Omar did not exercise. They ran toward the UN compound. Then the boy turned left. The path opened up to where the women collected their water. He saw a dark form on the muddy concrete pad against the hand pump. The chilling image of a marabou stork about to peck a human corpse flashed in his mind.

They stopped and looked at the body on the ground. "Be careful," Hamed whispered. "They told us they would kill anyone who helped her." It was Anik. Tangled black hair covered her face. Her long legs looked like cold ivory in the dim moonlight.

He cleared the hair from Anik's eyes. She looked to be asleep. He reached around her head and untied the gag from her mouth. Looking down, he saw a black pool between her legs.

An acid mist of terror hung in the air. Faces peered out of their huts from a distance but pulled back when he turned to them. Omar and Anik were both outsiders. No one would help him take her to safety.

"My mother told me to get you but to do no more." Hamed sprinted away into the camp.

Omar tapped Anik's cheeks with the palm of his hand, like in the movies. Her breathing was shallow and slow. She did not wake. She would die without urgent medical attention. He grabbed Anik under the arms and hefted her up. Her shirt was drenched with sweat. The lingering peril of the place boosted his strength, and he managed to get her over his shoulder. It occurred to him that she had lost weight in Dadaab. As he stumbled toward the clinic, he felt on his shoulder that she was still bleeding.

Just when he needed to put her down in the dust and rest, the UN compound came into view. A smell of smoke set off a new alarm in his mind.

"Sister! Help us!" he yelled with all his strength.

Hot air rasped Omar's throat, and he struggled for breath as he carried Anik through the open clinic door. Sister had a Kikuyu name, but he forgot what it was. Everyone just called her Sister. Her black eyes were wrought-iron hard. Her broad body and wide hips were a pillar of strength in a place of greedy diseases and feeble hopes.

"She was attacked. Where do I put her?" Omar asked, panting.

"Put her there. I'll help you. Then go." Sister pointed at a rusty metal bed. The other beds were occupied by impossibly thin women with sick newborns. The spectacle of a half-naked white woman made the other patients curious and nervous. Omar crouched until Anik's hips were level with the stained mattress. Sister leaned Anik gently back onto the bed. Omar slid her legs across, and Sister covered Anik's lower half with a ragged sheet.

"Take off your bloody shirt. Throw it in the garbage," she said. Sister felt for the pulse on Anik's neck with one hand. "Weak. Thready."

"Will she be all right?" Omar asked.

"I can't tell. She's in shock, and her blood pressure is low. Go. Come back tomorrow." Omar did not mind the sharp tone. Sister was a good person and a good nurse. She had probably exhausted her last reserves of easy sympathy many patients ago.

He walked back to the school in the dark. He had been solitary for so long. As he walked, his sadness mounted. With Anik he had found another lone soul who understood him on an intellectual and emotional level. She would leave now. The attack on her had killed a friendship that was about to take form. In the blackness of the night, no one could see or hear him. Invisible, Omar wept for his friend and for himself.

30

THE FOLLOWING MORNING, OMAR left a note for his senior teacher with instructions to run the New Light Madrassa in his absence and then went to the clinic. He found Uthman there already.

"*Salaam walekum*, Uthman."

The elder fingered his red beard as he stood outside watching the clinic. "*Salaam walekum*. You know what happened to the white woman." Uthman had already begun to chew qat and mumbled his words. He knew about everything that happened in the camp. There was no doubt that he knew exactly what happened to Anik.

"The attack was bad. Do you know who did it?" Omar asked.

"They tell me it was you. You were the one who helped the white woman," Uthman said.

"Yes, a boy came and asked me to help."

"I want to know who was this boy."

"I didn't know the boy," Omar replied. Hamed had said the assailants wanted no one to help Anik.

Uthman murmured dissatisfaction. "Tell her this. It's better if she leaves now. The community will understand if she must leave now. This is a difficult place for her. Too difficult. We will not think worse of her if she leaves. Tell her I'll be here when she comes out."

"That is considerate of you. I'll tell her."

Uthman grunted acknowledgement and stood staring at the clinic. Maybe he was sincere. Omar couldn't tell. Perhaps it was a sentiment Anik should hear.

The front of the clinic had a veranda with a corrugated metal overhang. Women and their sick children sat there patiently in hope of a turn. They did not talk to each other. Pessimistic mothers had stopped waving the flies from their babies' faces. No one met his eye.

Sister was attending to her overcrowded clinic when she saw Omar through the window. She went out to talk to him. Dark rings around her eyes told him it had been a sleepless night for her too. She wore a dirty lab coat over her jeans. He wondered if the stains were from Anik's blood.

"I don't want you in there," Sister said. "Neither do the ladies. Your friend is alive. Her friend, Sandra, is with her right now. She'll fill you in."

A few minutes later, Sandra came out. Her eyes were wide, as if terror were contagious. "This is the most awful thing I've ever seen," she said. "We come here to help, and look what happens!"

"Sandra, what happened? Do you know anything?" Omar asked.

"Last night the guards found papers, a computer, and clothes burning outside our fence. They thought one of us got robbed! Dr. Miroslav assembled all the UN personnel, and he sent a report immediately to New York—you know, to make sure his attention to our security was on file right away." Sandra paused. "Usually, Anik and I are in the women's shower first thing in the morning. She wasn't there today. I got a funny feeling and went to her place outside the compound. The door was open. They took everything.

That fire was her stuff. I told Dr. Miroslav, and then I came right here. When I arrived, Ubah was here. For some reason she said she had to leave right away and told me to tell Anik goodbye."

That was strange, Omar thought. Ubah was dedicated to Anik and the work they were doing.

Sister joined them. "She has regained consciousness. That is good news. She asked for three things. Post-exposure antiretrovirals, so she won't get AIDS. Well, we don't have that. Morning-after pills, so she doesn't get pregnant. We don't have those either. Then she asked for you, Omar. Make it quick."

Omar threaded his way through the women, back to the bed where he had placed Anik the previous night. Like an undertaker might arrange a corpse in its coffin, her arms were crossed chastely over her breasts. She lay with grim symmetrical stillness and stared vacantly past the rough wooden rafters into the middle distance. Heat waves radiated from the tin roof. A fly sipped at the tear duct of her blackened left eye. Omar stood beside the bag of saline solution that hung from a rafter and dripped into her left arm.

"Anik, I'm sorry for what happened to you."

The fly departed from her grimy face. Her eyes rolled sideways in her stationary head and met his. Her lips were dry, and the corners of her mouth were badly chafed. Two rough stitches closed the split in her upper lip.

"The community is sorry," Omar continued. "The elder, Uthman, said he knew about what happened. He understands if you need to go. He is waiting to see you outside."

"Who?" Anik asked, her hoarse voice trembling. "Who said something about me? Is he here?" She was suddenly alert and in a panic.

"Uthman. He's right outside. The elder with the red beard at your dinner. He said he understands if you choose to leave here."

"Can you get me out of here? Now! Now!" Her hand shot out of the covers to grab his with sudden strength. *"Je t'en prie."* [19]

Anik took a deep breath and covered her eyes with her hands.

19   I beg you.

31

OMAR DIDN'T KNOW WHAT to say to Anik. He averted his eyes. Of course, he could easily arrange a medical evacuation for Anik to a good hospital in the capital, or even get her to care in Europe. Money was no object. All it would take was a call to arrange a helicopter ambulance. Threatening consequences crowded his imagination though. He would be the one everyone saw arranging the landing location and escorting Anik. The costs of air evacuation would cast into doubt his false identity and everything he said about the school. Could he risk revealing himself? Should he risk the future of the New Light Madrassa for this one woman? Maybe it would be better to just walk away.

Omar looked down at her battered face and dirty hands. The shameful thought made him nauseous with self-disgust. Failing her would be to condemn himself to another eternal burden of betrayal. Then it occurred to him that the UN and the police would get involved. A report would be made, and he could be a witness. The simple request for identity papers could put him at risk of discovery. Omar had to get Anik out of Dadaab.

"I'll help you," he said. "I'll be right back."

The panic in her face lifted with relief. Her gratitude pierced her pain and shock with a faint smile. Omar's spirit eased with relief, like the first drink of a man dying of thirst. He had made the right choice.

Omar rushed to Sandra's UN office to use her telephone. He called Mohammed Dinar and told him the school playing field could accommodate a helicopter ambulance.

Twelve hours later they landed in Lamu, and Omar walked beside Anik as the stretcher was carried into the old stone house. Mohammed had brought in the best Indian doctor in Mombasa, who was accompanied by an American nurse.

"Quickly, quickly. Go up the stairs and into the room on the left. The doctor is waiting." Mohammed barked in Swahili to his men carrying the stretcher. "And then leave—and not a word about this to outsiders! I'll know if you talk!"

Omar stayed below with Mohammed as Anik was taken upstairs.

As soon as they were alone, Mohammed turned on Omar. "My hospitality for you is . . . unconditional. But these are not the proper things. People will see. I don't want any attention."

Omar couldn't meet Mohammed's hard gaze.

"First stolen gold. Now a strange white woman travels to my house by helicopter. What next?" It was the first time Omar had heard Mohammed raise his voice. He searched his mind for a way to assuage his friend.

"Muslims have a duty to rescue. It was my religious duty to help this woman," Omar said weakly. His anguish at exceeding the limits of his friend's hospitality struggled against his compulsion to help Anik.

"Ah, but the Koran also says the duty does not apply when there is undue risk of harm to you or those around you," Mohammed said. "This, my hasty friend, is a borderline case. In my opinion, you have done enough with your small school. Be serene in your virtue. She will be leaving shortly, I presume."

Black clouds of guilt cast another dark shadow over Omar's spirit. He felt somehow complicit and promised himself he would do everything possible to help Anik. It was the only path to atonement for this new outrage. He had known all along that she was courting retribution with her work. He had told her she should leave, then for his own motives he had brought her into the school and more deeply into Dadaab. He could have persuaded her to leave before this happened, had he been thinking about what was best for her.

"This must be up to Anik," Omar said. "She needs to be in a safe place and recover. I knew she was in peril, but I did not advise her properly. She was trying to help my people in her way. She did not have to be in Dadaab. She was beaten and raped because she was looking for truth. And then I was the only one who would help her. And you were the only one who could help me. There is a strange duty we share."

Mohammed's face went from a frown of disapproval to blank resignation. "So, it's God's will that this white woman is in my house, and it's God's will that we spend your gold for her benefit. Very well."

"I owe you a great debt, and I'll find a way to show my gratitude," Omar said. Mollified, Mohammed rested his hand on Omar's shoulder.

"Yes, yes. If I need something, I know you'll help me. I always knew that. Enough of this. What's done is done. Now I must arrange to increase the cash flow from your gold to pay for our new expenses. A customer is coming from Bombay. This man proposes to take some gold and pay through his Indian associates here in Kenya. It will give us Kenyan shillings with a 15 percent profit. My Bombay friend avoids the headache and heartache of customs and government intrusion into his personal financial affairs. We are starting with one million." Mohammed seemed relieved to leave emotional and moral calculations and step onto the solid ground of rational black market business dealings.

Omar needed to be near Anik. The only answer was to sit outside her door. He was the only one she knew. Omar climbed the stairs of the old house and sat in a chair outside her room by a large window to hold vigil.

He was there for a couple of hours before Diane, the nurse they had hired for Anik, came out of Anik's room. She had a Midwestern American accent. Even though the idea of North American competence was reassuring to Omar, he was suspicious of her youth.

"Hi. You can't go in yet," she said.

"How is she? What's happening?" Omar asked

"I gave her a course of morning-after pills to prevent pregnancy. Morphine will keep a lid on the pain, and we're keeping her on a saline drip. It's the best we can do to treat the blood loss. She has a catheter until she can stand and go to the bathroom. Broad-spectrum antibiotics should nip any infections in the bud. What's her name?"

"Anik, Anik Belanger."

"This is the first time I've worked this way—with a non-disclosure agreement. The money's fantastic. It was an offer I couldn't refuse. Thanks. And don't worry, I'll keep everything secret, like you said." Diane's eyebrows came together. "What can you tell me about Anik? And what's your name? Are you her boyfriend?"

"She's a Canadian lawyer—human rights is her expertise. This happened in a refugee camp where she was working. I'm her friend."

Diane gave a short nod. "Well, she looks pretty strong. I think she'll be okay physically. The psychological piece is the hard part. I saw a lot of gang rapes when I worked at the Detroit Receiving Hospital emergency ward. She'll be scared for a long time. She'll wonder why it happened to her. She may even blame herself. She won't trust men. She won't trust you."

Omar listened carefully to Diane's words. Evidently, she knew what she was talking about. He vowed to earn Anik's trust somehow. "Thanks for explaining that," he said. "I didn't know."

"Look, when the time comes, it's really important for her to be able to talk about it. This stuff doesn't just go away by itself. Doing nothing is not an option. I'll help you get ready for that, if you want. I mean if she wants. Anyway, I gave her a sponge bath and washed her hair. That's what I would want if it were me. Here's the doctor. He can give you more on the clinical side."

He was an older doctor with a lab coat and stethoscope hanging from his neck.

"What is your prognosis, Doctor?" Omar asked.

"She lost a lot of blood, but her blood pressure is getting better." He spoke with the gentle singsong accent of East African Indians. "The rape was extremely violent, and there was tissue damage, but physically she will recover. She is young and otherwise healthy. I don't think her recovery will take too long. I see contusions on her face, neck, arms, and ankles. She was struck many times. Fortunately, there were no broken bones and no internal organ damage. She is concussed."

"What happens next?" Omar asked. "What should we do to help her get well?"

"I would like to keep her on close observation. She will be quite comfortable here, as per your instructions. We have administered the required medications." He turned to Diane. "Nurse, you will please take a blood sample and send it to the Mombasa clinical laboratory for baseline tests. Tell them it's an urgent sexual assault case."

"Yes, Doctor. The nearest lab we can trust with that test is at the Aga Khan hospital in Nairobi. I'll send the blood sample there by air courier."

"All right. Please do that right away. Mr. Omar, unfortunately, sexual assault is too common in our country. But I must say, this is among the most vicious and violent cases I've seen. Usually with the foreigners it's a one-on-one sort of thing, or two maybe. I don't know how many were involved with your friend, but certainly many more. And it seemed like they were trying to hurt her. I wonder why they did not kill her afterwards. You should go to the police and make a complaint."

"Yes, yes. We have done that," Omar lied. There could be no official report for what happened to Anik without revealing his identity and all the dangers that entailed for him, for Mohammed, and for the gold.

"When will she be able to talk? When can I see her?"

"Anik is awake," Diane said. "She's not even sleeping. Sometimes victims want to postpone confronting their new reality." She turned to the doctor. "I think he can come in and see."

The doctor nodded his assent.

Omar softly approached the bed. Anik's right eye opened. The sapphire-blue iris was clear. Her left eye was swollen and blackened from the beating. It opened halfway. Half the white was blood red. She saw him and started to cry.

"Don't tell my papa and mama. I don't want anybody to know where I am. I'm too scared."

She closed her eyes again, but the tears kept coming, and her body shuddered with sobs.

32

IBRAHIM WAS SITTING ON a new cushion made from a Persian carpet. It was blue with intricate green-and-yellow geometrical patterns. It was the correct replacement for what he had before. Stuffed Chinese polyester blankets with loud flower patterns were alien to the austere Somali landscape.

He thought of how graceful butterflies emerged from ugly worms. He was assembling a cocoon of respectability to hide his inner brutality and crude usurpation of all political and coercive power in Merka. For this he was cultivating an image of tradi-tional Islamic leadership and wise gravitas. It would be his path to legitimacy.

Abdi entered looking disturbed by something. "General, we have come back from Dadaab to give you our report."

This was good news, and Ibrahim smiled with magnanimity. "I understand the hardships of the refugee camp, you know." He turned to his attendant. "Kill some chickens, and give them a proper lunch."

"And some whiskey? We would like that," Abdi said.

No more whiskey. It was not in line with his new image. "No, just orange Fanta today." It was a disappointing answer for Abdi, but it went unchallenged.

Abdi wrung his hands. "There's something wrong, sir. The Italians, they think we're strange."

"What do you mean? We're not strange."

"The peacekeepers delivered another captive for us to imprison and interrogate. He tried to enter their perimeter to steal food. The Italians saw two of our men walking across the parade ground holding hands as we do and burst into derisive laughter. It was disrespectful."

"Why?" Nothing was more manly or natural to Ibrahim's way of thinking. Of course, with his rank and position, he could only hold hands with men of comparable stature, such as the elders and notables of the region.

"I asked their translator—one of the ones we provided to them. They think we are all homosexual. Because we men hold hands."

Ibrahim thought about this in silence. Simmering rage displaced his initial shock and humiliation. This was the "respect" he got for helping the foreigners. He had been right to mistrust them. Clever exploitation was the only sensible way to approach his relationship with Cristiani.

"Get Gibreel. I want to hear his report now."

Ibrahim's lieutenant in Dadaab, Gibreel, was even bigger than he remembered. Ibrahim was displeased by the imported Chicago Bulls shirt. Gibreel's new Air Jordans were shamelessly huge, but so were his feet. The hat was official NBA merchandise. After he sat down, he pulled a cloth from his pocket and bent over to wipe the dust from his shoes.

"Don't tell me those were your work clothes," Ibrahim said. Gibreel was usually reliable. He obviously had plenty of money if he could afford such clothes. *I must be paying him too much.*

Gibreel grinned. "Do you like them? Everybody in Dadaab knows this is my trademark."

Ibrahim was not happy with this response. "That is not the good judgement I expect from my people. It makes you look arrogant." Gibreel knew too much and would have to be eliminated if his performance or attitude proved unsatisfactory. It would not be hard to find an adequate replacement. "You should dress in the traditional manner. Now give me your report."

Gibreel and Abdi remained standing, frightened by their leader's reproach. "The woman and her papers are gone, General," Abdi said. "She will not come back."

"How did this problem come to be in the first place?" Ibrahim asked.

"General, the insolence of the Canadian woman was unspeakable," Gibreel replied. "She was ignorant of our ways and spoke to our women without their men's permission. Then the women were disrespectful enough to give her information. They started talking to her and telling her our business."

Ibrahim felt frustration tighten his chest. He was flustered that new problems were always emerging, and his people were so unreliable. "Why am I only finding out about this now?"

"Uthman regrets that he didn't stop this mischief immediately. He didn't want it to become your concern. He asked me to apologize that you were troubled with Dadaab affairs when you have so many other responsibilities. He wants you to know he did his part. He even participated actively. He helped us find another five trusty men, and they were enthusiastic. He told them to show how hard they can work." Gibreel looked expectantly to Ibrahim.

"That's not good enough. It's not what I pay you for. I pay you to stop problems before they happen." Ibrahim scowled with rising anger. Things were complicated enough inside Somalia without worrying about Dadaab.

"I know, and I'm sorry," Abdi said. "But we achieved your intent, General Ibrahim. The UN camp guards and the Kenyan police were satisfied to take our money. They are paid so little that they have come to rely on our gifts. So, there was no one around when we told them not to be around. Nobody stopped us, and nobody came close. Our women won't forget either. I'm sure they got the message. Gibreel has the detailed report."

Gibreel took out his notebook and flipped through it. This at least was professional. The man was a dual national and had served in the United States Army. This was a good example to his other men. "We made extra payments that night of seventy-five US dollars just to be sure." Gibreel looked expectantly at Ibrahim. He probably wanted reimbursement. If he could afford clothes like that though, he didn't need more money.

Gibreel turned a few pages, consulted his notes, and continued. "General, at nine o'clock last night, we approached the target, and I divided the men into two teams. I ordered the first team to subdue, capture, and move the enemy to the site selected to execute your order. The second team removed and destroyed all enemy assets. The operation began at 9:15 p.m. following careful surveillance. The enemy was alone, and we fully exploited the element of surprise. The community was instructed not to interfere, and their cooperation was complete. Enemy assets were moved to a nearby location, covered with kerosene, and destroyed by fire. I confirm that all hostile intelligence records were eliminated, including the computer. All men participated in the punishment of the prisoner, in order of seniority."

Ibrahim saw that Gibreel was trying to look sincere and deferential to him. That was good.

"General, my role was to ensure full task completion, which I faithfully report to you. Sir, the operation was conducted in a way that was designed to have a demonstration effect on the other women of the camp. I'm confident that the effects will be long lasting."

"Did you kill her? What did you do with the body?"

"She has left Dadaab camp, sir. I believe she will not return. There has been no official complaint or publicity that we have been able to observe. This was a successful operation, and I'm confident, as I said, that the effects will be enduring."

"We left her for dead because there was no way she could have survived the night," Abdi said apologetically. "But somebody did interfere."

"Who was working with her? Was she alone?" Ibrahim asked with mounting frustration.

"She had a translator and a camp woman assisting her. They were gone the next day. We were not able to process them."

"I'm losing my temper," Ibrahim said in a level voice. "I need to know everything. Who helped her?"

"There was no police report; I've confirmed that," Gibreel said. "She left with the teacher. We don't know him. Nothing will happen."

"How did they leave?" Ibrahim asked. There was a long pause, so he repeated the question.

"Helicopter. Private helicopter."

"What? How could they get a helicopter? Did you get the registration? Where did it go?" Ibrahim demanded.

"I suppose she has a friend with a lot of money. We don't know where she went. Nobody thought to get the helicopter number." Gibreel looked down at his feet.

"What about the teacher? Who is he? What clan? Where does his money come from?"

Still looking at his feet, Gibreel shook his head. "I don't know."

Ibrahim glared at the man in his absurd clothes. "Your job is to protect my interests in the camp. I expect better than this. Much better. You are dismissed."

Ibrahim was uneasy that something was going on in his territory over which he did not have control. At least he could tell Cristiani that there wouldn't be any more reports. That was all Cristiani cared about anyway.

33

ANIK SHIVERED IN LOOSE cotton pajamas. Her back hunched and her elbows on knees, she held her head in her hands. She sat in a chair watching the housekeeper change the sheets. The previous night she had dozed fitfully, but she could not sleep. Her memory of the rape closed like a steel trap on her former self. All she wanted was the safe refuge of bed.

It was warm, and Diane wore a red tank top and long blue batik skirt. She seemed to know when Anik did not want to talk. They had been silent all morning.

The nurse put her book down and checked her watch. "How's it going today?" Diane smiled with encouragement and handed her a glass of water. "Do you want to talk?"

"I should want to talk, but I don't."

"That's okay. But you should keep trying."

Anik knew Diane was right. She took a sip and squinted through exhausted eyes. "I'm so tired. I'm still weak."

Diane drew the curtain against the stark white of the tropical day outside the window.

A lazy ceiling fan stirred the air and waved the mosquito net behind Anik. The cool coral walls urged her to go back to sleep. Like a little child, she could not master her feelings, and she hated it. Tears started to leak through her defences again. Anik forced a lifeless smile. "I feel all the things that happened to the rape survivors I met in Dadaab."

The bed was ready, the housekeeper left, and Anik shuffled over and slipped back under the fresh cotton covers. Her cold body moved slowly. She was stiff.

"There are some things I'm starting to remember. I remember the smell of the old man on top of me. Then the next one, the violent one. Then I remember the clinic. There was more, but that's all I remember. I want to . . . name them. They have to pay for what they did to me. For hurting me."

There it was again, that tightness across her chest and shortness of breath. Bursts of fear, unconnected to anything real, detonated in her gut and head. There was not enough oxygen in the room. Her heart accelerated to a triple time drumroll. Anik stopped talking and looked wide-eyed for help.

She felt Diane's soothing hand on her wrist, taking her pulse. "One sixty. Another panic attack. Breathe slowly. Take your time. You can do this. Inhale . . . exhale . . . inhale . . . exhale."

Anik pulled air as deep into her lungs as she could. Diane led her through the exercise for many long minutes. The tide of panic subsided. Her chest and shoulder muscles released a small measure of tension.

"In Dadaab I talked to women every day about what happened when they were raped. It was normal for me to talk about it. I never—ever—thought it would happen to me. How stupid could I be?" Anik asked.

"Don't beat yourself up about it. You didn't do anything wrong. Of course, you can't do anything about it either. The police don't give a fuck. In the States the chances the bastards get caught and tried are about zero," Diane said. "Here there's no way."

"What do you think I should do?" Anik asked.

"I think—and this is just me—you need to put what happened to you . . . you know, in perspective. You were the victim of a horrible crime. Don't hide from your reality. It's going to be part of you for the rest of your life. But it's not all of you."

Anik closed her eyes and struggled to concentrate. Faint flashes of anger sparked in the leaden clouds that filled her mind. She tried to think like a lawyer again.

"They weren't nervous. They weren't in a hurry. It wasn't hidden. They knew where to find me. They had a leader. I don't think this happened spontaneously, just for sex. Somebody planned it." She closed her eyes and shook her head. "The leader, the big guy, he wore a Chicago Bulls shirt. I remember that. He knew my first name and my last name. How would he know that? The women just call me Anik." She sighed. "I'm tired again. Can I stay here? I'm afraid to go anywhere else."

"For now, yes. But not forever. It's not up to me anyway. I just work here." Diane smiled softly. "Pretty soon you'll need to think about what comes next, Anik." Diane was right, again. But Anik wasn't ready. Not now. Not yet.

"On the plus side, you sure are rich, or at least your friends are, to fly you in and set up this high-priced personal care. You might be surprised how many problems can be solved just with money. I wish I had that much."

Anik's understanding of the situation was like a muddy river winding in random bends that made no sense. "I don't know where the money comes from," Anik admitted. "It's not mine."

Leather footfalls on stone approached. The heavy wooden door was ajar, and Omar's face peeked in. He had saved her. This was one true thing she could hang on to.

"Good morning, Diane. May I speak with Anik?"

Diane gave a questioning look to Anik, who nodded. "Sure, come on in."

"Diane told me to talk to people," Anik said. "I don't feel like it. But I do want to thank you." Her voice was tentative. She was using every last shred of strength to keep it together.

"You're welcome. I'm so sorry for what happened to you."

"I thought they would kill me. It hurt so much. It still hurts." Tears formed in her eyes, and she tried to hold it in. Anik covered her face with her hands to hide her shame and pain. When she could talk again, her voice was tinged with anger. "These are your people. Why did they do this? Why did they choose me? What did I do?"

"I don't know why or who. I just want you to be safe and get better."

Anik registered for the first time that he cared for her, though she could not imagine why.

She was startled by a new flood of panic, of something she had forgotten. "What about my work? Can you find out what happened to my work?"

"Those men who . . . who took you also ransacked your quarters and burnt your things. They either burnt or stole your documents."

She closed her eyes and covered them with her hands. Were her work and this ordeal all for nothing?

"Don't worry about that right now," Omar said. "Remember, the community understands if you don't want to come back. The elder, Uthman, the one with the red beard, told me."

She remembered Uthman was the first one on her. The implications started to emerge. They had wanted to stop her work. They knew what she had found.

Anik sat bolt upright. She panted in short, shallow breaths. "Oh, no. Oh, please, please no."

If they had done this to her, what would they do to others? She imagined Ubah and Jameelah being dragged to the water pump, their faces bloody and paralyzed with terror—all because they had chosen to work with her. Kamiis would relive what she saw happen to her mother.

"Settle down, calm yourself, Anik." Diane held her wrists and looked into her face. "Remember you are injured. Take it easy!"

"Where are they? Ubah, Jameelah, and Kamiis?"

Omar shook his head. "I don't know. Ubah left. She wanted Sandra to say goodbye to you for her. Jameelah and Kamiis are gone too."

"You mean you don't know where they are? We need to find them immediately and make sure they're safe." Then Anik thought about the women she interviewed. All their names would be known. Their accusations, names, and places were in the files. The bastards who did this might not be finished. "That hideous old man with the red beard, he was part of it. He wasn't the leader, but he was one of them. You know him. You said he was waiting for me outside the clinic."

She looked directly at Omar. He knew Uthman. Had he known what was going to happen to her? Could he be a war criminal too? Was he somehow part of it? She felt cold again.

Anik jerked free of Diane's gentle grasp. "I have to go back. Where are my clothes? Where are my things? Today. I need to go back to Dadaab today. I have to get back to work."

Omar and Diane stared at her as if she had lost her mind.

"Way too soon," Diane said. "You need to regain your strength first. This is enough for one day. Really, it's too much too soon."

Omar looked uncomfortable and puzzled. He didn't under-stand. Diane didn't either. Right now, only her enemies under-stood. Except for Uthman, she didn't even know who they were. With complete clarity, she decided she would find out who was responsible. Even if it was the last thing she ever did. Even if it killed her. She savoured the bitter anger, which displaced the sour despondence in her spirit.

She swallowed the pills and water Diane offered her. "Will this medicine get me out of here faster? I can't waste any time."

"It's a sedative," Diane said. "You need to rest."

"Don't you give me anything without asking!" Anik shouted. "I can't rest. Don't you get it?"

The lawyer in her wanted to get working. "I need pen and paper to write everything down. I need to work. I need a desk."

"Yes, yes, I'll get it. Right away. Anything you need," he said and then left the room.

"Let's get you on your feet a little bit tomorrow," Diane said. "Today we take it easy."

Anik decided she could not afford to be weak anymore. Then she felt drowsy, and the sedative put her to sleep.

34

AT SUNSET OMAR JOINED Mohammed for the fifth prayer of the day. Omar couldn't stop vibrating with anxiety that he would be discovered. Everyone in the camp would have seen the helicopter evacuation of Anik. How could he ever return to being a humble schoolmaster? He also worried about the news that Jameelah and Kamiis had left the school. His head teacher sent the message that they were gone, and nobody knew where they went. Omar didn't know what to do. He longed for the rhythmic words of prayer to push back the catastrophic possibilities that invaded his imagination.

After praying, the houseboy served them mango juice and two dates as an appetizer before the evening meal. Mohammed bit a date and chewed it thoroughly before speaking. It was maddening the way the man found comfort in food at such times.

"Surprises are not good for business, nor are they good for digestion. One should gently awaken the stomach and softly stimulate its humours before large meals." Mohammed took a sip of juice, and then regarded the plump, moist, ripe fruit with satisfaction "You just cannot improve upon the Saudi date," he said.

Omar refused to be drawn into a conversation of such exasperating superficiality. Mohammed did not notice.

"Omar, do you know Osman, my agent in Merka? I met with him earlier today to receive his monthly report."

"No. What did he say? Sometimes my students' parents talked about Merka. I heard things are bad there. What's the news?"

Mohammed picked up his second date and studied it with interest. "Sudanese dates are nice too, but it's difficult to obtain fresh ones these days. That pointless civil war of theirs has played havoc with our imports." He took a sip of his juice. "Do you want to hear the good news or the bad news first?"

"Start with the good news," Omar said. "I didn't know there was any."

"Business is good. The Italian soldiers are pouring money into this region as if it's their own country, or as if they want to stay. My business is benefitting from the so-called trickle-down effect. Our trade in food is doing well. The rice, wheat, and oil that the foreigners are giving have made food prices quite low. Everyone needs money, so there's good profit in buying food there and then selling it to the Kenyans here. You know what they say—buy low, sell high. The young general in charge, Ibrahim, runs the port, and we have a good working relationship with his organization. He's rather expensive though."

Mohammed shifted to find a better position on his pillow. He told his servant that they would be ready to sit down to their supper of coconut chicken and okra stew in fifteen minutes. Omar did not like the way the conversation was going.

"Omar, we all know that a man who cannot defend his family is not really a man. Somalis have always needed a good supply of guns and ammunition to protect themselves. With this UN arms embargo, prices are up, so it has become a profitable trade. Part of me feels uneasy about this business, but it's a high-performing sector and is even stronger now. Sometimes I think we have a responsibility to ensure weapons are available to those like your cousin, Bilal. Without his AK-47, how could he fulfill his duty to protect his family and community?"

The conversation was approaching a slippery slope. "In my view, the morality of the trade depends on the morality of the customer," Omar said.

"That is just the thing that makes me hesitant about a prospective good deal," Mohammed replied. "The customer is this Ibrahim Hussein. Frankly, I don't think people like him much. My man, Osman, said everyone is surprised and disappointed because they thought the UN peacekeepers would disarm him and make him go away. They thought the UN would be the new government for everybody. That would have been nice."

"That sounds crazy," Omar said. "With all their modern weapons and aircraft and money, they must have assumed complete control of the town. This is what is needed and what people would expect. Why else would these foreign countries be there if not to provide order and safety now that the state has failed and we cannot do it for ourselves?" Despite the gravitational force of his responsibilities for Anik, Jameelah, and Kamiis, he was hungry for news of his country and what could possibly be going on in Merka.

"Osman tells me that things have developed in a different manner. This is bad news, even though there's still money to be made. The most amazing thing is that the Italians give Ibrahim anything he asks for. It's as if they believe he's a sultan, and they're working for him." Mohammed laughed softly and shook his head in a gesture of fatigued amusement at the eternal ironies of human folly.

"Osman said, and these were his words, 'For this Ibrahim it's a dream come true, but for the people it's a nightmare come true.'" Mohammed raised his eyebrows to underscore the drama of a fine phrase. "He is controlling more and more territory in a hypocritical and dangerous way. I hear he's robbing even the notable families of the honour of their daughters. Then, of course, the families are disgraced, and the girls must be banished. Terrorized families abandon their properties to him. Can you imagine the pain and humiliation?" Mohammed shook his head in weary disgust. "Osman has two daughters and said the situation is completely un-Islamic."

"It's utterly un-Islamic and highly offensive," Omar said in disgust.

Mohammed nodded gently, and his humid lips curled into a knowing smile. Like a baby, the man's face had no wrinkles. "On the other hand, I feel a responsibility to keep this market for my business. Omar, it's finally my turn to ask a favour of you. Will you go to see what is happening and advise me? I need the counsel of a trusted friend."

This was the last thing Omar needed.

"Don't worry about your friend, Anik," Mohammed said. "We will take good care of her, and you will not be gone long."

After all Mohammed had done for Omar and Anik, there was only one possible answer. "Of course," Omar said. "Of course, I'll gladly do this for you."

Mohammed smiled. "Excellent. Now, let's eat."

35

ANIK DRANK HER BREAKFAST mug of sweet, milky tea in bed. She forced down a piece of bread.

Diane walked in the room with sunglasses over her forehead. "Good. You're eating. The way they make that tea will get your blood sugar up." She was dressed for the beach and had some clothes over her arm. As if she knew Anik was not going to reply, Diane kept talking. "Shit happens, and you can get over it if you want. That's my philosophy. I saw it all at the Detroit emerge. Drug overdoses, rapes, little kids hit by drunk drivers, punks shot by other punks. When I stopped feeling sorry for my patients, I knew it was time for me to get out of there. So, I took off and came to work here in Kenya last year. You can change your life if you want, you know.

"This place is so cool. Here in Stone Town, it's like we're still in the middle ages. A short walk down the beach, and there are millionaires and movie stars. Wait till you see the beach. Spectacular." Diane was trying hard to be cheerful. It came from the heart, and Anik welcomed it.

"We're about the same size, wouldn't you say?"

Anik looked at Diane appraisingly and nodded.

"Too soon for bikinis, right? But you must look good in one." Anik returned a wan smile to Diane.

"I brought a nice big T-shirt and a wrap skirt for you. Everyone around here uses flip-flops, and you can use mine until you get yours—they sell them anywhere. We got some bras and panties for you too; they're in the dresser. I'll leave you to get dressed. I'll be back with our friend Omar in about thirty minutes. He said he wants to come along."

Diane slipped out of the room, so Anik could get dressed.

Anik had not left the house since she arrived almost two weeks earlier. Most of that time she had stayed in bed. It took an act of will to swing her legs out of the bed. She stood up, got dizzy, sat down again, then recovered her determination and walked to the bathroom. She took off her dressing gown. In the mirror she saw that her face was gaunt, and the thin, translucent skin under her eyes was dark. The cuts to her face had left small but visible scars on her left cheekbone and forehead. Half of her left retina was blood red. A dark vertical scar bisected her upper lip.

Her body looked skinny and slack. Her muscle tone was gone, and she could see her ribs. She was not beautiful anymore.

The hot water of the shower was soothing, and it was a comfort to wash her long hair. Anik noticed that the high-end shampoo was accompanied by high-end conditioner. *Probably what Diane uses*, she thought.

She felt a little bit better after the shower and took her time brushing her hair. Another piece of her old self came back when she stepped into new underwear and snapped the bra clasp. She felt better and walked to the mirror. "*Maybe I can be beautiful, again. One day,*" she said to herself.

The skirt was light and loose. The shapeless T-shirt reached below her hips. She sat down and stared out the window. It was a bright, sunny morning.

The two knocks on the door were soft and hesitant. She waited, then heard two more.

"Yes?"

"It's me, Omar. Diane said you were going out for a walk. Going to see the beach. May I join you?"

"Okay," Anik said. She would have preferred to take this first step out of the house with Diane only, but she was too courteous to say no. She was his guest, really.

He was in traditional dress: a *kikoi*, safari shirt, and a new leather skullcap. He smiled. Omar was trying to look friendly and comforting. Anik wondered why. She had needed his help to get out of Dadaab and was grateful for it. She wasn't sure why he brought her to Lamu. She had no idea what he might want in return.

"It's a beautiful morning, the same as every morning here in Lamu," he said. "So, nobody talks about the weather. There's nothing to talk about." He smiled to see if she found the remark droll. She wasn't in a mood for stupid jokes.

"I'll take the weather here over a million conversations about Detroit winters," Diane said, trying to lighten things up.

"I want to show you the beach," Omar said. "Do you like beaches, Anik?"

"Diane, you're coming too, right?" Anik said.

Diane looked her in the eye and nodded. "Of course. This is your first time out of the house. It's a big day."

They went out of the house and down the narrow lane past donkeys, merchants opening their shops, and the odd tourist.

"It's nicest now, in the morning. The air is fresh, the sun is low, and everything's quiet," Diane said. "We go down this street to the dock, turn right, then follow the Corniche Path to Shela Beach."

Vendors with donkeys were headed to town. The animals were laden with green coconuts, bananas, and trading goods.

Anik shuffled slowly along the path. She looked to the left and saw a wall of mangrove forest on the neighbouring island. She tried to peer through the black and green tangle, didn't watch where she was going, and her flip-flop caught on a root. She tripped and fell to the ground. A piece of glass on the path cut into her knee. Embarrassed and angry, she struggled to her feet, refusing to take Omar's offered hand.

Diane bent to take a look at it. "Not too bad." She plucked the glass out, and blood began to flow gently. "It should scab over and stop soon. Do you want to go back?"

"This is nothing. We'll go where we decided to go," Anik said. They walked by an upscale tourist hotel.

"This is the Peponi Hotel. Small and exclusive. People come from all over to be on an island with no cars," Omar said. "Rich Europeans, mainly."

Anik watched her shadow feet meeting her real feet at every step. Her shadow body slouched pathetically.

The trickle of blood ran down her shin between her toes, and made a sticky spot between her foot and rubber flip-flop.

They reached the beach. Morning sun stabbed harsh shards of glare into her eyes. She slipped off her flip-flops, and the blond sand was cool and soft to her bare feet. Gentle waves slid over her feet to kindly wash away the blood. The beach went on uninterrupted for miles.

"It's beautiful, but I'm tired," Anik said. "Let's go back now."

"Do you mind if I go for a swim?" Diane asked. "I'll catch up with you later."

"Of course," Omar said. He turned to Anik. "Let's take a break at the Peponi. You should have something to drink."

They sat at a table on the beachfront terrace. Anik ordered a Coke and Omar a coffee. She looked out over the water as a small boat with a lateen sail slid by in the light breeze.

"Why did you do so much for me?" Anik asked.

"You asked me to help you." Omar smiled as if poised to accept her gratitude.

"I asked you to get me out of the camp. You got a helicopter, a doctor, and a nurse. Why did we come to this little island anyway?" Her voice was flat. She couldn't manage to put a friendly tone into her words.

"I have my good friend, Mohammed, here."

It didn't add up. He could have taken her to the hospital in Mombasa or even Nairobi. His demeanour changed, and Omar couldn't seem to look her in the eyes. Her legal experience told her that this was the conduct of someone trying to conceal incriminating evidence. He must have sensed that she didn't trust him anymore. A crescendo of tension rose in the stretch of silence between them.

"Oh," was all Anik managed to say. She didn't feel safe enough to confront Omar's shaky fictional story. Twisting in her chair she looked around for Diane. She clumsily knocked over her Coke, and the glass smashed into hundreds of pieces on the stone floor.

"Don't move," Omar said. "Don't move until this gets cleaned up." He waved a waiter over to sweep up the broken glass.

While Anik was trapped in her chair, Omar looked at her. "I have to tell you something. I need to go on a trip tomorrow. I'll be gone for a week."

"Where?" Anik asked.

"Merka."

Did this mean he was connected to the violence? How did he know when and where to find her after the attack anyway? He knew Uthman. Were they friends? Did he have anything to do with the attack? For the first time since her assault she was able to keep her feelings off her face. She noticed he was powerfully built and could hurt her. She tried to keep cool and not show too much interest.

"What for?"

"Mohammed has longstanding business dealings in Merka. He asked me to check some things for him. Please don't worry. Diane and the doctor will take good care of you. You can stay as long as you want. Just ask Mohammed for anything you might need."

Anik faked a smile. "Thank you."

Diane came up, still wet from her swim.

"I want to go back," Anik said. "Right now."

Omar paid, and they walked silently back to the stone house, Anik in the lead.

Pieces were starting to come together in Anik's mind. Omar knew that pervert with the red beard. Now he was going to a place connected with the epidemic of rapes. They did some kind of business there. What did he want from her?

As soon as they arrived at the stone house, she paused at the base of the stairs. "I'm going to my room."

Diane came into her room soon after. Anik was under her covers. She felt cold.

"The water is beautiful," Diane said. "You didn't stay long. Why not?"

"It was enough for one day. I don't really have much in common with that man. I should go back home."

"You're not going anywhere without a passport and money. Don't you need Omar to help you with that?"

"Yeah. I guess you're right. I'll wait till he gets back from his trip. Then I'll go home."

36

OMAR STOOD ON THE town dock and perceived a distant light at sea. It was Mohammed's dhow, which would take him to Merka. "This is something I prefer to do at night. No one needs to know our business," Mohammed said.

They stepped into the outboard launch and cast off. Mohammed told the boat driver to go slowly and quietly. The large twin outboards burbled at low power, and they sliced silently through the calm water.

Omar clutched a large duffle bag. It held a change of clothes and US$200,000 in $100 bills.

"Don't forget, every time you meet someone, tell them you're my new business agent," Mohammed said, like a teacher to a dull student. "This General Ibrahim is a man with ambition. I think he's going places. To show respect, the first thing you should do is pay a courtesy call on him at his headquarters and give him my gift. My man, Osman, will meet you on the dock. He'll be on the lookout for the dhow."

Omar didn't know how to swim and was feeling unsure about travelling by sea. "What about pirates?"

"Well, you might say that pirates need my services as much as anyone," Mohammed said. "Everyone knows the name of my beautiful dhow, pirates included. *Nur min Awa*—light of the sea. They won't touch it. Don't worry at all. It will be fine. It will be good. It's not so hard to be a merchant. It's in my blood. You're even smarter than me. You're an economist. It will be simple!"

The light on the vessel grew brighter as they approached.

"The main thing is to remember your budget and stick to it. Osman is a good bargainer, and he'll tell you if the prices are correct. Now let's make sure you remembered everything properly. What's your budget?"

"The gift to Ibrahim is thirty thousand. The port fee is five thousand. I give this to Ibrahim too. Two thousand is for the imam of the mosque for charitable purposes. I'll tell him it's the zakat of your business in Merka. Fifty thousand is hawala remittances for Osman to distribute to your clients. One hundred and thirteen thousand is for merchandise. Food and gum arabic."

"Very good. Please try to get as much vegetable oil as you can. The white people are giving it away in Somalia when it can fetch a nice price here in Kenya. The flour is of low quality, unless it comes from Canada, but the American rice is pretty good. And get as much gum arabic as you can. The market has been starved of it for a long time. Also, if you can get a Somali goat or two, we would enjoy that a lot, for old time's sake. Do you remember that trip when you were a boy and we met in Yemen? Do you still have the knife?"

"I do remember, but I had to leave the knife in Mogadishu."

"There is one other thing. I'm told that the people are short of ammunition. We can get our hands on a lot of bullets for the AK-47. I think that will be a welcome product for the Merka market. I have a supplier in Eritrea—Massawa. It became available after that hypocritical Ethiopian infidel Mengistu and his criminal junta fell." The outboard motor of Mohammed's launch shifted down to a quiet idle. "Well, here we are."

A single light bulb hung from a rusty crane on the large wooden ship. The broad hull was made of raw wood with salt patches and rust streaks. The sharp prow pointed heavenwards, and the vessel squatted under the rear-slung superstructure hanging over the stern. Written in Arabic behind the eye was *Nur min Awa*. The boat had gleaming blue eyes, like a living fish.

"Dubai-built," Mohammed said with pride of ownership. "My father commissioned it himself. It will return much lower in the water." He laughed happily.

"*Salaam walekum*, my brothers!" Mohammed shouted at the shirtless black figures looking down over the railing.

"*Walekum salaam*, Mohammed Sahib. Is this our passenger?" one asked.

"Yes, yes, Captain Kabir. I introduce my representative, Omar. Take good care of him."

"You are most welcome, Omar." The captain threw a rope ladder over the side. "Climb aboard, and we'll get underway."

A slender young sailor whipped down the ladder, jumped into the launch, and slung Omar's bag over his shoulder as he invited Omar to climb aboard.

"Goodbye!" Mohammed said. "Have a safe journey."

Once Omar was aboard, the engine let loose a great bellow. The captain smiled at him. "Cummins. Seven hundred horse-power. This won't be a long trip."

37

OMAR SLEPT ON DECK with the rest of the crew. He lay down on his thin foam-rubber mattress but couldn't calm his mind. Part of him felt a need to go to Somalia—to see what was happening in his country. To go as Mohammed's agent was the perfect incognito solution. He had grown a beard, and he would not be wearing a suit, so he figured the risk of recognition was low.

The captain turned the ship westward at about 4:00 p.m. the next day. The sun was in their eyes, and the city of Merka was an indistinct shadow against the bright horizon. A launch with an outboard motor sped toward them. Calculating young fighters with assault rifles squinted hungrily at them. Kabir shouted an order. Sailors scrambled for their weapons and trained them on the launch. It circled the slowing dhow and then headed back to shore.

"They like to know who's coming, so they can welcome us properly," the captain said. He looked alert and shouted commands in preparation for docking.

The sun set abruptly. The sea and sky darkened to a deep sapphire. The moon was full. The square shapes of the city and its pointy minarets contrasted with the soft roundness of the dunes behind the beach. Merka was so old that it looked like a geological extrusion.

The captain called back to the helmsman. "Go slow, slow. We don't know the depth anymore since they stopped dredging years ago!"

The city's stone walls came right to the sandy beach. Two rusty tramp freighters were anchored listlessly offshore with no sign of life on their decks or light behind the portholes. They flew no flag. They looked dead.

The Merka jetty was a cracked old cement platform on crumbling concrete pilings. Rusted rebar wept ochre stains on the salty surface. Light came from a corrugated iron shed on the dock. The engine gave a groan, and the boat's bow dipped when the mate put the engine in reverse to shed momentum. The dhow slowly glided to the dock. There were no other lights on the shore, just sporadic illuminated windows in the town.

As they sidled toward the old tires hanging against the dockside, a ragged handful of teenage toughs with AK-47s approached the boat. They called for the captain with happy voices. "*Salaam walekum, Nur min Awa*! What gifts do you bring us? Don't worry. We have our orders to take very good care of you. You are our guests. Come, everybody off. We must inspect! We must inspect!" Omar saw a bored group of peacekeepers ignoring the operation. Something was not right.

The captain returned the greeting. "*Salaam walekum*, my brothers. How glad we are to be again in the beautiful port of Merka. But I'm in no condition to receive you properly. Please be patient."

The powerful diesel engine rumbled into reverse thrust and stopped some ten metres short of the dock. The evening was still and hot.

Suddenly, two beat-up technicals raced down the dock, past the indolent peacekeepers, and stopped between the boat and the fighters. An energetic small man jumped out and started yelling and waving his hands. His head was like a large brown billiard ball.

"You thieves may not board this ship! It belongs to the Dinar family. It must be respected! Just wait until General Ibrahim hears about this shameful conduct. Back in your shed! I'm the authorized one!" He handed a plastic bag of qat to one of them.

With a sullen glare, the fighters turned and walked back to the shed. They sat down against the rusty corrugated iron wall and shared the twigs of bright green qat leaves, which would keep them awake through the night. The next morning Omar knew that they would be mired in a foul and angry hangover.

"Omar! Haji Omar! Are you there?" the man called. "Captain, you may dock now. I'm Osman. I'm the official agent who will assist you with your cargo. Please let me come aboard. Have the cook prepare tea, so we can converse like civilized people."

Nur min Awa came to and fastened thick braided cables to the rusty dock cleats. A woven mat was placed on the deck for Osman, Omar, and the captain to sit on. The cook served sweet spiced tea.

Osman's hands shot short abrupt gestures in all directions. His tone did not change much after he yelled at the fighters a few minutes earlier.

"You brought what we need? You brought the agreed amounts? Correct? Yes?"

Omar nodded. He did not wish to talk about large sums of money within earshot of others. He would be sleeping with the money on the deck again that night.

"The tea is good. Tomorrow morning I'll come at eight o'clock. Eight o'clock precisely. I've arranged to check the warehouse first. Be ready. Do you have any questions?"

Omar was in his own country, but this criminal economy with no rules was alien to him. He didn't know how to read the signals or assess the risks. One wrong step, and things could spin out of control. "Well, do you have any advice for me?" he asked.

"You need to be careful of General Ibrahim's warehouse boys in the morning. They are in a bad mood until they get their qat. I'll bring some for them. The sooner we can be done with them in the morning, the better." Osman gave a quick smile. "And don't make any sudden moves.

"Another thing, always call the general 'General.' Do it as much as possible. It appeals to his vanity." Osman gave a quick frown. "We need to have a very good relationship with him. Otherwise we can do nothing," Osman explained. "Nothing at all in Merka. Do you understand?"

Omar nodded as Osman peered into his eyes to confirm his sincerity. "Good. I'll see you tomorrow." Osman said.

At 8:00 a.m. the following morning, Osman drove down the jetty to fetch Omar in his technical. "You have the bag, yes? Good. Quick, quick. Let's go before these dock boys wake up."

When they got off the jetty, Osman's two escort vehicles fell in behind them.

"We'll go around the town to the warehouse."

A dusty track edged along the tattered outskirts of town. Omar looked out the window at a field crowded with thousands of mounds. Here and there small clusters of people huddled together.

"There are always those who don't quite make it through the night. Nobody wants a corpse in their house when it gets hot," Osman said.

Some mounds had a few rocks placed on top or sticks stuck into the ground as a fleeting memorial to lives buried in the shifting sands. As the lumpy field of shallow graves thinned out, they drove past a solitary woman slowly digging a hole beside a shroud the size of a cat. Just beyond a stone's throw, feral dogs sat and watched.

"We are a big town. More than two hundred thousand people. This is why it's so important for the Dinar business. Don't forget that. Mohammed would be furious if I—or you—damaged this market." They pulled up to a large, old concrete building with a rusty corrugated iron roof standing a few kilometres beyond the end of town.

A sullen group of scruffy teenagers sat on the ground with their backs against the building. They held their machine guns casually on their laps and glared at the visitors. One of them, probably their leader, grudgingly got to his feet and approached the vehicle. "What do you think you're doing here? Go away."

He came closer and squinted at the two men in the car. His thin lips stretched into a reptilian smile. "Oh. It's you, Osman. What have you got for us?" He sounded vaguely hopeful.

"Here is a small gift. My purpose is to view your goods." Osman held out a bag of qat. The guard brightened. It would be enough to take the edge off their hangover and help bridge to the next delivery.

"You are here at a good time. We just received new goods," the guard said. "Come, come inside."

Osman handed the bag of qat to the boy, who hurried to his comrades. Their irritable indolence shifted to eager expectation.

Inside, the warehouse was pitch-black at first. Looking up, Omar was reminded of bright stars in the night sky as the hot light from the morning sun penetrated bullet holes in the roof. When his eyes adjusted to the gloom, he saw tons of food.

Osman took out a small notebook and ballpoint pen from his pocket. "We can load fifteen metric tons comfortably in our ship," he said. "This looks like about six tons of vegetable oil, the highest-value item." Shiny tins with red, white, and blue colours gleamed in the darkness. They were marked with the image of shaking hands. "Those American cans travel well, and the market has a high acceptance for the quality of US food aid. We'll take it all. You go check out those bags of wheat with the maple leaf, and I'll see what else is here."

After examining the stock, Osman conferred again with Omar. "Nobody really likes that Japanese rice," Osman said. "Too sticky.

But the Canadian wheat sells fast to the bakers. There's a lot of that here, so we can take five tons. We haven't tried to market that UN soy biscuit product for children yet. They say it's nice and sweet, that it's good with a cup of tea. Maybe a half-ton is worth a try. Wait, what's that in the corner?"

They both walked toward a cluster of burlap sacks sitting upright and open at the top. Osman reached in and pulled out a handful of what looked like orange pebbles. He popped one in his mouth and started crunching, then chewing thoughtfully. "Nice, nice quality. We'll take this too. The market for gum Arabic is excellent these days. Okay. We can go now. That was good."

"Where are we going now?" Omar asked.

"I told you. Ibrahim is the one we do business with. What do we call him?" Osman quizzed.

"General. We call him General as many times as possible," Omar said.

Osman nodded. "I don't like him much, but never mind."

"Has he been a general for long? I thought our army was finished."

Osman told his escort to stay at the warehouse. "Don't let those uneducated boys sell our goods to anybody else." He chuckled as he slid behind the wheel and started the truck. "To what rank would you promote yourself? Of course he's a general, but it's his own personal army."

Osman drove to Ibrahim's compound with nervous alertness. He constantly looked from side to side and checked the rearview mirror. The roads were strewn with rubble. There was a surprising amount of traffic. Blasted-out concrete buildings walled them in. It was crowded and utterly chaotic.

"Everyone must see General Ibrahim for any problem they have. This is why there are so many vehicles when we approach his compound. I'm sick of this traffic." Osman scowled. "No one has a licence or insurance. No police. Only guns."

At one intersection they saw a black technical about to butt heads with a tan one. The enraged drivers screamed at each other to give way.

"Maybe different clans. I can't tell," Osman said. "A matter of honour, perhaps. We wait."

A burst of gunfire silenced the furious exchange as fighters from the black truck rushed out of the rear bed, AK-47s at the ready. Osman put the vehicle in reverse and told Omar that they needed to find another route to the compound. Osman sighed. "There will be a settling of accounts. It seems to always happen in this neighbourhood. We are on the border between the Hawiye clan and the Bimals. They're constantly disputing control of this intersection. It's strategic because it controls access to Ibrahim's compound. I don't like the looks of this situation. These young boys with trucks and guns, you never know what they'll do. Especially before the qat comes. Then they can chew and calm down."

Osman found another way through and pulled up to the opaque face of a massive steel gate. It was painted blue with a bright white Somali star in the middle, like the national flag. A dozen or so men and women stood to the side of the gate. "What are these people waiting for?" Omar asked.

"They are supplicants. They need something from the general— or must ask his approval for something. Every day people line up in the hope he will agree to see them for a moment."

Omar looked to the side and saw fleeting silhouettes crossing in front of a blast hole in the ruins next door. It could be perimeter security, or it could be squatters.

The guards at the gate pointed their weapons at Osman. "What is your business here?"

"I'm Osman, Mohammed Dinar's agent. I have business to discuss with General Ibrahim. He knows me well."

They relayed the information inside by walkie-talkie and then slowly obeyed the order to admit the visitors.

"Now they will search us." Osman spat out the window. "It's undignified, but nothing can be done."

He drove through the open gate, and they both got out of their truck. Omar followed Osman to the guard post and, like his companion, raised his arms for the pat down.

"You tell Mr. Dinar that I'm getting too old for this kind of work. I need a better assignment," Osman said.

Omar's eyes widened, and his heart sank when he saw a poster on the guardhouse door. It was professionally printed and showed photographs. President Barre was at the top. In large letters it read, "If you see these war criminals, immediately make your report to General Ibrahim. A large reward will be provided." Omar was one of the photographs in the second row under Barre along with the rest of the cabinet ministers. Half of them had an X through their pictures and "Deceased" written under their name. He was clean-shaven and wore a suit and tie in the picture. Would his short beard and traditional clothes be sufficient disguise? On the bottom of the poster was the Italian flag and UN symbol.

Omar felt as if he had bumbled naked into a pack of rabid hyenas. He turned to the wall and kept his face averted from the guards as they patted him down.

"Wait outside the headquarters," the lead guard said. "You'll be called when it's time."

Osman began the long walk across the sandy surface of the compound toward a large ornate house. As they walked, he explained the layout to Omar. "We are walking across the parade ground, as the general calls it. You see those concrete buildings along the wall? Barracks for his fighters." Omar saw a tidy row of Hilux technicals next to perimeter wall. "The oil barrels you see are full of gasoline for the general's vehicles and generators. The Italians give it to him."

Three shipping containers were next to the barracks. "The prison." Osman said. "It's bigger than the last time I was here."

"How hot must it be inside?" Omar wondered aloud.

"Hot enough to kill. That happens sometimes on warm days. The prisoners are not normally released. Once the general has what he wants from them, they are finished." Osman grimaced. "So, we all try hard to please him. That is the best."

Ahead of them was an undamaged villa, its concrete walls freshly painted yellow and white. It had terraces and arches, like the house of a rich family.

"And this is the headquarters. Nice, is it not? He refurbished it recently. It contains his living quarters, dining area, and the meeting room where we will talk."

"Is that a clinic or a women's residence next to the headquarters?" Omar gestured to a low building with women lounging in the shade of the veranda. Omar was stunned to see that the young girls had red lipstick and black kohl around their eyes. "What are those women doing?"

"This is his harem, as he calls it. He takes the daughters of his enemies as whores for his army. I don't like it, but what can you do?" Osman turned up his nose as if he had just been served rotten fish.

They entered the antechamber, which was ringed with white plastic chairs. Two peacekeepers were looking over a set of papers and chatting in Italian. With reckless curiosity, Osman sat next to them.

"*Buongiorno, amici.*" They ignored his greeting. He looked over at their papers. "And what business brings you here?" he said amiably in English. "Those look like contracts. We are also businessmen. Perhaps we can be of assistance to you."

The younger soldier seemed pleased with the opportunity to converse. "Hello, we are from the finance unit of the battle group. We have contracts with General Ibrahim. He manages the port and food delivery. What is your business, sir?"

Before Osman could answer, a fighter came out to usher the peacekeepers into Ibrahim's presence.

"How interesting," Osman whispered to Omar. "The business opportunities are big with these peacekeepers. At first I thought they would do everything themselves. Now I see they can buy what they need from Ibrahim. He must be making a fortune. There's no competition."

"What does that mean for Mohammed's business?"

"It means it would be crazy for us to compete with Ibrahim," Osman said in a sad whisper. "Someone could get killed. Probably me."

They waited in uncomfortable silence for their turn. About ten minutes later, the door opened, and the soldiers left. Ibrahim stepped into the antechamber. His eyes were cold and intelligent. He had the manner of a carnivore atop the food chain of his natural habitat. With a jolt, Omar realized he knew him from somewhere.

Ibrahim spoke to them in educated and formal Somali. "*Salaam walekum*, Osman. How are you? How is your family? Please come into my office. Sit, and tea will be served."

The voice surfaced a memory. This was the young man who often accompanied his powerful father, the chief of intelligence, to the presidential palace. They had been introduced. Ibrahim was a former military intelligence officer. Ibrahim would have a mental file on all men of consequence from the collapsed regime. Omar quelled his rising panic. It was essential to remain calm.

Osman made a show of respect, formality, and deference. They sat, and a servant poured spiced tea from a brass teapot into small glasses.

"My family is well, thanks be to Allah," Osman said. "And thank you, General. I trust your business is healthy and prospering. As always, I'm grateful to you for receiving us."

Ibrahim's face darkened. "Please introduce me to your companion. I'm not accustomed to dealing with strangers in matters of business. You did not advise me that you would be accompanied. I must be informed of my visitors in advance. You did not do this."

"Yes, yes, General Ibrahim. Please forgive me. Haji Omar is the personal envoy of Mr. Mohammed Dinar. He has come with Mr. Dinar's trading instructions. His presence is a token of the personal esteem with which you're held by Mr. Dinar." Osman looked expectantly for Ibrahim's reaction.

"If his esteem is so high, I would have imagined that Mohammed would be here with us in person." Ibrahim's eyes narrowed. "Tell Mohammed to visit me soon. Of course, I'll personally guarantee his security and profitable transactions. I have future plans for our relationship. But today you bring me this stranger." Ibrahim turned to Omar. "Tell me about yourself. What is your clan and family? I'm sure a man of your station and qualifications must have personal friends with whom I'm acquainted. In fact, we have probably met before."

"General Ibrahim, I also thank you for receiving us, and I present to you the compliments of Mohammed Dinar," Omar said. He pulled from his bag the money Mohammed had given him for Ibrahim and handed it over. "He especially asked that I express the esteem in which you're held by Mr. Dinar with this gift. You don't know me because my family has been many years working in the Gulf. We have a small trading and financial business in Dubai and long business relationships with the Dinar family. Our fathers were friends and business associates." Omar couldn't tell if Ibrahim was buying his story. "We are from the Ishaaq clan. Originally from the north. But my family left prior to independence in 1960. These are the reasons you may not know me."

"How is it you speak with the Mogadishu accent, like me?" Ibrahim asked. "You don't have a northern accent."

Omar scrambled for an answer. "This is the accent of the Somalis in the Gulf, as you must know. You have been there, yes?"

Ibrahim did not answer. Omar felt Ibrahim's eyes crawling like spiders all over his face, probing for a trace to rouse a recollection. Then he let it go. "With time I'll find a connection between us. With time. Meanwhile, business is business."

Ibrahim slowly and carefully counted the money Omar had given him. As he did, Omar recalled the first time he had seen Ibrahim. Years earlier they had been at a wedding of one of the president's nieces. Ibrahim's father escorted young Ibrahim around the crowd, introducing him to future high-level contacts. Omar was in a bad mood that night, unhappy to be at the marriage of a couple he neither knew nor cared about. He was particularly irritated by the president's nepotism, which kept burdening him with incompetents as the country's economy spiralled downward. So, when the chief of intelligence had asked him for a favour, to receive his son on a visit to the ministry and discuss his work, he had answered churlishly. He recalled his words vividly. "I'm afraid that won't be possible. I don't have anything to do with military intelligence. Isn't that a contradiction in terms, in any case?"

Those around them had laughed. The puzzled anger on the father's face and Ibrahim's crestfallen expression told Omar that he had humiliated them. They turned away wordlessly. All of his future encounters with the chief of intelligence had been stilted and cold.

The money counted, Ibrahim looked up. "Yes, that is the correct amount. What do you want to buy?"

"Five tons of oil, seven tons of flour, one half-ton of those biscuits for starving babies, and all of your gum arabic," Osman said.

Ibrahim nodded. "Fine. Now tell me if you have arms for sale."

Omar answered along the lines Mohammed had instructed. "You are indeed a valued client, General. As you know, our financial company has many customers and many contacts up and down this coast, as well as in Yemen. Following the collapse of the Ethiopian army to the rebels, an impressive supply of weaponry has come on the market. What do you need?"

Ibrahim smiled. "This is good news. I need to diversify my suppliers. For some reason my international friends are not as generous with weapons as I had hoped. Some nonsense about a UN arms embargo.

"While my personal preference is for the American M16, the Kalashnikov is the most suitable for my men and this environment. Of course, ammunition must be included in any package. Rifles without sufficient ammunition are of no value. Additionally, rocket-propelled grenade launchers are useful to me. I want the RPG-7, Chinese-made."

"Your needs correspond nicely to our supply." Omar said without having a clue what he was talking about. "What is the amount that you're thinking about?"

"To begin with, let's say one thousand rifles and five tons of ammunition. I'm told you have visited my warehouse. Take your food as a down payment."

Omar found himself in unfamiliar territory and hesitated. He did not know if he could deliver guns or when. Mohammed had been vague on details. He wondered what plans Ibrahim had for the weapons. They would allow him to outgun the peacekeepers and any other players in the region.

"Can you tell me more about your plans?" Omar inquired. "Perhaps there are additional items that we can provide to you."

"How long have you been outside your country, Omar?" Ibrahim replied with the impatient irritation of a man unaccustomed to explaining his actions. "Wake up! This country needs a leader with an iron fist. Can you do this or not? If you cannot, tell Dinar that I prefer capable partners with the goods that I need. I'm certain there are others besides Dinar. I intend to grow my organization rapidly. Come back soon, and we will finalize details, like price. Goodbye."

There was no more to be said. They left Ibrahim without shaking hands. Osman was unhappy.

"That went badly. You had better be able to deliver those guns and RPGs!" Osman's hands punched and pulled the air for emphasis. "And come back soon. I have no experience in this ugly line of trade. But I have to live here with this mess. My family too. Think of my daughters. I don't like it." He shuffled his feet and rubbed his face as he walked back to their vehicle.

"Why does he need so many guns? Who is his enemy? What business are the peacekeepers doing with him?" Omar asked with a feeling he was being naively blind to something.

"It's simple. Everything goes through Ibrahim. He's the most powerful man by far. Who better for a client? And who else would you have the peacekeepers deal with? But what do you want? To do business or question our clients? Be serious. Ibrahim always pays on time. Mr. Dinar has decided to do business with him, and that's why we're here."

A gust of super-heated wind blew dust in their faces. Omar's eyes stung. Osman sneezed and stopped. He pulled on Omar's sleeve. "Since when have we enjoyed the luxury of choosing our rulers?" he asked. "Since when can we only do business with the virtuous?"

Osman paused for effect, pointed a finger to the sky, and looked at Omar with wide eyes. "Since never—that's when! And those dogs who let this country fall apart, where are they now? Where are Barre and his band of traitors?"

The words stung Omar, and he felt a return of the dizzying guilt that he had tried to extinguish with the New Light Madrassa. There was nothing to be said.

"Apparently, you have nothing to say. Well, this conversation will lead us nowhere." Osman concluded. "Tomorrow you can depart. Let's organize the loading of our goods."

"No, take me to the mosque," Omar said. "I wish to perform my evening prayer with the community. I'll be back and wish to conduct myself properly."

"Very well." Osman looked at his watch. "It's three o'clock. I'll drop you off and pick you up after prayers. There's a nice mosque by the water, close to the dock. Be ready to go immediately after prayers. I don't like driving at night."

Four fighters ran up with their weapons trained on Osman and Omar. "Halt! The general requires your presence. Go back!"

38

OMAR AND OSMAN WERE shoved back into Ibrahim's presence. Osman tripped and sprawled face-first on the floor. The fighters laughed.

Ibrahim had dealt out so much terror that he could sense its presence and calibrate its intensity with precision. Sometimes it resembled the penetrating odour of turpentine. Sometimes it felt like an icy wind. Today fear was an aura of light in the dusty air.

Osman stood up, and a yellow light of growing peril illuminated his anguished face. Omar appeared to be summoning his strength to resist the fear within him. Ibrahim assumed they were both cowards. Nonetheless, it was always instructive to see how far their courage took them. Everyone was different.

Ibrahim got off his cushion and examined Omar's face. "In my position, it's wiser to suspect betrayal than to offer trust. This is why that foggy explanation of your past is no good. You're lying to me."

He put his hand on Omar's shoulder and felt it twitch. "I know you from somewhere. Don't you remember me? Perhaps you don't want to talk about it. But why would old acquaintances not renew their relationship?"

Omar glowed orange. "You must be confusing me with someone else." It was a naked and feeble lie.

"You know me, and you know my family, General," Osman said, his voice shaking. Ibrahim listened with pleasure to the stutter and quiver in his voice. "We have never been anything but loyal to you."

Ibrahim studied Osman's face, reading the contours of sub-surface panic like a surgeon deciding where to make an incision. "Yes, I know your house. Your wife is plump and juicy. Your three young daughters are fast approaching ripe womanhood. I know all about you, Osman."

"I was here in Merka and welcomed your arrival. I've been here many years, and I'll stay here," Osman said.

"Indeed, we have known each other from the beginning of my government. Tell me, when did your mysterious friend, Omar, join the Dinar business?"

Osman glared at Omar, seething with rage and fear, happy to betray. "Early 1991, my dear General. Omar came to Mohammed Dinar's house in 1991 and then did some kind of charity work in Dadaab. A school." Osman reminded Ibrahim of a nervous fat dog, unsure if it was about to receive a caress or a beating.

Ibrahim looked at Omar with fresh interest. "That is shortly after Barre's criminal government fell. Did you perform a service for the Barre government? That government of traitors?"

"No, I did not. This is the first time I've been back to our homeland, in the service of commerce."

Lying again. The glow of terror turned red. Ibrahim called out to the guard at the door. "Bring me the poster."

Ibrahim looked over the poster for a few seconds. This was an outstanding piece of good luck. "You look like Omar Khalil, Minister of Finance." He took his gold Cross pen from his shirt pocket and slowly drew an X across Omar's photo. "You know, I saw your vehicles leave that night. I was waiting with my father as Barre's convoy left. I know what was in the convoy. I remember that night as if it happened an hour ago.

"After you left, the chaos became even worse, if you can imagine. You should try to imagine. Imagine you were not too cowardly to run away. My father's dignity did not permit him to run. You remember him? The chief of intelligence?

"The families of our 'guests,' as my father liked to call them, went immediately to look for their loved ones in our prison. You see, he asked me to close things down properly. I did, and when the brothers and wives saw the bodies, they went to our house and dragged my father there. They found an imam at some mosque nearby. Of course, they said my father was guilty. He was sentenced to immediate beheading. There were guns, but nobody had the necessary sword. So they used their hands. They say he screamed and cried. I don't believe that part. I do believe that enough strong men can twist and tear a head off a body. I was not there, but I can see it clearly, nonetheless."

"We are so sorry for this terrible misfortune. Our deepest condolences," Osman said. "Knowing this tragedy and your unshakable fortitude, General, we will redouble our efforts to serve you. I'll make a full report to Mr. Dinar, and you will never be troubled by this man again."

"Osman, you go now. But do not leave your house. I'll send some of my people along to keep you company. To inform me of your actions and movements."

Osman scurried out. Ibrahim turned to Omar. "You have something I want. Where is it?"

"Barre took it," Omar lied.

"I don't think he kept it. If he had that gold, the Kenyans would have been much kinder. They kicked him out after two weeks. He is in filthy Nigeria, living like a pariah. You are not motivated enough to tell the truth."

Four fighters came in. Two held their assault rifles on Omar. Smiling, the other two took his arms and dragged him outside. The sun was blinding. The men and boys lounging around the compound all stared at him. Some laughed and shouted taunts.

"Now the fun begins!"

"Don't cry!"

"Time for the box!"

39

WHEN IBRAHIM ENTERED THE shipping container that they used for interrogation, Omar was tied with duct tape to a filthy steel office chair. The chair was fastened to the steel-plate floor with rusty bolts. Automotive and electrical tools were scattered on the floor, interspersed with bloody rags. It smelled like an outdoor toilet. The fighters exited, and the two gates to the container were left open to the parade ground. Curious onlookers peered in.

Ibrahim closed the container and switched on a bare bulb hanging from a wire. He didn't want others to hear what Omar would tell him.

Ibrahim reached for Omar's left hand, and Omar made a tight fist against the steel armrest. Ibrahim picked up a pair of grimy needle-nose pliers and gripped Omar's little finger between their jaws, prying it apart from his fist. He grabbed Omar's finger and pulled it back, dislocating it at the bottom knuckle. First was the popping noise from his hand. Then a wave of pain flooded his hand and climbed to his elbow. An involuntary howl escaped his lips. He stared in horror at the unnatural angle of his finger against his fist.

Ibrahim looked around the container, walked into its back, and picked up a black plastic garbage bag. He pulled it over Omar's head and held the corners tight around Omar's neck. Omar tried to take shallow breaths at infrequent intervals. His panic rose from the solar plexus to his heart and expanded to fill his chest. Omar thrashed his head back and forth in desperate uncontrollable terror. His body was starving for oxygen. Involuntary survival instincts took over. Omar's bladder evacuated, and he blacked out. Ibrahim had eliminated his free will rather easily.

Omar recovered consciousness, and his aura shone the intense red that only appears when a person thinks his or her life is about to end.

"You soiled yourself, Minister."

Terror mixed with defeat and exhaustion in Omar's face. It was not enough. More was needed to avenge the humiliation he had caused. Something permanent.

"For theft, the hands should be chopped off." Ibrahim said this for his own amusement. He had no intention of doing it. It had to be done for an audience, but he did not have one to appreciate the spectacle. Also, it usually killed from loss of blood or gangrene, and he needed Omar alive.

"For your hypocrisy and lies, the fitting punishment is removal of your tongue."

The aura turned deep purple. Ibrahim realized Omar was more afraid of losing his tongue than dying. In any case, Ibrahim needed him able to talk.

"Tell me where the gold is. That is your only way out."

"It's on Lamu." Omar said with abject defeat. "Some of the gold is in Lamu. Some has been traded." Omar's need to survive pushed his dignity out of the way. "Will you let me go?"

"Is it in Mohammed Dinar's house?"

Omar nodded. Ibrahim's face transformed into a kindly smile. "Tell Dinar to bring it to me," he said softly, "along with the weapons you promised."

"If he thinks you will kill me after you have what you want, maybe Mohammed won't do it," Omar said.

Ibrahim did not want blood on his clothes. He opened the doors and called in a fighter. "Right hand index finger." He instructed. The fighter found a pair of metal shears.

"What knuckle?"

"At the hand. Clip the whole finger off."

There was a crunch, a bellow of pain, and then sobbing from Omar. The fighter untied him and handed him a rag, which Omar clutched to his mangled hand to staunch the bleeding.

"This will help you and Mohammed understand that I'm serious. But I'm also restrained and reasonable. If others ask what happened to you, tell them this is the kind of workplace accident that often happens on ships.

"Now go to Dinar, and then come back. You'll bring me the gold. If you don't, we'll kill Osman and his family. They are innocent, but it will be as if you killed them yourself." He looked into Omar's eyes to make sure he understood. "And when I kill them, or perhaps take the women for my harem, everyone will know about Mohammed's betrayal of his own people. His business will suffer. Tell him to think of it as a business decision."

Omar nodded.

"My men will take you back to your ship. The loading should be finished soon."

40

OMAR WAS AT PEACE. The morphine felt so good. So did the bed and the gentle breeze of the ceiling fan. He opened his eyes and raised his arm to see a bandaged paw. He looked up and saw Diane looking down at him. The strange blue cloud around her head resolved into a hairnet. Diane was wearing blue scrubs. The expression on her face was dry and professional.

"Welcome back to the land of the living. Don't move. You have an IV in your arm. Any pain?"

He shook his head. "No."

"There will be. Tell me when it starts increasing, and I'll give you another dose."

He wanted to return to the numb oblivion of sleep. "I would like more now, please."

"It's nice, isn't it? You can't have one quite yet. Just be quiet, lie down and relax."

He looked at his bandage again.

"You still have four fingers," Diane said. "I don't think you'll lose the hand. Anik wants to see you. Don't move that arm, I said."

"Yes, I need to see her too." But who would he say he was? A war criminal who enabled crimes against humanity? A coward who didn't have the guts to get out while there was still time? He did save her life. That would surely weigh on the right side of the balance. The chemical comfort of the morphine dripped away and then vanished under a rain of physical and spiritual pain. He was lost and alone in a desert of failure. There was no honourable place to hide.

Diane returned with Anik. He could tell she had been sleeping from the way she rubbed her eyes. Anik had a notebook and pen. She sat on a chair beside him. She wore a clean white button-down blouse and faded jeans. There was a bit of colour on her tan face. The stitches had been removed from her lip. The red in her left eye was still livid testimony of what she had suffered through. The concern for him in her gentle gaze was the first ray of light to enter his black hole of solitude. He decided to shed his burden of deception and tell her everything.

"It's time for me to go," Anik said. "I need to put my life back together. I don't really think there's anything I can do here. Not anymore. Not after what happened. But before I say goodbye, I have questions for you. I'm so sorry for your injury," she added as an afterthought. "What happened? Are you ready to talk? Diane, is he?"

"Sure—if he wants. I just don't want him to move that damn hand," Diane said.

"I have things I need to tell you," Omar said. "I'm not who I told you I was. I was hiding, and I was discovered."

"What's that supposed to mean?" Anik asked, her brow furrowed with confusion.

"I was a minister in President Barre's government. I was pretending to be someone else. I pretended to be a schoolmaster. I pretended to be a business agent for Mohammed. I was discovered by Ibrahim Hussein. He controls Merka." It was a relief to get that out, but he feared her reaction.

Anik's smile faded to a neutral expression. She looked at her list of questions and then back at him. He was afraid of scaring her. She was calm. She was not frightened by him.

"Ibrahim Hussein. Women said that name. That he was involved. That he directed assaults on them. Is it the same person? Why did he want to hurt you?"

"He was with the Barre government too. Ibrahim and his father were in military intelligence. When Mogadishu fell, I escaped with President Barre. Ibrahim was left behind. He said he killed his prisoners and escaped to Merka, where he took over. He tortured me for revenge because I escaped with Barre, and he was betrayed by the president. He wanted information from me. He wanted to know about the gold."

Anik wrote in her notebook. "Is it the same person who directed the rapes?" Omar had feared that Anik would interrogate him like a war criminal. She hadn't done that, at least not yet. "Women said that a Colonel Ibrahim Hussein directed his men to perpetrate gang rapes as a weapon to intimidate, extort, and terrorize families and neighbourhoods. Could it be the same man?" A look of single-minded determination came over Anik's face. He could see that she was still driven by her work in Dadaab.

Nothing of what she described would happen without Ibrahim's approval. "Would he be capable of planning and ordering a sexual assault? Without doubt. He was unchallenged at the apex of power and control of Merka," she wrote.

Anik spoke to herself as she wrote in her notebook. "Means, motive, and opportunity. Armed men at his command are the means. The motive is extortion, intimidation, and social control. Unchallenged territorial control of Merka is the opportunity." She looked into Omar's face.

A spike of pain shot from his hand to his elbow. Omar grimaced. "That's right," he said through clenched teeth. "It must be him. It must be the same man who tortured me." He tried to keep his suffering off his face.

"Do you want that dose now?" Diane asked. Omar nodded.

"Don't give him too much, Diane. I need him to concentrate. I'm not finished," Anik said.

"Okay, okay. I'll just give him a touch. That should take the edge off. Men have lower pain thresholds than us, by the way, so you should cut him some slack," she muttered as she prepared the syringe. "Come back in fifteen. That Ibrahim sounds like such a motherfucker."

Omar felt the welcome sting of the needle in his arm and braced for the pain to recede. His loneliness receded first, and then he floated away from his grievous reality on a narcotic raft of wellbeing.

Anik returned in what felt like seconds.

"Was that fifteen minutes?"

"Yes," Diane said. "Back to work for you."

"How do you feel?" Anik asked.

"Diane is a good nurse," Omar replied. "Let's continue."

"Please listen carefully. Do you remember when we had dinner that night in Dadaab?"

"Yes. I remember we talked about your work. I said reports about the situation were not enough. Something should be done to change things."

"Right. The next day I gave my report to Zanov. He sent it to the UN in Mogadishu. It had the names of the victims and the assailants. In many cases Ibrahim Hussein was the accomplice. The report had my name on it. It showed that rape as a weapon didn't stop after the peacekeeping mission began.

"Ten days later I was attacked. The leader identified me by my first and last name. No refugee in the camp knows my last name. They destroyed my work and took my files. In my interview with Jameelah, she was scared that her rapist, and by extension, Ibrahim, had influence and presence in Dadaab. The report and my rape are linked. This leads me to conclude that the UN gave my report to the criminal who ordered my attack. The senior UN commander in Merka must, therefore, be the intellectual author and prime suspect. This is General Cristiani."

"They wanted to shut you down!" Diane exclaimed angrily.

"Osman told me that the peacekeepers work with Ibrahim," Omar said. "I saw them in his compound."

"In Detroit when crooked cops work with the mob and somebody smells a snitch, they shut it down—permanently. I don't see why it would be different in this Merka," Diane said.

The report would go from the UN to the area commander, Cristiani. How could it be any other way? "For the UN commander, this Cristiani, your report is devastating," Omar said. "If it became public that he was working with a warlord who uses rape as a weapon against people they are supposed to protect, it would be the end of his career and an international scandal for his country."

Anik nodded. "So, Cristiani had the means to direct the attack on me through Ibrahim's people in Dadaab, and he had the motive because of my report and the threat I would continue. The opportunity was his influence on Ibrahim. It fits now." Her eyes had a stainless-steel glint in them. "It's unforgivable."

Omar was not alone anymore. Now he and Anik shared an anguish and a growing rage. Perhaps retribution could bring them together.

"You said something about gold," Anik said.

Omar yanked the IV from his arm.

"Jesus Christ, Omar! What are you doing?" Diane said.

He got up, swayed, and then recovered his balance. "Help me down the stairs," he told Diane. Anik followed them.

In Mohammed's office Omar took a set of keys from a drawer. They went out the front entrance, across the front of the house, and through a dark, narrow walkway. The dank stone walls closed in. A rat scurried through the trash at their feet. They stopped in front of a low door. It was massive, ancient, and looked abandoned.

Thick iron hinges were fastened by hand-beaten rivets. The door was secured with a weighty padlock.

With a turn of the key, the lock snapped open. The door yielded to their entry with a groan. Cold, moldy air wafted into Anik's nose.

Omar placed a thick steel bar across the door and flipped a switch with his shoulder. A florescent tube hanging from the vaulted stone ceiling illuminated a slimy green stone stairway. The steps were smooth and sloped from countless feet bearing centuries of Indian ocean trade.

Water wept from the walls. He flipped another switch, and the cold light lit rows of stone pillars and arches bearing the heavy house above. Thick green fungus covered the porous coral walls like leprosy.

He was getting tired and leaned heavily on Diane as they went to the far corner of the cellar. "Anik, please take that tarp off." She gingerly pulled the frayed canvas tarp off of the stack of khaki ammunition boxes. "Open one." The gold ingots gleamed warmly, as if from an inner light.

"Twenty-five million dollars," Omar said. "To buy some justice."

41

IBRAHIM CHEWED FURIOUSLY ON a twig of qat. When he was stressed, he needed to chew. He always felt so unfairly judged by the foreigners. What would be praised and celebrated as the finest hospitality in Merka would have these infidel Europeans turning up their noses. They couldn't get used to eating with their hands, and they were uncouth in their clumsy attempts to do so. Quality food was hard to find, and he had killed one of his best young camels for Cristiani's farewell dinner that night. European tastes were incomprehensible to him, even after all these months with Italians for neighbours. There could be no wine or whisky. That would offend the elders. There would be spaghetti. Cristiani should like that anyway.

He started to feel the pressure of the masticated green leaves on his inner cheek. He stopped nibbling before there was a visible protrusion. He didn't want green dribble on the fine clothing he had purchased especially for that night.

The darkening compound was full of his fighters doing their best to follow his order to look disciplined and serious. He had invited the notables of Merka and a dozen of his trusted accomplices to the dinner. They stood together talking. Their chatter came to a halt when they heard the shrill creaking of the steel hinges of the heavy metal door to his compound. Sand crunched as the heavy armoured vehicles rolled up in the hot, humid evening. *The bastard better not forget to call me General,* Ibrahim thought.

As Cristiani descended from his vehicle, Ibrahim put on his best smile and spread his arms in welcome for everyone to see. "My fren, my fren, General! Please be welcome to my home. Come, we talk before dinner. Come with me."

Cristiani winced when Ibrahim took him by the hand. Ibrahim was once again baffled that these educated people still didn't understand this masculine custom. Two soldiers entered Ibrahim's building to do a security check before Cristiani entered. They came back and reported to Cristiani. Ibrahim saw that the bodyguards were nervous. He knew from his own military training that retreat brought vulnerabilities and could be a dangerous moment.

"Doan worry so much. Your guards can stay outside my office. No problem. You need them, you call them. Come." Ibrahim led Cristiani into the meeting room.

Ibrahim had arranged chairs and a table in his office for the occasion. Unfortunately, the only thing he could get was the ubiquitous white extruded plastic.

They both sat down. Cristiani started talking without even the pretense of a customary greeting. "Colonel Hussein, our partnership has been good. But it's over now, and my mission is complete."

"Please remember, I'm a general. Have you told your new general about our arrangements? Also, tell him I'm a general, same rank like you."

"These arrangements are between you and me. It will be up to you and him to work out what comes next. I took risks to support you. I overlooked things that came to my attention about the way you do business. Ugly things. I don't expect he will support you as

I have. In fact, his main task will be to pack up and leave. We are finished here."

"You should help me more before you leave. You should thank me more." Ibrahim was asking for just this one small thing, a signal of UN approval of his control and authority.

"We had a mutually beneficial relationship for a defined period of time," Cristiani replied. "The concessions and contracts I gave you for the seaport and airport and food distribution were part of an agreement for a limited time. That time is coming to an end. The contracts end with my departure."

This was bad news, and Cristiani's haughty tone was infuriating. It was as if he had never understood how dependent he was on Ibrahim. He never understood how Ibrahim permitted him to operate successfully there. Now when he needed Cristiani to do one small thing for him in front of the elders, all he was getting was arrogance and hypocrisy.

"Remember, Ibrahim, you would be nothing without me. Think about how much our arrangement helped you grow, helped you with money. Your political future is not my concern," Cristiani said. This was the wrong thing for him to say. He had learned nothing.

"But maybe you would be dead without me too," Ibrahim replied. "We need each other. You need to tell people about me. You need to make sure our arrangement continues."

Cristiani shook his head. "That's not the way it works. When I transfer command, everything is up to my replacement. Our contract ends now, as do our arrangements."

This was not what he planned. Ibrahim had control of Merka, but there were no guarantees for the future. He worried about challenges from neighbouring warlords. They would covet his territory, weapons, and men. Once the peacekeepers left, there would be dangerous new rivalries. He couldn't afford to start over. If he lost his position, he would be killed, perhaps as his father had been.

Ibrahim wanted to organize an immediate, painful, and public killing of Cristiani and his men. It would give him great pleasure, satisfy his sense of fairness, and increase his stature in the community. Of course, it would be too risky and could undermine his longer-term political strategy.

"You better be careful about cancelling anything. You should keep doin' what work so well. Maybe I start telling Merka people you soldiers shouldn't be here. What if I start tellin' people I doan care they steal from you? What if I doan care if they shoot you soldiers?"

"I don't understand. You wouldn't do that. You couldn't do that," Cristiani said, a frown of confusion on his face.

"I need you tell everybody. Tell UN and Americans that Merka is my town, that I'm the governor of Merka. You must tell them support me. You tell them Somalia need me." He saw doubt and weakness in Cristiani's face. It was time to exert some leverage.

"Maybe I have things to say you doan wan. You never asked me what happen to the prisoners you give me. You never asked me about you soldiers fucking my women. You never asked me about a lot of things. You never asked me how I stop those reports about Dadaab. Doan you wanna know about Anik Belanger? I send my men on mission to rape her. They do it for you. It worked, right? No more reports."

Cristiani's head fell in his hands. Then he looked up with a blank face. "Are you blackmailing me?"

"Little bit. I doan wan to. I doan haff to now. But I need you help me. I told you what I need. Merka is my town. My country needs me. I know how to keep the people quiet. Keep things under control and safe for you. Tell everybody that. Tell everybody call me General."

Cristiani's frown deepened, and his eyebrows furrowed in anxiety. "I'll do what I can."

Ibrahim was exasperated and impatient, but there was nothing more to be gained from this conversation. "My guests waiting. We go in now," he said. Cristiani glared angrily at him.

They walked into the main receiving room. It was spread with carpets, and on the carpets sat platters of food. Ibrahim had decided that Cristiani could sit on the floor like everybody else. He gestured for him to sit beside him and with his hand served stewed camel hump, raw camel liver, and spaghetti with tomato sauce and a banana onto his plate. There was no cutlery.

Ibrahim stood up and addressed the crowd in Somali. "Today we bid farewell to my friend and fellow general, Giancarlo Cristiani. He came with his soldiers from a distant land to bring us assistance when we needed it. This man also showed the wisdom to listen to us, to respect our customs and way of life. He is my friend, and he asked me to convey a message to you. He said the United Nations and the United States wish me to be recognized as governor of our region. His excellency General Giancarlo Cristiani requests that you accept this and give me your support. It will soon be time for the foreigners to leave, but they need Somali leaders who can take responsibility for security and food aid. This will be me. Please express to me your agreement by clapping."

The elders knew better than to debate, and Ibrahim received a warm round of applause.

Cristiani gave a phony smile, stood up, and applauded, nodding toward Ibrahim. It was good enough for the purposes of showing support for Ibrahim's position.

"What did you tell them?"

"I tell them what a wonderful work you do here. Now we must make democracy and free market from you example. Please eat."

They ate in silence. The food was consumed quickly. Cristiani only took a bite of his banana.

Afterwards, Ibrahim walked Cristiani back to his vehicle.

"Goodbye," Cristiani said.

"Doan you wanna say thank you? Doan you wanna see me again?" Ibrahim asked.

Cristiani did not reply; he just climbed silently into his armoured personnel carrier.

Ibrahim had a sad feeling of rejection. He walked soberly back into the building and sent for his accountant. His money was running short, and he had to ration qat to his fighters. Morale was going down too. Things would be changing, and he needed to plan for the future.

"How are the finances?"

"You have approximately two hundred and fifty thousand in various currencies: US dollars, Saudi riyals, French francs, Kenyan shillings, and Ethiopian birr. Also, you have the largest and finest camel herd in Somalia now."

"I don't want to liquidate my camels. The old men respect camels when all else fails. What about commitments and liabilities?"

"The news is not good. Our projected cash liabilities for the coming year are five times that."

"So, you're saying we need more revenue?"

"Yes. And soon. The peacekeepers have stopped providing fuel for our vehicles and generators. You have a large account receivable from Mohammed Dinar. He took vegetable oil and other food products on credit. I believe you had a swap for arms. In the ledger, it says he owes us one hundred and thirty thousand."

"Call it in. Tell him we will be wanting our money back plus 10 percent interest. Remind them about Osman. If we don't get the money, it's time to start killing Osman's family."

42

CRISTIANI LAY IN HIS hotel bed. In his mind he played with the idea that he had changed planets. Planet Rome was safe and beautiful. Planet Somalia was ugly and treacherous. But it could never touch him again. Fine linens caressed his silk pajamas, and a top-quality mattress held him in a seductive soft embrace. Good wine tasted better than ever. The Roman women carried themselves with sensual elegance, as if it was their civic duty. He was tired though and conscious of his need to maintain focus. It was time to cash in his sacrifice and success in Merka for his next step up in the world and in rank.

At fifty-five, Cristiani felt his age and took his time getting out of bed. He had navigated his nine-month tour of duty with no explicit missteps—or at least none visible to his superiors. True, there was some messiness and a few loose ends with Ibrahim. *C'est la guerre*, it didn't matter now.

For the day's meeting he put on his new non-combat uniform, made to measure by his longtime tailor. He had lost some weight, and it fit well.

Breakfast arrived at his room. He was uncharacteristically pensive. Peering into his coffee, he considered the fact that his military career had consumed his entire adult life. He was separated from his wife. There was no point even calling or visiting. The marriage was loveless and childless. The estrangement was saturated with mutual recriminations, leaving no space for reconciliation.

He took another sip of black, bitter espresso. In a moment of sincere self-awareness, it was clear to him that his self-esteem depended on his rank and advancement. Could it be that he did not have a sense of self that was independent of his dominance over subordinates and his obedience to superiors? He looked at his feet. His critical eye could find no flaw in the gleam on the brown leather shoes that he had instructed the hotel to shine with special attention.

He had five medals for his UN campaigns attached to his medal bar brooch. He carefully attached the medals to the right breast of his uniform jacket. He expected the chief would award him two more: one for Operation Restore Hope and the War Merit Cross for his leadership in combat. That would make for an impressive second row of medals. His spirits began to improve. He picked up his empty briefcase and went down to the lobby.

His official car was waiting. Cristiani took in the magnificence of the architecture that culminated in the approach to the Palazzo del Quirinale. Like a celestial body spiralling toward the sun, he felt the gravitational pull of state power.

They drove around the presidential residence to the headquarters of the armed forces, where a major was waiting to escort him to see the chief of staff. After a brief wait in the lobby, he was called into the chief of staff's office. Cristiani strode into the room and gave his best salute. The chief looked older and fatter. He looked tired too. From behind his desk, he returned the salute and motioned for Cristiani to sit down.

"Well, Giancarlo, here we are again. Welcome home."

"Thank you, sir. It's good to be home."

"I haven't read your report yet. What did you conclude about your mission?"

Giancarlo had expected a friendlier tone. He had expected some more warmth and gratitude. He adopted a more formal tone. "I reported that we must adapt to a new kind of war, one without victory or defeat. In this new war, we must search for and find allies in the population and enable their success. This gives us the conditions that we need in order to leave.

"These allies will not be the darlings of the NGOs, but they will have the ability to keep from getting killed, to command the respect of their compatriots, and to control territory.

"We created those conditions in our area of responsibility with Ibrahim Hussein. My relationship with the Americans was constructive and without friction. I believe my mission was, therefore, successful."

"And, of course, the mission of your men, I'm sure you mean. We ask them to give their lives or their health or their sanity for these missions. Never forget that," the chief said with irritation. "Nobody died, is that correct?"

"Naturally, the mission of my men as well. There were few casualties. No fatalities. I consider it a major achievement."

"The application of Machiavelli to the work of peacekeeping," the chief said. "Well done, I suppose. At the same time, I don't imagine we will have any monuments for this war, or whatever it is. No victory and no statues. Those days are over. You'll get your medals, of course."

Cristiani smiled at the well-deserved recognition of his intellectual and strategic contribution. "I conducted our operation with political sensitivity to the realities of Rome, Washington, and Somalia—simultaneously, as you ordered me to do. We compared well with other nations and brought credit to our country. Especially after that humiliating American debacle with the helicopter crash and pandemonium in Mogadishu."

"Well, congratulations are in order. It has been a long time since a military man in our country has enjoyed such a positive media profile. Remember when we first talked about this in Washington?"

"Vividly. Whatever happened to our ambassador there? I lost track."

"Julius was a good man. He retired shortly thereafter. Then he died. Without his diplomatic career, there was little to live for. Sad, but not surprising.

"I forget, Giancarlo, did you thank me when I gave you your command?"

"It's not necessary to thank commanders for orders."

"Right. Now I remember." The chief's tone was dry and businesslike. "Well, you should thank me. Somalia got you your next job. It's in NATO. I think they will like your ideas, and Brussels will suit you.

"I've lined you up for the position of director general, international military staff. Our European colleagues are intrigued by your low-combat/low-casualties approach and want to hear all about it. It's a good position and sets you up for something even better in the future. You'll be going there in a couple of days to present yourself. They need to see you in person before it all goes through. Tell them about your Cristiani Doctrine." He paused. "What is your ultimate ambition, Giancarlo?"

Cristiani had thought about this on the drive to the meeting. He could do two more assignments before mandatory retirement. Something with international profile, prestige, and positioning for lucrative consulting contracts would be best. "I would like to be head of UN peacekeeping. I like New York, and I'm attracted to the UN's global scope."

"That's usually held by a civilian, but why not? You seem to cope with Africa too, where most of these civil wars are for some reason. Who knows what the future holds for us military men? Sometimes I think we'll be out of business before too long. The

Berlin Wall is down, and the Russians have backed off. Reports are even coming out of Oslo that the Israelis and Palestinians are ready to shake hands." The chief shook his head in wonder. "What about leave? Are you taking a vacation? You need one. I insist."

"I thought I would spend some time with my family," Cristiani said. He had no intention of doing any such thing, but neither did he have any plans. Now he regretted his inattention to organizing a personal life for himself.

"I don't recommend you go straight to your family," the chief said. After an assignment like you had, it's better to take some time alone to decompress before your family sees you. Time to get back to the way you were before all this. Did you ever go to Mombasa, where your men took leave?"

"No, sir. I took no leave during the deployment."

"It's such a beautiful part of the world. In fact, there's a little hotel on an island not too far from there. The wife and I just loved it last year. Very exclusive. No one will recognize you, and you can just forget about everything for a week. It's called Lamu. Go there right after your NATO presentation. I insist. We'll make the arrangements from here. You'll go on one of our regular flights to Mombasa. Don't argue. You deserve it."

"Yes, sir." Cristiani smiled. A vacation would be nice.

43

BEFORE HE LEFT FOR Lamu, Cristiani was to make a presentation and take questions in NATO's main conference room. The huge circular table was dotted with delegation microphones and surrounded by a rich carpet in which the four-pointed star of the North Atlantic Treaty Alliance was woven. He had a seat in the area for the Italian delegation. He stood up and watched from behind the US delegation as ambassadors and their military advisors gossiped, traded secrets, and fished for intelligence in the minutes before the meeting was called to order. In the US delegation he saw Samson in a new blue suit and red silk tie. Samson met his eyes and motioned him to the side of the room.

"Not bad, not bad at all," Samson said. "Director General, International Military Staff. That's a good job, and a big one."

"Thank you very much, Randy. As you know, it hasn't been announced yet. I can't take anything for granted."

"Don't worry, we've intercepted more than enough of these . . ." Samson surveyed the room, "so-called secret cables to know you had it in the bag all along."

Cristiani had been pretty certain it would go his way, and this gave him full confidence that everything was on track.

"We figure it's a kind of quid pro quo for you coming on our team in the Somalia campaign. It's good to have someone we know as intimately as we know you in that kind of job." Samson showed his teeth in a grin. Cristiani shrugged off a small shiver. Samson knew everything about him, including the reputational risk of those rapes in his area of responsibility.

The secretary general tapped the microphone to call the meeting to order. "Excellencies, I'm pleased to announce the new Director General, International Military Staff, Major General Giancarlo Cristiani. General Cristiani distinguished himself in Somalia with an innovative strategic vision and operational skill in the management of complex operations in our new threat environment. The position of DGIMS, for which Italy has put him forward, is responsible for policy advice and strategic direction to the Military Committee. As you know, the Military Committee advises the political leaders of our countries on military actions. General Cristiani will be a key player as we build our capabilities and elaborate plans to face the threats of the twenty-first century. General, you have the floor."

Cristiani approached the podium with the gait of a top commander. His back was straight as a steel girder. The steps of his glossy shoes on the thick carpet were even, purposeful, and unhurried. He was happy and confident in his abilities. The Brussels position would give him what he wanted for the next two years. It would be an excellent platform from which to secure the pinnacle of his ambition: head of UN peacekeeping.

At the lectern, he turned his educated British accent up a notch. "Mr. Secretary General, your excellencies, generals, friends, and colleagues. I'm honoured to be my nation's nominee for the position of director general, international military staff. Please allow me to share with you my sense of the strategic climate and tactical challenges the members of this great alliance will share in the coming five-year planning period.

"Our operation in Somalia signals a fundamental geopolitical transition. We no longer face threats posed by strong, unified nation states. We must prepare for the amorphous new threats of weakness and governmental collapse.

"It's too soon to claim victory in the Horn of Africa or in the Somalia campaign. The gains we have made are yet to be consolidated. Challenges remain, and improvements to the humanitarian situation are incomplete.

"And so, it's too soon for us to leave. Of course, these decisions will depend on the UN Security Council. At the same time, in my view, and based on my experience, the North Atlantic Treaty Organization must rapidly shift gears to our new strategic environment. I believe the alternative to vigorous Western military political leadership will be stagnation, chaos, and new threats to the civilized world from failed states.

"We cannot ignore the democratic shortcomings of colonialism, but it did have the advantage of political military organization on a global scale.

"With the end of the Cold War, we have an opportunity to give new structure and direction to the geopolitical landscape. My contention is that the military perspective corresponds most closely to the reality of our new challenges and should play the policy leadership role.

"We learned in Somalia that it's not the diplomats, and it's not the aid workers—it's the military commander who is closest to the Somali community and understands the needs best. It's the military that has the training and capabilities necessary for operating in the non-permissive theatres of civil conflict. Whether it's in the Balkans, Somalia, or the Middle East, we will be going to failed states. It's the international military leader who has the strategically decisive relationships with the strategically important local leaders. This is what explains our success.

"As you know, I want to bring my hard-won experience to benefit security affairs more broadly in NATO. I want to bring the lessons we learned to the new challenges that we, the military leaders of democratic countries, face in future campaigns. Thank you."

He received warm applause. It was longer and louder than he had anticipated. He felt a surge of pride and satisfaction that his provocative new thinking was right on the mark. He felt more than ever that he could transform his Cristiani Doctrine into international policy. Samson would approve of forward-leaning military solutions. That would be good for spies.

A junior diplomat from the Danish delegation was the first to ask a question. It was cheeky not to wait for his seniors, Cristiani thought.

"The warlords have a terrible reputation for cruelty," the young man said in a high and self-important voice. "What about human rights, and what about international humanitarian law? How do these factor in to your new strategic concept?"

Cristiani did not hesitate. "Has the distinguished representative of Denmark been to Somalia?" The surprised diplomat shook his head. "You must understand that when states collapse, there is no law. No elections, no parliament, no police, no judges, and no trials. All that remains is power. If the right people have the power, like we do, the rest follows."

He looked around and saw in the expressions of his military colleagues both sympathy for what he had said and an interest in where he was going next.

"And so the task of the expeditionary campaign in these settings is to identify who has power over the people. This is the critical enabler for anything you wish to do. My choice, and I believe the chief factor of my success, was my working relationship with the local leadership.

"You see," Cristiani continued, secure in his intellectual authority on the subject, "we want to leave. We do not wish to occupy, and we must empower, shape, and instruct the local leadership to assume their responsibilities once we have stabilized the situation and addressed the humanitarian need. I believe this merits consideration and reflection at the level of doctrine and strategy. What you call a warlord is, in reality, an emerging leader."

The Secretary General gave him a warm smile and started to clap. Starting with the Italian delegation, then Samson, the room came to its feet and a warm round of applause washed over him. The Secretary General shook Cristiani's hand and said for all to hear, "Congratulations. The job is yours."

44

THE SUN DEGRADED FROM violent pink to smoldering umber. Ibrahim stood with his deputy in front of his quarters. He observed the dusty parade ground, watching the gate.

"The peacekeepers are only patrolling around their base and at the port where they're loading up," Abdi said. "They don't come into the city anymore. Everybody is asking when their last day is. Why don't they tell us?"

Ibrahim was frustrated and impatient with his deputy's ignorance of basic military principles. "They are keeping it an operational secret. A military unit is most vulnerable in retreat. That's when your back is turned, and you have nothing in reserve." Of course, it was the same for Ibrahim. He could never leave or show weakness. He was bound to this path of cruelty and terror as a matter of survival. And now his forces would look small and vulnerable without his alliance with the peacekeepers. That would be all right if all he had to worry about was controlling Merka. But now the predatory General Mohammed Hersi Morgan, who controlled the port of Kismayo down the coast, was eyeing Merka. If Morgan took Merka, he could monopolize all shipping and piracy down to the Kenyan border. Other warlords were circling like sharks, ready to exploit any sign of weakness. Ibrahim's political gambit would infuriate Morgan and the others he excluded, but creating a coalition was the one thing that could improve his chances of survival and, just maybe, satisfy his ambitions.

Money was another agonizing problem. "Did Osman get on the boat to Lamu?" Ibrahim asked. A gust of wind blew dust and generator diesel fumes in his face. If he didn't get that cash from Mohammed Dinar soon, he would run out of fuel for his technicals. It was a shame to cancel the arms order, but cash was more important at the moment.

"As you instructed," Abdi said. "He will bring payment for the food when he returns on the next boat. We are keeping one daughter hostage as a guarantee. The little one. I think I should fuck her. It's only fair. To send a message."

"You are incorrigible. I told you no. We need this business relationship. What's more important—your prick or our money? Don't you remember how difficult it was to control the men when Mohammed schemed with his corrupt merchant friends and cut off our qat supply? Don't you remember how we had to lock up the weapons until the negotiations to release Osman were concluded, and we could resupply?" Ibrahim was furious. He also felt lonesome trying to lead under these impossible conditions. "Think about if we were attacked by Morgan at a moment of weakness like that. People would come looking for you first, Abdi. I have a mind to throw you naked into the street. The people would castrate you first, shove your genitals in your mouth, and then rip you to shreds. And you would deserve it."

It would be so different if he had that gold. At the moment though, it might as well be on the moon. There was no way he could mount an operation on Lamu. He probably couldn't keep such a thing secret anyway. The temptation to betray him would be irresistible. He couldn't help being sorry for himself.

He glared at Abdi. "You need to control your conduct." Chastened, Abdi looked at his feet.

"I don't have any more time to indulge in this nonsense," Ibrahim continued. "Remind me, what is the disposition of our vehicles?"

"Three technicals are here in the compound. The rest are out in the field, General. Of the twelve that are out, six are positioned to meet the elders when they enter our territory and provide them safe conduct. The others are guarding the sensitive intersections."

Ibrahim hid his anxiety behind the mask of command and worried about his own vulnerability. Others would see it too. He needed to project as much strength and confidence as possible with what little was left at his base. As usual, he had to think of everything.

"They will come. They will come soon," Abdi said.

"When they come, direct them to the parking spots we selected, and keep them as far apart from each other as possible. There is great hatred in the group—including for us."

Abdi reviewed who would be on the east wall, who on the west, who next to the armoury and so forth.

"Put their vehicles sideways against the wall, so we can control them until the meeting begins," Ibrahim instructed. "Station our vehicles outside the gate, heavy weapons pointed to the side. Mass all our fighters with their weapons in the parade ground. Under no circumstances are they to point their weapons at the visitors unless the order comes from me personally. I'll wait inside until I receive the signal that they're all here."

"What if they want to bring their fighters in with them?" Abdi asked. That was a good point. Ibrahim would never enter such a gathering without personal protection.

"Only one. They can each bring one armed man with them."

Abdi stood there, waiting.

"Move! Do it now!" Ibrahim shouted, then turned to take his place in the receiving room.

Everything had been arranged with symbolism in mind. The furniture maker had made seven chairs upholstered in blue velvet. They were overstuffed and opulent. The one for Ibrahim was six inches taller than the rest and had a white star glued on the back. Its smaller brothers were arranged in a semicircle, each facing the white star and accompanied by an ornate side table. Oriental rugs covered the floor. He bent down and adjusted one to hide the raw cement floor showing through. Heavy red drapes covered bricked-over windows. New air conditioners hummed chilled air into the room. The northern wall had an enormous framed colour photograph of the black basalt Kaaba of Mecca, covered by its stately tapestry and orbited by legions of believers. No unplanned object intruded on the perfection of the scenario for Ibrahim's meeting with six carefully chosen elders from the regions of southern Somalia.

One after another he heard voices and the crunch of gravel as Toyota Land Cruisers pulled into his compound, each with their technical escorts. He heard Abdi arguing with them about how many bodyguards could enter the meeting room. Abdi lost control of the situation. Like a knot of vipers, elders and their bodyguards writhed through the doorway, ceremonial staffs knocking AK-47s, and moved into the room. Once inside, they gave each other space and glared at Ibrahim. There was a blend of hostility, suspicion, and expectation.

"*Salaam walekum*, dear brothers, and thank you for honouring me with your presence in my home. We begin our council with prayer." He nodded to a boy peering around the doorway, who slipped away with a walkie-talkie to tell the muezzin to begin the pre-arranged call to prayer.

All the elders had a prayer bump in the middle of their foreheads from so many years of five prayer prostrations per day. Two of them had red henna beards. Ibrahim worried that the slow growth of his own beard diminished his ability to command respect. He had applied a smudge of brown shoe polish in the centre of his forehead to imitate years of piety.

Ibrahim and the elders knelt, bowed, and pressed their foreheads to the ground in the direction of the Kaaba photograph. Having completed the ritual, Ibrahim took his place and gestured for the old men to sit in their chairs. As Ibrahim had planned, the prayer forced their silence, but soon he was challenged.

"Tell us the meaning of these chairs. Are we not all equals? Are we not your senior?" the elder from Juba region demanded. His worked leather skullcap was the shade of old bone. Grey tufts of short hair poked out from under its rim. His bright crimson beard had been freshly dyed for the meeting. He had the face of a man who had raged against many famines.

"Respected bother, I thank you for this excellent question." Ibrahim adopted a formal tone to convey statesmanship. "I'm troubled by the foreign flags of infidel intruders insulting the dignity of our nation. I thought to recreate the magnificence of our flag with these seating arrangements in honour of your presence in my house. Your chairs symbolize my respect and admiration for your regions. My chair carries the single star of national unity to which we aspire."

The elders reacted with confusion as each one silently calculated his comparative status and what seat he should take. After jockeying for the seat to Ibrahim's right, the Juba elder sat there with two armed fighters behind him. The others followed suit.

Seven fighters brought in seven trays, each containing a can of Coke, a glass, and twigs of moist, glossy qat leaves. The leaves gleamed bright lime green. They had been selected from the ends of young shoots, and their quality was indeed superior. Ibrahim picked up a twig and examined it carefully before he selected several choice leaves, placed them in his mouth, and began to chew.

"Please enjoy. It's fresh. I had it flown in this morning from Ethiopia for this meeting. I prefer the qat from Harar because it's the fifth-holiest city of Islam. I thought it would be a propitious choice for our council tonight." The elders acted in unison, examining the product, carefully selecting individual leaves to place in their mouths, and then chewing with deliberation. The room was quiet.

Qat could turn even the most taciturn of elders into a chatterbox. Ibrahim waited for the stimulating juices to lower inhibitions and induce talking. When a wad of satisfactory size was lodged in one cheek, sips of Coke would be taken.

"General Ibrahim Hussein," said a sleek, fat elder from a merchant family up the coast. His voice was high and nasal with an unfriendly, sardonic tone. "Our national philosophy is equality. Why is your chair taller? Is this an insult to us? Where is my star? As you know well, we can buy our own qat and converse happily with our friends and brothers. We are busy men."

The merchant had three guards standing behind him. They fingered their weapons. Ibrahim had neglected to assign himself personal protection. Regretting that oversight, he struck his most conciliatory tone. "Respected brother, my chair represents the leadership that is required for our country to recover its unity, territorial integrity, and sovereignty. Our unity was undermined when that pig, Barre, abandoned our traditional values and Islamic ideals. Our sovereignty was usurped by the atheists of the United Nations. Their plan is to separate Somalia from the Arab Islamic nation. Our infidel neighbours in Addis Ababa and Nairobi lust after Somali land."

Tapping into their shared xenophobia and chauvinism was working; Ibrahim could see it in the animation of their faces and brightening eyes. The qat was beginning to take effect too.

"My friends, our country will soon have the burden of heathen occupation lifted from our land," Ibrahim said.

"What are you talking about? What do you want from us?" the Juba elder asked. Others murmured agreement.

"The foreigners failed to corrupt us. Soon we will resist, and they will leave. I have a political proposal. It will protect our positions and our interests in the new Somalia. We must put our arrangements in place now, or our country will once again be a playground for the mischief of outsiders."

"What do you mean about our positions and our interests?" the crimson-bearded elder from the neighbouring region of Baidoa asked. "You know nothing of these things." It was time for Ibrahim to present his proposal before he lost any more ground.

"My idea is a simple one," he said. "Our people understand religion, and they understand clans. My proposal is to create an Islamic caliphate with strict adherence to sharia law. You, as the clan elders, will be the emirs and judges responsible for political and security affairs in your region and for all people in your individual emirates. Emirs shall appoint their male heirs to succeed them in emulation of the perfect example of the Prophet, peace be upon him. This concept will appeal to our people and will bring unity. Even the harshest laws are preferable to the chaos that has plagued us and sent our brothers and sisters into exile."

"Harsh laws, you say," the elder from Baidoa hissed. "I know who your father was and why he faced a just and fair Islamic penalty. My nephew was his prisoner. His fingers were taken. All of them. He had done nothing, but came home crippled in body and mind. Is this the way you plan to treat us and our people?"

It was a betrayal, but it had to be said. "I'm not my father, and we no longer live in those times. I sit before you unprotected. I've invited you here because of my patriotic sentiments, my Islamic faith, and my respect for you. Now is the time, and it's our only chance to combine forces according to our shared obedience to Allah's will." It was impossible to tell from the impassive faces before him if his message had been persuasive.

The fat merchant slurped his Coke and belched. "Verily, God is truly great. Please indulge our age. Leave us to confer amongst ourselves on your unusual proposal. Thank you."

If this meeting failed, he would have revealed his ambitions and created six new enemies. "Of course, my brothers. With your permission . . ." Ibrahim rose from his chair. He strode out of the room with the rhythm and air of decision that he had learned from General Cristiani. He moved to the adjacent room to listen on hidden microphones.

There was a long period of silence. Finally, a non-committal voice spoke. "The time of the caliphate was a golden age. Youth respected elders, and women knew their place and duties."

"It would help everyone if our people had a religious duty to obey us," another added. "We will interpret the Holy Koran for them. I would have that upstart so-called general stoned to death if I found him in my territory, but I like his idea."

"If all of us do this at the same time," another said, "if we announce our emirates all at once, we will reinforce one another. If we don't do it together, there will be confusion and conflict."

"It will be good for security. When executions or amputations are required, we can use God's law to justify and explain."

"Ibrahim has been successful with his import and export duties. If we organize this way in our regions, our incomes will grow. We cannot fulfill our political and spiritual duties without money." Ibrahim could tell that was the fat one talking.

"Ibrahim is too ambitious, but I like his idea. I think we should support him. What is our alternative? If we don't organize together, we will soon be at each other's throats. If he wants to be caliph of southern Somalia, let him try."

"What could it hurt? If Ibrahim turns out to be a hypocrite or too greedy, together we can kill him."

When there were no more dissenting voices, Ibrahim returned with the bearing of a worthy young leader and accepted their support.

45

POURING RAIN BROUGHT A welcome cool to Lamu. It helped Anik concentrate on reconstructing her notes and evidence.

The houseboy came up to invite her to take tea with Mohammed, Omar, and Diane. They sat together on the veranda. She sat at the massive wooden table. The air was motionless. Milky tea and biscuits were placed in front of her.

Anik was lost in thought about recovering her evidence. It was not going well. The full names, specific dates, and places had escaped her. She had been in Stone Town long enough—too long, really— and felt the need to leave. She would be leaving in defeat, a damaged and diminished person after the failure of an obscure and quixotic project for people that nobody cared about. She could go back to her parents, maybe find a job with the municipality or something.

She couldn't tell if Omar was in a morphine haze or lost in his own thoughts. Diane was reading a lurid paperback at the table. She looked kind of bored now that Omar didn't need any active treatment.

"Well, if nobody is feeling talkative. I have something interest- ing," Mohammed said. The merchant was obviously annoyed by his guests' lack of sociability. "The Peponi Hotel is buzzing with news. A famous general is staying with them, but it's to be kept secret. Very secret. Security demands it, you know. This is what my cousin's husband, the security manager, told me confidentially at the mosque. He considers this a great honour and a mark of respect for him and the hotel."

"Who is it?" Omar asked, his interest piqued.

"A high-ranking Italian. He said the man is a Christian. A rather stupid remark, seeing as he's coming from the land of the Pope. But then again, my cousin's husband is a stupid man." Mohammed became absorbed in the soft dough of the *mandazi* he was eating.

"Could it be that his name sounds like Christian?" Anik asked, her heart starting to beat faster.

"Possibly. Perhaps my cousin's husband misinterpreted the information. He is thick. I told her not to marry him. But he found the right job. I mean, how hard is it to manage security on an island with no cars and where everyone knows everyone else? I avoid him when I can."

"Could it be him?" Anik asked. "Could it be the Cristiani from Merka?"

"You mean the friend of that son of a hyena Ibrahim Hussein?" Mohammed asked with distaste. "Can you believe that greedy Ibrahim insisted on one million dollars for Osman and his daughters? At least we were able to negotiate him down to 25% of the original demand. Now that we have secured their release and have relocated them to Mombasa, I'll have no more dealings with Merka." He pointed to the ceiling for dramatic emphasis. "Not for one hundred years."

"We must know the name of that general," Omar said. "Please call your cousin now, and ask him the general's name."

Mohammed shrugged at the request. He went to the telephone and called the security guard.

"*Salaam walekum.* It's Mohammed. I have a question. What is the name of your general?" Mohammed listened carefully, and then said a brusque goodbye. "His name is Cristiani. You were right." His eyes winced in concern, and the corners of his mouth turned downward.

"This must be the same man who was in command in Merka," Anik said.

"Did he have anything to do with the attack on you?" Diane asked.

Anik nodded. "Yes, I think he was behind it. I must confront him. I need to question him."

"So, this is the Italian general our troublesome business client Ibrahim works with?" Mohammed asked. "Umm . . ." Mohammed looked up and closed his eyes, as if beseeching God for guidance on a risky financial transaction. "Of course, taking into account what happened to Miss Anik, to whom we have provided shelter and protection, there are certain demands of honour involved as well," he said. "As distasteful as this conversation is, and notwithstanding that you have ruined my tea break, let us discuss this further, so I may put this insane notion in a deep grave, where it belongs."

"Your security man. Could he help us get to Cristiani?" Omar asked. "We have a score to settle with him. I don't know how, but he needs to pay."

Mohammed shook his head. "He would lose his job. His prospects elsewhere would be weak, for reasons I've explained. All he knows how to do is hurl abuse and rocks at some of the beach peddlers and then take bribes from the others, so they can sell to the rich tourists. He has a family. A man without self-restraint, he also has countless filthy children. He would never do it. His wife would not allow it."

"So, it would be expensive," Omar said.

"Yes. Very expensive."

"A gold ingot?"

"No!" Mohammed exclaimed. "A half. A quarter. A tenth. That would be plenty."

"It will be a good use of gold. Mohammed, we must see him urgently. Let us go now."

Mohammed thought for a moment and then nodded. "Very well. As this is a matter of honour . . . Oh, and there's an envelope for you from the head teacher. He gave it to the driver who took the weekly food delivery to your school."

Omar opened the large envelope and looked inside. It contained a note from Ubah, which he handed to Anik.

> Dearest Dr. Anik,
>
> We are sad and downhearted because of the terrible crime that befell you. It was a crime against all women. We are sorry and ashamed that we were not able to help you. Please forgive us for running away. Those men would also do the same to us.
>
> We are hiding, and afraid. We hope you will understand that we cannot put our location in writing. I'm with Jameelah and Kamiis.
>
> Truly yours,
>
> Ubah

"What is the date? Who delivered it?" Anik asked. Her relief that the three were out of Dadaab sank under the cold realization that she was unable to help them.

"There was no other information on the note," Omar said, turning it over. "Maybe I can find out more from the school, but I'm doubtful. It looks like they're trying to hide. I don't think we could ever find them. And our time is short. We must focus on Cristiani while he's here.

"This is also for you," Omar continued. "I sent a message asking Sandra to get it out of Zanov's office. I told her that you were recovering in seclusion."

Anik's heart stopped beating for a couple of seconds. It was her report.

46

ANIK PITIED HERSELF. SHE had tried to make a difference, so the strong would protect the weak. Her daydreams about success and a ground-breaking contribution to international law had been absurd. What had faith in the law and justice gotten her? In Ottawa, it had cost her a job. In Dadaab, it had gotten her gang raped and left for dead. She wasn't dead, but her dedication to the law was. Her spirit was maimed to the bone. Justice was a joke—stupid, even.

Anik did an autopsy of her former self. Her faith in law and rules had been poisoned by the toxic shock of her attack. It was like the idealistic part of her identity had become gangrenous and had to be amputated before it infected the rest. After that, a different diamond-hard self could emerge.

Alone with her elbows on the ancient wooden dining table and her head cradled in her hands, Anik stared at her papers. There was her report to the UN in the middle, crumpled and collapsed. It should have been on the front page of the *New York Times*, not timid and hidden like she was. Around it were pages of notes she had carefully prepared. One stack described how Cristiani cohabited Merka with Ibrahim in an intimate illicit relationship. Another stack detailed Omar's torture and mutilation by Ibrahim. And there were the detailed notes of her attack.

She couldn't release the report without saying what happened to her and where she went. That would bring Omar into it. To reveal his identity would be to sacrifice the life or the freedom of the man who had saved her. It would be an unforgivable betrayal. And anyway, it was impossible to disentangle Omar's culpability from the picture. Any reasonable person who didn't know him would think the former finance minister of Somalia was as bad as—if not worse than—Ibrahim.

These dangers, risks, and contradictions were a garrote choking the women's voices, leaving accusations unsaid, evidence buried, and smashing Anik's solemn promise to bring justice to them.

She looked at the report and at her reference to Canadian Criminal Code provision 273, Aggravated Assault. She was so far beyond the reach of courts and police that it was laughable to think a Canadian law could have a molecule of relevance to Dadaab. Ruth had asked her what her endgame was. Well, here it was. Tomorrow she would send off a letter of resignation saying she was unable to complete the work—*force majeure* or something like that.

The more she thought about Cristiani, the more she was depressed by ice-cold frustration. Anik pushed back from the table and thought about the difference in guilt between Ibrahim and Cristiani. Cristiani was worse. The ecosystem of war was Ibrahim's natural habitat. He was behaving rationally in his niche to exploit the available opportunities to the maximum. He was not far away from Lamu in kilometres, but his impunity was absolute. He might as well have been on another planet. A path to punishment for Ibrahim was inconceivable.

Cristiani, on the other hand, had been sent to protect and symbolize the values of the international community and bring hope. He had accepted that role. His shameless dereliction of responsibility to protect was a breathtaking violation of the ideals of nations. She didn't know either of them and wondered what they looked like.

"Don't kill yourself. You've been in here all night." Diane said. Anik hadn't even noticed her enter the room. "You better go get something to eat, then lie down."

"I can't. This rape is a cage." Anik kept looking at the papers on the table, as if they could give her an answer. "I can't get back to who I wanted to be. I can't get back to who I was." She rested her hand on her report to the UN. "They did it because of this. They attacked me because I found out what was going on. The UN commander in Merka is responsible."

Diane sat down beside her and laid her hand on Anik's shoulder. "Just go back home and start over. What's the matter with that?" Her kindness and concern was different from her normal blunt practicality.

"I can't stay here, but I can't just walk away either." Anik gestured at her papers. "I can't just walk away from what they did to me. I'm stuck."

"You know that stuff about the stages of grief when someone dies?" Diane gave Anik's shoulder a soft squeeze for emphasis. "It's like that. Anger is a stage. You need to get mad at the bastards who made this happen. You need to get furious before you can move on."

"At least in a courtroom, I can look the perpetrators in the eye and say what I need to say. At least I can confront them and tell the judge and jury what they did. Even if I don't win, the truth will go on record." Anik paused. "Cristiani's coming here."

"Don't let him scare you," Diane said. "He doesn't know you're here, and he doesn't even know what you look like."

Anik stood up and started to pace. A knot of fear inside her let go. "I want to confront him. I need to do it. I want his confession."

Diane looked interested, intrigued even. "Me too. I hate the idea of that fucker getting away scot-free. To get a confession, he would need to be tricked—or trapped." Her eyes shone eagerly. "Or kidnapped, ha-ha. But you won't get what you need from him over a friendly beer. Hey, wait a minute. Are you really thinking about kidnapping him? It would be risky."

The insane idea was in the air now. The thought of having Cristiani in her power surprised Anik with a thrill of adrenaline. Anik clutched the idea and then it stuck in her like a barbed hook. She needed Diane on her side. She seemed close, but not all the way there yet.

"Kidnapping is not the right word. What we're talking about is a citizen's arrest. We have all the facts of the crime, but the police won't do anything, so it's up to us. That's what justifies a citizen's arrest." Anik knew this was dishonest, but Diane's face relaxed a little. It worked to reassure her.

Diane's eyebrows curved in a provocative arch. "You could lure him here. This would be a good place for it." Now Diane was thinking about it, imagining how their crime could be staged.

Anik couldn't repress a bitter laugh when the idea came to her. "Seduction. That's how I get him here. Entrapment. Hoist him on his own fucking petard."

Descending deeper into their shared conspiracy, Anik moved into talking about practicalities. "We couldn't stay here long. The island is too small. When he goes missing, somebody will try to find him. It will be too dangerous for Mohammed. We'll have to get Cristiani off Lamu."

"Can I do something to help?" Diane's smile had a reckless tilt. "But like I said, it would be risky." Doubt cast sudden shadows across her face. "I didn't tell you this, but I need a new start too." Her voice quavered. "I kind of left Detroit under a cloud. I got fed up and just walked away from my last job at Detroit emerge with no notice and no forwarding address. It's hard to get references after that. My visa expired here in Kenya."

"How can I help you?" Anik asked.

"If you double my pay, that would be enough for a nice little place in California. I don't mind delivering some pain to this creep. I can't be a part of killing anyone though."

Anik's mind gave way to a wave of heavy fatigue. She was too exhausted to be rational at a time that called for all the cunning and intelligence she possessed. In an impulse of gratitude, she embraced Diane. "I'm going to lie down. We'll bring Omar and Mohammed into this later."

47

AFTER A DEEP SLEEP, things were clear in Anik's mind. She climbed the stairs and found Omar on the rooftop terrace, looking over the coconut palm trees at the clouded and windy Indian Ocean. He cradled his wounded right hand in his good left hand.

"I need Mohammed to make some arrangements for me." Anik had carefully written down all the things she would need for her meeting with Cristiani. "Could you give him this list?"

Before long, Omar returned with Mohammed. The trader's face had a pinched and worried expression. "I don't like this idea. It's against my better judgement. It's not proper for a Muslim man to involve himself in the intimate affairs of women."

"Mohammed, you know what happened to me. I must do this," Anik said. "I have to try."

"I'm a respected bachelor," Mohammed replied. "I would be a source of jokes. Put yourself in my position. I live here. My business is here. It's unthinkable." He looked to Omar for support and found none. "I have never set foot in a beauty parlour for women. Within five minutes, everyone will talk. It would be unbearable.

My business requires me to be sober and serious at all times. I cannot contaminate my reputation by doing business with a women's beauty shop."

Anik rolled her eyes at his protests. "I understand your position. Can you contact someone outside of Lamu? Someone who will not gossip in Lamu about this?"

"Well . . . that might work. If it's not someone on the island it might work. I have a friend down the coast in Malindi, and he can say it's for the niece of a friend who is visiting."

Anik jumped to accept his wavering as consent. "Thank you so much for helping me, Mohammed. I'll never forget this. Tell her to come fully equipped to work in my room. Tell her I'm a size-six dress." She went on to explain that she needed beach outfits. "And tell your person that I want to look sexy."

Mohammed had a coughing fit, excused himself from any personal knowledge of these things, and told her that all her arrangements would be put in place, and a beautician would meet her at the appointed time.

Two days later at midmorning, Mohammed escorted Anik to the hotel to make sure everything went smoothly. The front desk gave her a room with no need to present a passport or enter a name on the register. No signature would be required for food and drink either.

Her second-floor room opened over the aquamarine serenity of the Indian Ocean. Handwoven carpets contrasted ochre and saffron against the cool beige coral. The look was austere and elegant. The privacy and luxury were delicious to her after so long.

It was only noon, so she had time to rest. The slow breeze of the ceiling fan cooled her. The cotton sheets were crisp on her skin. She lay down to plan the encounter. The idea didn't disgust her, she kept telling herself. This was the logical solution to the problem. The more she thought about meeting Cristiani, the harder it was to concentrate. The stakes were high, and the consequences would fall upon her friends. Her heart began to pound faster. It struggled against her tightening chest, as if it wanted to escape. Cristiani was the author of her torment. When she looked in his eyes, how would she control her terror and rage? Her pulse reached a crescendo in her skull like a crazy jazz drummer.

She couldn't keep the gate to her memory closed. Ugly images challenged her inner defences. Oh, God, it was happening again.

Another flashback blurred the corners of the ceiling. She panted for breath, and a dense red fog obscured the furniture and the windows. She was chilled. The room spun. In a dizzy panic, Anik tried desperately to remember what it was she had promised the refugee women. Punishment. She promised punishment for rapists. She needed to run home to the safety of her mother and father, but her legs were numb, and the door vanished. She went dizzy with vertigo.

She started at the sharp knock on the door. She looked at her hands and touched her face. She was alone. More insistent knocks. With all her mental strength, she pulled herself out of the flashback and into the lifeboat of her room. She put her feet on the floor, and stone reality held the flashback at bay.

"Come in. It's not locked." Anik hugged herself to get warm.

The beautician entered with two cases of equipment. A bellboy behind her carried a large garment bag. Anik was shaking and could not face this just yet. The beautician looked friendly and a little concerned.

"I'll take a quick shower while you get organized." Anik said.

"Don't worry. Take as much time as you want. I'm here when it's good for you. My name is Faith."

Hot water on her skin rinsed away the imaginary filth and grounded Anik, so she was capable of returning to Faith.

The Kenyan woman was about forty-five years old, Anik figured. She wore perfectly fitting jeans and a loose white cotton shirt with a low-scoop neckline. Her short hair was clipped tight with a peppering of grey. Her coffee skin was flawless and her makeup just barely perceptible. Anik felt Faith's expert eyes inspect her up and down.

"They told me you were beautiful, but you could be more beautiful." She smiled and laughed quietly. "Much more. Let's get to work." Anik saw clothes laid out on the bed and beauty equipment carefully placed on a table. She shuddered when Faith's hands touched her face.

"First, I think a little massage," Faith said.

Anik closed her eyes. The gentle kindness of a soft human touch settled her. As a little girl, Anik loved when her mother brushed her long hair, and the comfort of it returned. Faith's fingers carefully rubbed Anik's temples, and her eyes relaxed, then her jaw. Faith worked the knotted ropes in Anik's neck and shoulders until they were untangled and untied. When she finished, after a quiet moment, Anik opened her eyes and saw Faith smiling gently.

"Now I think we are ready. Okay?"

Over the course of the afternoon, Anik's hair was conditioned, trimmed, and straightened, so it fell sleek and glossy below her shoulders. A full facial replaced a sullen tinge of grey with a clean, healthy glow. Hot wax hurt after such a long time, but she knew it was necessary for what she had set out to do.

"These are the outfits I brought for you. Let's try some on." Faith's manner was businesslike and efficient. "Is there a special man you have in mind?"

Anik nodded. "Yes, there is."

"What setting? Day or evening?"

Anik had received advance information from Mohammed about Cristiani's routine at the hotel. He was regular in his habits and had been going to the bar at 5:30 sharp since he arrived three days earlier. He took three gin and tonics before dinner. Mohammed said he was of middle height with rather short legs, brown hair, and extremely well-polished shoes.

"Sundowners tonight," Anik said. "In the bar."

Faith looked Anik up and down. She picked a long loose skirt in a deep midnight blue and a white halter top that set off Anik's olive skin.

She told Anik to sit down and then carefully applied mascara, light-blue eye shadow, and deep-red lipstick.

"It would be better if you took off your bra. The halter is enough." She gave a light laugh.

Anik followed this advice. She looked in the mirror. She wore her calculated beauty like the camouflage of a predator. She imagined a python's concentration when a fox moved within striking range.

Anik left her room at 5:50 p.m., calculating that Cristiani would be into his second drink by then.

He was sitting at the bar. She recognized him from behind. His chestnut hair was precision trimmed above the ears. Brilliantine kept the comb strokes in tight martial order over his scalp. The back of his neck was clean-shaven above the collar. His muscular forearms were thick with dark hair. He had an untanned strip on his wedding ring finger. He wore a white button-down short-sleeve shirt, khaki slacks, and black loafers with tassels. Sitting alone and erect on the barstool, he lifted his drink to his mouth without bending his neck.

Anik approached him from behind. She took a deep breath, held her head high, and gave a loose swing to her hips.

She sat on a stool one away from Cristiani. He regarded her with faint interest. She fought against the rising nausea that roiled her guts and tossed him her most winning smile. "Gin and tonic? Do they make a good one here?" Anik steeled her mind and body to be bait.

"Not too bad," he answered. "When I arrive in a new place, I always tell the barman to keep the gin in the freezer. I like a cold drink after a hot day. I recommend it." Cristiani smiled. He spoke to her in a smooth, cultured, and courteous tone. There was an arch to his eyebrows, and one side of his mouth grinned. He was curious, which was good. Against his friendly voice, the protrusion of his fleshy upper lip added to her hatred of him.

"I hate to drink alone. May I join you?" she asked.

He smiled and nodded. "By all means."

Anik ordered a gin and tonic from the barman. She took a large swallow. Her nerves were frayed from his physical closeness. The icy bite of quinine on her tongue and the burn of alcohol in her throat braced her for this risky moment.

She turned to face him directly. His gaze jerked up from her breasts, and he looked away. She needed to pull him back. She decided to touch him and offered her soft hand. "Very nice to meet you, my name is Marie."

His features remained relaxed, but not as confident. Behind that she saw a spark of arousal in his light-brown eyes. He held her hand for a moment, as if to gauge something, then released it. Anik was slow to pull her hand away. She expected his hand to be strong and the skin to be tough. Instead it was soft and moist. His fingernails were manicured. She moved to sit next to him.

"Enchanted to meet you. I'm Major General Giancarlo Cristiani, Italian Army." He lowered his eyelids. "Please call me Giancarlo."

"I've never met a general before. What's it like?" In her experience as a prosecutor, Anik had found that open questions were the best way to get someone talking. She held her head high and her shoulders back. Her eyes projected undivided attention.

"There are not so many of us." His oily smile was an invitation for her to continue.

"Were you ever in a combat situation?"

He nodded. "Yes, I was. In fact, I completed my tour of combat duty just this month."

"Where? I didn't even think we were in any wars anymore after the Berlin Wall came down . . . three years ago, right?"

"I'm afraid you're much mistaken. I was stationed close to this island here, leading our mission in Somalia. It was a new kind of battlespace. Our Cold War standoff with the Russians was much simpler," he said with a patronizing chuckle.

"Can you tell me what is was like?"

"In a war zone, you carry the responsibility for life-and-death decisions." He delivered this dramatic message in an even tone. He had said it many times before. Anik decided to pull on this thread.

"Tell me about Somalia. Were you really able to help the people? I remember some stories on the news. I saw pictures of stick people and starving babies. That was Somalia, right?"

He warmed to the topic. "My work was to give aid to those starving people. It was a humanitarian mission. I was the lead humanitarian. We left our theatre of operations much better than we found it." He took a pull on his drink and looked intently at her. "There may never be statues and monuments to glorify us, but it was extremely rewarding work."

Anik placed her hand softly on his forearm to test his attraction to her. He looked down at her hand and smiled at her again. "I would love to know more about this," she said. "I hope none of your men were hurt."

"We did not take casualties, although I was prepared to. You see, my job was not to fight and defeat the Africans. We bring peace and stability to countries that cannot govern themselves. Adult supervision is required." He chuckled.

"I'm sorry, but I don't understand. Can you explain this to me?"

"The people knew we were there to help them and to protect them. So, they did not fight us. Of course, it would be utter foolishness for a primitive tribal fighter to confront a modern soldier. They would be slaughtered." He grinned at the absurdity of the idea.

"Wasn't it lonely? You were so far from home with no one to talk to about how you feel. And you need to make such hard decisions." Her voice was low and slow.

Like a trout fixing on a brightly coloured lure, he registered her sexual magnetism. He took a couple of sips of his gin and tonic. "Lonely? No one ever asked me that before. Generals are only permitted to show satisfaction when orders are obeyed or anger at disobedience. Sometimes we can show hatred of the enemy and affection for the common soldier."

He looked at the table, and there was a long pause. Anik worried that she was going too far too fast. Was talking about emotions a mistake? Cristiani was pulling back from her. She had probably offended him. Needles of pain stabbed her temples.

"It can be dangerous for a commander to show other emotions," he said, looking away. "Emotions are signs of weakness. How can you expect a soldier to risk his life on your orders if you're emotional or have doubts? Mine is a solitary occupation." For a microsecond, his chin quivered, his lips drooped, and his eyes closed. Then she saw him vanquish the flash of self-pity, stiffen his back, and recover his martial bearing.

"Your feelings are not a sign of weakness," she said. "We all have emotions, even if we need to hide them sometimes." He smiled wistfully and raised his eyebrows.

Anik looked out over the Indian Ocean. "The sun has already gone down!"

"Will you join me for dinner?" Cristiani asked. "I'm enjoying our conversation. I want it to continue."

"I want to, but I can't. I have a deadline at midnight for my magazine."

"Are you a journalist?" Cristiani leaned back from her, and his face became neutral.

Anik laughed. "Yes . . . for a fashion magazine. I'm sure you've never heard of it. I'm doing a piece on beach fashions. But what about tomorrow morning? Have you visited Stone Town? I found this wonderful setting for a photo shoot in one of the old houses. Can I show it to you? I would love to know what you think." Anik leaned forward and touched him again for emphasis. "I want to get to know you better too, Giancarlo." She saw Cristiani twist a little on his stool, reminding her of a dog receiving strokes from its master.

He leaned forward again. "They say I cannot leave without seeing Stone Town, and my flight is the day after tomorrow. Would it disturb your workmates?" Between moist lips, the grey tinge of his small teeth showed his age. Mid-fifties, Anik thought, like her father.

"Don't worry, nobody will be there." She took a large skeleton key out of her purse and showed him. "Just you and me, together in a big empty house."

"By all means. I'm totally free tomorrow morning. Shall we meet at, say nine o'clock in the lobby?" She had done it. He wanted her.

"That would be perfect. See you then."

Anik finished her drink and turned to leave. Her jaw and eyes ached from suppressed rage. She let her mask dissolve into the hate she felt. She blinked back tears as she hurried back to be sick in her room.

48

THE NEXT MORNING ANIK stepped into the lobby a little after 9:00. Cristiani was seated on a rattan wing chair reading a faxed copy of the *International Herald Tribune*. He was wearing the same outfit as the previous night but with crisp new creases. Maybe these were the only kind of clothes he wore. Pathetic.

She willed her features into a look that was expectant and excited at seeing him again. "What a beautiful morning for a walk, Giancarlo!"

He smiled knowingly when she offered her cheek for a kiss. The previous night he must have drawn the correct conclusion that she was seducing him. He licked his lips and pressed them to a spot touching the margin of her lips. His horrid saliva so close to her mouth turned her stomach. His musky cologne had an edge of cat piss.

"Indeed, indeed," he said. "My entire day is free." They stepped into the hotel's front garden. "I put myself completely into your hands."

"Into my hands, hmm . . . I hope you're sure about that!" She laughed. "I have so many more questions for you. And maybe you can help me with my work too. How do I look?" Anik did a pirouette. She was wearing blue shorts and a red sleeveless blouse. Her hair was in a high ponytail off the back of her neck. Mirrored aviator sunglasses concealed her eyes.

"Spectacular! I dare say you even look perfect. You look ready for an adventure—for anything that could happen!" He laughed.

She smiled. "I thought you might like it. You look ready for anything, too."

They stepped out of the hotel and down the lane that led to Stone Town, a short kilometre away. Anik felt a patina of sweat under her arms and over her lip. She couldn't tell if it was because of the mounting heat of the day or if the situation was making her feverish. She tried to cope by taking deep breaths.

"You said you had questions. I'm completely off-duty. Since military affairs are so new to you," he grinned at his vulgar pun, "perhaps you'd like to know more about them." He was being provocative. He anticipated sex. Good.

She smiled playfully at him, grateful he could not see her eyes behind the sunglasses. "You read my mind. Tell me how you became a general. I guess not many men make it so far. Maybe they're not prepared to make the sacrifices you have."

They waited for a donkey cart full of green coconuts to pass by on its way to town.

"Let me start from the beginning. I come from an aristocratic family in Italy. The second-youngest son, I was not in line to assume the hereditary rank of count or the leadership of the family, like my older brother. But I'm happy—in a way—about that. My brother did not fully develop as a person. He has difficulty keeping things afloat. I'm the person of last resort who keeps our family's estate intact. You would be surprised how much is involved in maintaining one's position." He was completely disarmed and unguarded. She would never have a chance to talk to him like this again.

"You must be the kind of person who takes responsibility seriously. I guess generals need to be responsible for everything that happens around them."

He nodded. "They do. Military responsibilities and family responsibilities too. Perhaps one day you will come and visit our small palace. I invite you. Please come."

"I'd love to see your palace!" There was no time to waste on this empty, silly line of conversation. How could she get this on the right track for the information she needed?

"I grew up in our palace," he said, "schooled by a governess. I asked to go to English boarding school when I was ten. School was not easy, even though I'm an aristocrat. The English believe themselves superior to the rest of humanity, and my schoolmates did not understand that the Romans—who brought civilization to the British Islands—are my direct ancestors."

"When you're commander, does everybody come to you? Do you have to decide everything?" Anik asked.

The lane turned away from the shore and into town. They stepped down a narrow, empty alley paved with flagstone. It was squeezed on either side by the walls of tall, ancient houses. Centuries of salt air had oxidized the coral to dove grey.

Her fawning encouraged him, and he was utterly absorbed by his story. He described his excellent training at the Modena military academy and how his perfect English made him the ideal candidate for UN missions. He also explained how his diplomatic success in Washington positioned him for his command in Somalia. Anik was relieved he did not probe her once or even ask about the blood in her eye.

"You said you helped the people there. In Somalia." Her tone was serious now. "That's so important. It touches me. Tell me how you did it."

"I'm proud of that, very proud. Do you understand what strategic vision means?"

"Not really," Anik said. "Like the big picture?"

"It's more complicated than that. It means seeing clearly what you want and how to get there with the means at your disposal." He waited for Anik to nod before continuing. "I wanted success for the people. We knew from the beginning that we were not going to stay longer than we were needed. I wanted to create the conditions for success for the people in my city, in Merka. That was my strategic vision."

"But wait, I don't get it. What did you do differently?"

"Leadership. I found and nurtured and supported their best leader. I mentored him, guided him, and told him what decisions to make. You see, people in childlike societies need strong leaders. And their leaders need to be led. Democracy and human rights, these are western concepts that might be fine for us, but they mean nothing if you're starving."

"Did he do what you asked of him?"

Cristiani puffed with pride. "Very much so. He responded well to my leadership."

"What was the name of your leader?"

He looked at her in surprise. "Are you really interested? Well, it was Ibrahim, Ibrahim Hussein. I was his partner, and I guided him in everything he did. His future will be my legacy, really."

"Here we are! I think you're going to love it. I can't wait to hear your reaction. Just let me get the key."

Anik pulled the key from her bag and inserted it in the keyhole of the massive wooden door. The lock opened with a clunk.

"Close your eyes, and give me your hand," she said, then kissed him swiftly on the lips.

49

CRISTIANI WAS GETTING HOT. He had arrived in Lamu with hopes for a fling, and Marie was the first available white girl he had seen. He hoped his sweat and body odour did not dampen her arousal. He had showered scrupulously and generously applied Hermes cologne and underarm deodorant.

He had not been with such a beautiful woman for at least ten years. At age forty-five he had lost interest in emotional satisfactions, except for his career. The ashes of his marriage had turned so cold that his wife didn't care if he was home or in a war zone. Divorce was out of the question for his kind of Catholic. He usually wore his wedding band still. He decided not to humiliate himself—or his wife—with visible affairs, other than the infrequent call girls international hosts arranged at overseas conferences.

This girl's innocent admiration was exhilarating. He walked a little straighter and prouder than usual. Her vital radiance put a spring in his step as they entered the quaint little town.

He used the walk as an advertisement for himself, feeding off her fascination. Normally, he was indifferent to the views of people outside the military hierarchy. He surprised himself by caring very much what Marie thought of him. Could this be the beginning of something new for him? She admired and respected him; he could tell that already. Could she come to love him? He dared to imagine she might follow him to Brussels if their day went well.

Cristiani had often wondered what female secrets lay inside the suggestive covers of the *Cosmopolitan* magazines he gazed at on newsstands. This might be his chance to find out. What would this girl's erotic expectations be? Some of his colleagues told him that martial bearing and the mystique of high rank could open legs better than a handsome face and strong physique. He worried his sexual techniques might be a little rusty, but he would do his utmost to satisfy her.

She led him to the entrance of a magnificent, ancient three-storey stone house. Its front door was massive hand-hewn wood. It gave right on to the quiet laneway. He imagined that the house had belonged to an African version of nobility at some time in the distant past. Marie had good taste in more ways than one.

"Here we are." Her voice was light and melodic. "It's the best house in town. I think you're going to love it! I can't wait to see your reaction. Just let me get the key," she said, struggling to contain her excitement.

He was heading into the unknown with confidence in his ability to master any situation. Initiative was a principle of military advantage, and he decided to take the lead as soon as they were in private. His imagination came alive with visions of the sensual skills of liberated women.

She inserted an antique key into the wrought-iron keyhole. There was a clunk, and she swung the door open. His eyes were accustomed to the bright tropical sun. Beyond the threshold was a black void.

"Close your eyes, and give me your hand." Her voice had the tone of a silver flute. She kissed him swiftly on the lips, and he sucked her fragrance to the bottom of his lungs. "We'll go to my special room first, so you have the full impact," she whispered.

He swallowed. This playfulness was taking him into new sexual territory, but he was a willing captive. Young lovers experiment, he had heard. Eyes closed, he took her hand. She gripped him hard, impatiently. The door closed behind them. The air had a cool, clean scent of old stone.

A fist smashed his nose. Pain exploded across his face. Blood poured into his gasping mouth. His eyes opened wide as a hood was shoved over his head and pulled tight around his neck with a cord. Blind and confused, he was shoved to the rough floor. Two figures held his arms behind his back, and nylon cable ties were tugged tourniquet tight across his wrists.

He writhed to get to his knees. If he could get to his feet, he could run where he thought the doorway should be and into the lane.

"Help!" he howled with all his strength.

The door slammed. A sharp kick between his shoulder blades knocked him onto his belly. He couldn't breathe, and he started to get dizzy from lack of oxygen. Then he remembered his training. *Conduct after capture for general officers. Keep calm and orient yourself. Develop situational awareness. Collect intelligence. Cooperate, but under no circumstances reveal operational secrets.* He lay still and slowed his breathing.

"Who are you?" he asked. "What do you want?"

"Shut up!" someone yelled. Where was the girl? Had they both walked into an ambush? "Shut up and do what we say," the voice continued. "You're going on a trip. We won't kill you, and you can't escape."

It was a terrorist kidnapping. *Do not anger your captors. Cultivate their sympathy. Give them the minimum necessary to prevent torture or execution.* He lay there passively, tasting the blood in his mouth. His face throbbed, and razors of pain slashed his sinuses. The terrorists would learn nothing from him.

50

CRISTIANI WAS TIED TO a stretcher, sedated by Diane, gagged, and under a sheet. If anybody saw him, they would think he was a corpse on its way to burial within the twenty-four-hour time limit required of Muslims. Mohammed assigned a trusted guard to go with them—the one he used for collections from tardy debtors. He knew how to operate the AK-47 they were taking, just in case.

Anik embraced Diane at the dock as they loaded Cristiani. "You brought me back to life. Thank you so, so much." Anik still felt numb after the kidnapping and was unable to express the depth of her gratitude.

"Hey, you're welcome. I made a new friend," Diane said and hugged her back.

"Where are you going to go?"

"After I pick up my pay, wherever I want. Let's get together again sometime. I'll let Mohammed know where you can find me. You better go now. Me too. Don't worry. I tranquilized him for a good eight hours. You'll be Okay."

When the boat reached the mainland, they put Cristiani into the back of an old snout-nosed Bedford truck, and Mohammed's man drove them five hours north over a bumpy dirt track to this abandoned colonial farmhouse.

The sun came up, and Anik looked in the cracked mirror over the plastic washing bucket in her room. Her hair was pulled back. It was dusty from the previous night's journey. Her face was drawn, and her eyes were red. She wore jeans and a man's work shirt with the sleeves rolled up.

Anik felt like a high diver. She had climbed up the ten-metre platform and was looking over the edge. She had completed the first moves properly, and now Cristiani was under their control. The next moves—his interrogation and penalty—would be harder to execute. Going face-to-face with Cristiani in an interrogation supercharged the emotional degree of difficulty.

She moved into the main room and leaned against the wall next to the doorway to the bedroom where they put Cristiani.

Omar walked up beside her. He held himself at his full height and strength. Then he stepped into Cristiani's room. "Don't move," Omar said to Cristiani. He turned to Anik. "It's up to you."

The moral shock of the kidnapping hit her. Her stomach rose to her throat when she remembered the crunch of Cristiani's nasal cartilage. Anik had struck him with a furious strength that she didn't know she possessed. The reverberations of her own rage and hate still stunned her. The sweat and hair of Cristiani's muscular arms had adhered to her hands from the struggle to bind the man. She winced at her memory of Cristiani's sharp intake of breath when Diane yanked the nylon straps around his wrists. Cristiani had frantically flopped on the floor, trying to get to his feet. Looking down on him that night, she saw the blood begin to seep out from where the sharp plastic ties had sliced through his skin.

The animal violence of the scene made Anik realize she was a felon now. Criminal Code 279. Everyone who, without lawful authority, confined, imprisoned, or forcibly seized another person was guilty of an indictable offence and liable to imprisonment for a term not exceeding ten years. This last thought was too much, and she pushed it out of her mind. She was the key witness, the prosecution, the judge, and victim. Executioner too?

She took a basin and towel and stepped into Cristiani's presence without a mask of courage. There was no room in her mind or spirit for pretending. Her face was grim, her heart empty and cold.

"Here. Wash your face."

He moistened the towel, then dabbed softly at his face. From his grimaces she could tell he was in pain. That was fine. The red-hot rage that had driven her fist into his face had cooled to icy malice.

He cleared his nose into the bucket. Black clots of blood and snot floated in the dirty water. He wiped his face and looked up at her.

"You were part of it all along," Cristiani said. "Tell me what you want, and I can help you get out of this mess. It's not too late. In fact, nobody needs to know." His tone was gentle and rational.

"Does it hurt?" Anik asked.

"Yes, very much so." His eyes were black, his nose bulbous from the swelling.

"Here are some painkillers." She handed him three Tylenols, and he downed them with a swig from his water bottle. They looked at each other silently. Something moved in the corner of her eye. Anik looked to her side and saw a pair of large cockroaches climbing into the can of sardines he had been given for breakfast.

"Why do you think you're here?" Anik asked.

"I have no idea why I'm here." The broken nose made his voice nasal. "Who are you?"

"Think carefully. You're here for an important reason. I'm sure you know what it is. I want to begin by hearing how you understand it."

Cristiani looked from side to side. He took a considerable time to think before answering. She told herself to respect his intelligence and to listen carefully to his story, to listen for the lies.

"Perhaps you have a grievance with my government. Perhaps there's a political issue. Or maybe an economic question. You may have financial needs."

"You are guilty of crimes against humanity in Merka," Anik said.

Cristiani's eyes widened in surprise. He stood up. Then he recovered his self-discipline and control over his posture and his face. He sat down again. He was fighting against any breach in his emotional armour.

"You've made a mistake," he said after a long moment of silence. I'm a decorated Italian general. I've always worked in the service of peace. I've only been in UN-sanctioned peacekeeping missions. I repeat, UN-sanctioned. There were never any war crimes. War crimes are impossible when the purpose is peace. We were not fighting a war against anybody. This was not a military occupation. You are an intelligent, well-informed person and must understand this. Your allegation is not logical."

Anik noticed a gecko walking along the raw brick wall, oblivious to the force of gravity. An ungainly hornbill squawked an angry reproach to the world and perched on the acacia tree outside the window.

"We are both in an unfortunate situation. You can just let me go, and that will be the end of it. I'll say I was mugged—it happens all the time here—and everyone will believe it."

Anik waited for him to go on. They had all day—even all week, if necessary.

"The Italian government will not spare any resources to find a high-ranking military leader like me. Think of my poor wife. Soon she will be frantic with worry." Cristiani gripped Anik in his stare and spread his arms to underline his point. "I advise you to reconsider your actions." His voice was friendly and warm.

Was this misdirection, or did he truly not know? Anik had not entertained the possibility that he might be oblivious to his role in the crisis that defined her life, sucking her spirit from her like a black hole. A hint of doubt must have shown on her face, and he pounced.

"You see, you do see!" Cristiani said with fervour on his battered face and conviction in his voice. "You don't know why I'm here either! These mistakes can happen. I'm sure your cause, whatever it is, will be best served if you release me. Perhaps you want to speak to your friends about this."

"Tell me about your time in Somalia. What did you do there?" Anik asked.

"Why do you want to know?" Cristiani replied in a neutral tone. "Can you tell me your name? I think I deserve to know it. Tell me what you want. Maybe I can help you get it. You seem like a reasonable person. I want to understand how we can both get out of this situation. You know who I am. I should know who you are."

"We'll get to that later," Anik said

"Why am I here? I really have no idea."

"Crimes against humanity," Anik repeated.

"This is a mistake," Cristiani protested. "It's impossible."

"I'll listen to you if you listen to me," Anik said. "If it's a mistake, we'll take you back, and this is over. I'll say I'm sorry. We'll work that out together, okay?"

"Yes, yes, of course." She saw a flash of relief on his face. She was amazed that he didn't seem to know—or didn't know what she knew.

Anik clicked on a tape recorder. They both listened to the dry scratch of plastic gears.

"Let's get the facts straight. You are General Giancarlo Cristiani, correct."

Cristiani nodded. "That is correct."

"The Security Council said your mission was to create a secure environment for humanitarian assistance. It said there were grave violations of international humanitarian law in Somalia. That was why you and your soldiers were sent. You told me that you were in charge. You told me that Ibrahim Hussein was your partner. Correct?"

"Yes, I told you that. What of it?" He was not afraid now, she saw.

"His militia controlled Merka. You knew that. Correct?"

"Obviously. I told you that too. He was the local leader. This is not important."

"You gave him the food aid to distribute."

"So?" Cristiani spread his arms expansively. "It was the best way. If you dump food in a starving city, people will tear each other apart over it. Do you expect us to walk around town giving alms of food to a country of starving beggars? Please be serious. We maintained control with our partners. You cannot simply parachute into a place like Somalia. You need to work with those who can make things happen and are strong enough to protect themselves. They are the only ones still alive, anyway. The weak leaders got killed."

Cristiani lowered his head and looked hard into her face. "I told you these things when you were trying to get into my pants. I'm a general. You have no right to question me."

"I have eyewitness reports that Ibrahim sold that food," Anik said

He paused, and his face betrayed a flicker of uncertainty. He broke eye contact with her.

"He ordered weapons with the money," Anik said. "There's a UN embargo on arms exports to Somalia. You conspired to break the Security Council resolution." Anik had to catch her breath before she could continue. "You were part of a conspiracy against the Security Council of the United Nations. This is how I would describe it." She was working hard to stay rational.

His face darkened. "What kind of political game is this? You tried to pick me up, remember?" His eyes sparked. "I thought you wanted me to fuck you. I thought it might be nice to fuck you. And now . . . now you want to talk about international humanitarian law after you assault and kidnap me? You're being ridiculous. Let's end this sick joke."

"You thought it might be nice to fuck me?" she asked.

He was unable to conceal his arrogance and contempt for her. "Yes, but I didn't know your game," Cristiani said with slow deliberation. "I can see that now. But I'll keep my word. Let's bring this farce to an end. I'll keep this secret. After all, it will look like I have trouble keeping my trousers zipped if this story gets out."

He stood up. Her fear instinct spiked. She jumped up. "Omar!"

Cristiani sat down before Omar entered. She gathered up her threadbare willpower and sat back down.

"I'll stay," Omar said.

Anik refused to be defeated by Cristiani's feint of dominance. "No, I'll do this alone," she said. Omar withdrew.

"What are you afraid of? Tell me about your friend . . . Omar." Cristiani was trying to take the upper ground, testing his margin of movement and trying to gather information about them. She reproached herself for giving away Omar's name. He scared her, and she was badly rattled. If Omar had not been behind the door listening, she would have fallen apart from terror.

He leaned back in his plastic chair. "Where did you get this ridiculous information? You're making a silly and groundless accusation."

"I'm going to say it again, and then I'll move on. Your mandate was to provide humanitarian assistance, and you gave it to a criminal who sold it. This is contrary to international humanitarian law. You are guilty of this."

"I'm guilty of nothing but protecting people and serving my country. I'm proud of it. I repeat, you can take me back now, and there will be absolutely no consequences." A thin trickle of blood wormed from his left nostril onto his lip. He tasted it with the tip of his tongue. "Besides, who are you to call anybody a criminal? You're guilty of kidnapping and assault."

"Ibrahim systematically ordered the rape of women as a weapon of war. He did this to accumulate property, to intimidate, to terrorize the population, and to recruit soldiers."

Cristiani scoffed. "This . . . this has nothing to do with me. I certainly had no idea of any sort of thing like this. It can't be true."

"It's true. I know it's true. I collected evidence from some of the victims. The crime is sexual assault. Aggravated sexual assault. You are guilty of conspiracy. When you conspire, you're guilty of the same crime, and you face the same penalty."

"What is this, anyway? Let me go. You're crazy. Even if there were a grain of truth to these allegations—and there's not—our rules of engagement do not allow us to get involved in the family disputes of local people. I'm only subject to Italian military law in a properly constituted court martial of the Italian army." He started to look a little worried. A drop of blood slithered from his right nostril. His blood pressure must be rising. Anik was glad.

"We have information that your men participated in sex slavery. I admit this is hearsay, but I find it convincing."

"What do you mean, you find it convincing? You have no right to judge me." He wiped his nose with the back of his hand, smearing blood across his face. He had become hunched. Anik straightened her back and held her head high. After feeling impotent and imagining Cristiani as invulnerable, his grotesque and pathetic face gave her newfound strength.

"And yet here we are," Anik said. "A report on the systematic use of rape in your area was submitted to the United Nations. Did you receive it?"

His lips were taut, and his eyes narrowed. "Perhaps. There were too many reports to read. I had a mission to complete. I was not there to read reports."

A waft of sweltering, dusty air pushed through the window. It made Anik tired, as if it contained no oxygen. Her hair blew into her eyes. Sweat trickled from her underarms down her sides and from her temple down her cheek. Her throat was scratchy and constricted with thirst.

Cristiani forced a smile. "But really, how can one be expected to take these NGOs seriously? It's all so political. There's no end of complaints, but what is their basis in fact?"

"How did you know it was an NGO report?" Anik asked.

"I totally reject your fictitious claims. It would be laughable in any court anywhere. This is not proof or evidence. You seem to be an intelligent girl. Come now. Consider your position, and let me go. You can just drop me off on the highway." He was bargaining again, but now he sounded worried.

"Stay there." She stepped out of the room, and Omar handed her the envelope. She came back in, sat down, and held it in front of Cristiani's face. "I wrote this report," Anik said. He flinched and sat back. The arrogance melted from his face.

"I interviewed those women, and I did these case files. Yesterday you told me that you mentored Ibrahim, guided him, and told him what decisions to make. That means you conspired with him to commit these crimes."

"So that's who you are. Anik Belanger. And Omar," he added.

The logic of their dialogue arrived at Anik's inescapable moment of truth. "Shortly after I submitted the report, I was gang raped in Dadaab camp."

Anik had a falling sensation, as if she had stumbled off the edge of the ten-metre platform. As if her moves were jerky and panicked. As if there was no water in the pool. Her heart raced. "It was by Ibrahim's men," she said, struggling for breath. "Therefore, it was by your orders." Anik forced herself across inner rivers of fear and revulsion to look deeply into his eyes. "You are the intellectual author of this crime." She studied his face for the verdict.

He touched his nose and grimaced in pain. His eyes looked down and to the side.

"What did you do when you saw my report?" Anik demanded. Then she saw anguish, shame, and defeat in his eyes. That was enough. He knew he was guilty.

From a labyrinth of crushing terror and utter failure, she had found her exit.

51

OMAR WAITED FOR ANIK to stop panting, for her panic to settle. "And we are certain?" he asked. "Now we can sentence him?"

"Absolutely," Anik said. "He's guilty. I prepared a written confession for him to sign."

"I don't need it," Omar said. "It would be better to kill him. It would be the right thing to do, and so much simpler. So many have died and lost everything." He looked at his tortured hand. The pain and fear to which he had been subjected in the steel container flooded his memory. The dark part of his spirit required retribution, and this was the perfect opportunity to secure that recompense.

Anik looked at him with rock-hard eyes. "For this to mean something, the world must know. And the countries who care reject the death penalty. Omar, an execution would make us terrorists."

She didn't understand his needs at that moment. She didn't understand that in the humanitarian wasteland of his failed state, leniency for a malignant actor like Cristiani would be absurd. Immoral.

"You told me yourself, Jameelah's children died because Ibrahim's men raped her, and she had to leave. They died on the road to Dadaab. Kamiis had to witness the rape and murder of her mother. Cristiani could have stopped that plague of rapes. He could have stopped Ibrahim's terror. He could have saved people. His cowardice and irresponsibility are unforgivable."

With a sudden overwhelming sadness, Omar realized there would never be another chance for his country. When the peace-keepers left, Ibrahim and those like him would be the future. Cristiani had enabled it and squandered the opportunity to lift the curse of criminal intimidation from hundreds of thousands.

"The death penalty is customary in my country, where the crimes occurred. We will have acted in accordance with the requirements of traditional Somali law, of Islamic principles, and we will have stopped future crimes by him. For my people, this will be satisfactory. It will also be much safer for us. It's the best we can do."

Omar thought about how he would do it. He had never killed a person before. He had never even committed violence against anyone. He had no training on how the AK-47 operated. There was a lever on the side to select single shot or full-automatic operation, but which was which? If Omar was the one advocating the execution, it would not be ethical to involve others in the killing. It must be done by him alone. He visualized tying Cristiani to a chair and dragging him outside. There would be a struggle. If, by mistake, he pulled the trigger on automatic, the close-range carnage would be horrific. Major Moussa's crushed body returned to his mind. Could he put Anik through that? What would she think of him then?

Anik broke a silence, which was becoming too long. "I'm not responding to what you say. The moment I do—as soon as I talk about an execution seriously—I'm guilty of conspiring to first-degree homicide. That's one place I won't go. Do it, and you also bring in Diane and Mohammed as conspirators. I can't have that on my conscience."

Omar knew he couldn't inflict such pain and suffering on Anik. Nor did he want to add any more poisonous cargo to his own inner burden of guilt. The distance to redemption was already so far. He nodded. "I understand."

He could see Anik calculating something in her mind. He had not seen this scheming look on her face before. She started to talk to herself. "Cristiani feels shame, but not guilt. He isn't capable of deep remorse. He regrets getting caught, but he doesn't regret his conduct. He doesn't behave as if we would hurt him. He expects to be released." She looked up at Omar "I don't think he's scared enough for what we need. It would help to get his signature on the confession if he thought we were capable of killing him. Can you do that?"

"Yes, I can." Seeing the fear of death on Cristiani's face would be some recompense. Omar retrieved the assault rifle and stepped into the interrogation room.

Cristiani was a wreck, barely able to hold himself upright in the plastic chair. Snot and blood dripped from his nose.

"General, now you have to choose how you pay for what you did. I think we should have killed you already," Omar said. "Execution by a single shot to the back of the head. By me."

That shocked Cristiani into wakeful attention. "No, no. You don't have to do anything of the sort. There's law, and there are international treaties. You can't do that. Don't do that. I'm a prisoner of war."

"I don't care about those things. This is between us now. You and your army say you help the starving, and yet you play into the hands of butchers. The hypocrisy is breathtaking. Those UN resolutions didn't help people. You didn't help my people either." Omar was calm, fully engaged in this cruel theatre. "You have a choice. If you sign a confession, we will let you go, and we will make it public. Otherwise, I will execute you, and that will make everything much simpler."

"What will you say about me?" Cristiani probed.

"Probably nothing." Omar said. "If I kill you, the price is paid in full for what you did. That will be enough. But my friend prefers you to make a written confession, so everyone will know the truth of what happened. In words signed by you. That way it might not happen again. People need to know about this. But it's your choice."

Cristiani raised himself up. "You can't do anything except let me go. I have rights, and I insist on them. If you have evidence, give it to my government. That is what you need to do."

"We wrote the confession for you," Omar read from the hand-written paper Anik had prepared.

Confession of Major General Giancarlo Cristiani

I am guilty of conspiring in the following war crimes: murder, torture, and rape. I have also abetted grave offenses that have not yet been legally defined as crimes against humanity

In the exercise of my duties as Commander of UN peacekeeping forces, I was given responsibility for the Merka area of operations. In the conduct of my duties, I associated and allied my forces with the local warlord, Ibrahim Hussein. Therefore I am guilty of conspiracy in the commission of his crimes. I have heard and accept the evidence against me as true and factual.

- I knowingly permitted my soldiers to engage in sex with women and girls kept against their will by Ibrahim Hussein.

- I directed my officers to transfer detainees to Ibrahim Hussein without concern for the risk that they would be tortured and killed.

- I deprived distressed and vulnerable people of humanitarian assistance and facilitated its uncontrolled sale in barter for arms to be purchased in violation of the Security Council arms embargo.

- I allowed and conspired in the use of sexual assault as an instrument of armed conflict.

I recognize that my actions constitute grave war crimes. Furthermore, negligence in protecting the Somali citizens in my area of operations put them at risk of systematic human rights abuse by Ibrahim Hussein.

With my signature, I confirm that this confession is true and have accepted that it become public.

Omar handed Cristiani a sheet of paper and a pen. "Sign the paper, or not. I'm done talking to you.

Cristiani shooed the flies from his bloody face with the paper, then read it carefully. He shifted in his chair, and then took a drink from his bottle of water. "You need to inform the Red Cross about me. That is your first obligation."

"Sign it." Omar said, and flipped the safety lever of the AK-47.

Cristiani looked up at Omar. "These are not capital crimes," he said in a voice wavering between rational argument and supplication.

"Sign it," Omar said. He set his face with the stone-hard contempt he carried inside.

"How could I have possibly known Ibrahim Hussein's intentions?" Cristiani asked.

"Don't be a fool. If you're not ready to die, sign it."

The last quivering ray of hope faded from Cristiani's eyes. He signed the paper on his knee and gave it to Omar. "This was done under duress and will not be credible in court. Let me go."

"We leave at sundown." Omar left Cristiani alone with his thoughts.

52

CRISTIANI'S INDIGNITIES WERE ABOUT to end. He would keep quiet, and they would drop him close to the hotel. He would get the hotel physician to attend to his injuries, wash up, call his embassy, and get the manhunt started for these terrorists, Anik Belanger and Omar. They must be operating on a shoestring budget if this was the best they could do for a safe house. Those amateurs wouldn't get far. He rehearsed how he would describe the woman's oval face to the criminal sketch artist in Rome: aquiline nose, high cheekbones, blue eyes, and black hair. Identifying scars—split on the upper lip and blood mark in the left eye. Spoke with a French-Canadian accent. The African was an ethnic Somali, two metres high and approximately eighty kilos. Hair going grey, short beard, Arabic influence on nose and lips, deep-black eyes, domed forehead with receding hairline. Identifying scars: missing index finger on the right hand. Spoke with an educated American accent. In Lamu two days earlier. With an Interpol Red Notice,[20] they wouldn't be hard to find.

20   A Red Notice is an international wanted persons notice.

"You have three minutes. Take a piss and drink some water!" Omar shouted from behind the door.

Cristiani urinated into the plastic bucket. Flies scattered. Cristiani smelled the ammonia stench of the day's urine fermenting in the heat. He opened a plastic water bottle, drank deeply, and waited. His sour sweat still carried a sulfurous note of fear.

"Climb in." Omar held the gun on him, though it was completely unnecessary. Cristiani heaved himself into the back of the enclosed truck. A flashlight hung on a string from the roof and swung a weak yellow light around the dark interior. A couple of mattresses were on the scruffy sheet-metal floor.

"Sit in the corner," Omar said. "Don't say anything. Just shut up." The AK-47 rested across his legs. The Belanger woman sat next to him.

Maybe there would be a way. Maybe this misadventure could work in Cristiani's favour. He would say they were part of an international terrorist cell—Islamic fundamentalists, probably. This could be a new group, previously unknown to authorities. They interrogated him for military secrets. He was kidnapped for his coming position and interrogated about NATO plans and procedures. The business of human rights was just a ruse. It was just propaganda to discredit the West. He would say he gave them nothing of value. His broken nose would testify to his bravery under extreme duress.

The ride was interminable. The jarring over potholes and stones produced a chaotic rolling din inside the old truck's wooden plank walls. The exhaust brayed like a bad trumpet, and the air brakes shrieked right under them. Diesel fumes, carbon monoxide, and cloying dust snuck past the rear flaps into the box in which they travelled. A piercing headache jackhammered the interior of his cranial vault. He covered his ears with his hands.

The woman held out a bottle of water and three pills. "Painkillers. Take them." It was a kindness. The pills were strong and dulled the pain.

When he could think again, he thought about his confession. Samson would know what was true. Samson wouldn't like that he had signed it. Samson had told Cristiani to clean up his mess.

The sinkhole of his responsibility opened before him. Generals were responsible for outcomes. Intentions were irrelevant. The upper echelons of the international peace and security establishment would shun him. He had no future as General Giancarlo Cristiani. A sad apathy extinguished the flame of ambition and smothered his drive to survive this ordeal.

He thought some more. They would make his confession public. The leftist anti-military press and human rights groups would jump on it. Maybe it would make the *New York Times*. There would be calls for an inquiry. It would be worse if Omar and Anik were captured and told their story. He would not give names or descriptions. He would say they kept him blindfolded. No one needed to know how he was lured into the trap.

The truck stopped. It was dark. The driver opened the back. The smell of charcoal and roasting meat wafted into the truck. Cristiani's mouth watered, and he realized he was hungry. Why were they stopping to eat in the middle of the night?

"Get out. Go." Omar ordered. The woman glared at Cristiani with a withering righteousness. He looked back at her with shame and loathing. Ibrahim should have killed her.

Outside he saw goat carcasses hanging from a dead tree. Strips of meat roasted over charcoal fires on the roadside. Men were drinking beer. Some had girls draped over them, and he saw women lounging on the stoops of shacks behind the fires. He heard wild laughter and angry sounds of fighting in the darkness. "Where am I? I deserve to know where I am. What country is this?"

"It's a brothel for long-distance truckers," Omar said.

"Get out," Anik said. "If the police come, you can tell them whatever you want. They'll draw their own conclusions about what you're doing at a brothel, why you got beat up, and why you have no money or ID with you."

Cristiani climbed out. He watched the truck drive down the road. It had no licence plate. Men got up and started yelling at him in a language he didn't understand. His life sentence of disgrace had begun.

53

ANIK STAYED INSIDE MOHAMMED'S house for two nights and a day between getting back from the abandoned farmhouse and travelling to Nairobi for the long flight home to Canada. Drained of emotion and energy, she sank into an exhausted sleep. At dawn she woke to the tangled calls of the muezzin and roosters. Her confused mind strained to wrench itself out of a terrible nightmare.

She had dreamed she was in an airport. A mob of sobbing women wailed their grief and blocked the airline counters. Their long colourful dresses were soiled, bloodied, and hung ragged from emaciated shoulders. Ten-litre cans of Castrol oil tumbled from the women's frantic heads, spilling dark-red blood onto the dusty ground. The women's shuffling feet stirred blood and dirt and shit into a morass of stinking, sticky mud. It clung to Anik's feet like glue.

Anik stepped out of her shoes and with all her strength dragged herself forward. The airline attendants turned their backs to the crowd under a sign that read "All Departures Cancelled." Anik pushed her way through the howling women. She shoved one out of the way. The woman fell to the ground. Anik looked down at Jameelah and watched helplessly as Jameelah's face slowly sank below the filth.

Covered with the women's blood, she finally reached a counter with a sign that read "Canada." She tapped the back of the huge uniformed attendant. The figure turned to face her, and she read the nametag on his jacket. It said, "Chicago Bulls." Anik sucked in all her breath to scream, but his massive hand clapped over her eyes, nose, and mouth. In an eruption of panic, she suffocated in the dark.

Shaking, she sat up in bed and shifted, so her feet were on the ground. The cool floor assured her that she had returned to reality and a place of safety. Anik pulled a dressing gown around her shoulders and stepped across the hall into the bathroom.

She searched for herself in the mirror. They would notice the upper-lip scar first. With a dark lipstick applied just so, like when she seduced Cristiani, the flaw was hard to see from a distance. In her life before Dadaab, a lover had told her that she had a Mona Lisa smile. Now a heavy sadness pulled the corners of lips into unhappy creases. She slowly stroked her cheek, looking for the soft silk complexion of before. Her skin felt like paper, baked tough in the oven of Dadaab. Her hair was matte black, the ends fraying and dry. Squinting and worry had drawn the edges of her eyes into faint crow's feet. The hemorrhage in the white of her left eye had not faded. Not even a little. Inside, the stain of her outlaw torment of Cristiani was still there, like a botched prison tattoo under a see-through blouse.

This was her new face. It had been shaped by the experience of desperate terror and the courage to exact her measure of retribution. To hide what had happened to her would infect her new self with a lie. To own the shame that belonged to her enemies would betray Jameelah and the other women. There was something else. Her heart was getting stronger with recovered dignity, and she was ready for the long journey back to her old world.

She stepped into the scalding shower. When she was done, she put on her jeans and a T-shirt.

On the small prop plane flight from Lamu to Nairobi, she turned to Omar. "Where do you think Ubah and Jameelah are? How can we find them?"

"Ubah is from Nairobi, and I imagine she took Jameelah and Kamiis there. To Eastleigh. That's where Somalis in Kenya go. Especially if they have to hide. It's too dangerous to try to find them. For you and them. And for me. Ibrahim will have people there, like he did in Dadaab."

She looked down, discouraged by her haste to get the hell out as soon as she could. "No. Not now. I don't think I could manage it anyway. Not yet. But . . . could you find Ubah and give her a letter?"

"It might take time. We will have to be careful. Mohammed has contacts in Eastleigh. We'll try."

"Thank you, thank you. I'll write it tonight. I want her to know where I am in Canada. Maybe there's some way I can help her."

Mohammed had arranged Anik's tickets and insisted that she use one of his trusted drivers to take her from Wilson Airport to her hotel. They arrived late morning and checked into an upscale hotel in Nairobi. Mohammed had reserved separate rooms for them. Nairobi was a dangerous city, and she appreciated this kindness. He bought her a British Airways business-class ticket to Montréal via London.

She was travelling light. She had an overnight bag and an IBM ThinkPad that Mohammed had acquired through his network. That afternoon Anik got passport pictures from a photographer and then went to the Canadian High Commission. She was ushered into a small room with a counter and a consular officer on the other side of bulletproof glass. The officer was about the same age as Anik.

"What happened?"

"I was mugged," Anik said. "I lost everything."

"Were you hurt?" The woman's brow furrowed with sincere concern.

Anik wanted to say yes, but she didn't. "No. They just took everything."

"Well, you're lucky. These robberies can be violent, especially the carjackings. Most people come in here shaking and scared. Actually, it happens a lot. Some women have been terribly hurt. Raped, even." Anik wanted to start talking to this sympathetic woman—someone from her own country, whose job it was to help. "If you get a police report and give me permission to contact your family in Canada, I can probably manage a replacement passport in about ten days or so. Otherwise, we'll have to go with the emergency passport. It'll get you home, but you'll need a new one after that."

"No, no. I just need to go home. I'll gladly take the emergency passport. One-way is perfect. Thank you so much."

The officer smiled kindly. "Well, actually, that's probably easier for everyone. The police never catch anyone anyway. You can get a new passport back in Canada. For when you need to travel again." Another item on the long list for putting her life back together. The diplomat sighed. "Airlines here are used to these one-way documents. We issue a lot of them. Just have a seat out in the lobby, and I'll get it ready right away. Of course somebody is probably going to try and sneak into Canada on the one they stole from you. Our big problem is Somalis. They'll do anything to claim refugee status. I don't blame them though."

Anik sat down, flipped through some old *McLean's* magazines, and in thirty minutes had her temporary passport.

Mohammed's driver was waiting for her at the curbside along with Omar. It was overcast, and a grey, grimy drizzle filled the air. They wove through chaotic city traffic. Hawkers shouting from the sidewalk demanded they buy candy, cigarettes, and snacks.

Outside the city, dun-brown fields opened up, dotted with acacia trees. Then the raw concrete terminal of Jomo Kenyatta

International Airport came into view, and the driver pulled up to the departures zone.

Omar stood beside Anik as the driver got her bag out of the trunk. She had her computer case over her left shoulder and her overnight bag in her right hand.

Omar looked her in the eyes, and Anik felt his gaze, steady, firm, and kind. Even his mangled hand felt that way. Feelings streamed into her mind. Relief, guilt, gratitude, fear, and affection wrestled with each other in her agitated mind.

This place had almost killed her. Anik was starved for the shelter, security, and familiarity of Canada. The more she craved her home, the more guilt burdened the farewell she must give to Omar, and the more she dreaded turning her back on him.

He smiled gently. "I'll never forget you. I want you to come back. But later, much later." He looked down. "I haven't had a friend for a long time. You're my best friend."

She gave him a sad smile. "I don't know what I'll do next."

He looked up in surprise. "Really? I thought you had a job at home. You're a lawyer. Go back to your work. It's a job you can feel good about. Nobody wants to hurt you there. That's what I would do if I were you." Omar's smile broke. "I wish I could." He was right. She did have a place to go. She would be a fool to waste it.

"What will you do?" She had been thinking only of herself, and the question was too casual. Omar didn't seem to notice. Her question made him hesitate and think.

"It's not clear for me yet. I must do the right thing. I'll keep the school going and build another one on the other side of the camp. Fifty-fifty, girls and boys. Or have it built. I don't think I can show my face again in Dadaab. It would be dangerous for me, and dangerous for the project. I'll have to work at a distance.

"I'll stay with Mohammed until I think of something else. I'm not done yet, and the gold's not done growing yet. We have more than we started with. I want to find a way to make shelters for women like Jameelah, women who seek refuge, alone and

destitute. Here in Nairobi could be good. No one would recognize me, I don't think. Maybe it will lead me to Ubah, Jameelah,
and Kamiis."

Anik put down her bag and took Omar's hand in hers. She held
it lightly so as not to cause him any pain. She felt a soft squeeze
back. She remembered the first time she held his hand. It was in
Dadaab, at the dinner with Ruth. She tried to define what they
shared now, to summon the right words out of the tangled thicket
of her emotions.

Omar spoke before she could gather her thoughts. "Thank you,
Anik. Thank you for saving me."

The surprise yanked her out of her reverie. "What do you
mean? You saved me."

"No, you saved me," Omar insisted. "What we did. What we
saw. Now I can begin to atone for what I did to my country and
the harm I caused. It will never be enough, but I could not have
come this far without you."

"I can't tell people what we did. I can't tell them what happened."

"You need to say something," Omar insisted. "There are some
things that must be told. You have a long flight to think about it.
Goodbye." She felt him relax his hand. She let it go.

"Goodbye." Anik said. "Be well." She wanted Omar to feel love
and comfort from her smile. He was more alone than she was.

54

ANIK WALKED INTO THE airport. A brisk uniformed attendant at the business-class desk checked her one-way passport without comment, issued her a boarding pass, and told her the location of the business-class lounge. Once through security, she found a seat right by the departure gate behind a concrete pillar.

Soon they boarded the plane. Anik had a window seat. She slid across the knees of her neighbour, a ruddy-faced British tourist in a loud batik beach shirt. At the click of her seatbelt, a tightly sprung tension began to unwind, and she balanced herself on the rocky edge of a river of tears. She tried to empty her mind of everything but calm.

"Fantastic, just fantastic, init!" he said. "What safaris did you do? I did Amboseli and Masai Mara. Those luxury tents are incredible. Even those amazing toilets. Total luxury." He grabbed two champagnes from the stewardess. "I got the big five twice. How about you?"

"I'm afraid I don't feel well. I must have picked something up. I'm going to try to get some rest." She turned her face to the window and leaned her forehead against the cool plastic of the airplane wall.

"Suit yourself, love, suit yourself," he said and then called the stewardess for another drink. He took off his sandals, put on the slippers from the business class toiletry sack, and unsnapped his pants with a groan.

She declined dinner. The lights of the aircraft dimmed, and her neighbour fell asleep. Anik pulled the laptop out from under the seat in front of her and started typing.

> Memorandum
>
> To: Minister of Justice
>
> From: Anik Belanger, War Crimes Unit (currently on leave without pay)
>
> Subject: Rape as a Weapon of War—Testimony from Dadaab Camp
>
> Victim 1: Criminal Code Provision 273, Aggravated Sexual Assault.

Prompted by the lists in her recovered report, things came back to her in a flood. The particulars of Jameelah's case were etched in her mind, as were others. At first she was proud of herself for her recall; that had not been robbed from her. But then she realized something was missing. She scrolled up and wrote at the top of the page:

> Purpose: The purpose of this memorandum is to provide evidence that sexual assault was used in Merka, Somalia, as a weapon in a strategy of systematic commission of war crimes to gain power and territorial control through terror against women. This strategy was known and evident to the International Peacekeeping Mission.

From there her knowledge flowed clear and cold onto the page.

55

ANIK WAS BACK IN her apartment, drained, depressed, and a bit drunk. It had been a joy to see her parents again, but after three days she couldn't stay in her childhood bedroom any longer. It hadn't changed since she went to university. It made her feel juvenile and dependent. And three days were enough of hearing how her parents had worried about her. She met their criticism about not writing enough letters by saying she had been too busy with work. They didn't really understand what she had been doing or why or where it was anyway. Now that she was in Canada again, they said getting that good government job back was the important thing.

The memo to the minister wasn't something that she could just put in a mailbox or send by courier. She had gone to the minister's office herself to drop it off. He had said he wanted to talk about her ideas. He had seemed to care—or at least he did before the deputy swamped him with political issues. That meeting seemed like a lifetime ago. Anik didn't know what she would do if the minister forgot that he had asked to see her again. At least he was still in the same job.

She took the first sip of her third glass of wine. It tasted good. It was seven, and she should be feeling hungry for dinner, but she didn't have the motivation to go out of her apartment. Anik walked over to the mirror. The hemorrhage in her eye was a blackish brown, and it wasn't going away. The scar from her split upper lip twisted her smile. Should she get her face fixed? There was that cramp in her lower abdomen again. Next week she would make an appointment for a check-up.

The news came on the radio. The Québec separatists planned another independence referendum to break up Canada. Yasser Arafat was back in Palestine. The guerrillas and the government in El Salvador had begun to talk about a peace agreement. There was something about ethnic clashes in Rwanda.

The shrill ring of the phone startled her. That was funny. She wasn't expecting any calls. Anik topped up her wine in case it was her mother again. She let it ring two more times before she picked up.

"Good evening. Is this Madame Anik Belanger?" It was a woman's voice that she didn't recognize.

"Yes, that's me. Who is this?"

"I'm calling on behalf of the minister of justice. He would like to know if you're available for a meeting with him tomorrow morning at ten."

He had read her report. Then she remembered the treatment she was given by the deputy minister and her boss the last time she met Minister Sandy MacDowell.

"Who else will be there?"

"Just you. And him."

"Thank you," Anik said. "I'll be there." She was relieved to get the call—but why so soon? What did it mean?

Anik finished her wine and decided to go out for a meal. She felt like comfort food. The deli down the block served a good smoked meat sandwich and barley soup.

That night, lying safe and warm in her bed under a sky-blue duvet, her mind raced. What would she say to the minister? Politically, she liked and admired MacDowell. She knew he had the background of a prosecutor, like her, but she didn't know him personally. She didn't know what he really thought about things. Then Anik started to worry.

How would she hide what she had done? If she were connected in any way to what happened to Cristiani, she would be out of a career forever. She would need to cover her trail. What if he called Justice Before Peace for references? Eventually, long past midnight, she fell asleep.

The following day she walked into the imposing and gothic House of Commons, down the hall, and went up in the wood-panelled elevator. The secretary showed her into the richly carpeted office furnished with old, heavy government furniture. Minister MacDowell was a tall, slim man. She thought he had more grey and less red in his wiry hair compared to the last time she had seen him. His formerly athletic frame was a little more stooped than before. He was hunched over her memo.

"Take a seat, please." She sat in one of the two armchairs facing his desk. She had no idea what he was thinking, or what it would mean for her future.

"Explosive," he said.

Had she gone too far?

"It's explosive. I mean politically explosive. What are you going to do with it?"

"It's for you. I can't publish it. But maybe you can do something, or start to do something."

"We can't do nothing," he said. "We have to do something!"

She took relief and comfort from the anger in his voice.

"But there's one thing I don't understand. Why didn't you name any of the perpetrators—or victims, for that matter? What happens to those men? Is anybody doing anything about it?

Where did this take place? Don't we need specific evidence to do something?"

"It's too dangerous. There could be a risk of reprisal. Maybe it's too political."

"Does that mean they get off? It's outrageous. What about the UN soldiers? Was that just a waste of time and money? Didn't they do anything about it?" The minister paced his office. He hadn't looked at her or shook her hand yet.

"No. This time they didn't."

The minister pulled his hands over his face. "In God's name, why? That's what we all thought this was for. What the hell happened? We're talking about a crime scene the size of a country. It was like the police were asking the criminals for permission to do their job. This isn't a war for soldiers. We need something different. Something new." He looked at her. "Do you want your old job back?"

"I don't want to be a government lawyer anymore."

"I need to know more. I can give you a job. I want you as my political assistant."

"What will I do?"

"For a start, let's try to make sure this never happens again. You'll be my special investigator on crimes against humanity— the ones happening now, like in your report. I want you to go out there and bring in cases. You'll be my private detective for crimes against humanity." He smiled at her.

Anik laughed. "I'd like that. Crimes against humanity need a detective."

MacDowell lifted his head and stared at her. It felt intrusive. "You look . . . different."

"The sun is strong out there. I think it probably toughened my skin." She knew it sounded lame.

"Is that blood in your eye? What's wrong with your lip? What happened?" He was suddenly concerned, and it was genuine.

Anik didn't know what to say. She held her expression firm. Thoughts swirled in her head. If she didn't say it now, in a safe place with a person of power she trusted, there would never be another chance. If it didn't come out now, everything that came after would be a professional lie. But if she did, then she might expose herself and Omar for what they had done to Cristiani. She blanched again at the realization that she was a criminal—or would be if charges were ever laid.

"Are you okay? Do you need a glass of water or something?" MacDowell asked.

She spoke without thinking, "I was gang raped. That's what happened."

"My God! I'm so terribly sorry. Did you receive proper care? Do you know who did it? Did they catch the perpetrators? Can we help?"

Anik wanted to trust MacDowell, but she knew better than to give trust easily. She studied the line of his brow for signs of insincerity and the cast of his lips for a repressed sneer of duplicity. They were not there. Maybe she could trust him. Until she was sure, she would open herself in small doses. "I survived, and I'm getting psychological help. That's what matters now," Anik said. "When do I start?"

"Make sure you take care of yourself, Anik. When you're ready, wrap up your commitments with that NGO. Let's meet here next week. Same place, same time."

Omar was right. She did have a good job to go back to. She just never imagined it would be this.

56

ANIK HAD ONLY RECEIVED her replacement driver's licence the day before, and the pimply young rental car agent was nosy. She explained that her ID had been stolen when she was travelling. He had no idea where Kenya was.

"The credit card is new too," he grumbled suspiciously. Then he asked how long she had been in Québec, and if she really lived in Canada. She hated lying and felt cornered on shaky ground by his questions. She felt a cold dread that she would be caught out. Finally, he gave her the keys to a blue Ford Taurus sedan.

She thought about the child and went back into the rental car office. "I forgot something. Do you have a booster seat?"

"We don't do that. There's a Walmart down the street. You can get one there."

It felt like a long time since she had driven, and she picked her way slowly and carefully through the crowded parking lot. Parking lots were the worst place for fender benders.

In the store, she selected the prettiest booster seat: the one with pink flowers.

Anik pulled into her driveway after grocery shopping. The previous week, she had moved into her new house. It was comfortable and had room for some guests, but it needed more furniture and kitchen stuff. She had decided on a place on the Québec side of the river. Prices were cheaper, and it was a short commute to the Department of Justice in Ottawa. Anik preferred to be in a French-speaking environment. It was more tranquil and close to a park. She loved to skate, and Brewery Creek was just down the street. It was a good neighbourhood for kids, and she saw that immigrants lived on the block—probably refugees from the civil wars in Central America, based on their looks. Anik would buy herself a bike to get to work. She looked forward to pedalling along the Ottawa River bike paths. The trees were changing colour, and the air had a hint of an autumn fragrance from the fallen leaves on her small front yard.

As she unpacked, she worried that she had forgotten something, so she crossed things off her shopping list: four litres of milk, spice tea, cookies, three kinds of breakfast cereal, eggs, rice, chicken, goat meat, flatbread, tomato sauce, vegetable oil, hot sauce, bananas, mangos, carrots, okra, tea, and sugar. Good. Everything she needed for the first couple of days was present and where it belonged. She usually shopped just for herself, so it was strange to stock up for more people.

She wanted a glass of wine, but decided against it. At just 11:00 a.m., it was too early. Maybe in a few days. She had a five-hour drive ahead of her. The booster seat stayed in the trunk.

She knew the way to Montréal by heart. She crossed the rust-encrusted Champlain Bridge over the St. Lawrence and headed through the gentle maple forest and fields of the Eastern Townships to the American border. The limits of Canada were imperceptible but felt more real with each kilometre south. So strange how people's rights on one side were different from their rights on the other; one step over the forty-fifth parallel changed lives and destinies. For her, it would be another step toward redemption.

In the late afternoon, Anik came to the Québec border town of Stanstead and parked to look at the map. It showed the border with Vermont as a straight red line drawn right through the village. She drove around the little town to reconnoiter. The neighbourhood streets crossed back and forth without concern for the frontier of the mightiest country in the world. This was a border between rich countries, she thought. No disorder or refugees in sight. No wonder it was unguarded.

A steady flow of traffic funnelled through the Canadian and US border control stations. Drivers entering Vermont offered up their identity and car registration documents for inspection by the US customs officers, and those coming into Québec did the same for the Canadian officers. Some were told to pull over and had their trunks searched.

Anik thought Laurier Street would be the best choice for what she needed. It went through a residential part of town and right into the US with no controls. She parked about one hundred metres back and waited, watching. She had hoped there would be little traffic at her planned crossing, and she was right.

After about fifteen minutes, a car with Québec plates crossed over and stopped at an American grocery store. The milk and gasoline would be cheaper there. It was time to make her move.

Anik entered a heightened state of awareness of everything around her. Her moist hands gripped the padded vinyl steering wheel as if her life depended on it. Her right foot was rigid on the accelerator, and she constantly checked the speedometer to fix her speed at exactly forty-five kilometres per hour—fast enough to avoid attention while keeping under the speed limit.

A large white sign with aggressive black lettering came into focus: "You may not enter the United States on this street. Violators are subject to a $5,000 fine and/or prosecution. All visitors to the United States must pass through Border Control on Smythe Street."

Thankfully, nothing happened. She crossed over the invisible line. Nobody noticed her, and she continued down the road through the countryside. Rich-looking pastures full of black-and-white dairy cows slid past.

A short twenty kilometres south, she slowly drove into the first American town, Newport, on a picturesque northern blue lake. Tidy summer cottages with small floating docks were scattered along its shore. She wheeled her car into the Texaco gas station and asked for a fill and directions to the bus station.

The bus station was attached to the post office six blocks down on Water Street. She easily found it and parked where she could see the bus arrive. Anik had an hour to spare. Heavy clouds scudded low across the steely lake, spitting chilly drizzle.

She shuddered in a panic attack. It was a recurring side effect of the gang rape that she couldn't completely shake. A tremble in her hands made her clutch the steering wheel. She thought a walk along the shore might help, but her legs were jelly. A sinkhole under her heart sucked in her courage and confidence.

Anik rolled down the window and practiced the deep-breathing exercises her psychiatrist had taught her. After thirty breaths, composure inched back into her mind. Her thoughts struggled out of the quicksand of panic and registered her surroundings. It was the end of fall. Leaves had lost their life-giving chlorophyll. The maples they had nourished all year cast them off in betrayal to rot in the dirt.

Anik had faced betrayal in Canada and then in Africa. She had been expelled from the Department of Justice, then violated and left for dead, as if her life was worth nothing. As if she could do nothing but fall down and fail. But she could not let depression hold the reins of her spirit.

She was alive. She had found and revealed a hideous hypocrisy and a terrible crime. It was something no one else had managed to do. She felt the presence of the water-bearing women in Dadaab, and a meaning began to emerge in her heart. She had survived and had borne witness. It came back to her what the women had said at the water pump. In her mind she heard Ubah translate, "For justice, there must be punishment." Some punishment had been delivered. Not much. Not enough. But some.

The righteousness she wanted to feel was muddied by guilt and a recurring fear that her own crime against Cristiani would be discovered. At some point in almost every day, she had a flashback of the desperate women she had interviewed. Then she remembered the smell of smoke, her files burning, and the attack.

She wrestled her mind onto a path of logic and searched for a rational exit from these dark feelings. She pulled the autumn air into her lungs with all her might.

Lost in that jagged tempest of cruelty and greed, there had been no one else but her and Omar. They had delivered a piece of justice and a message of truth.

Following hard on the heels of his NATO appointment, Cristiani had been exposed and humiliated by the international coverage of his confession. Italian newspapers reported that his location was unknown, and he could not be found for questioning by the commission of inquiry into the affair.

In a letter, Omar said that Ibrahim was still in control of Merka and secure in his position. However, Anik had a new chance to move forward with her mandate to investigate crimes against humanity.

A front opened a patch of blue sky to the south. The sun radiated a little warmth on her shoulder. A fragrance came from the forest floor. It reminded her of spiced tea and fresh bread. It made Anik smile.

A sharp honk from the bus yanked Anik into the present. She hurried out of her car and pulled her down jacket tight around her.

She stood as close to the steps of the bus as possible without blocking the exiting passengers. Two American soldiers in uniform got out—boys with bad complexions and weary eyes. Next was an old couple. The man tangled his walker in the retracting door, and Anik felt a flash of impatience.

A woman came down in a green tracksuit with a baseball cap over a tidy afro.

"Dr. Anik?" It was Ubah! Anik felt her sadness vaporize in the warmth of their hug. It was happening. Her secret plan with Omar was bearing fruit. It had seemed too crazy and impossible to come true, but Ubah had made it.

Ubah turned to the bus and spoke in Somali. Jameelah carefully stepped down, looking this way and that. She was disoriented. Clutching her hand was Kamiis, small and skinny in an oversized set of pink OshKosh B'gosh overalls. Her eyes were wide with wonder and trepidation.

"*Bonjour*, Tante Anik," the little girl said in a high, wavering voice. Jameelah smiled and stroked her hair proudly.

Anik stooped to eye level with Kamiis. "*Bonjour, ma chére.*" She felt the thin arms around her and the girl's head rest on her shoulder. Tears rose to her eyes. "Come, let's go home," she said.

Ubah went to pick up the duffle bag, and Jameelah took Anik's hand as they walked to her car. Anik opened the trunk, got out the booster seat for Kamiis, loaded the duffle bag, and seated Jameelah next to Kamiis in the back. Ubah was next to Anik in the front.

Ubah started telling Anik about how Omar had found them in the Eastleigh neighbourhood of Nairobi. They had been in hiding and terrified that the men who attacked Anik were looking for them. Mohammed had secured them Kenyan passports with counterfeit us visas.

Anik had to interrupt. "Ubah, it's better that we cross into Canada without going through the border controls. We might have trouble. Let's talk after we cross. It's not far." Ubah explained this to Jameelah, and the car fell silent.

Anik motored at precisely forty-five kilometres per hour as she approached Stanstead and turned onto Laurier. In the darkening evening, the pretty houses carried the menace of a suspense film. Anik imagined unfriendly residents picking up phones to report a suspicious woman transporting three Africans. The street was empty, and she passed a sign in French and English ordering all travellers to report to Canada customs. Anik didn't stop until she reached the outskirts of town.

Kamiis and Jameelah were whispering in the back seat. They sounded worried. Of course they were worried. This must be like landing on a strange planet for a little girl, a war orphan with different-coloured skin and a different language from everyone else. It would be baffling and scary for her. Anik would find psychological help for Kamiis as soon as they were settled. She had so much to do. It started to feel like too much.

"*Pouvons-nous faire pipi?*"[21] Jameelah asked. So that's what they were talking about. Her worries and the tension in the car melted into laughter.

"I have to go too," Anik said. "Are you hungry? Let's get something to eat." Up ahead Anik saw the illuminated head of a grinning rooster. Fried chicken would be good. They would like that.

Their first stop was the women's washroom. They walked through the door, and the two Somali women stopped and looked at Anik expectantly. Kamiis turned her head this way and that nervously, fiercely gripping Jameelah's hand.

"We are still not used to these western toilets. They are cold on the bottom," Ubah said with a smile.

When everyone was finished, they found an empty booth. They looked fine, Anik thought. They would be happy in Canada.

A young waitress handed out menus, and Anik ordered barbecued chicken and French fries for everyone.

When the food arrived, she cut the thigh and drumstick off the bone and into pieces, like her mother did for her when she

21 Can we stop to pee?

was a little girl. Kamiis looked at her with deep seriousness. Anik smiled and nodded. Kamiis picked up a piece with her fingers, tasted it with caution, and then ate in earnest. She must have been famished.

Jameelah and Ubah ate more slowly and carefully, also using their hands.

First in English for Ubah and then in French for Jameelah, Anik explained what was going to happen. "Tonight I'll take you to my house. It's a long drive—about four hours from here. You are my guests for as long as you want. I'm so happy to see you again. You are in Canada seeking asylum as refugees.

"Tomorrow we will make your claim at the office for refugee claims. I've filled out your forms. Jameelah, your rape by Abdi as a weapon of political intimidation and the risk of reprisal if you go back is your basis of claim. Ubah, after what happened to me, your risk of reprisal is clear. I'll testify for both of you."

Kamiis hesitated at the French fries. Anik squeezed a puddle of ketchup onto the plate, dipped a fry into it, and ate it to show Kamiis. Kamiis did the same, grinned, and picked up another and another.

"If you want, we can begin an application for citizenship as Canadians. We can also look for work in a medical lab for Jameelah. Ubah, I'd like you to work with me. When she's ready, Kamiis will go to school. She will meet other girls like her who had to leave their country and come to Canada."

Kamiis gently pulled on Jameelah's sleeve for attention. Jameelah smiled and nodded. Kamiis reached across the table and took Anik's hand. "*Merci beaucoup*, Tante Anik." She turned and said something in Somali to Ubah.

"She says you saved our lives. She is right. You did."

Anik smiled. A warm bloom of pride and redemption began to heal the injured place in her spirit.

AUTHOR'S NOTE

Anik, Omar, Cristiani, and Ibrahim tread their fictional paths through real historical events. Let me spell out for you what was real in *Moral Hazards*.

Mogadishu, the capital of Somalia, fell in 1991, and President Siad Barre fled with the country's gold and currency reserves. Among my crazier diplomatic experiences was a mission to Mogadishu in 1991 to meet the warlords and make a political assessment of the situation before Canadian peacekeepers were deployed. I was accompanied by two great colleagues from the Canadian High Commission in Nairobi: Chris Cooter and Chris Liebich.

We hitched a ride into Somalia on a Canadian Forces transport plane loaded with food aid. We rode with humanitarian agencies across the battle lines of the wrecked capital to the headquarters of the warring factions fighting for the capital and country. Besides the veiled threats and false commitments to human rights that we heard from the warlords, we heard that President Siad Barre took the nation's gold reserves when he fled the country. I thought that could be a pretty good start to a story, but I doubted its veracity.

Later I saw it confirmed in a document posted by the UN. Now I choose to believe it's true.

The peace operation Restore Hope did take place—and it was a fiasco. In the famine and power vacuum that attended state collapse, Somali warlords harassed and attacked humanitarian aid organizations. In 1992, a UN peacekeeping mission (UNOSOM) was deployed. UNOSOM was pathetically ineffective, and the situation stayed bad. I was the desk officer for the Horn of Africa in the Canadian government at that time. Western governments couldn't just stand there and watch the catastrophe unfold on TV. Something had to be done—or so we thought. President Bush felt that way too, and the US put together a military solution to the suffering and chaos. The operation was named "Restore Hope." The US, Canada, Italy, Germany, and Belgium were major troop contributors

The military contingents entered Somalia ill prepared for this new kind of mission. They exited in disgrace and humiliation. US efforts will be remembered by the horrific downing of a Black Hawk helicopter and the death of eighteen American soldiers at the hands of hostile militias and mobs. The Canadian Armed Forces were subject to a public inquiry after news that a Somali teenager under interrogation by two Canadian soldiers was beaten to death. Photos emerged of Belgian paratroopers apparently torturing Somali captives. Two Italian generals resigned over reports that their troops tortured, sexually abused, and killed Somali civilians.

Ravensbruck was a Nazi camp for women. The Nazis had a concentration camp for women called Ravensbruck. Some women were forced into sexual slavery as a cruel and cynical incentive to get more out of slave labourers. The background for Edith's story was inspired by descriptions of the camp from Sarah Helm's book, *If This Is a Woman: Inside Ravensbruck: Hitler's Concentration Camp for Women.*

In 1992 Dadaab was the largest refugee camp in the world. It's still there. Hundreds of thousands of Somalis fled their country because of civil strife and state collapse. Many went south across the border to Kenya, and in 1991, the Dadaab refugee camp was established. It grew to become the largest refugee camp in the world. Now it's both a refugee camp and the fourth-largest city in Kenya. As of this writing, the largest refugee camp is in Bangladesh, populated by Rohingya refugees who fled Myanmar. Rohingya refugee women are also victims of rape as a weapon of war.

Rape as a weapon of war is now a crime against humanity. Anik wanted to be the one to make rape a war crime. The Rome Statute, which defines the crimes for the International Criminal Court, came into effect in 2001. It includes the kinds of systematic sexual violence described in *Moral Hazards* as a crime against humanity. This is what it says:

> For the purpose of this Statute, "crime against humanity" means any of the following acts when committed as part of a widespread or systematic attack directed against any civilian population, with knowledge of the attack:
>
> (a) Murder;
>
> (b) Extermination;
>
> (c) Enslavement;
>
> (d) Deportation or forcible transfer of population;
>
> (e) Imprisonment or other severe deprivation of physical liberty in violation of fundamental rules of International law;
>
> (f) Torture;

> (g) Rape, sexual slavery, enforced prostitution, forced pregnancy, enforced sterilization, or any other form of sexual violence of comparable gravity . . .

There has been one conviction for rape by the ICC. It was a Congolese warlord for the use of rape as a weapon in the Central African Republic. He appealed and was acquitted.

Two slow-motion outrages drove me to write *Moral Hazards*.

First, armies strike dark bargains with local power brokers (or warlords) when they bring military solutions to failed states. It's logical. Imagine you're a brigadier general taking 600 young men and a UN resolution to a remote, obscure, and dangerous country. You don't know much about its history or culture. You don't speak the language. You won't be there long before your next mission. Maybe a year. So, you're in a big hurry to complete your assignment and get credit. You need someone to work with. Someone ruthless enough to survive and powerful enough to make things happen. If you were that general, you might enter a marriage of convenience with your local warlord.

I saw this problem bedevil NATO's mission to stabilize Afghanistan. But don't take it from me. Here is what the American Special Inspector for Afghanistan said: "When they arrived after 9/11 in Afghanistan, the US chose to ally with warlords . . . to push out the Taliban. And, in the years that followed, rather than break those ties and widen the circle of power, NATO got to be ever more dependent on these men."

Second, rape is still used as a weapon of war. We may think of it as a relic of the past, and yet it persists into the twenty-first century in Congo, Colombia, and Myanmar, to name a few places. Even if the problem is not getting better, the international community is getting better at recognizing and talking about it. Here is what the UN Secretary General said about Somalia in his 2018 report about Women Peace and Security. "The following patterns have emerged regarding conflict-related sexual violence:

it disproportionately affects displaced women and girls from marginalized groups; most perpetrators are described as men in military uniform; most cases involve rape or gang rape . . ."

I hope you enjoyed *Moral Hazards*. My hidden agenda is this: the next time we see our military deployed to a distant crisis, let's ask them about those with whom they will partner and how they will protect civilians, especially women and children.

ACKNOWLEDGEMENTS

Thanks to the Buenos Aires writers group for their warm friendship and cold, hard criticism. Helen Coyle coached me on how to bring strategic structure and direction to the book. A positive reaction from my first beta reader, Joanna Richardson, gave me the confidence I needed to publish.

My friends and neighbours in Minaki bought the first limited run of twenty copies and have been a constant encouragement.

Michiel van Wyngaarden's amazing creative vision transformed the story into a beautiful and haunting cover image.

My family helped with love and practical guidance. My mother instilled a love of books that continues to this day. My father showed me that it is more important to understand people than to judge them. Daughter Jena, a nurse with forensic training, checked for clinical accuracy. Daughter Natasha encouraged me from the beginning with creative and editorial advice. My loving wife, Fatima, never got tired of listening to me and never stopped believing in *Moral Hazards*.

Printed in Canada